THE ELEVENTH HOUR

Tavian Brack

ACKNOWLEDGEMENT

I would like to give a special thank you to Courtney and Jocelyn, you know who you are. The two people who took such an interest in my work. Thank you, Samantha, for being my quasi-editor and cheerleader. I hope you are proud of this work. Thank you to Panera Bread for the endless long use of your cafes and for the coffee that I needed in order to get through this. For all the people who will read this work and the others to come. Thank you to all the authors who inspired me and continue to do so: Bernard Cornwell, George R.R. Martin, C.S. Forester, Harry Turtledove, J.R.R. Tolkien and so many more. Thank you to Timothy Zahn for writing me back when I was twelve years old. I'm still your biggest fan man.

I really, truly believe that creation, in all its forms, is a reality. Take from that what you will.

TABLE OF CONTENTS

PROLOGUE

There was a dull pain in his right arm. He could feel it in his sleep. Slowly and with all his effort he began to open his eyes. He could hear voices in the room but could not understand what they were saying.

"Where.....?" He asked in a soft tone, barely able to speak.

Through the blurred vision he saw movement, a woman he thought, dressed in white walking away from him.

A half minute later another image appeared, this time a little bit clearer. A man was approaching, a doctor's coat on him and a stethoscope draped over his neck.

"Mein Führer," the man began. The doctor thumbed open Hitler's eyelids. "Can you hear me, Mein Führer?"

"Ja," Hitler whispered back to him. He struggled to move his mouth. His vision was blurry, but his mind was even more so. He could feel the stethoscope placed over his chest and fingers grasp his wrist.

His vision went blank, and he was unconscious once again.

More voices began to speak, and he could feel people stirring around him.

He forced his eyes to open with all his strength. This time his blurry vision cleared up as he opened his eyes. He breathed heavily through his nose.

The doctor was still standing over him but there was something different about him this time. His tie and shirt had been changed; Hitler had noted.

"Where?" He managed to whisper out.

The doctor stood over him and smiled at him. He was a heavyset man wearing glasses and smelling slightly of what Hitler thought, was a rather cheap cologne.

"You are in the hospital, Mein Führer," the fat doctor answered. "I am Doctor Edinger."

From the doctor's left another man stepped into view. The unmistakable Hermann Göring. Göring stared on over the doctor's shoulder.

"Göring. . . ." Hitler whispered then trailed off. His lips were dry. "Hospital?"

The doctor stirred uncomfortably then turned slightly to look at Hermann Göring who stepped forward and the fat doctor moved aside.

The overweight air marshal looked down at his Führer and put his hand on Hitler's.

"What happened?" Hitler asked, this time his voice a little bit stronger. "Why am I here?"

Göring cleared his throat audibly. "What are your last memories?"

Adolf Hitler moved his eyes around the hospital room and thought hard for a moment. It was all very hazy. He struggled to clear his mind, but it wasn't easy. He inhaled sharply through his nose then let it back out. Rain, he remembered. There was rain outside of the Reich Chancellery. He had just attended a meeting of political and military leaders. Göring was there, so was Himmler, his generals. What were they discussing? Poland. . . .

He fixed his eyes back on Göring. "Poland. The invasion. . . ." there was a tone of urgency in his voice. "What happened with the attack?" He whispered out.

Göring looked at him and scowled. "Mein Führer," he began, "the invasion was halted."

Hitler could scarce believe his ears. He attempted to move his body and sit upwards but found he had little strength. He looked down at his hands to make sure that they were still attached to his body. They were still there but he was too weak to move himself.

The fat doctor stood back over him on the opposite side of the hospital bed as Göring. "Lie still, Mein Führer. You are still too weak.

"How long have I been here?" He asked throatily.

After a moment's hesitation the doctor answered. "Almost three months. You awoke the first time two days ago."

Hitler gasped and let out a sigh. Awoke two days ago? That would explain the doctor's different appearance. Three months in a hospital. His mind began to settle, and he looked down at his body. His hands and arms were still attached and working, as were his legs and feet he noted as he looked between his legs and moved his feet slightly in either direction.

"Why?" He asked. His voice was becoming sterner and more focused.

"Mein Führer," Göring began, "you were in a horrific auto accident. Do you remember? Your car spun off the road."

Hitler shook his head slowly and closed his eyes. The rain he remembered, that night in Berlin after leaving the Reich Chancellery.... His eyes popped back open and he looked at Göring with steely eyes.

"What is the date?"

"Today is December eleventh," Göring told him. "You were in a coma for quite some time."

Hitler took that in and settled back into his pillows. He cursed himself inwardly about speaking out loud of the planned attack on Poland in front of Herr doctor. Few outside the top political and military leadership knew of it. If the fat doctor had any sense at all he knew to stay quiet. *He would either be silent or else he would be silenced*, Hitler thought. He shook his head and looked back at his Air Marshall. Göring, sitting at his bedside in his sky-blue uniform glared down at him wearing that awkward smile that he so often had.

"Leave us," he told the doctor in a stern voice.

The doctor bowed his eyes and silently left the room. Hitler waited to hear the click of the door handle before looking at Göring again.

"Three months I have been here," he spat out. Göring could hear annoyance in his voice and also something else.... concern perhaps. "What has happened since? Who is in charge?"

Göring's brow furrowed, and he shook his head slightly. "In charge, Mein Führer? You are still in charge. There have been no leadership changes made." *Although it had been discussed*, he thought, though that would never be brought up to the Führer.

"And the plans? For Poland? There was no attack?"

Göring swallowed. "It was decided that we would postpone the attack. Wait until you had recovered from your injuries."

Hitler grunted. *You mean wait until you see if I survive*, he thought to himself. Then the context of Göring's response sunk in. "Injuries? What injuries?"

The fat man hesitated. He took a small hand mirror from the table next to the bed and held it up for Hitler to see. His face had a scar going from the right side of his face, next to his eye all the way to just under his nose. His nose also was crooked, obviously broken from whatever automobile accident he'd been involved in. His face was slightly swollen. His eyes stared coldly back at the reflection of himself in the mirror. *The ugliness of it*, he thought. He pushed Göring's hand and the mirror away.

He closed his eyes and tried to remember what he could. He remembered having dinner with Ribbentrop that evening, discussing Russia as well as British and French plans for retaliation. There was a later meeting with his military planners that ran well into the night. It was raining hard, he remembered that. He remembered the rain pelting the windows of his meeting room. He did not recall anything beyond that.

"The people, do they know?" Hitler asked.

"They do. We could not hide your absence forever, Mein Führer. However," he hesitated before finishing.

"However?"

"Goebbels used the incident to further increase public support. It is widely believed that foreign agents have attempted to assassinate you, Mein Führer."

Hitler let his words sink in for a minute. Leave it to Joseph Goebbels, Hitler's head of propaganda, to capitalize on just such an incident. *Foreign agents attempting to assassinate the Führer of the German people? Yes*, he thought, *this could work.*

It was now nearly the middle of December and soon the snows would be falling across Eastern Europe. The army could not effectively launch an attack now. It would have to wait until the spring thaw, April or even

May. *The army would like that,* he thought. Although the delay was not to his liking it would add to their strength come the spring.

The so called 'attempted assassination' would also help to rally the German people. He would need to focus their energy on this. To do that he knew his people would need their Führer, they would need to hear his voice again. Stronger and more determined than ever before. The Führer put his hand on Göring's and squeezed as hard as he could.

"Bring me a radio," he said in as strong as a voice as his exhausted body would allow. "I must speak to the people."

CHAPTER ONE

London
March 1940

The curtains flew open, and the first rays of sunshine shone into Churchill's bedroom. His butler drew back the drapes and went about his business of tidying up Winston's mess from the evening before. Notes and papers, hastily scribbled memos, telegraphs that had arrived overnight were scattered here and there about his bedchamber.

Sitting up in his bed, breakfast tray in his lap, Winston was already busy reading the morning newspaper and puffing away on his cigar, the first of many throughout the day. He'd grunt and grumble as he read through the headlines. India was, of course, first on the *Times* front page, followed by the national recovery, some rubbish concerning the young royal princesses or some such thing that he thumbed past, news about President Roosevelt across the pond and more news about yet more atrocities by the Japanese Army in China.

The butler finished cleaning and quietly exited the bedroom, picking up the finished breakfast tray on his way out. For a moment Winston lay in his bed alone before another light knock at the door.

"Yes," he bellowed, acting seemingly annoyed at whomever it was knocking. Although he knew already before the door opened.

The door opened and in stepped a young woman, dark haired, fair skinned and thin, as they all had been. Churchill continued smoking his cigar, barely bothering to look up from his newspaper. The young lady stepped forward, sat herself at a small, cushioned chair and began to set up her typewriter machine.

He finally folded up the paper and threw it next to where he was lying. After a moment he looked up at the young lady and grunted something incoherent at her.

The young lady looked at him confused. "I'm sorry?"

Plucking the cigar from his mouth he repeated himself. "Who are you?"

The young woman, no older than twenty blinked and visibly gulped. "Miss.... umm....I'm Miss Robinson, sir," she replied nervously.

Seconds passed by as the older Churchill stared at the young lady. It became quite uncomfortable for her after a short while.

"Miss Robinson," he repeated. "Where is Miss Pruitt?" His voice had a seriousness in it.

"She...she....umm," the woman's voice teemed with nervousness.

"She.... umm...umm," Winston boomed. "Get your tongue together girl."

"You fired her, sir," she told him. "Umm.... last week. You fired her."

Winston puffed away again on his cigar then grumbled. "Hmmm. Alright then." He gazed around the room as if he were expecting someone else to walk in but then returned his gaze to Miss whatever her name was.

"Well Miss....uh," he waved his hand as if it would revive his memory of her name.

"Robinson," the young woman stated.

"I know your name!" he bellowed. He tossed the bed sheets from him and with wholehearted effort, threw his legs out and blew noisily as he heaved himself up.

"So.... What are you waiting for?" He said as he looked at her. *Stupid girl*, he thought. They were all stupid.

"You haven't told me what you would like to me do, sir."

More puffing on his cigar, already halfway finished and still only now seven o'clock. His morning ritual these days was to have letters and telegrams dictated. Although he'd been out of government now for several years, he had continually sounded the bell about Hitler and his ilk across the Channel to anyone who would listen. Lord, lady or commoner.

He had warned them. Warned them all in government back in '38 after Munich. He'd been in the minority of course, nobody else wanted to poke the bear, when he called out the government for failing to act decisively. What good were treaties if you did not act on them when they were continually violated, he'd tell them. What the government needed, what the country needed was stronger leadership, not the cowardly types who were in charge now. It shocked him that his own Conservative Party seemed to lack any backbone these days.

He stood up from his bed, grabbed his morning robe and swung it around his heavy frame. "Let's see," he said, put his finger on his temple and started tapping. "To my dear friends at the Admiralty.... Sirs.... It is my continued wish.... umm....." He stopped. He did not hear any typing and shot a look at the young Miss Robinson, a cold stare. "What are you doing?"

Her lips trembled for a moment. "Nothing, sir. Do you want me to begin?"

"Of course I bloody well want you to begin typing. Stupid girl." His voice carried well through the door and the girl began nervously typing. "If I'm speaking, you should be typing! Are you daft?"

Miss Robinson continued typing as fast as she could, tears now visibly running down her cheeks.

"Where was I? Oh yes, the Admiralty. Umm....it is my continued wish to see that more and more additional resources be spent on the construction and upgrading of our fleet, particularly of our smaller class of ships. Destroyers, frigates, etc..... I genuinely fear for the continuation.... no strike that, survival of our island nation when it comes to the threat of German submarines operating in the North Sea and North Atlantic Ocean." Again puffing away, he mumbled some additional words that Miss Robinson could not quite make out.

She coughed. "Excuse me, sir?"

"What?"

"I didn't.... I didn't quite catch that last part." She couldn't bring herself to blink.

Churchill stared coldly at the young woman. "Couldn't make it out?

The young girl was now visibly trembling with both hands and lips, her eyes reddening as more tears began to swell up and run down her cheeks ruining her makeup.

The door swung open, and Churchill looked over as his wife Clementine strode into the bedchamber. He went silent. Her eyes were fixed upon him and gave him a look that he'd become all too accustomed to see. She then swung her eyes down to the young lady trying desperately to hold in her cries, her hand over her mouth.

Clementine Churchill stepped forward and placed a hand gently on the girl's shoulder. "Would you give us a minute please dear." Her voice was as sweet as a mother speaking to her child. Miss Robinson nodded, clearly glad of the reprieve. She quickly got up and exited the room, Churchill watched her until she left the room.

Clementine looked at her husband and shook her head gently. She folded her arms together in front of her. "Dear," she began, her voice stern but not loud, "You simply cannot keep going through secretaries this way." She approached him, placing her sweet, soft hands on his non cigar hand. "Otherwise, there will be no one left in England willing to come work for you."

Winston grumbled, stared at his beautiful wife then relented as he always did. He chuckled slightly, putting the cigar back into his mouth then patted her hand.

"You are right, my dear. As usual."

She smiled back at him. "Now," she began, "I must insist upon some restraint. You've much to do today and must get moving."

"To do?" He shook his head in confusion.

Mrs. Churchill sighed. "Dear, you are to be in Westminster later today. Parliament, remember. If you would not get so worked up with these young ladies, your memory might work better."

"Parliament!" He exclaimed as if his memory had returned. "Was that today?" He muttered slightly as he turned and began to disrobe out of his sleeping clothes.

It took Winston nearly another hour to groom and dress himself. In that time, he'd finished his seven o'clock cigar and had begun with another. He stamped downstairs and into his living room where his wife and personal butler were waiting for him.

Mrs. Churchill greeted him with a warm smile, she picked at tiny pieces of lint on his coat.

"My dear, what would I ever do without you?" He asked affectionately, patting his wife on the hand and kissing her on her cheek.

"God knows," she replied.

Winston smiled then took the proffered coat from his butler, snatched his bowler hat off the wall then turned to march off to the car waiting for him outside the home. As he was leaving the room, he noticed Miss Robinson standing near the door. He'd missed her completely as he'd walked in.

Winston looked at the young girl as he walked out of the room, paused in front of her and lifted his hat ever so slightly to her. "Madame......." He trailed off. She was quite a beauty this young lady of perhaps twenty. In some way she reminded him of his dear Clementine. "Good morning," he finished with as much kindness in his voice as there had been anger earlier.

Miss Robinson's lips flickered slightly in smile. "Good morning, sir," she replied then looked downwards.

Winston quickly adjusted the cigar in his mouth and stomped off.

He didn't keep track of time as he left his home on the way to Westminster, he was far too busy reading reports, scribbling notes and grumbling to himself.

Although he was no longer in government, he'd kept his seat in the House of Commons and had used his position and connections to those still in government to keep up to date with the important affairs of diplomacy and military preparedness. He'd spoken out bluntly against the policy of appeasement and on the need to keep a strong-armed service at home and abroad. While many of the higher-ranking military people silently nodded their agreement with him in private and hushed circles, the major policy makers had ignored him completely.

There had been more than a few heated discussions with his contemporaries about the happenings in Europe and the Far East. He openly opposed the Munich Agreement, and everyone knew it, Parliament, the

Government, even the king himself. Frustrated he'd confronted Neville Chamberlain before and after the agreement with Hitler had been signed. Thus, when the new cabinet had formed Winston had been left out in the cold completely, even though, in his mind anyway, he'd been more than qualified for a variety of different posts.

Who knows, he thought, *maybe the opportunity will present itself again and perhaps sooner rather than later.*

The opposition was chomping at the bit over the appeasement policy of the Chamberlain government and there was a good segment of his own Conservative party that was not happy about it either.

The car came to an abrupt halt, he barely noticed it, his driver exited and came around to open his door. Still scribbling notes furiously for a moment, he sat there as his driver endured the cold wintry air. Finally, plucking the cigar from his mouth and letting ashes fall on the car floor, he threw himself out of the car, put his bowler on and charged for the entrance.

The hallways of Parliament were as busy as ever, MP's and aides walking this way and that. Mail women pushing carts of envelopes made their way around. As he passed certain MP's he made sure to tip his hat in respect. Most he did not know, some he did, some disliked him, and he knew it. Always there were those who spoke softly to each other as he would pass by.

"Here comes the bulldog," some would whisper. For others it was "The fat pig." None of it bothered him, not much anyway. Most of them weren't even babes yet when he'd made his daring escape from a Boer prison camp in South Africa back in '99. More than a few of them spoke openly about Winston being far too old to be of any use in government and that the "old man" should hang up the hat and retire to Blenheim to take up gardening.

Finally, he came to the very door he was expected at. The Foreign Office.

"Good morning," said the young man sitting behind a small wooden desk as Churchill walked in.

He removed his hat and threw his coat over his arm. He grumbled a good morning back.

The young man stood up and reached out to take his coat and hat. "The Foreign Secretary is waiting for you already, sir. Allow me."

Winston gave up his belongings then started toward the inner door.

"Umm, sir," the man coughed slightly and indicated to Churchill's cigar.

"Hmmm? Oh yes." He gazed around for an ashtray, saw none, then put the cigar on the man's desk, still burning. He turned and walked into the adjoining office.

The man sitting in the room was a lean, bald-headed fellow. His face was gaunt, and his eyes were stern. Glancing up at Winston there was not so much as a glimpse of happiness in the man's look. He quickly returned his gaze downwards and continued writing on some papers. He was Winston's rival, his nemesis, his sometimes friend and his complete and polar opposite. Edward Wood, 1st Viscount Halifax, Britain's Foreign Secretary.

Standing for several uncomfortable seconds Winston coughed a fake cough and inched towards the man. He'd not been offered a chair and he'd be damned if he would ask for one.

After a long minute of silence as the Viscount finished his papers, he placed his pen down and gazed up at Winston. For a moment the two held a long, unyielding gaze at each other.

"Winston," he finally allowed. The tone in his voice monotonous.

"My Lord," the reply equally monotonous.

The false pleasantries done with; Viscount Halifax gestured for Winston to sit.

Churchill grinned then indicated that he would rather stand. "Far too much energy to sit still."

"Fine. I'll come to it then," Halifax said. "It is possible," he emphasized the word possible, "that there may be a position for you in the near future in government." The man clearly struggled to get the words out and Winston took note of it. He pursed his lips then added the word, "Unofficially."

Winston stood silent and stern. "Unofficially. Meaning what?" Parliament's session this morning had been a closed-door affair, he knew. It was possible that Chamberlain's government was beginning to fray. "I'm not familiar with unofficial government positions."

Halifax sat back in his rocking desk chair and scowled. His tongue pressed the inside of his cheek, and he crossed his right hand over his left prosthetic one.

"The PM is in a position to receive advice of a nature to which you hold a great deal of experience. He's asked me," he sighed at that last, "to speak with you about becoming an informal advisor on continental affairs."

Churchill grumbled and nodded his head slightly in understanding. He was no fool or amateur in this game. The Liberals and Labour parties were against Chamberlain and had, no doubt, asked for Winston's return. "I see. Advisor on continental affairs," his voice trailed off.

Hitler's aggression on the continent was placing a great deal of pressure on the government and on Chamberlain directly as the PM himself had negotiated directly with the German Furher. The situation in Europe was falling apart every day and the blame was falling more and more squarely on Chamberlain's shoulders. The opposition in Parliament were outraged and had no doubt offered Chamberlain a way out. The old man, too proud and too foolish to simply resign had probably been pressured by his cabinet to bring Churchill back into the fold.

"I'm not sure what service I may be, Mister Secretary," Winston stated bluntly. "Not in an unofficial capacity." They were bent and he knew it.

The back-and-forth political niceties that had been a part of British political history was a long and intricate dance and Winston knew it well. He'd been around too long and had made more than his fair share of mistakes and blunders to not recognize it when it came around. The difference between him and all the others who fell victim to this, was that he was still around and most of them were not.

If a fight broke out in Europe Chamberlain's government might well find itself the first casualty and both men knew it too. Halifax was no fool either. He was as much of a master politician as Winston. In more ways than one the two men were alike. Both the sons of lords. Both had committed to government service as young men. The difference between them was that Halifax's career up until now had been nearly spotless and Winston had stumbled and fallen out of government more than once. If they were calling him in now, the situation was desperate.

My chance at last, he thought to himself. "I'm sorry, Mister Secretary. But I am not sure that I can be of any assistance in this matter." He stared into the Foreign Secretary's eyes. "I do, however, wish you and the PM much success in the future." He grinned slightly to the man. The last was as much a warning as it was a rebuke.

Lord Halifax stared at his rival coldly, not uttering so much as a word as he watched Winston march out of his office.

Recovering his coat and hat from Halifax's secretary, he made sure he took a moment to pull out another cigar from his coat pocket, cut off the end and light it up prior to leaving the office.

The entire drive home had gone by for him nearly unnoticed as he stared out the window at the people passing by his car. He puffed away on his cigar and watched Londoners going about their daily business. He feared that their lives would change before the year's end and not for the better either. He'd hoped he was wrong but each day it seemed the newspapers brought more and more grim news. He was surprised that conflict had not begun already quite frankly.

His car pulled into the driveway and his driver opened the door letting Winston out.

He took off his hat as he entered the house. Clementine smiled as her husband returned and gestured for his hat. He handed it over.

"Well. How did it go?" She asked him.

Winston removed his coat, grinned broadly at his wife and said, "I've got the buggers right where I want them my dear."

CHAPTER TWO

The general staff snapped to attention as Herr Hitler walked slowly into the large briefing room, his entourage of personal aides and staff behind him. He walked slowly, taking care to hide the minor limp in his step, a leftover effect of his automobile crash last year. The large underground bunker of the OKH, army headquarters, had been completed last year and had become the preferred spot of all of Hitler's top secret military briefings. Designed to look like traditional housing from the air, it was several kilometers south of Berlin proper. It's larger companion at the OKW, the successor of the Reich Ministry of War, was in the same complex of buildings but was still under construction.

In the center of the enclosed room was a large table with an equally large map of Germany and Poland that was spread out across it.

There were numerous block markers laid across on the map marking the various locations where army and air force units stood ready across Germany. On the Polish side of the border the known locations of major Polish bases and airfields were marked in blue. A long line of X's on the French side of their border indicated the Maginot Line, the series of bunkers, pillboxes and fortifications built following the Great War to prevent another German invasion of that country.

In the room were Generals Halder and Brauschitsch, Chief of the General Staff and Commander-in-chief of the Army, Admiral Erich Raeder, Commander-in-chief of the Kriegsmarine, Hermann Göring, the overweight chief of the Luftwaffe, Germany's air force, in his sky-blue uniform with an obscene number of ribbons and medals, General Keitel and his deputy Jodl, Heinrich Himmler, the stone cold head of the SS and various aides and staff for each. Also present was Albert Speer, Minister of the newly created Reich Ministry of Armaments and the man in charge of Germany's war production.

Hitler placed his hands on the table to steady himself. His eyes shifted around the room and at the large map before him he finally gave a signal for them to proceed.

General Halder cleared his throat and adjusted his eyeglasses. "Mein Führer, allow me to first congratulate you on your miraculous recovery. With your leadership again guiding us, I feel there is very little that we cannot accomplish." There were various nods of agreement from the men around the room. Hitler gave the faintest of smiles then motioned for Halder to proceed.

"Case White Two is what we have named this operation, an update on the original plan for the attack on Poland," Halder continued. "In the months after our briefing on this matter last August, we've made considerable strides and gains in our logistics. As you may recall, Mein Führer, at that time we had planned for an offensive of some sixty divisions and over twenty-three hundred aircraft. Due to the delay of the operation our original plan for attack has been revised as we now have additional military resources to bring to bear."

He held up a pointing stick and indicated to the groupings of markers placed around the large map, each indicating a division, an army or army group and their corresponding headquarters. Black markers indicated land forces, red for airfields and Luftwaffe wings. On the Polish side of the map, Polish units were indicated in yellow and blue.

"In the last eight months since the original postponement we have added some nine divisions to our ground forces along the Polish border, including three more panzer divisions. Two more Luftwaffe attack wings have also been factored into our new plan. We now have seven hundred more aircraft available for the offensive. In addition, Army Group North," he indicated it with his pointing stick, "has received another five hundred of our Panzers Threes and Fours and Army Group South will have another four hundred. Because of the increased number of trucks available and with the technical assistance we've provided to our Slovak allies we've solved some of the logistical problems that we were faced with before. Supplies should move much faster now from our rear areas to our front-line forces.

"Several of our infantry divisions have also recently been upgraded with more motorized and mechanized units which should make traversing terrain easier and faster, thus allowing more of our infantry to keep up with their armored counterparts. Our previous total of commitment to this campaign was roughly two million men. Our committed forces should now number closer to two million four hundred thousand. We've equipped many of our divisions with additional engineering equipment and units that should also make the crossing of vital rivers much easier than previously planned upon.

"The offensive looks much like the original Case White but with two major differences. Here along the eastern Polish corridor, we've moved elements of the Fourth Army eastwards towards the city of Danzig. Any Polish forces caught in the corridor between Pomerania and East Prussia will be cut off from their base of supplies will either quickly surrender or be annihilated. Our ground forces there would then be tasked to act as the leftmost wing of our forces driving towards Warsaw.

"Furthermore, we've assigned six of our newer divisions, including one armored division to Reichenau's Tenth Army here. Their strength added to the Tenth should allow them to push deeper and faster into Silesia upon crossing the border. Their primary objectives are Katowice and ultimately Lodz. Securing those cities should cut off large amounts of Polish forces from retreating eastwards once their logistical support collapses." He straightened back up. "Our intelligence services monitoring Polish forces indicate little to no change in their positions and it seems likely that they do not suspect an attack coming, otherwise they would have begun to entrench and fortify their positions already."

Hitler looked over the map then grunted as if he'd taken it all in, continually tapping his finger on the map. "Luftwaffe?"

Herr Göring leaned over the huge table. "We have over three thousand three hundred aircraft in position and ready. Our first primary targets shall, of course, be the airfields of the Polish air force. Establishing air superiority quickly will be essential for our ground campaign. I've assigned enough bombers to each initial target that I feel quite assured we shall crush most of their aircraft while still on the ground, within the first twenty-four hours. Along the entire front our Stuka dive bombers shall provide close aerial support to ground forces, particularly where our own artillery cannot be concentrated." Göring moved some markers around the map as he imagined the air war would go, removing the Polish markers as each one was eliminated. "The Polish aero planes are antiquated and not much of a threat to our higher-flying bombers and faster flying fighters. A few British planes here and there," he waved it off, "but they are too few and too far between to effectively contest the skies."

Hitler remained silent. The fat man was always so confident it annoyed him. "How long for a complete victory?"

General Brauschitsch acknowledged the question. "Our timetables and estimates, based upon our most recent intelligence of Polish military positions, is three to four weeks from the first of our troops crossing the border. The Poles have very little in the way of effective defenses against our panzers and virtually nothing against the Luftwaffe."

Hitler noted Herr Göring puff up visibly. He picked up one of the markers and held it up in his hand for a few moments. He looked around the map and nodded as if to say, this is what I would have come up with as well.

"Ribbentrop has assured me that the Russians stand by to honor the agreement that we made with them last year," Hitler stated. "Eastern Poland to the Bolsheviks and the rest to us." He looked up from the map at Admiral Raeder, his naval chief. "What of your naval preparations, Raeder?"

"As you know, Mein Führer, Poland's navy is vastly inferior to our own. Their only port, of course, is Danzig and once the army has taken that, they will have no base from which to hurt us from. Nonetheless, I've stationed several additional warships to the operation to ensure that we keep control of the waters surrounding the port."

"And support from England or France?" Hitler asked.

Raeder nodded. "I've consulted with Admiral Canaris and we both agree that neither the British nor the French will be in position to do anything to stop the city from falling. Much of the French fleet is still based in the Mediterranean Sea and the British base at Scapa Flow would be too far to sortie with any real chance of successfully breaking our blockade. Besides, with our forces simultaneously capturing Oslo and Copenhagen, the risk to their warships would be too great to gamble on passing through the Kattegat Strait. Once we seize airfields in Denmark and southern Norway our aircraft would pounce on them, and they would know that."

Ah yes, Hitler thought about that. Upon his release from the hospital, he had repeatedly argued with his generals concerning Denmark and Norway. After his crash last year and subsequent postponement of the Polish campaign he had been eager to make up for lost time. There had been an additional eight months of military production and preparation, which meant more troops, tanks, planes and U-boats and Hitler felt confident that the Wehrmacht could pull off both campaigns at the same time.

So, beginning May 3rd, his troops would cross the border into Poland. Upon the declaration of war from England and France, one that he knew they'd be forced to make, his forces would then launch northwards to capture Denmark and Norway, the other blonde-haired people. *If anything*, he thought, *they were in a far better position now than they had been back in September*.

With Denmark and Norway in German hands, the Royal Navy wouldn't dare come to Poland's aid for fear of the Luftwaffe.

The other benefit of last September's delay was the increased amount of time and resources that the Kriegsmarine had to counter Britain's expansive navy. Since September, the number of serviceable warships had increased as had the number of U-boats in his arsenal. Twenty-two additional U-boats were now operational with another seven more being commissioned before the end of the month. That would almost double the number of submarines Germany would have operating in the North Atlantic. Hitler felt that this new strength would be enough to strangle the French and British from their overseas supply lines.

Hitler eyeballed Himmler for a moment. The Chief of the SS stood motionless and expressionless, as he always had before. They'd had their own meeting yesterday and had reached an understanding about the SS role in the forthcoming campaign. Though nobody else in the room would know the details of that meeting, all that they needed to know was that their respective branches of service would be required to cooperate fully with the SS chief and his minions.

Hitler looked over at Reich Minister of Armaments, Speer. The man, in his black Nazi party uniform, had just recently been given his title and the power to oversee all of Germany's war production. He'd succeeded the late Fritz Todt when that man had been killed in the very automobile accident that had almost taken Hitler's life as well. The young Speer had wasted no time in expanding Germany's industrial power since taking control. Every bullet and every bomb produced in factories across the country were now his responsibility. "Speer. You've now had almost a year to put our industry on a war footing. What have you done with all this time?"

"Mein Führer, we've made a great deal of progress in our war production in the past few months in order to meet our current demands." He pulled a small notebook out from his pocket and flipped it open. "Since last September we've increased our production of mechanized and armored vehicles as well as heavy aircraft in order to meet the goals set by the OKW. The Panzer Mark One, now being operationally obsolete, has been phased out and replaced with the much better Panzer Threes and Fours. We've handed over to the army another six hundred and thirty new tanks since January and we'll have another one hundred and fifty more by the operational date. Furthermore, we've retooled many of our factories that were making civilian consumer goods. Factories that previously made house ware products are now producing parts for our aircraft, rifles, submarine torpedoes, etc...

"Since December the Luftwaffe has received an additional seven hundred light and medium bombers and sixteen hundred of the newer Messerschmitt fighters. By the end of this year alone, we fully expect another eight hundred of the Bf-110's and a thousand of the 109's. By the beginning of 1941 our expectations are to be able to have all our factories currently scheduled for retooling to be operational. As our military grows, our manufacturing base must grow with it to meet the demands.

So, I've ordered a number of new projects to begin. The shipyards in the north will undergo an expansion in the coming months to increase naval production and we have begun a program to expand our industry in Austria and our Czech territories. These things together will take full advantage of our available labor force and we will see a steady rise in industrial output over the next year.

"Unfortunately, however, our industrial expansion is meeting with limitations. Obviously with the higher demand for more production comes a higher demand for the raw resources we need in order to accomplish this. Certain materials, such as rubber for instance, are becoming harder and harder to come by. Oil production in Germany is much lower. . . ."

"Yes, yes!" Hitler waved his hands. "I've heard this before. Rest assured Fritz, those resources shall soon be in our hands. Ribbentrop is even now negotiating with other countries. Soon we will be receiving more oil from Romania. Very shortly we will have the resources that we need to fuel your precious factories. Before summer's end you'll have enough raw materials to keep our industries roaring for years to come. Now gentlemen, are there any other details that I must know? I am expected to be at a party function later this evening."

He looked around the room, all were silent. He nodded his final approval then set down the marker he'd been holding in his hand. "I expect a total victory in the east! I have full confidence in the quality of our brave soldiers, and I look forward to hearing of their heroic exploits." He breathed loudly. "These are rightfully our lands." He slapped the table. "This will be a brief and sharp conflict. I do not see either the British or the French putting up much of a fight, if any at all. They do not have the will to fight a long war." He went silent for a few moments. His head bobbed up and down as if he were deep in thought and agreeing with the thoughts in his own mind. "I mean to undo the stain of Versailles," he whispered, barely audible to the men in the room. "The stain of Versailles."

CHAPTER THREE

Gwen's body shuddered and she reflexively dug her nails into the back of Johnny's neck, then let out a last gasp of pleasure and a long, exhilarating sigh of relief. He put his head up and held her gaze, her hands fell away as if she no longer had the strength to keep them up. He kissed her lips softly; she moaned and turned her head away and he continued to kiss her lightly on her cheek and neck.

Johnny rolled off her and together for a long moment they lay next to each other. Finally, she threw her arms across him and laid her head on his chest.

"That was amazing," she whispered then bit him teasingly. "Care to go again?"

He smiled then slowly ran his finger up and down her spine.

"Of course I would, Baby," he replied. "Sometime after my coffee and breakfast."

Gwen ran her fingertips over his torso. It was so good to feel her touch. It was always good to have her close to him. To touch her skin, her hair, to feel her breath on him.

He'd gotten back to the city just two days ago and they'd barely left her apartment in Brooklyn in that time. A fact, he'd noted, that had not gone unnoticed by Gwen's neighbors. The elderly woman next door, Mrs. Simmerson or whatever her name was, giving both a sneering look of disapproval as they'd walked by her in the hallway yesterday, Gwen being an unmarried woman and all. Then there was the pounding on the wall as her other neighbors were reminding them just how thin the walls in the building were.

Oh well. He didn't much care and he knew she didn't either. He liked Gwen and she liked him. They'd known each other for years. She had been a onetime girlfriend of one of his fly boy buddies and they'd always had a little flirtation with each other. After his buddy and she went their separate ways, John had wasted no time in filling that void. The difficulty came when the army had given him orders to pack up and ship out to Honolulu last year, so they had mutually decided that a steady commitment wasn't a current option. But whenever he'd gotten some leave time, he would return to her in Brooklyn, and they'd pick right up where they'd left off.

"What would you like for breakfast?" she asked, running her hand up along the side of his torso.

"Hmmmm.... Bacon and eggs sound good. Coffee."

"Okay." She kissed his chin then got out of bed, threw her silk robe over herself and walked out of the bedroom. "Water's hot if you want to shower."

That sounded good, he thought. He tossed aside the sheets and got up. It must've been nine or ten o'clock he knew. The sun had been up for a while and people were coming and going outside, the trains could be heard whistling by just a couple blocks away and taxis running up and down the street honking their horns as they went by. *Noisy*, he thought. He was originally from a small town in Pennsylvania, a farming community. There were no buses or trains, or for that matter sidewalks for people to walk. While he didn't care that much for Brooklyn, he liked Perry Township Pennsylvania even less, so he hadn't been back there in ten years.

He enjoyed Manhattan's nightlife and culture, the plays on Broadway, the clubs and taverns, Times Square, all of it. A good-looking guy with a few bucks in his pocket could have a good time in Manhattan, Honolulu too for that matter. He'd lucked out when the army had stationed him at Hickam Field in Hawaii.

John turned on the water and waited for it to heat up. Took a quick look at himself in the mirror and ran his hands over the stubble on his face. A hot shower and a shave later he stepped out of the bathroom, put on his pants and walked out into the living room.

Gwen's apartment was small, just what one would expect for a girl who waited tables at a local diner during the day and moonlighted as a cigar girl at some Brooklyn nightclub, but it was homely and not a mess. It consisted of one bedroom, bath, a living room and a tiny kitchen with a table only big enough for two. It looked like just about every other apartment in Williamsburg Brooklyn. Small.

She was standing behind the stove cooking when he walked in, wrapped his hands around her waist and kissed her from behind.

"Your coffee," she said, handing him a steaming cup.

He took it and seated himself at the table. The newspaper was waiting for him, he unfolded it and went right to the sports section, leaving the rest of it for her. He loved having his morning coffee and newspaper with her. It had become their little ritual.

"Feller pitched a perfect game yesterday," he told Gwen as she put his plate in front of him then sat down across from him and took a sip of her coffee.

"Who?"

He chuckled. "Baseball, Baby. He plays for the Cleveland Indians."

Her eyes rolled as she picked up the front page and took a bite of her bacon. "Sounds important," she said sarcastically.

Gwen was a smart girl. Used to being independent and taking care of her own life, rather than relying upon a man as most girls her age and with her looks did and Johnny liked that about her. She was a damn good-looking woman, a slender, dirty blonde with green eyes. She never put on a lot of makeup, she didn't need it and quite frankly he didn't care for it on her. She could swear and drink just as well as any guy he knew but she also kept a ladylike quality that he liked. She enjoyed getting flowers, nice dinners, romance novels and kids. A New Yorker, born and raised, she was tough when she needed to be and sweet when she wanted to be.

Reading through the newspaper Gwen sighed. "These poor kids in China, those Japanese are killing so many of them."

He grumbled in agreement but said nothing. He didn't know any Chinese people back in Pennsylvania or in any of the places in the Midwest or Pacific Northwest that the army chose to stick him in. He hadn't even seen a Chinaman until he'd gotten to San Francisco on his way to Hawaii last year. There were Japs in Hawaii, a whole bunch of them and he'd found it impossible to distinguish between the two. Chinese or Japanese in his mind were kind of the same thing anyway. Besides, he'd heard from some of the other guys in his unit that the Chinese were different than we were, less intelligent, more like animals or something. He wanted to believe that so that when he heard about all the horror stories about Japanese atrocities, it made it easier to dismiss, but deep down he didn't like what was going on either.

"So much killing," Gwen went on. She enjoyed sharing her opinions and John, unlike other guys, didn't mind. "That man in Russia, Stalin, he's doing the same thing, murdering people just because they're not communists. It worries me that people like that could take over the world. Maybe even come here."

"Nobody's coming here to take over the States Hun. We've got two great big oceans between them and us." He outwardly played cool and coy, but he did agree with her.

John had voted for Roosevelt both times, partly because he agreed with the President about these dictators, Stalin and Tojo, Hitler and Mussolini, all trying to grab more and more land. He genuinely felt bad for the people in those conquered countries, but they weren't his people, and it wasn't his country.

"Still, it worries me," she went on. "I remember my dad avoided talking about the war when I was little. He never said much about it, I don't think he liked to. Whenever it was brought up, he'd just get this look on his face. Mom always told us to forget it. A lot of our guys died over there. Was your dad over there?"

John shook his head. "Nah. Too old. My uncle went over there, though. Fought in Italy."

"Well, eventually I think that somebody is going to have to step in and stand up to these people. The world can't keep going through this.

Look at what those Nazi' are doing persecuting those Jewish people like that." She shook her head.

Johnny smiled and took another sip. "You're an idealist, Baby. The world is a tough place."

He finished up his eggs and bacon then pushed the plate away.

"Hey, let's go out," he tried to change the subject. "We'll do lunch, maybe go see a motion picture or maybe Coney Island."

She eyeballed him and squinted. "Trying to change the subject?" she said pointing her fork at him. There was the smallest frown on her face, but her voice was playful.

He grinned at her. "No of course not."

"We will, lover," she told him and rubbed her hand along his arm. "You're on leave for the next two weeks and ummm.... It has been six months since you were here last." She smiled that beautiful smile that John loved.

Bobby cupped his hands together and blew hot air on them. It was cold, damn cold, even this late into April. The wind off the East River blew hard and sent a chill through him. He finished his cigarette, tossed it on the ground and stomped it out. A tug liner blew its horn as it passed by. He stayed outside for a few minutes longer. It was a nice day today, other than the temperature. The sun was out and right now he wished that he were anywhere else but here. Here being the Turner and Co. Ironworks of Brooklyn.

The metal door behind him screeched open and a voice called out to him, "Skaggs, you on vacation or something?"

Bobby looked down for a moment at his crushed-out cigarette then replied, "No, Mister Goldman. Just grabbing a quick smoke is all." He turned back to the man.

His middle-aged and overweight supervisor stood in the doorway staring back at him. His sweater vest was hanging open and his cheap white pocketed shirt betrayed the fact that the man both drank too much coffee and never seemed to clean his white shirt. He was all of five foot six, fat faced and balding and close to three hundred pounds, most of which he carried in his bulging stomach. He wasn't the most intimidating guy in the world and Bobby always let Goldman know it too. Not with sarcastic wit or bland insubordination, but just by sheer force of will.

He stepped closer to his boss, then closer still until he was right on the man. His six-foot three-inch, lean and hardened frame imposing over his stout boss, he stared right into the fat man's dark eyes. Goldman blinked then gestured for Skaggs to come back to work.

"Alright," the man said in a voice similar to that of a schoolteacher talking down to some schoolboy who was misbehaving in class. "Well.... break's over." He stepped aside to let Bobby back into the run-down warehouse where they worked along the river.

They went back inside, and Goldman struggled to shut the large metal door behind them, its rusted bottom scraping eerily along the concrete ground.

"What'd you do, smoke a whole pack of Lucky's?" Goldman commented. "Look.... I like you Bobby, I really do. You're a good worker and I've never really had a problem with you. But I've got quotas to meet just like everyone else and there's plenty of work to do. You get me? So, give me a break will ya. Back to work."

"Yes, sir, Mister Goldman," Bobby replied dryly. He'd gotten this talk more times than he cared to remember since he began working here, everyone had. Goldman's attitude towards workers was to make sure they knew he was boss, which meant berate them as much as possible and let them know just how lucky they were to have a job these days. "I'll get right on it, Mister Goldman." He walked away.

"You know," Goldman began, Bobby already knew what was coming next, "you're lucky to have a job here. A lot of people out there looking for jobs."

Goldman was a wimp and Bobby knew it. He'd seen a thousand guys like him throughout his life. Guys who thought that they were just a little bit better than others, but he knew they weren't. They were more insecure with themselves than those poor bastards that guys like Goldman kept pushing around like sheep or cattle. He'd take any one of those fellas who'd braved those cold nights lining up to get work back in the early days of the crash over some plump faced guy from New Jersey who probably never knew what it was like to have his heat shut off in January.

But he was right in one sense. Bobby was lucky to have the job he had. He'd worked as a welder at Turner now since the summer of '38, a job provided to him by the great state of New York. It was tough work, but he liked that about it. The harder, the better. Although, he'd never welded a day in his life prior to getting this job, he'd lied and told the state employment people that he'd welded on the family farm when he was young. In reality he'd grown up just a few miles away in Flatbush, his father had been a schoolteacher and his mother worked in a department store.

He'd been fortunate though, his first couple of weeks he'd been assigned to an older guy, Milton, or Milt as he was affectionately called, who had quickly recognized the truth that Bobby had no previous experience welding iron. The two of them connected well and Milt taught the younger man everything he could about welding rather than ratting him out to the bosses. His crash course lasted a few intense weeks, instead of the many months it might have taken another guy to learn. Bobby had always been a fast learner, you had to be quick when you practically grew up on the streets.

He walked back to his work area. He was farther ahead in his work than half the other guys he worked with, both he and Goldman knew it too. A lot of the others milked it, took longer and worked slower so that Goldman didn't hassle them too much. Bobby did his job right the first time and got it done more quickly and didn't give a shit what the fat man said to him.

"Fucking propellers," he said to himself as he gazed at his workspace. His company molded and produced propellers for navy ships. He didn't care very much for the job, but it did pay well, better than a lot of other jobs out there. He'd stood in line for food and unemployment too many times and often in bad weather for him to cry and complain about his job. Here, at least, he had a roof over his head, warmth from the cold and a steady paycheck week after week.

He picked up his welders' helmet, sparked his torch to life and set back to work, albeit slowly. He just didn't want to hear the fat man's voice again today. Bobby might just strangle the fat bastard if he did. It took him nearly an hour to do what he would normally do in about fifteen minutes.

Other guys usually worked in small groups, but not him. He preferred to work by himself. He didn't dislike his coworkers, but he also didn't go out of his way to get to know them either. If one of them needed a day off, he'd have been the first to cover for him, he just simply preferred to work alone. It kept uncomfortable conversation to a bare minimum, and he was good with that.

"Hey Bobby," came a loud voice and a tap on the shoulder. Bobby shut off his torch and lifted his helmet up. "Hey, look at what my kid gave me." It was Neil Earleman.

"What is it?" Bobby looked down at the small comic Neil was holding.

Neil chuckled. "Just something my kid left in my lunch box. Batman." He laughed. "Who's ever heard of such a thing huh? A guy dressing up like a bat."

Bobby nodded and took off his helmet. Neil was an okay guy. Bobby was 35 and Neil was a couple of years older than that. Neil was a family man, three kids and a wife. He was one of the few that Bobby chose to talk with now and again. Neil didn't ask too many questions.

"Funny," Bobby replied. "How old's your boy now?" He already knew how old the kids were, but he knew Neil always loved to talk about them anyway.

"Andrew? He's eight. Molly's eleven and the baby's five." He shook his head. "They're growing so damned fast I can hardly keep up. Before you know it...." He spread his arms out. "I'd make three more of 'em but Janey...." He shook his head and let out a laugh.

Eight, Bobby thought to himself, *Sarah would've been eight herself.* He pictured his own little girl playing with Neil's kids at a park somewhere. It got to him, and the old pain resurfaced as it always did. He licked his lips and grinned back at Neil, putting a bright face back on.

"Yeah," was all he could come back with.

Neil patted him on the shoulder. "Hey, listen, why don't you come on over, maybe this weekend. Janey's younger sister's in town from Philly.

They do a great dinner, a real feast. Her name's Rosalie." He made gestures with his hands. "Nice and curvy. Big tits."

Bobby grinned back at him. "I'll let you know. Maybe."

A whistle blew. Quitting time. He pulled his work gloves off and tossed them onto his work bench. Other guys were doing the same and picking up their personal belongings to make their way to the locker room and showers.

"How about this," Bobby told him, "I've got some business to take care of Saturday. If I get it done with, I'll stop by."

Neil smiled broadly. "Yeah. Great. I'll let Janey know. Maybe we'll listen to a Dodgers game."

"Sounds great."

He patted Neil on the shoulder and walked off to the locker room. Most of the guys had already been through and grabbed their stuff. There were a bunch of tables pushed together in the center of the locker room, it's where a lot of the workers ate their lunch. The room was littered with trash and food of all types. He almost never ate with the other guys, preferring instead to keep working.

He popped open his locker, exchanged his rubber apron for his flannel coat and hat. He grabbed his own lunchbox then closed the locker. Turning to make his way out the door, he looked down, grabbed a copy of the New York Times lying on the table and left.

Bobby walked a few blocks from work on his way home. It was already dark out and thought he'd grab a cup of coffee before taking the train back to Ridgewood. He ducked into Carl's Diner, a little place right off Driggs Avenue that was never too busy this time of day. A little bell on the door jingled as he walked in and the waitress, Sue, waved at him as he did. He hung up his coat and hat then took a seat at the counter. Sue was already pouring him a cup of joe.

"Hey, Hun," she smiled as he sat. She was chewing on her favorite bubble gum as she always did. Her lipstick was a bright pink, and her dark brunette hair was naturally curly. She always wore a bit too much French perfume and he noticed it as he took his seat.

"No Gwen tonight?" He smiled back as she topped off his cup.

"I think she's got herself a boyfriend or something." She eyed him and smiled then stuck her shoulder out at him. "But I'm just as cute."

He nodded. "Yeah. Yeah, you are, darlin'." He liked Sue.

"Eating tonight?"

He shook it off. "Naw. I always eat dinner at home. You know that."

"Yeah, I know. But the day I don't ask is the day you want a steak and potatoes."

Bobby grinned, unfolded the newspaper and started scanning the articles. Fenner had pitched a perfect game against the White Sox, something about some guy named Chamberlain over in England and the economy was looking better and better.

"How 'bout you buy me dinner some time?" Sue interrupted. "There's a little Italian place right around the corner from my place." She smiled; her lipstick had smeared her teeth.

Bobby smiled. "Yeah. Sounds good. Maybe Saturday."

"You're sweet," she replied. She looked down at the paper he was reading, and the smile fell away. "Sad what's going on over there in China. All those kids and all."

He looked down at the article and the photo of a small Chinese girl crying.

"Yeah, it is," he agreed. "Somebody's going to have to do something about all that."

CHAPTER FOUR

Across the wide, flat expanse of open land the huge, armored formation moved forward, a few tanks in the center at first and then more and more across the flanks as the entire regiment moved forward in a giant V shaped formation. Their targets were nearly four hundred meters ahead of them now.

Lance Corporal Ernst Krauss stood half out of the turret of his brand new, straight off the assembly line Panzer IV and gazed through his binoculars. The regiment's formation looked good; each tank rolled along just as they'd practiced for months now. His tank was fourth from the center on the right of the line. The third and fifth tank to his left front and right rear were a perfect eight to ten meters apart from him and keeping up a good speed.

The lead tank, a Panzer III, was closing in on the first target, three hundred meters was the effective firing range. The lead tank fired a hit! The two flanking tanks, both Panzer IVs, fired on the stationary targets almost simultaneously. Ernst just had time to shift his view to see both rounds go right through their targets, sending the two vehicles ten feet up in the air and bringing them crashing down, chunks of metal debris flying everywhere.

As each tank came within three hundred meters of its scoped target it fired, nearly all of them a hit. The panzers passed through the damaged wreckage on all sides, like cavalry of old charging through the gaps in some old-fashioned line infantry formation.

"Fire!" He screamed through his throat mike.

A heavy shudder ran through the tank as the giant gun fired a 7.5 cm round ahead of its advance. A blink later the target exploded off the ground and the wreckage came crashing down with a hole in its side. Everywhere the field was littered with broken trucks and vehicles of all types, all smoldering and smoking.

Krauss held up his microphone to his mouth. "Left. Pass left."

The tank bore down on its victim and passed by the burning hulk's left. Over his vehicle headset he could hear as tank after tank radio operator reported in their hits. Nearly all of them hit their targets on the first try, most of the rest on their second. Those tanks that did not hit their targets, well, *God help them*, he thought to himself. General Veiel, commander of the 2nd Panzer Division, would probably have their heads. There was precious little room for error in the panzer units.

Ernst had been assigned to command a tank in the 2nd Panzer division only a week ago and as such he'd had precious little time to get used to both his new tank and his crew. At only age nineteen some of that crew were older than he was, and he often felt their eyes of disdain upon him whenever he was shouting orders. Private Nicholas, the loader, was the youngest at seventeen, Privates Schmidt and Mayer, the driver and the radio operator, were both older than he at twenty and twenty-one respectively. Then there was Private Albrecht, his gunner, a young man of just eighteen who'd graduated from tank school as one of the top gunners. He'd hoped that going into combat, if they ever even did, his expert gunner would be a great asset to them all. And there was not a doubt in his mind that all the men under his command were complete professionals. Besides, he didn't believe there was going to be any war, and nobody would ever see combat anyhow, unless the Allies started one.

Krauss had enlisted just two years earlier, in the spring of '38 at only seventeen. He'd been scared of course but he'd found, to his own amazement, that he excelled at soldiering. Having never even fired a rifle before joining up, he'd quickly mastered the arts of small arms, map reading and radio operation. By the time he'd finished tank school last year, they'd promoted him to the rank of lance corporal. While most of his schoolmates, many of them older than he, were still privates. Upon being reassigned to the 2nd Panzer Division, he'd been given charge of his own crew and one of the brand-new Panzer IVs. It was more than the son of a Dresden shoemaker could have ever hoped for.

"Second target coming up," he called into his microphone. "Four hundred meters ahead, ten degrees right, mark!" His gunner was ready, the turret shifting to keep the new target in its front sights.

The large heavy Panzer IV barreled in, keeping its formation with the rest of the force. Nobody had broken formation. . . . not yet anyhow. Since the targets were stationary and didn't fire back there should be no reason to break ranks. Three hundred seventy, three hundred fifty, three hundred twenty, three hundred meters.

"Fire!"

Another explosion fired from the short gun barrel, sending a single round down field at 385 meters per second. It passed right through the immobile target like a bullet through a sheet of paper. The target broke nearly in half and the round burrowed into the ground, sending up a plume of dirt and earth.

"Hit!" He bellowed.

"Pass right," Krauss ordered. The tank shifted its huge body to pass the target on its right. Ernst grinned proudly as he watched the burning wreckage pass him. "Good job, boys. One more to go."

He looked around the field, the rest of the regiment was rolling along through the muddy field just as they'd planned. Other tank commanders surveyed the field just as he was, their black clad panzer uniforms stained from mud splatter and earth that had fallen on them as they'd passed by their destroyed targets.

"Target three, five hundred meters ahead," he called. "Twenty degrees to left."

He wiped the sweat from his brow and adjusted his side cap, peered through his binoculars and zeroed in on the final target.

His panzer closed the distance on the target, four hundred, three seventy, three fifty, three twenty-five, three hundred. . . . "Fire!"

The tank shuddered again as a heavy round fired out of the main barrel. Ernst brought his binoculars up to view the target. The round exploded just to the right of the target, sending up a hail of earthen debris that fell harmlessly down.

"Reload, reload!" He yelled. The loader acknowledged. "Target two hundred meters, twenty-five degrees left." The turret shifted to the new bearing. "Fire!"

The round passed right through the target this time, sending the door of the destroyed vehicle flying off and catching the rusted wreck afire.

"Pass right!" The burning wreck passed harmlessly a dozen meters off Ernst's left. He watched it burn for a moment, grinning broadly with pride at how his crew had performed.

The resumption of live fire exercises had recently become the normal routine among the venerated panzer divisions. Training exercises using live ammunition, although costly as well as potentially dangerous, did have the advantage of drilling actual combat conditions into the men as well as allowing the officers to better gauge their troops performance. It also gave the boys the opportunity to scratch their itchy trigger fingers now and again.

The lead tanks had completed their run and were heading off the firing range and towards the assembly area. The remaining panzers fired the last of their rounds, finishing off the "opposing force" before being ordered by the commanding general to cease their live fire and assemble on the edge of the firing range. One by one the tanks rolled into parking formation and shut off their engines. Crew by crew began to exit their vehicles and greeted each other enthusiastically on their performance.

Most of the regiment was made up of younger men, like Ernst. Some of the men were conscripts but most, like himself, had signed up voluntarily to serve the Fatherland. It was, after all, every real German's duty and honor to serve Germany and the Führer.

"Regiment to formation!"

The men each jumped to and the regiment, nearly five hundred men total, formed a large square, officers in front, enlisted men behind.

Two cars pulled in front of the formation, their regimental commander Colonel Rohm exited the lead car, a serious look on his face. Rohm was a lean man in his mid-forties, a professional to his core. He wore a typical panzer officer's gray tunic and cap with gray trousers and standard high boots, signature Luger P08 sidearm on his hip.

The colonel was a veteran of the Great War and had seen much combat during those times, Verdun in 1916, the Argonne and the Marne in '18. His wispy brown hair was flecked with gray despite being only forty-five, his left arm hung slightly limp from where he'd taken shrapnel during that war. His eyes were still keen, and his manner was always that of a clear-thinking professional fighting man.

He had been an early supporter of the mobile warfare doctrine who had served under men like Guderian and Manstein and had helped to write the manual on tank warfare. Rumors among other men in the regiment was that Rohm was being groomed for general a few years back but had been passed over due to repeated disagreements with Berlin OKH over the development of the tank corps. Also, it probably didn't help that the Colonel had refused to join the party, Hitler's party.

"Men," Rohm spoke loudly and clearly, years of military professionalism in his Prussian voice, "you have performed well. You have performed just as good soldiers should. Just as good Germans do when it is asked of them. I know that if we were called upon to make even more sacrifices," he paused and looked around at the faces of the men of his command for what seemed like a long moment, "I know that every one of you would be willing to do it. Because.... that is what soldiers do.

"Tomorrow we begin the task of moving all of our equipment east of here. Our orders are that the entire division is to participate in additional training. Service your equipment this afternoon. Any man needing medical treatment should do so immediately, you may not be coming back here for a while. I am proud of you men. The Fatherland is proud of you." He nodded to another officer then turned and walked back to his command car.

"Dismissed!" The officer hollered.

The regiment began to break up.

"Moving east again?" Private Mayer, the tank radio operator stated. He shook his head. "More war games and field training. Just like last fall. They moved us all, had us sitting around on our hands, then moved us back again."

Private Mayer was the oldest of his tank crew. At twenty-one he had failed to make any reasonable impression on anyone. He was the radio operator of the crew and manned the forward machine gun while in combat. He was good at both but had shown a series of disciplinary problems in the past, prior to Ernst's arrival to the 2nd Panzer. He had the age, experience and time in service to have been promoted by now and it was very clear from the start that he was mildly hostile to Krauss, whom he saw as a younger up-jumped kid.

Ernst had been with the 5th Panzer last September and remembered half the army packing up and moving east towards the Polish frontier. No explanation had ever really been given, some said the Poles had crossed the border and attacked some German town or some such thing, turned out to be nonsense. But then again, the Führer had been involved in an assassination attempt around that time too.

Maybe it was all connected, Ernst thought.

Radio Berlin said that the attempt had been made by some Poles and Communist sympathizers. The entire nation was in shock over that for quite some time. Germans everywhere fretted at the prospect of losing their beloved Führer, especially those who belonged to the party.

For days there were vigils held for Hitler in the streets of every major city in the Reich. He remembered the recruiting bonanza that erupted after that. Young German men from all over had flocked to recruiting offices to sign up as fast as they could. The ranks of the Wehrmacht swelled so quickly last fall and winter that recruit depots had to be formed in schoolhouses and public parks became parading grounds for the army.

"Fall in," Krauss ordered, and his men obeyed. "You did very well today, and I mean that. Training on these new tanks has been difficult. Most of us trained on the twos but in these last few weeks we've made real progress together. I told you when we were first assigned together that given time, we'd master this beast, and we have." He looked back at the huge tank then back to his crew. "Do a quick equipment check. As soon as it's done you can rest for the remainder of the day. They have no. . . ."

"Krauss!" A voice bellowed; a thick bodied, mustachioed sergeant walked around from behind a tank. Krauss turned to look. "Go see Captain Hofer!" The sergeant shouted and continued walking.

Krauss turned back to his men, hands clasped behind his back. "Carry on men."

The men broke up, Private Mayer held Krauss's gaze for a brief second before turning away and joining his comrades.

Krauss made his way over to the small group of officers standing around a wooden table near a tree. Captain Hofer was the company commander, an Austrian by birth and a member of the National Socialist Party, the man had been absorbed by the Wehrmacht when Germany had annexed Austria in early '38. A tall, lanky man he had little muscle, but he had the sharp eyes, nose and chin that displayed his Aryan blood, the Germanic look that party members liked to see in their servicemen.

"Lance Corporal Krauss reporting as ordered, sir!" He stomped his boots into the grassy ground beneath them. He brought his right hand up in salute and waited for his commanding officer to return the gesture.

Captain Hofer put down the papers he was looking at and saluted him in return. "At ease. I've been reading through your performance evaluation, Corporal, since you've been with us and while you were with the 5th Panzer. I remember telling you when you first got here, that your previous company captain thought very highly of you and that I also had high expectations of you." He paused for a moment; his face betrayed no emotion whatsoever. "You've been in the army now for what. . . . two years?"

"Yes, sir!"

Hofer nodded slightly. "And you've made lance corporal since then. Not bad at all, Krauss. It takes most men three or four to make that in peacetime."

"Thank you, sir!" Krauss fought to contain a grin; officers never liked when an enlisted man smiled.

Hofer held him in his sights for a moment then raised his left arm, a piece of paper in his hand. Krauss hesitated for a moment, unsure whether he wanted to know what the was on the paper. The tone of Hofer's voice betrayed nothing. He took the paper from his captain, opened it up and read it over.

"A letter of recommendation?" Krauss said in a low voice. "Thank you, sir." He looked back up at his officer.

"Don't thank me, Lance Corporal. It's only a recommendation, you haven't gotten the promotion just yet. Also, with higher rank comes more responsibility, but I think you can handle it."

"Yes, sir. I won't disappoint you, sir." Krauss replied, all the professionalism in his voice that he could muster. Papa was going to be so proud.

"I believe you," Hofer told him. "You're dismissed, Lance Corporal." He held his right hand up, palm outward. "Heil Hitler!"

"Heil Hitler!"

CHAPTER FIVE

The teletype had been busy all morning long by the time Archibald Norwen came into work at the Naval Planning Office. Long rows of ticker tape had been cut and pasted together onto a readable report that was waiting for him by the time he'd finally arrived at work, over twenty minutes late. His aide, a young man named Daniel Towman, had already put the report on his desk and had a pot of hot tea water ready to go.

The office was nothing more than a confined workroom in the bowels of the Admiralty building in Whitehall, which consisted of an open workspace for the dozen people who worked in it, a large conference table along the far right wall that was often where large maps were splayed out in overlapping layers, and a small enclosed room in the far left corner where the teletype was daily spitting out reports from all corners of the British Empire.

It was just a small part of the Operations Division and had often been considered a dead end for those who had the unlucky fortune to be assigned to it. Its position within the Admiralty building itself had earned it the nickname "The Closet", for those few who went in seldom came out and were often forgotten about afterwards.

However, for those naval and civilian employees who worked inside its walls, there was a good sense of camaraderie and cheerfulness to the work that they were doing there. Its primary function was to disseminate information from a variety of sources concerning the naval operations of foreign nations that may be considered hostile to Britain, to make certain recommendations for countering such threats, and then to kick those rec-ommendations up the ladder. Too often, though, the office was seen by the very captains and admirals to whom those recommendations were sent as being redundant to naval planning. Intelligence, some believed, should pass directly from Section 6, the country's premier intelligence agency, straight to the admiralty, who then would make their recommen-dations to the cabinet and so on and so forth.

In the mind of the man who'd been tasked with overseeing the Closet, Commander Norwen of His Majesty's Royal Navy, Section 6 was an intelli-gence gathering apparatus that spent little time contemplating long term naval policy. Furthermore, naval intelligence had too often been seen by the politicians who cut the checks as less vital and not as important as its army component. With the British Empire spread across the globe, on six continents and four oceans, this would seem to be a fatal flaw in strategic thinking.

"Good morning," Commander Norwen said as he entered the office, hanging his hat up on the wall and putting his wet umbrella in the corner stand. "Apologies. April showers and all that."

There were various nods and smiles of greeting from the staff work-ing around the office as the boss settled in behind his wooden desk near the back wall.

"Good morning, sir," Towman greeted him. He placed a cup and saucer on Norwen's desk, steam rising from the hot tea. "Your morning report is ready for you, sir."

Commander Norwen settled in and took a sip of his morning Darjeel-ing tea, a wedge of lemon bobbing up and down in the cup. He took the green folder in hand and began to scan through the overnight reports.

His office had been established back in the '20's but nobody had taken the time to put together any real procedures for how things got done in the Closet at first. As so the first few years of its existence was spent shuffling papers around meaninglessly and only rarely, if ever, passed along recommendations. When Archie, a fifteen-year veteran of the Royal Navy, had been given charge of the office he'd quickly found that it existed for no real reason other than to act as yet another meaningless paper pushing unit that was too often trying to justify its own existence.

Within a year of arriving, he had changed all of that, quickly establishing operation protocols and procedures, fired anyone who did not take the job seriously and brought in people that he knew would get the task done. Despite his effective streamlining of the information process, he had never really gained the trust or approval of many of his superiors. Even those who had praised his work at untangling such a tangled knot had still failed to show any real belief in his department as an actual viable one within the navy.

"The teletype has been going all night long, sir" Towman informed him, nodding to the back room where the sound of ticker tape could still be heard drumming off.

Towman was a young man with no social life whatsoever. A civilian worker who always took to calling Commander Norwen "Sir" out of respect. The young man was well educated and seemed to have a limitless supply of energy, often arriving at work well before his scheduled time and staying long into the night. He was detail oriented and quick on his feet and Norwen appreciated the lad.

"Did we get an information update from Section 6 last night?" Norwen asked, he turned his head from the teletype room back to his aide.

"No, sir," was the reply. "Not that I've seen. This is all from civilian sources. My understanding is that MI6 is still working on deciphering last week's transmission requests."

Odd, Norwen thought. Typically, when information was coming in at this rate it was because Section 6, otherwise known as MI6, had decoded foreign transmissions and were passing along relevant information to his office, but that only happened once or twice a month. Last week's coded Japanese naval communiques, picked up by listening stations in Hong Kong and Singapore, had been the latest package to be received and thus far had not been fully cracked by the cryptographers.

Norwen flipped through the report sitting on his desk and began to read attentively. His staff routinely pieced together ticker tape printouts, creating readable reports so that it was ready for him when he arrived for work and today was no exception. One of the procedures he'd implemented upon taking charge of the Closet.

The Foreign Office had relayed a report by the Danish government which had informed them of a body of German surface vessels that had passed through Öresund near Copenhagen yesterday. At least a dozen vessels, including one battleship, had been observed by the Danes. Another report came from a civilian pilot flying a weather aircraft northwest of the Hebrides. The man reported to authorities that he had spotted no less than three cylindrical shaped vessels bearing southwest towards the Atlantic. When attempting to investigate further the three ships suddenly disappeared without a trace. He read on. Another report came from a Norwegian fishing boat who reported sighting a submarine surfacing near their location. The most concerning report came from an American submarine operating between the Azores and Portugal that reported to its base that it had picked up coded radio transmissions coming from that area. The American's transmission had been intercepted by the listening post in Gibraltar and relayed to London.

Suspicious....but not a loaded gun.

There had been a lot of German naval activity late last year that raised some red flags, such as mass movements in the North Atlantic and North Sea and indications of ships in the Baltic Sea. He had sounded the bell back in late August about that suggesting to his higher ups and anyone else that it could indicate a planned German offensive. The Admiralty had not taken him seriously then and when his supposed German offensive never materialized, his suspicions were mocked as that of an insecure or inept officer. He had privately stuck by his decision to ring the bell, however, it did hurt his credibility and he wasn't too interested in reliving that mistake again.

Norwen opened the top drawer of his desk, pulled out the pack of cigarettes he kept in the office and lit one up. He told his wife he'd quit months ago but when he needed to think he would often light one up.

"Daniel," he said and exhaled a puff of smoke. "I want you to call over to Section 6. Ask them for all they have on recent coded transmissions. Particularly in the vicinity of the North Sea and Atlantic. Then send a courier over to pick it up ASAP."

Towman nodded his understanding then picked up his desk phone to set to work.

Archie stood up and walked over to the large conference table covered in maps. He began flipping through them until he came across the one he wanted, the North Atlantic zone between the Azores and the Franco-Spanish coasts. Took the last drag of his cigarette then stamped it out in an ashtray. He traced his finger between the Azores and Portugal. The American had reported coded transmissions from that area. Navy vessels on maneuvers perhaps?

"Also...." he continued out loud while hovering over the map. "An American submarine off the Portuguese coast transmitted a radio message last night that we picked up on. See if we can get a full text of that message. Gibraltar station listened in."

"Right away, sir," he heard Daniel reply. *Good lad*, he thought.

Even if British Intelligence had not yet put any resources into deciphering those transmissions, he was willing to bet the Americans had. All they really needed to know was the when and where in order to rule out French or British navy vessels. Typically, there was some sharing of information of naval activity with their American counterparts, but that didn't mean definitely. An American submarine commander might not be aware of Allied warships operating in a certain stretch of ocean, but the Royal Navy would have kept precise details on their own as well as French movements.

He straightened up and walked to Daniel's desk, the young man speaking to another voice over the telephone. He tapped his finger on the desk lightly.

"Check with Operations, see if they know of any ships that were operating west of the Bay of Biscay yesterday."

Towman was still speaking with the other party but heard and acknowledged his boss's request. Norwen patted the young man on his shoulder before returning to his own desk.

It took a couple of hours for a courier to arrive from the intelligence office, carrying a bundle of cardboard tubes and a large leather carrying pouch, inside there was an accordion folder marked top secret, with a shuffle of papers inside. Towman signed for the receipt of the paperwork from the courier then the man left the office. Daniel went right to work unbundling the package and thumbing through the documents inside.

The concoction of paperwork inside were in no order and took a good deal of time and effort from most of the office staff to piece it together and make sense of it all. It wasn't until near 3 o'clock that afternoon that any semblance of a picture was beginning to come together.

Part of the problem with intelligence was that one department usually did things one way while others did things another way and causing serious lack of overall organization. Some had tried to correct this over the years, that Churchill character for instance, but their cries too often fell on deaf bureaucratic ears.

By 4 o'clock Norwen had smoked near half his pack of Benson and Hedges. He had marked out on the large map on the conference table the locations of British and French vessels that were operating near the American submarine yesterday. Only one, a French frigate, was even close and there had been no transmission sent from that ship all day yesterday at all.

What little MI6 had sent over concerning non-deciphered transmissions was also beginning to paint an interesting picture. He suspected some intelligence officer over there was sitting on more but was choosing not to share it. The information was scant and, in some cases, random, reinforcing his previous theory. MI6 was good at their job, damn good, and he found it impossible to believe they were simply sleeping over there.

Daniel, pencil in hand, made some X marks on the map indicating the probable locations of coded transmissions picked up by listening stations around the country. Five marks in the North Sea, west and northwest of Stavanger, two marks in the area between Iceland and the Scottish islands, three more X marks in the area southwest of Ireland known as the Western Approaches.

Norwen, having been in the navy now for some fifteen years, knew that the Western Approaches were a sea of death during the last war. German U-boats had been quite successful in destroying British shipping in that area during the conflict. It was reasonable to assume that if hostilities were to resume, that would most likely be an area that the Kriegs-marine would have their U-boats waiting.

Archie sipped on another cup of hot tea as he took in the picture. Ships operating in the areas surrounding Britain, the French and Spanish coasts and all the way down the west coast of Africa, sightings of surface vessels sailing past Copenhagen, too many things were pointing to a bad omen. *What a way to start the week*, he thought.

"Commander Norwen, sir," another aide said, handing Norwen another printout from the teletype machine.

He took the message and put his teacup down as he read its content. *Good lord!*

He read the report aloud. "Two RAF pilots flying back from Oslo had reported to their commander upon arriving home of observing a large warship in the Skagerrak Strait. Photography to be developed." He put the message down. Photography. The squadron commander had kicked the report up the chain as he was supposed to. He wondered how many others would have simply ignored such trivial things.

Daniel put an X mark in the stretch of sea between Denmark and Norway.

"A large warship. . . . could be a battleship," he commented to no one in particular. "Pieces are beginning to come together." He looked at the young man, Daniel looked back at him and nodded slightly. "Put on some coffee, lad. I think we're going to have a long night."

It was a long night indeed. The entire staff was busy all afternoon and well into the evening as more and more reports came in. Nobody dared to leave the office right now, it was too important and besides everyone's adrenaline was up, their blood pumping like crazy. An almost exuberant sense of excitement hung in the room as they continued their work. Additional couriers came and went till all hours of the late night.

Norwen was sleeping on a leather couch next to Daniel's desk when the young man shook him awake. Archie rubbed his eyes as he sat up.

"What is the time?" He asked.

"Ummm. . . . near midnight, sir. I knew you'd want to see this though." He handed Commander Norwen yet another printout from the office teletype machine.

He'd been sleeping for over an hour now. He forced his mind clear and took the paper in hand. It was from Acklington, an RAF airstrip on the Northumberland coast, they'd finally developed the pictures taken by their pilots earlier in the day. The pictures were passed along to naval identification experts who had confirmed just what he had guessed. A German battleship, most likely the *Scharnhorst*, had steamed through the Skagerrak Strait. Unconfirmed reports had placed it now roughly sixty kilometers from Kristiansand.

"Some tea, sir." Daniel was a blessing. The young man extended a cup of hot Darjeeling. Norwen stood up and took the offered cup of tea.

He patted his young aide on the arm. "Get Captain Fleming on the phone. I need to speak with him. Urgent."

He sipped on his cup of tea and put the message on the edge of Daniel's desk. Dan picked up the phone and began making his call.

CHAPTER SIX

Prime Minister Neville Chamberlain put his elbows on the table and placed his face in his hands. A sudden headache had come over him and he felt slightly dizzy. He rubbed his temples then looked up at the men sitting around the large rectangular table. He knew his cabinet was watching him and could sense his weakness. He had to show strength, now more than ever.

How could I have let things get so out of control?

He'd read the communique twice just to make sure that he had not misread it. He hadn't. It was unmistakable. The Polish government had made an open and public declaration against Germany, accusing it of preparing for an invasion of their country. Germany, of course, was denying it entirely. But the Poles weren't accepting the denial and had ordered a full mobilization of their armed forces just this morning. There was no mistaking what was happening here. War.

Chamberlain and his French counterpart, Daladier, had fought long and hard for peace on the continent, despite detractors and opposition, sometimes by members of his own political party. Now the house of cards seemed to be falling apart and quickly.

He had wasted no time in calling an emergency meeting of his cabinet. Though he tried to keep the meeting secret and out of the public eye, the matter had leaked to the press and there was a crowd of London onlookers that was gathering outside to watch the cabinet ministers arriving one by one. More than one shouting obscenities at them as they entered the Prime Minister's residence.

The Foreign Secretary, Lord Halifax, sat across the table from Chamberlain, biting his lower lip, legs crossed and steely eyed, he portrayed no emotion whatsoever. Chamberlain did not know whether the man was in shock, though he doubted it. Halifax was as tough a man as there had ever been in politics.

"The French have been in contact with the Polish government hoping to deflate the situation," Halifax informed him, his voice betraying his feelings on the matter. It was moot now whether the French were trying to talk the Poles into a reversal, the damage had been done. It was like trying to talk a jumper from a high ledge right after the man had leapt off.

"Herr Hitler won't care," Chamberlain came back. He shook his head. "He'll use this as his casus belli. The Poles may have just signed a declaration of war." He tapped his finger on the communique.

Even a full mobilization of Polish forces would have little effect against any actual German invasion of their country. Germany had spent the better part of the last decade rearming and modernizing their armed forces. Fast moving tanks now replaced old cavalry, monoplanes surpassed the older and slower biplanes that made up the bulk of the Polish air force. Germany had both while Poland possessed very few modern units that would be able to stand up to the Wehrmacht.

"Our options?" Chamberlain asked, looking around the table, his eyes inevitably falling across the table on Lord Halifax.

Halifax raised his eyebrows slightly then leaned forward in his chair and crossed his fingers. He let out a long heavy sigh before replying, "Herr Hitler could undoubtedly use this as his casus belli. If the French are unsuccessful in persuading the Poles.... today may go down in history as the day a new war starts. If Hitler attacks Poland, we'll have no choice but to honor our alliance with the Poles. If the Germans launch an attack...." he chewed his lip, "they'll crush the Polish army in a matter of weeks. On the other hand, if we were to offer Hitler another option, he may back off."

Chamberlain nodded his head in a defeat. "You mean offer him a compromise. Swaths of Poland perhaps?" His voice was full of desperation and aggravation.

"It's no secret, Prime Minister," Halifax replied. "Hitler wants Danzig, he wants the Polish corridor connecting east Prussia to the rest of his country. If he could have it and we can avoid another war, it might be enough."

Chamberlain sighed slightly. *More appeasement, hadn't Munich been enough?*

He looked around the large conference table as if begging someone, anyone, to offer him another option. Anything at all.

"We could condemn this action by Poland," offered Leslie Hore-Belisha, the Secretary of State for War. Halifax shot an outraged look down at the man sitting at the end of the table.

"Come out against the Poles?" Halifax asked, slightly angered at the remark. "Come out against our ally? British credibility would be shot."

Chamberlain wanted to hear more and motioned for Hore-Belisha to continue.

"Publicly declare against Poland's mobilization," the man continued. "We can then put pressure on Warsaw to fold their cards before the situation goes too far. If the Polish government believes that we may not stand with them on this, it might be enough to bring everyone to the table. Negotiate with Hitler."

But they'd already done that, and it hadn't worked. This government had pegged its entire foreign policy on appeasing Hitler in Berlin in order to keep another war from igniting. Chamberlain had given his 'peace for our time' speech following the Munich Agreement a year and a half earlier when they gave Hitler large territorial concessions in Czechoslovakia. That hadn't stopped the man from taking the rest of that country just six months later. Could they do that again and hope to have the government survive? What would that mean for Poland?

The Prime Minister sank back in his chair, ran his fingers through his gray hair. A negotiated settlement with Hitler would never pass with the opposition, or for that matter some in his own Conservative Party in

Parliament. The King would likely not approve of it either and Labour and Liberal alike may well call for a vote of no confidence in him.

But the nation was not ready for another war.

Lord Halifax reproached the suggestion. "Prime Minister, if we decry Poland's armed mobilization, we will not only break our alliance with them, but quite possibly with the French as well. That would leave us isolated from the rest of Europe. However, if Germany attacks Poland, the French will undoubtedly intervene on their behalf. If we fail to act in concert with our allies, again we risk isolation.

"Signor Mussolini has offered to work with us on this issue in the past. I believe he would welcome it now. We negotiate through Mussolini," he waved his hand. "Some territorial concessions on the continent, perhaps even in Africa. We could do that and wouldn't have to come out publicly against anyone. My office could make arrangements, perhaps a meeting in Venice or Milan."

"Another settlement?" Chamberlain sighed. *How many more?*

"To avoid war," Halifax told him bluntly.

They'd already given Hitler everything he'd wanted and even looked the other way when he'd taken lands without their consent. It seemed that diplomacy simply was not working with this man in Berlin. His appetite for neighboring countries appeared to have no limits. But the other option was just as uninviting. War. Consultation with the military leaders had been less than encouraging. Britain simply could not raise the army it needed in an adequate time to repel any German attack on the west. There were less than two hundred thousand men under arms in country as it was. If they had recalled additional troops from India, they risked losing that territory in exchange.

Is this what madness feels like? Chamberlain thought.

Finally, the elder statesman nodded his head. "Very well, My Lord. Contact Signor Mussolini at your earliest convenience." His voice had lost all confidence. *He* had lost all confidence. "However, I will be forced, quite soon I think, to order our military leadership to begin making preparations for the possibility of transporting our own forces to France. If we can arrange a sit down with Herr Hitler, I want it clearly understood from the beginning that we mean business."

"Gottverdammt!" The Furher slapped his knee as he happily took in the news. Members of his personal staff and the inner circle were laughing along with their glorious leader as he smiled broadly.

They could not have asked for a better gift from the fool Poles. Nobody would ever accuse the Polish of being a smart people. This gave him exactly what he'd wanted to begin with, an impetus for invasion. Now he could make it all look as if the Polish government had been the ones to start a war with Germany and not the other way around. Combined with several incidents that had been planned by SS operatives that would also make it look as if Poland launched attacks into Germany, he'd have all the provocation he needed.

Last night he'd been briefed by his generals again on the preparations. The army was in place and ready. The extra eight months of preparation, due to the postponement of the original Case White, did wonders for German logistical preparation. Reichsmarschall Göring had assured him of a swift victory in the air and the Kriegsmarine had put to sea under cover of radio silence. The chess board was set, and his pieces were in place.

Blitzkrieg would be tested in the coming weeks. With luck and the gods on his side, German forces would be in control of Poland, Denmark and Norway before the allies could even respond. He held out his teacup for his attendant to refill.

CHAPTER SEVEN

It was 0338 in the morning when the wheels of the first bombers lifted up from Luftwaffe airfields in Germany. Before daybreak hundreds of medium Heinkel He 111's and the lighter Dornier Do 17 bombers would ascend skyward fifteen to twenty thousand feet, then level off and head east into Polish airspace. They would be joined by hundreds of fighters, agile Messerschmitt Bf-109's and the heavier 110's would escort the large bomber fleets deep into enemy territory to knock out Polish airstrips, with any luck, well before the Poles would even know they were there. Squadrons of German fighters would knock out of the sky anything that the Polish air force was able to get off the ground.

Additional waves of Luftwaffe aircraft would be made up of combat close air support, mainly the Junkers Ju 87s. The terrifying dive bombers would descend from the skies, their signature shriek heard well before their bombs fell on the heads of Polish tanks and fortifications. On this day death would come from above.

By 0400 in the morning the very lead elements of the Fourth Army had crossed over the frontier into Poland. The tanks of Heinz Guderian's XIX Corps made up the spearhead of this force.

Any soldier standing on the ground during the early morning pre-dawn hours could just faintly make out the sounds of a thousand aircraft flying high above the earth. Just before 0500 those sounds became distant booms, as if some great god creature was beating a large drum in the sky, the sound reverberating for miles. Across the flat land, in the far-off distance there appeared to be lightning strikes that rose straight up from the ground.

Blitzkrieg had begun.

At 0534 the lead tanks of the 3rd Panzer Division, Lieutenant General Schweppenburg commanding, fired their first shots at defending Polish forces.

To the flanks of the great advancing German army, some fifteen hundred pieces of field artillery began shelling enemy army positions, allowing Guderian's tanks to punch through with little resistance. Some three hundred Panzer III's and IV's broke through the Polish forces, what few there were just as the dawn sun was breaking on the battlefield.

Those panzers were followed by a long, streaming line of motorized and mechanized infantry units that stretched back for miles. The ground of the Polish countryside had been churned up by the advancing tanks and trucks that by the time the foot born infantry units had arrived they were stumbling in ankle deep muddy roads.

Two command cars, traveling with the 5th Regiment of the 3rd Panzer Division, pulled off the road as the bulky tanks rolled past. General Guderian leaned over the side of the first car and quietly observed the advancing troops. Their formations were in good order. The tanks crews had trained hard for months and that training was well evident now. Fire and advance, fire and advance.

Half a dozen Bf 109 fighters flew by overhead, providing cover for his force in case of an aerial attack by Polish planes.

His aides were busy at work, studying maps and pointing to far off spirals of smoke in the distance. He wasn't listening, he was observing his troops as they kept moving forward. Some of the men saw their General but knew better than to make any gesture. He was a professional soldier, not some theater actor on a stage in Berlin and he expected his soldiers to act as professionals also. From what he'd seen so far this morning he hadn't been disappointed.

He scanned the horizon with his field glasses. The 5th Panzer Regiment was his lead unit, their new Panzer IVs armed with the heavier 7.5-centimeter barrel guns could easily take out anything that the Polish Army had. The tank formation was spread out over a two-mile wide front, behind them hundreds of motorized vehicles followed: motorcycles, trucks and even some of the older Panzer II's to provide infantry support if needed.

Thus far, however, the attack had gone nearly unimpeded. Some reports of fighting farther south had come in via radio, but the Luftwaffe had seemingly cleared his front remarkably well. Here and there they had passed some bodies lying on the roadside, dead Polish soldiers and horses, the wreckage of some armored car or some wooden carts that had been upturned with its contents spilled over, but no major resistance.

Guderian knew that would change and that resistance would become heavier and heavier the deeper they drove into Poland. They'd had surprise and preparation on their side. Before the day was out, surprise would be all but gone and most of the experienced officers knew it.

He took his pocket watch out, popped it open, it was only now 0910 hours. He put his watch back into his pocket. By his reckoning they were approximately six kilometers east of the German border.

The plan had called for his troops to push twenty kilometers into Poland by day's end. His force was the spear of the entire northern front. His armored force was to cut a swath across northwestern Poland, close off the so-called Polish Corridor, link up with the XXI corps, which was pushing west from Prussia and trap the Poles in a northern pocket. Once cut off from the main Polish army in the south, they could be picked off easily.

"Let's go!" Guderian told his driver then pointed south.

400 kilometers to the south of Guderian, Lance Corporal Ernst Krauss wiped the sweat from his brow then took a short sip of water from his canteen. He peered through his binoculars at the long row of tanks ahead of his own Panzer IV. It stretched for as far as he could see. Far ahead of the column there were several tall spires of black smoke on the horizon.

Just fifteen minutes earlier he'd seen several Stuka's fly overhead, heading back towards Germany. He'd surmised that the smoke up ahead came from the unfortunate victims of those Stukas.

The division had been on the move constantly since around five this morning and was making an unceasing advance in Poland. He and his men had not yet seen any action, but they'd certainly heard it in the distance.

All morning long there had been a steady stream of Luftwaffe bombers flying overhead, bombing and strafing enemy positions far ahead of the army's advance. There had been a brief enemy artillery barrage about an hour earlier that had slowed the column's advance. One of the older Panzer III's had taken a hit and they had passed a truck a short time after that had been hit and upended. The driver, or what was left of him, had been torn apart by the shell hit. A small price to pay for the hurt they'd inflicted against the enemy.

Ernst looked upwards as another half dozen heavy fighters flew by overhead, about five hundred meters off the ground, flying eastwards covering the ground advance.

He hadn't seen any enemy aircraft but obviously they were up there somewhere. Several Messerschmitt's had been seen dueling with something earlier, bobbing in and out of the clouds. Ernst was glad that those fly boys were up there. If there was one thing that the army was lacking, it was anti-aircraft guns.

God these Poles are stupid, he thought. Word had spread quickly that some Polish soldiers had illegally crossed the border this morning and attacked some radio towers on the German side of the border but had been driven off before doing any damage. Word came down that the Führer had broadcast to the entire country about the incident and that he'd ordered an immediate counterattack.

His tank was pushing forward at a good 30 kilometers per hour. He wasn't positive, but he figured that they were at least that far into Poland by now. He dug into his pocket and pulled out his watch, the one Papa had given him. 10:00 o'clock. He wiped more sweat off his forehead. The sun was beating down on them and the heat coming off the engine made it worse.

The XVIII Corps, of which the 2nd Panzer Division was the forward tip, formed the elbow of the entire southern front. The majority of the Fourteenth Army was to their east and driving upwards into central

Poland with the objective of flanking the Polish army in the west. The 2nd Panzer Division had been assigned to push out from the German-Czech-Polish border and engage the main body of Polish forces.

So far there hadn't been much to engage, and deep-down Ernst had hoped that it would stay that way. The Luftwaffe had done a good job today driving the enemy out of their positions and as far as he was concerned, they could be the heroes.

By 1030 hours the column's progress had begun to slow. Tanks were seen maneuvering past the destroyed wreckage of several vehicles, including two of the so-called tankettes that the Poles had in their arsenal. The tankettes were nothing more than half tanks that sat two men, one driver and one gunner that sported a low caliber machine gun that couldn't punch through a brick wall much less a German armored vehicle.

There was a series of loud booms from the southeast. Ernst held up his binoculars in that direction but couldn't see anything for a moment, then he saw it. About a kilometer off he could see bursts of earth erupt upwards and then the loud sound of an explosion washed over him. There were more bursts and then more. Artillery he knew. He couldn't see where it was coming from but it hadn't hit anything. . . . yet.

The lead tanks began shaking out into battle line formation. He swallowed and let out a long, nervous breath. Battle was ahead.

"We're going into action," he shouted down to his crew. He tried to keep his voice calm but inside he was tense.

The one hundred fifty strong tank regiment maneuvered out into a solid line formation nearly a kilometer wide. A mile and a half ahead of the panzers was an elevated ridge extending across the immediate horizon that rose perhaps a hundred feet then plateaued before rising up again in the center by a further forty or fifty feet. From a distance it seemed to be a giant man-made earthen castle, with marshy wetlands and woods that had recently been cut down protecting its northern and southeastern sides. The entire position offered excellent defensive ground. God only knew how many soldiers were up there waiting and what was waiting beyond that.

To the right of the formation more incoming artillery shells fell, fired from unknown positions. Far off a motorcycle took a hit, the vehicle and its rider sent ten feet off the ground and then sent slamming back down to the earth. Another round hit the treads of an older Panzer II, sending the vehicle tumbling to its side, churning up mud in every direction, the small tank stuck and unable to move further.

From above two Stukas dove down on the hill ahead, machine guns firing down on the enemy defenders before releasing their 500 lb. bomb loads. Fireballs rose from the center top hill. The dive bombers pulled out of their nosedive and left their high pitch shriek wash over the battlefield before leveling out and flying off.

Ernst looked around the skies in wonder but saw nothing besides those two Stukas which were now on their way back to a German airfield.

Where could the rest of the air support be?

In between the walls of tanks dozens of trucks and half-tracks were mingled in, carrying platoons of infantry in their rear. The men ready to jump into action the moment they were needed. The distance between the ridge and the approaching German line was closing now to half a kilometer and that's when Ernst caught his first glimpse of movement. Peering through his binoculars he could see what looked like ants running this way and that along the crest of the ridge and the plateau below. From a distance there appeared to be a good number of them up there.

The panzers kept closing, came to within a third of a kilometer of the ridge then the first of them opened fire with their main guns. The rounds landed softly against the ridge or passed overhead doing nothing but sending up small plumes of soil. A few enemy machine guns opened fire at this range, the small bullets harmless against the armored units hurling against them.

In the cupola of his tank Krauss ducked low to avoid any lucky bullet that may stray his way.

The lead tanks hit the bottom of the hillside then started up the embankments. One by one they rolled upward, their own machine gunners beginning to fire on the enemy as they advanced, trucks and half-tracks following meters behind the tanks, using their armor for their own protection. In a dazzling display of bravery, or stupidity, Polish troops kept firing away at the Germans with everything they had, rifles, machine guns, small anti-tank rifles that did nothing. A few rounds found their way to a truck driver driving his vehicle behind one of the tanks. A few more pierced through the engine blocks or hit the rear of a half-track, killing a man here and there but doing nothing to stop the wave of German tanks climbing up the side of that hill.

At the center of the ridge the Polish troops fell back as the first tank, a Panzer III, roared over the crest. Krauss could only just make out the back of that tank as his own was now hitting the bottom of the hill and starting its way up. The overlapping sound of machine guns firing was all that he could hear. He descended into his tank, locking the hatch above him and peered through the forward view slit.

One at a time the German tanks were reaching the plateau and rolled slowly forward, the defenders fleeing back into some defensive works that had been throw up. Felled trees and abatis works stood between the lip of the plateau and the hill in the center of it. A solid line of fortifications blocked the panzers from moving farther passed the top of the hillside. As a result, all the tanks below were forced to cease their advance as they were running out of space on the top of the ridge between its edge and the enemy fortifications.

Polish infantry were pelting the armored vehicles with everything they now had. Small mortars dropped shells on the Germans. One shell caught a truck's side and sent the vehicle toppling over, the riflemen in its rear crawling out dazed. The German advance had stopped, but the panzer units already on top of the ridge were firing away at the defenders. Machine guns ripped wooden barricades apart and the tank's main guns were loading and firing as fast as they could, trying to blow holes wherever they could in the enemy line.

A Polish machine gun position took a hit and got shredded by the huge tank round, men in trenches were being riddled with machine gun bullets. The Poles were dropping like flies and getting in precious few hits on the armored Germans.

German infantry began to deploy from the rear of the trucks and sprinted up the hillside, rifles in hand and machine guns in tow. The two sides began trading small arms fire. A German soldier got hit, then a Pole, another German... The mortar shells then started to be exchanged. But the Germans soldiers were protected by the armor of the tanks they were surrounded by, and the Polish troops were in an increasingly precarious position defending that ridge.

The fight almost looked like two lines of battle out of some eighteenth-century European war with the armies slugging it out with each other, firing round after round in the face of the opposition. Except gone were the days of single shot musketry. Dozens of Poles fell to the combined fire from the German tanks and infantrymen. The Poles from atop the higher hill fired down but they themselves were becoming out-matched by the better weapons the Nazis had. The Poles simply didn't have anything that could stop a tank. Infantry guns from the deployed German troops were firing in overlapping streams towards the hilltop.

The Panzer IIIs and IVs inched forward again ever so slowly, infantry advancing along with them one small step at a time. Krauss could hear the occasional ping of a bullet round striking against the thick armor of his own Panzer IV, then an explosion just meters away followed by another. Enemy mortar shells were now dropping onto the vehicles still making their way up the side of the hill. More rounds fell. One tank took a direct hit but just kept on going, the small shell doing no damage. But still the shells kept dropping.

Ernst, still peering through the viewing slit, saw the forward tanks halt again and he became panicked, could feel his pulse racing harder and harder. He didn't know what the hell was going on up there. Infantry were running upwards between the panzers, machine guns were going off everywhere, enemy shells kept bursting around his tanks, the sounds of death. He'd become so focused on what he was looking at that he barely registered the voice in his headset.

He touched his hand to his right ear.

".... position.... All panzer units hold your position!" It was Colonel Rohm's voice coming through loud and clear. "All panzers to hold your positions! Do not advance! Infantry to fall back immediately!" The order repeated itself.

The battle line came to a stop, infantrymen then rapidly fell back between the tanks and retreat back down the hillside for cover. Polish snipers picked off a couple of them. Then came the familiar sound outside. Even through the tank hatch he could barely make out that high pitch winding sound coming from high above.

"Stukas inbound!" someone from outside called out.

The signature shrieking noise got louder and louder, like a siren going off from some loudspeaker somewhere. The whining cry reached a high point a few seconds later only to be replaced by the sound of bomb after bomb being dropped on the hilltop. A series of loud booms and the earth shook, then fireballs rose from the ground across the top of the ridge. The Stukas dove down like vultures and released their bomb loads right on top of the enemy positions before pulling out. The boom of exploding bombs was absolutely deafening and after several dozen large impact there came an eerie silence on the battlefield.

Ernst, taking a chance, popped open the turret hatch and stood up half out of the tank. A wave of hot air washed over him. The mortar shells had ceased and there was only the sound of an occasional rifle popping.

After a minute the infantry, which had been withdrawing off the ridge, were now advancing forward again. The lead platoons charging straight into the defender's positions. A general cheer went up from the men on top of the ridge and from one of the forward tanks, its commander looked back down behind him and grinned then pumped his fist into the air in a sign of victory.

It would take another hour after the Luftwaffe had subdued most of the enemy resistance before the regiment had secured both ridges. The right wing of the division had moved off into the distance to secure the area where some Polish artillery units had been placed.

Krauss's Panzer IV sat atop the right end of the long ridge, overlooking the valley beyond. He climbed down from the turret, gave leave for his crew to get out of the hot tank and observe the battlefield. In the valley behind them German infantry were marching away the hundreds of Polish prisoners taken. Along the entire ridge he could see his fellow soldiers counting the number of dead on both sides, the bodies now lying in the midday sun.

Walking down the hillside and away from sight of all the carnage he found an isolated muddy dike, unzipped his trousers and relieved himself. In the far distance was the sound of faint artillery fire, but it was quiet where he was, and he took a quick moment to listen to the birds singing.

As he stood there relieving himself into the grass, he felt the beating of his heart, could feel it's rhythm and it gave him a moment's pleasure in the realization that it was, in fact, still beating. He finished his business but stood there for a few seconds more. It was wonderfully quiet now and he stood with his eyes closed and felt the sunlight on his face.

"Who are you?" A loud voice asked, it took him by complete surprise. Completely startled he'd turned towards the person shouting then realized he was still holding his cock. "What are you doing over here?"

Ernst frantically zipped up. The man was tall with blonde hair and bright blue eyes. He was slender and well built, wearing an officer's uniform. Two other men were standing a few steps behind speaking to each other, barely acknowledging Corporal Krauss.

"Major Zant," Krauss said in a stammer. Zant was the regimental executive officer. "Sir," he gasped, "I was. . . . I was. . . ."

Zant looked at the young man with an almost amused look on his face. "Pissing?"

Finally, Krauss nodded his head. For some reason that he could not explain, he felt tense. "Yes, sir. We've been on the move all day and I. . . ."

Zant waved a dismissal. "I understand, Corporal. . . . . .?"

"Lance Corporal Krauss, sir!" He finally came to a belated attention.

Zant nodded. "Lance Corporal Krauss. Are you finished pissing, Lance Corporal?"

"Yes, sir." He'd felt embarrassed. Zant was known to be a hard ass.

The older man looked at the young corporal then the faintest smile came across his face. He took a few paces forward. "Well, Corporal Krauss," he began and turned his head towards the ridge where the earlier fighting had taken place, "did you fight earlier?"

Krauss nodded slowly. "Sir, yes, sir!" In fact, he had not done a damn thing but sit in his heavily armored tank as Polish infantry had been slaughtered outside.

"Good," Major Zant replied in a gentle tone, his harsh demeanor dropped. "How old are you, Krauss?"

"Nineteen, sir!"

"Nineteen and already a lance corporal. You did your duty today. Do you know what the first duty of any soldier is?"

Ernst thought to himself for a moment. *What would a good officer want to hear?* "To kill the enemy, sir!"

Major Zant stepped closer to Ernst, looked him square in the eye for a few second then finally shook his head. "No. The first duty of a soldier is to survive the day." He nodded his head towards the dead Polish bodies being hauled off the ridge top. "They failed in their duty. You did not. At least not yet. But the day is still early, Lance Corporal."

Ernst looked back into the older man's eyes. There was no indication of harshness or maliciousness in the officer's voice and eyes.

"Off you go," Major Zant ordered. "We'll be moving out in a little while."

Ernst snapped off a salute which Zant returned.

CHAPTER EIGHT

WAR!

Every newspaper in the country was writing about it, every radio broadcast was talking about it and every citizen in all Great Britain from Inverness to Cornwall were learning about it. The British government had given Germany an ultimatum to withdraw from Polish territory by eleven o'clock this morning. The French had delivered a similar ultimatum but giving Hitler until five this afternoon. Berlin had ignored the British ultimatum entirely and it was likely that they would give the French the same courtesy.

Britons everywhere had tuned in their radio sets as Prime Minister Chamberlain had delivered his speech from the House of Commons in Parliament just moments earlier. The mood of the country was obviously somber. There was a heaviness that lay across the old city and Churchill had felt it on his drive to Westminster this morning and could feel it now in the halls of Parliament.

He knew that this was coming, had told them it was coming. Too many of them had either held out absurd hope or ignored things completely for too long. He'd warned them. Warned them all.

Yesterday he'd gotten the telephone call early in the day, right after breakfast in fact. He knew it was coming and did not feign surprise when he got it. To his disappointment it was not the Prime Minister, nor even Halifax, who had phoned him, but rather Samuel Hoare, the Home Secretary who had informed him that he was being recalled to government service.

Winston had awoken early this morning. Clementine, bless her heart, had made sure that his suit had been pressed and his signature bowler hat well brushed for today. They had even shared breakfast with each other this morning, something they rarely did as Winston often ate in bed. Being the good wife that she was, she'd schooled him on how to behave when he met with the Prime Minister today to discuss his future in government. She even went so far as to swat down his, admittedly joking, suggestion that he have a large breakfast this morning so that he arrived to meet with Chamberlain extra flatulent.

Now, standing in the large waiting lobby outside of the Commons Chamber, pacing back and forth as inside the Prime Minister was giving the most difficult speech of his life and quite possibly the last of his political career.

Churchill and Chamberlain had both been from the same Conservative Party but had split on foreign policy, particularly the appeasement policy that Chamberlain and Halifax had been pushing. They had been vocal opponents on the matter, even adversaries, both privately and publicly. But there was a part of Winston Churchill that felt sorry for the man. He was not a bad man, although his name may very well go down in history as the man who let civilization itself fall to a madman.

The door to the Chamber creaked open and the Prime Minister of the United Kingdom entered the lobby. His face was gaunt and white, obviously he had not slept much, and he walked slowly as if he lacked the energy to move his legs. His eyes were deep and dark, and he was understandably quiet.

He came to Winston and stopped, stared at his political enemy and remained silent for a good half minute. It felt awkward for both, Winston was sure.

"Prime Minister," Winston finally said in a respectful tone. He knew that he would have to bite his tongue today and not let his temper get the better of him.

There was no need to bring up their differences, nor give him the "I told you so" treatment. Both men understood well what was about to happen and he felt no overwhelming need to rub the man's nose in things.

Chamberlain's eyes seemed to drift past Winston for a moment as if looking at some ghost then came back to him.

"It seems that we are now at war, my friend," Chamberlain told him in an oddly low voice. Churchill was shocked at the phrase "my friend". They had never been friends.

Chamberlain finally took a deep breath and let it out, looked at Churchill with all seriousness.

"I need you back, Winston," he had found his voice again, more confident this time, more like his normal self. "The country needs you."

Your government cannot survive with me, Churchill thought to himself. *No doubt the Liberals and Labour are pushing you to shake up your cabinet. An ultimatum of their own perhaps?*

"I am here to serve, Prime Minister," Winston said, all the respect in his voice that he could muster. "What would you have me do?" Always best to get straight to the point and now was not a time to delay and politic.

Chamberlain bit his lip slightly, "We need strength. We'll have to meet strength with strength. I'm prepared to offer you your old position of First Lord of the Admiralty. Full control of the Navy." He ended it bluntly, dangling the offer out there. He knew Winston would take it. Give him the Navy, include him in the cabinet and make his opposition in Parliament happy. He'd do it for the country.

Churchill grunted slightly, looked down at his well shined shoes on the polish floor. He brought his gaze back up to the Prime Minister.

"First Lord of the Admiralty," he commented. A good position within the government and he knew it, he'd done it before and done it well. The only reason he'd left was over his own failure over the Gallipoli campaign in 1915, but he had not been driven out, he'd voluntarily left to go fight in the trenches of the western front.

"Although I am honored to serve," Winston began, "and to be considered for First Lord...... I believe that I would be of much better use to you and in fact to the country....... As Secretary of War." He looked at Chamberlain, his eyes unblinking, his facial features stern.

"War?" Chamberlain's jaw dropped open and he shook his head. "That I cannot do. Hore-Belisha is too entrenched, too popular with the King. Winston, I need you but not for that! First Lord is what I can give you. Stanhope is willing to step aside and take his position with the Lords. I can support you at the Admiralty."

"I can do more as Secretary of War than I ever could at the Admiralty. This country is in more dire need than I think many realize. I can better serve you there." He waved a hand. "Besides, Hore-Belisha is unpopular with Parliament and with his own commanders, the Imperial Staff."

Chamberlain rubbed his eyes and shook his head. "No. If I give you War, I could face resignations from other cabinet members. Be reasonable. I'm trying to keep this government together! We're hanging by a thread. If we falter, we risk losing a Conservative majority in Parliament. Take the Admiralty. You can be back there this afternoon." The faintest of smiles came across his face.

Winston stood silent. The large chamber through the thick wooden door was full of people, many of whom did not want Chamberlain in power anymore. Liberals and Labour were screaming for new blood, Churchill's blood, he knew that and so did the Prime Minister. Although the Conservatives still held the majority in that chamber, it was pieced together by a fragile truce of peace doves and war hawks. Those hawks had been in Churchill's camp, and he was willing to bet on them coming to his side if it came down to it.

Would the Liberals and Labour parties follow me also if I stepped up? Can I risk it? If I lose, the Conservatives will lose their position and quite possibly government as well. Bluff it!

Winston grinned slightly at the other man; the room deathly quiet as they both stood there.

"Our nation stands on the edge of a cliff, sir," Winston told him, his voice steady and calm. "Our strength has dwindled in recent years. Across the North Sea the Nazis have ruthlessly prepared their own country for war for seven years now. Our own army is a shambles." He waved his finger in the air. "The General Staff themselves have said as much. Leslie is unpopular with them. He's usurped their authority and disregarded their advice. A good man yes, but not equipped to handle the task."

Chamberlain had considered sacking Hore-Belisha once before but had decided against it. The man was a member of the Liberal Party, he'd been seen by many as an olive branch by Chamberlain to reach across the floor. Unpopular with members of Parliament yes but the King was an ally of his and his dismissal could cost him with the Monarch. On the other hand, James Stanhope, the First Lord of the Admiralty was a Conservative, like Churchill. His departure would keep the delicate balance that Chamberlain had kept in his coalition government.

Churchill could see the internal struggle on the man's face, his features shifting slightly. Winston stood there silent as a rock for a moment, not quite yet ready to offer the other man another option. He'd have to be pushed a little bit more.

"Prime Minister, we're now at war. The King will not dissolve Parliament, there will be no new elections. This government will survive or fall based on the strength that it shows now. Waver and the opposition will call for a new government to be formed. Show strength and...." he shrugged, "maybe it shall survive." By call for a new government, Churchill had, of course, meant that Chamberlain would be forced to step down.

Chamberlain knew this too. His government was coming apart at the seams as it was. He knew that if he failed to bring this man back into the fold, it would mean the end of his own political career. As it was, he was coming ever closer to the end of his own life, but nobody had yet been told of that, not even the King.

Winston turned away for a moment then made a grunting sound, turned back to Chamberlain. "I'm not sure that I have another option, Prime Minister. Unless you do.... I'm not sure where this leaves us."

Chamberlain eyed Winston for a moment, gave serious thought about turning away and walking back through those doors behind him and inform party leaders that no agreement could be reached with this man. A third of the Conservative Party would howl and pull their support for Chamberlain's government before midnight. Clement Attlee, the Labour leader, would call for a new government and that would, he knew, be the end of him.

He rejected that option. He did not wish to resign while there was still the possibility of bringing peace. If the French mobilized their army and the British joined them on the continent, there was still a possibility of bringing Hitler to the table to negotiate a peace.

"Minister for Coordination of Defence." Chamberlain's voice was stern and full of as much authority as he could muster. He could live with giving him that. If Churchill had refused, then Chamberlain could honestly state that he offered two positions in government and on the war cabinet and that Churchill had turned them both away. Any blame would not lay on Chamberlain's shoulders.

Churchill mulled it for a moment. "Minister? Supervision over the three branches?" Chamberlain nodded slightly in reply. "I'd have to have authority to make final decisions on military leadership.... Second only to yourself of course."

Am I giving this man dictatorship? Chamberlain thought. *No. Churchill is many things, ambitious, eccentric and arrogant, but not a Julius Caesar.*

"Second only to myself," Chamberlain agreed.

The two men, two adversaries, eyed each other wearily then shook hands. Their immediate political futures were now tied to each other, and they both knew it. Churchill would now be committed to this man and that meant that he'd both have to support as well as depend upon him for his own future.

CHAPTER NINE

Poland was collapsing. Everyone present knew that the situation was dire, and that German victory was a near certainty. Hitler had tried to sell some story about Polish troops crossing into Germany, but nobody was really buying that, at least not here in America. It was clear through the swiftness of the German Army advance that the campaign had been planned and prepared for weeks or even months ago.

It had been a week since the invasion had started and when news reached the United States the following day, there had been a sense of outrage by the public, but that outrage had been short lived, and the mood of the country was quickly returning to normal. The vast majority of Americans certainly weren't willing to go off to war for some place that many of them couldn't find on a map.

The Polish embassy in Washington had been overwhelmed by requests for information by civilians looking for any news they could get about family and loved ones. So far, the news from the Polish government had been next to nothing. The government in Warsaw was having a hard time getting any information out. The German invasion into their country was moving so fast it was practically impossible to get any accurate information.

Britain and France had honored their alliance with the Poles and had declared war on Germany two days later. It seemed that Europe was once again falling into chaos. America, for its part, had swiftly condemned the invasion, but that was as far as it was going to go for the foreseeable future.

"Mister President," the voice was General Marshall. "Are you okay, sir?"

Franklin Delano Roosevelt brought his attention back to the men gathered in the briefing room today. His cigarette still burned in his mouth. He answered, "Yes, General. My apologies. My thoughts were elsewhere."

He had been thinking about all the Polish Americans and immigrants from that country who were this day, thinking and worrying about their families that were now fighting for their very lives.

How many more will die in the coming days and months, maybe even years?

"Please continue, General."

General Marshall nodded and continued to give his briefing. There was a large map of Poland that had been placed against the wall, markers placed where German and Polish military units were estimated to be.

"Right now, sir, we estimate that roughly a third of the country has fallen to the Nazis. From what intelligence we've been able to gather about the situation we know that most of the northern part of the country is occupied, including the city of Danzig. Most of the Polish resistance is here, in the southwest of the country, the Silesian region. We've identified the main force driving towards Krakow as the Fourteenth Army. Most of their newer tanks are with this army and they're moving hard and fast.

"This area here, between Pomerania and Warsaw is quickly being overrun by the Wehrmacht. The Polish Army is retreating from this area, falling back towards Warsaw." He shook his head gravely. "It'll be hard for them to establish defensive lines in time to repel any German attack on that city. If the Germans follow traditional military thinking they'll lay siege to Warsaw within a week, ten days at the utmost."

"Mister President," Secretary of State Hull spoke up. "Our embassy in Warsaw has advised the Polish government that they have already begun removing some of their personnel and resources out of the city. We'll be completely out of there in the next twenty-four hours."

"Warsaw has been bombed by the Luftwaffe every day since the invasion first began," Marshall continued. "Our counterparts in London and Paris have informed us that the Polish air forces are all but decimated. The Luftwaffe is now in almost complete control of the skies. We're looking at the future of warfare, Mister President. The role of air power on the battlefield is greater now than ever."

The President nodded his agreement. He'd seen the reports of new German aircraft, the monoplanes that could out fly anything the British and French and for that matter the Americans had in their arsenals. The vast buildup of bombers that could fly hundreds of miles and carried as much firepower as an artillery battery and could destroy targets on the ground from twenty thousand feet in the air. The results of that build up were now evident as events were being played out in Poland.

General Henry Arnold, the head of the Army Air Corps, had been a proponent of newer aircraft and a vastly expanded air force. He'd been heard running around Washington talking to any general, senator or congressman who would listen and been laughed away at every turn. Now it seemed that someone had been listening to his arguments, but those people were in Berlin and not DC.

"What kind of support are the Poles getting?" Roosevelt asked.

General Marshall took to his seat. "Not much, sir. Practically nothing in fact. German warships cut off the port of Danzig in the opening hours. The major airfields have all been either bombed or captured. Any supplies that may get in would probably go through Hungary or Romania. But I doubt they'd get much through that way. Too far away from the British and French."

"The French Army has mobilized," Secretary Hull added. "The Royal Navy has taken to sea and there's already been some minor engagements. The Polish Navy, such as it is, has been sent to Britain. It seems likely that the British and French will take up their traditional positions along the border with Germany and Belgium." He made a scowl. "It's unlikely that Germany will take the bait and redeploy their forces from the east."

Chamberlain doesn't have the stomach for war, Roosevelt said inwardly. *He's still hoping for a negotiated peace deal with Hitler. Fool. Damn fool!*

Roosevelt shook his head in dismay. He did not like the idea of war, but he more disliked the idea of letting Europe fall into anarchy, or worse, fascism.

"How long can the Poles last?"

"Not long, sir," Marshall replied. "Our thinking is two weeks at best."

"It seems, gentlemen, the world is at times coming apart at the seams. Millions dead in China, Soviet purges and this." Roosevelt puffed on his cigarette, sat back in his wheelchair. "I fear that someday we may have to fight this man in Berlin. I fear that very much."

"There's still a chance the fighting can end before it goes too far," Hull said. "I've spoken with Joe Kennedy, our ambassador to London. He's been advised by the Brits that their Prime Minister has been in communication with Mussolini in Italy. Apparently, he seems to think that there's a chance for a negotiation with Hitler."

"Hard to negotiate with a hungry lion," Roosevelt told him. He shook his head. "Hitler won't be interested in negotiating a peace. At least not a long-term peace. We're going to need to act. We can't keep letting that man get away with whatever he wants without consequences."

"There's not much we can do, sir," Hull said. "We've sanctioned Germany, we've sanctioned Japan. Hasn't done anything to slow their momentum. Can't sell them military arms either, as much as I think we should, Congress wouldn't allow."

Roosevelt snatched the cigarette out of his mouth. "Won't they? I've spoken with the Speaker of the House and the Senate Majority Leader, and they both seemed to agree that the Neutrality Act revision will make it through Congress. The Republicans in the Senate should be on board. If I must, I'll wheel myself onto the floor of the House Chamber and get it passed myself. Neutrality, gentlemen, is tantamount to cooperation with aggressor countries."

At times Franklin felt more crippled than just a man in a wheelchair. The existing neutrality act forbade the United States from supporting any side of any conflict that the United States was not embroiled in. Hitler's aggression in Europe and Japan's war on the Chinese were going totally unchecked and millions were now paying the ultimate price for it.

Roosevelt had seen firsthand the price for America's neutrality. He'd toured the battlefields of the Great War back in 1917. Seen the displaced people, the starving, the homeless, the dead. America, he knew, might have made a difference if they'd gotten involved in that war earlier than she had. This time the price would be worse, far worse.

"If it does, sir, we could sell war materials to the Brits and French," Hull began, "but it would have to be on a cash and carry basis. No credit given. That'll be the law."

Roosevelt nodded. "Well, it'll be a start. Gentlemen, I believe that if Hitler is left unchecked, it'll mean a Nazi regime across Europe perhaps even Africa."

"If the British and French can't keep the Nazis at bay, that could very well be the case," General Marshall stated. "Right now, as it looks, neither one of them seem that interested in doing that. There's two million men in the French Army. So far only a small portion of them are well equipped enough to take on those Nazis. One on one the Germans are a lot better armed."

"Well, one thing at a time," Roosevelt replied. "We get that revision put through Congress, then we can begin to lend our aid. Which means, for you George, that we'll have to put together whatever we can for our friends over there. And for you too Admiral Stark. It'll be your job, obviously, to protect our shipments to Europe from being sunk halfway on their way over."

Admiral Stark, Chief of Naval Operations, cleared his throat. "Mister President, General Marshall and I have conferred several times and we both agree with you, sir. We should and must aid the British and French as much as we can. However, I'd like to point out just two things, they both concern Japan. First, their war in China aside, we have intelligence to suggest that they have designs on British and Dutch possessions in the Pacific and they have the power to take them. Secondly, the Japanese have been on a naval binge for a few years now. They may have as many as ten carriers built.

"Sir, if they decide to come at us from across the Pacific or hit the Philippines with that, they could wipe out our bases before we could even get our ships past Hawaii. Sir, I've put together a memo on just such a case and I've spoken with the Secretary of the Navy, but I'll bring it up here and now. I believe that we need to move the bulk of our Pacific Fleet westward to meet any such threat."

"Where?" Roosevelt asked.

"Honolulu, sir," was the reply. "Naval Station Pearl Harbor could house our Pacific Fleet."

"What are your thoughts on that, general?" Roosevelt asked. He always liked to get Marshall's opinion on subjects. He found the General to be a good levelheaded man and officer.

"It makes sense, Mister President. It's far enough from the West Coast to give us a good defense if we needed one. Also, a good launching off point for offensive actions if we have to go to war in the Pacific. We could make it work."

War in the Pacific? Was the entire world to become embroiled in war?

"I'll confer with the Secretary of the Navy about the matter," Roosevelt said. "If he agrees then I'll approve of the move. As long as you believe moving the fleet to Pearl Harbor saves American lives."

Winston read the report that he'd just been handed by his military aide-de-camp, Lieutenant Commander Charles Thompson. He mumbled the words as he read each line, when he finished reading, he picked up his cigar and puffed it back to life.

"One day," he exclaimed grimly. "Denmark goes in a day." He looked at the three naval officers standing before him in his office at the newly renamed Ministry of Defence. His eyes settled on the man standing third in line. "It seems, Commander Norwen, that your suspicions have proven to be correct." He exhaled, a smoke ring rising upwards from his burning cigar.

Captain Fleming, Norwen's immediate superior, nodded then hung his head down. Captain Fleming had received Norwen's report on a suspected possible attack on Denmark and Norway, just days before the German attack on Poland, but had dismissed the man's suspicions as nothing more than just paranoia. He'd practically censured Norwen that day. Turned out that the man's instincts had been good.

Churchill sat quietly for a moment, looking at the officers, puffing on his cigar.

"What do we know is going on in Norway?" He finally asked.

Fleming and Thompson both looked over at Norwen.

"We have reports of German paratroopers landing near Stavanger," Norwen reported. "Some airfields have been seized. It would follow that additional German forces will land by sea transport near Oslo. We've also received intelligence of German Naval forces sighted off the coast heading towards Narvik. From the descriptions, it seems likely that they're battleships."

Again, the room became silent. Churchill looked over Norwen, then Fleming. He began to chew the end of his cigar.

CHAPTER TEN

The loud winding screech of the opposing Messerschmitt Bf-109's engine made Flight Lieutenant Christopher Sharp wince suddenly as his aircraft and the German flew passed by within just feet of the other at a nearly 700 mph combined speed. They'd flown so close to each other that he swore he could smell the German's aftershave.

Sharp took a quick moment to scan the aerial battlefield around him. The situation was not looking good for the Poles and the foreign pilots flying with them. The Luftwaffe outnumbered their Polish counterparts by no less than twenty to one. They'd launched a predawn bombing run against Polish army forces to the east of the city of Lodz, troops guarding the southern approaches to the capital of Warsaw.

The Polish squadron, of which Sharp was assigned, had scrambled to meet them but had been overwhelmed by the German bombers and their escorting fighters from the very start. Out of the fourteen fighters that had taken off eight were newer British built Spitfires or Hawker Hurricanes. The remaining six were the Polish built PZL's, which, as fast as they were, lacked the firepower and maneuverability of either the British or German fighters.

By the time that the squadron had moved in to engage the German bombers, they'd been pounced upon by a flock of Messerschmitt Bf-109's and the Polish aircraft had been the first to take hits. Four had been knocked out of the sky before even a shot was returned by the allied aircraft. Today's engagement had certainly taken its toll. Of the fourteen fighters that lifted up this morning, five were destroyed in the sky, three had taken hits and been forced to retire from the fight. Most of the squadron was, of course, Polish, but a few British and Canadian volunteers had been assigned to it as well and those were the pilots who had gotten in the precious few hits on Luftwaffe aircraft. Four of the Do 17 light bombers had been hit as had one of the medium Heinkel He 111's. Three of the escorting Messerschmitt 109's had also been shot down, in return, two of the Hawker Hurricanes had been lost, a third forced to retire. All in all, today had begun just as every day for the past ten days had, with unsustainable losses. The Germans were simply too much.

Sharp pulled back of the control yoke of his Supermarine Spitfire and pitched his fighter skywards climbing at thirteen meters per second. The Messerschmitt he'd passed, by contrast, began a banking turn along the same altitude and started to come around in order to try and get in behind Sharp.

He spun his head around to try and get his eyes on the German. He was climbing skywards and away from his enemy at 340 mph trying to gain altitude on the other. He spotted the German. He was halfway through his bank turn and looked as if he meant to chase after Sharp.

The Bf 109 was an excellent fighter. It was agile, reliable, well-armed and could climb faster than anything the British had. But after this German had flown passed him, he had decided to bank his airplane around rather than gain altitude. That little indecision was what was now going to give Sharp an opportunity to fight his way out of this and maybe even survive the day.

Off to his right two Hawker Hurricanes were tangling with a pair of 109's. To his left the main body of the Luftwaffe bombers were barreling eastward in their standard three plane formations. It was a solid phalanx of over three hundred of the light Dornier do 17's and their heavier Heinkel He 111 brethren. He must've been just outside of their combat box otherwise there would be the visible tracer fire coming from their flanking bombers.

From the middle of the bomber formation, he could make out one of the Polish PZL's diving down and firing rounds at one of the Heinkel's. The Polish pilot drove his plane hard through the formation of enemy bombers and kept on speeding towards to ground, a German fighter breaking formation to chase after him. A trail of white smoke followed the bomber where the PZL had gotten in a hit.

Sharp decided he had gained enough altitude and timed an Immelmann turn to coincide with the Messerschmitt completing his own turn and climbing skywards, straight towards him. He dropped his left wing and swung around in a tight half loop bringing his aircraft aiming down towards the German fighter, now giving Sharp the advantage of coming down on his enemy, picking up speed as he dove.

The German plane could climb faster than a Supermarine Spitfire could climb, but the Spitfire was faster on a level plane. With the altitude advantage Sharp was moving faster than the enemy was by nearly 100 kilometers per hour and if by some chance neither pilot was able to kill the other in this duel, he could simply disengage and have the speed to exit the combat zone before the Messerschmitt could ever hope to catch up to him.

Tracer fire was coming from the German fighter, and they were closing the distance between them at a combined speed of now well over 700 mph. Sharp lowered the nose of his fighter and lined up for the shot, put the enemy plane square in the center of his sights and squeezed the trigger. The sky between the two fighters filled with a steady stream of machine gun rounds flying in both directions.

The German rounds came dangerously close to the underbelly of Sharp's Spitfire, the 13 mm rounds darted past him on his dive. But in the end Sharp's eight Browning machine gun rounds saturated the air around his enemy and a few of them found their way to their target and ripped into the 109's fuselage. A sharp explosion from the 109 then another, the German simply fell apart in midair. The plane broke apart at 15,000 feet and toppled over in the sky.

He cut his fire and gently pulled his aircraft away from the smoking enemy plane and watched for a brief few seconds until he saw the German pilot fall out of the aircraft and his parachute open. He breathed out a small sigh of relief, a small courtesy afforded to the other pilot, as he watched the parachute drift slowly earthwards.

There was still a fight going on in the sky and his mates were fighting as hard as they could, hopeless as it seemed to be. His fighter drifted back towards the fleet of bombers and the few pilots who had the gall to oppose them.

The streets of Warsaw were as desolate as they could be with only a few civilians running this way and that looking to get to shelter as fast as they could and volunteer fire fighters waiting for the inevitable time in which they would be called into action. The majority of Warsaw's population were huddled together in basements and underground shelters spread throughout the city.

It was the fourteenth day that the city had been bombed, or was it the fifteenth? It had become difficult to tell anymore. The Germans had begun bombing raids over the city on the first day, which had sent a terrifying panic throughout the capital by civilians and government officials shocked at the use of the German Luftwaffe in such a way. The bombardment of opposing capitals was not unheard of in war, but this was profoundly different. Large fleets of bombers flying high above the earth unloading their arsenal of bombs of the city of over a million people, 99 percent of which were unarmed civilians, had become the new norm in this conflict. It seemed that military thinking in Germany had not only conceived of the indiscriminate murder of women and children but had strongly swung towards it.

Anthony Joseph Drexel Biddle Jr. the American ambassador to Poland stared up into the afternoon skies and took that thought in. *Is this how things are going to be now? Are we looking at our future, a constant way of war in which civilians are now targeted for extermination?* A cold shiver ran up his spine as he thought about that.

The American embassy had been hit by bomb debris six days earlier and much of the west side of the building was now off limits and its windows and doors had been boarded up. The ambassador and several of his staff had gathered on the roof now, watching the bombers fly off to the south, setting the southern part of the city ablaze.

The Polish government, such as it was, had sent word to the foreign embassies that they fully expected the city to be surrounded by no later than Thursday. Two days from now. As it was, German troops were already shelling the very outskirts of Warsaw and its hastily erected defenses.

In his breast pocket Ambassador Biddle had the folded-up transmission from Washington which had come in just this morning. President Roosevelt had ordered them out. The embassy was already being emptied of vital documents and American personnel were busy gathering personal and diplomatic belongings, packing them into several large trucks that the Polish government had lent them.

Two planes were sitting on the tarmac of Okecie Airport, fueled up and ready to evacuate the Americans to neutral Hungary. Most of the non-essential American personnel and visiting citizens had been evacuated in the first few days of the conflict. The embassy was now down to a bare bones staff and even they were now leaving.

In the distance there were the sounds of more bombs exploding. In the streets surrounding the embassy the people of Warsaw had been almost completely cleared by police and fire fighters.

"We'd better get going," Ambassador Biddle said in a low, depressed tone.

He and his aides made their way down the stairwell to the executive floor. The embassy hallways and offices were almost vacant. The flags taken down, government documents boxed up and the picture of President Roosevelt removed from the wall and put aboard trucks.

"Alan," Biddle turned to his young aide and motioned for the telephone sitting on the office desk. "Please get the Foreign Minister on the phone. Mac, I want you to personally make one last walk through of the building. I don't want to miss anything or.... anyone."

A third embassy aide entered the office they were occupying. It was Milton Crain, his personal head of security. "Sir, a car will be pulling up to the east gate shortly. I've already got your personal belongings crated and headed for the airport. I've also spoken with both the Polish Air Force attaché' and our own pilots. We're going to take off just as soon as we've been assured there are no German fighters around. We've notified the German government that we'll be evacuating, and they've given assurances of safe passages, however, I'm not willing to chance it. Some Nazi son of a bitch pilot decides he wants to shoot down an unarmed transport plane. . . ." he shook his head. "The Belgians made it out just fine yesterday and so will we."

The ambassador patted the other man on the shoulder.

"Sir," Alan Johnson, said from behind. He was extending the phone out. "The Foreign Minister."

Biddle took the phone. "Josef? Yes, I wanted to call you before we left. Uh huh. Yes, I'm sorry as well. I wanted you to know, Josef, that I've communicated with President Roosevelt, and he wanted me to tell you that. . ." he paused a second "...we're going to do everything that we can do for you." He forced out those last few words, hated it, regretted them, knew how empty they were. Worthless political promises and both of them knew it.

"I understand how that sounds. I understand how you must feel right now. I wish that I could do something more right now. I know you do, I know you do. I understand, Josef. Josef, I have to be going. We'll be leaving shortly for Hungary. Thank you, sir. I will pray for you as well. Yes. Goodbye."

He kept the phone in his hand for a few silent moments then hung it up. There was nothing else left to do. The room was silent except for the dull thunderous sound of distant bombs.

Biddle sighed heavily, let it out. Putting his fedora on and taking the briefcase Alan had just handed to him, he nodded and looked around the now empty office of the now former embassy of the United States.

"Alright, let's get going."

Sharp's Spitfire had been running on fumes by the time that his landing gear touched down on the patch of ground that was now serving as an air force landing strip. It was really nothing more than an empty spot of land that had been used as a hunting lodge. The former lodge itself had been turned into makeshift barracks and the spotting tower was now manned by aerial observers looking to the skies. The ground was just firm enough to accommodate the Polish and British planes that now made this home, what few planes that were left anyway.

The Spitfire came to a stop, and he killed the engine, took his goggles and summer helmet off, inhaled a long, deep breath and let it out slowly. His watch said just past 4 o'clock. They'd taken off at just before noon and there was still plenty of daylight left.

The Luftwaffe had been relentless since the beginning, and it was only getting worse. Each day there were fewer of them and no matter how many of the Germans they knocked out of the sky, there seemed to be a never-ending supply of them. Today's engagement killed ten of them, four more forced to retire. But it wasn't near enough to stop the three hundred and fifty plus bombers from reaching their targets.

The ground crews made their way out to the fighters as they came into parking positions. Fuel trucks began to move out to refuel the squadron.

Sharp jumped up from his cockpit and climbed down from the wing of his Spitfire, gave his craft a good look over before the ground mechanics got there. A few holes from German machine gun fire but nothing that would keep her from flying again.

He looked around the airfield. Five other planes, two Hawker Hurricanes, another Spitfire and two of the Polish PZL's had taxied into park. The pilot of the other Spitfire, Harry Alexander, a Canadian volunteer pilot spotted Sharp and gave him a small two fingered salute from his cockpit which Sharp returned.

The strain of constant fighting combined with the heat and humidity had taken its toll on the fliers and ground crew. Sharp had been in Poland for several weeks now, having been assigned by the RAF to help train Polish pilots in the use of the British planes they had purchased. At first the assignment had been almost pleasant, before the conflict had erupted with Germany. The climate in this part of the country was not unlike Southern England, warm spring days and cool, pleasant evenings. Now, two months later with summer beginning to show itself, the humidity was starting to be felt and the clouds of black flies had become something of a real nuisance, particularly to the foreign pilots who were unused to them.

The ground crew ran up to Sharp and began to get to work on the Spitfire.

"Alright boss?" A soft voice asked. The young man named Tomasz, whom the British and Canadians had dubbed 'Tommy', walked up. No more than fifteen or sixteen he was a scrawny, blonde haired kid from Warsaw that had become one of the best aircraft mechanics in the squadron.

Sharp grinned at the boy and nodded. "I'm alright, lad."

Tommy reached into his back pocket and pulled out a small tin flask, unscrewed the top and offered it to Sharp. The older man raised an eyebrow and chuckled. He liked the kid. He didn't at first, found him to be quite annoying when he'd first been forced to entrust his plane to an orphaned kid from the streets of Warsaw, but the boy had grown on him and eventually gained his respect. The kid had shown a real ability to learn quickly, and he never seemed to sleep either. He was up at all hours tinkering away on mechanical parts.

He took the proffered flask and downed a quick swig. Polish vodka was something else that Sharp did not like at first either, but in lieu of nothing else it became something that he'd learned to at least live with. His own supply of Scotch whiskey had run out weeks earlier.

"We'll be going soon, boss," the kid said, his English had gotten much better.

He handed the flask back to the lad and his forehead creased. "What do you mean?"

"The officers, there," he pointed his thumb back to the shed that served as the airfield radio shack and HQ. "they say we'll go soon. Away from here."

Sharp eyed the group of Polish officers around the HQ shed. There did seem to be a lot of activity going on around the shed. The commanding officer, Colonel Wojcik would probably be found inside.

"You help the other lads," Sharp told the boy. "Refuel the planes. Reload the ammo. Understand?"

Tommy grinned and nodded. Sharp rubbed the kid's hair and then walked over towards the HQ. Several Polish officers were bustling around the building, couriers were coming and going on bicycles. The Poles barely acknowledged the Lieutenant as he made his way into the HQ. The airfield CO, Colonel Wojcik was indeed inside, a phone held up against his head, his staff busy writing out orders on paper. Lieutenant Frederick Brown, the British liaison and translator, was also present, puffing away on one of the stinking American cigars that he loved so much.

"Frederick," Sharp said as he entered the small, cramped room that served as HQ. It was really nothing more than an old wood and storage shed that had been equipped with two small desks and one large map on the wall.

"Chris, good to see you." He let out a long puff of cigar smoke. "Bloody affair today. Bloody affair."

Sharp only nodded. Brown was a young officer, born just outside of London. He was one of those wide-eyed young officers who thought that they knew it all, were full of naivete and eager to prove themselves. He'd been posted to Canada prior to this assignment, which is when he'd picked up his habit of smoking American cigars. He'd never so much as fired a shotgun prior to enlisting in the army where he'd excelled as an office clerk. His only redeeming quality right now was that he spoke fluent Polish.

Sharp, on the other hand, had enlisted as a seventeen-year-old, straight out of common school in the north of England. He'd spent five years in the ranks in India prior to becoming an officer and electing to attend flight school in England back in '37 when a slot had become available. Since earning his wings, it seemed like he'd been posted to anywhere that the Union Jack flew. Malta, India, Africa and Gibraltar. Now he was here.

Colonel Wojcik made brief eye contact with Chris, then continued his phone call. Sharp did not understand Polish, try as he had, he simply couldn't get it down.

"What's going on?" He asked Brown.

"Looks like we're pulling out. The Jerries are bypassing Lodz. Damn panzers will probably be passing by here sometime tomorrow. Colonel's got orders to move the squadron."

Sharp knew that the Germans were moving fast, but not this fast. The Wehrmacht had a lot of newer motorized units that could move faster than the Polish Army could, and their Panzer units were moving faster and hitting harder than anyone could possibly have imagined.

Entrenched Polish troops had initially held them up when the fighting had begun, but the Germans, learning quickly, simply bypassed those entrenchments and encircled the Polish infantry, allowing the Luftwaffe to bomb them into surrender.

The map on the wall showed the location of both allied and enemy units. The blue marked Polish Army units were gathered mostly in clumps to the west, southwest and north of Warsaw on the Vistula River. The German units, marked in red, seemed to be everywhere else. The German Fourteenth Army was cutting deep into the Galicia countryside, towards Lwow in southeastern Poland. Resistance to them had all but collapsed. The Eighth and Tenth Armies were pushing hard towards Warsaw from the south and the Third Army from the north. Vital defenses and choke points were simply being hammered to death by the Luftwaffe. Death from above.

"Pulling out to where?" Sharp asked.

"Not sure. There seems to be a lot of confusion. Bombers are hitting Warsaw every day." Brown took a puff on his cigar again. "Our embassy has closed, so have the Frenchies and the Belgians and the Americans. There's some word that the government in Warsaw has evacuated as well."

Sharp shook his head, looked at the calendar on the wall. It had barely been a fortnight since the fighting had begun. He marveled at just how fast the Nazis were moving. *German efficiency,* he thought.

Colonel Wojcik slammed the phone down and swore openly, the other officers barely stopping to notice. Wojcik was an older man, an old veteran who'd fought against Russia during the first war. His thick hair was graying, and his mustache was thick in a traditional Polish fashion. He was heavy set around the midsection and chain smoked his cheap Polish cigarettes. The man did not speak a word of English either, hence Brown's present assignment.

The Polish Colonel spattered away at Brown, stopping every few seconds to catch his breath. There was an exhaustion in his voice, the sound of a man trying hard not to let himself break down. Whatever he'd been on the telephone about, it didn't seem to be anything good. But it had been quite some time since any of them had had any good news come down the chain.

Brown nodded then turned to Sharp. "The government is evacuating from the capital. The general staff thinks that the city'll be under occupation sometime in the next few days." The Colonel went on, slapping his thighs and looking down at his feet as he spoke. "We're moving out to an airfield outside of Lublin. Trucks are on their way now to load up the equipment and men. As soon as they've loaded everything up, we'll move them out under the cover of night. You might want to catch some sleep, Lieutenant. As soon as your planes are serviced and refueled, you'll be wheels up."

Christopher Sharp looked at Brown then to the Colonel. He reached into his pocket and pulled out his pack of Pall Malls and lit one to life.

CHAPTER ELEVEN

A chorus of exuberant laughter went up around the chamber from the men assembled in the large briefing room at the OKH. The top officers of the three service branches and their aides were loosely arrayed around an immensely large table in the center of the room, a map of Europe splayed out across it with markers indicating the current placement of their forces. The mood in the room did not quite meet what they would call 'military professional', but Hitler allowed it. This was a good day for Germany, and he'd allowed for a less formal atmosphere.

The German Army had pushed deep into Poland with unexpected speed, encircling or destroying the defending armies. A few disorganized Polish units had escaped destruction and had either fallen back on Warsaw or had fled east. The invasion had moved so quickly, quicker in fact than the military planners had initially thought, that there had been a serious concern that the forward divisions, particularly the panzers, would find themselves cut off from German supply lines. A two day slow down actually had to be ordered just to get supplies caught up to the fighting units.

At sea the Kriegsmarine had scored several victories as well. Three British warships torpedoed in the opening salvo of fighting and now Hitler's prized U-boats were slipping past the Royal Navy and escaping into the wide open Atlantic. Soon they would begin the task of cutting the island nation off from its own vital overseas supplies. Oil tankers from the Middle East, rubber from the East Indies, food supplies from Canada would all need to be decimated in order to keep the British at bay.

In the air Göring's Luftwaffe had done just as the fat man had boasted and secured supremacy in just days. Fleets of German bombers sortied daily deep into Poland, destroying airfields, supply depots, decimating front line troops and bombing the major cities, particularly the capital Warsaw. The boisterous, overweight head of the Luftwaffe seemed to be like a schoolboy who had kissed his first girl, his face at times blushing. The overall success of the invasion had gone better than his planners had anticipated, and losses had been lighter than expected.

The spear has pierced deeply, now for the death blow.

Hitler sipped on his tea, bent over the large map and gave the go ahead for Keitel to begin.

General Wilhelm Keitel, his hands clasped behind his back, stood ramrod straight and began his briefing.

"Mein Führer, I am pleased to inform you that the invasion so far has been very successful. Our forward units have driven into the very heart of Poland. As of this very morning units of the Third Army have begun a general artillery bombardment of Warsaw. Army Group North has secured the entire northern half of the country and linked up with our units in East Prussia. General Bock will now be pushing straight into the central part of the country. His panzers are moving virtually unopposed at this point. In fact, General Guderian's panzer troops have leveled the few remaining fortifications north of the city. His biggest obstacle right now is the number of prisoners that he's taking.

"Rundstedt's forces in the south control everything from our borders all the way east to the Carpathians. Supplies for Army Group South are flowing through Slovakia and our Slovak allies have taken control of many of the bridges and roads which we are now using to transport our supplies through. Here, the remnants of the Polish forces around Lodz and again here at Poznan, have been completely cut off. Tenth Army's tanks have bypassed the fortifications around Lodz and have moved around the flank of the entire Polish army in the western half of their country. Warsaw is now completely encircled, and our forces are fighting in the outskirts of the city. The city did not have adequate time to gather supplies. We expect a full surrender within a matter of days."

Keitel sprung up and down on his toes in a gesture of success. He grinned broadly when he looked at Hitler.

Hitler groaned but said nothing, looming over the large map like a god might stand over his new creation and nodded in silent satisfaction. Denmark had fallen in a single day, Copenhagen was now occupied, his troops were quickly subduing Norway and meeting with little resistance on that front as well. With Poland falling, his forces would be masters of the Baltic. His agreement with the Soviets would soon come to pass and prove to be the dagger through the heart for the fool Poles.

The secret agreement that he'd signed with Stalin and the Soviet Union last summer had called for Poland to be divided up into thirds. The western third of the country was to be annexed directly into Germany proper. The eastern third of the country, which bordered the Soviet Union, was to be ceded to that country, as well as the three small Baltic states in the north minus the traditionally German city of Memel. The central third of Poland was to be the buffer zone between the two powers and controlled by a German friendly puppet state. Despite a near year long delay in the original invasion plan, Stalin had stood by the original agreement.

Hitler continued. "What news of Britain and France?"

Keitel grunted. "The French have begun a general mobilization of their forces. Although, Mein Führer, I must say they are going about it very slowly. Their army is occupying the border forts of the Maginot Line." He swept his hand across the French-German border, a land occupied by hundreds of small fortress defenses, stretching from the Swiss border in the south to Belgium in the north. "Neither country has taken any concerning action yet. Despite its immense size, the French lack the logistical capacity to move their army with any speed. The British.... more likely their Prime Minister, is still hoping for a negotiated settlement. Although, we now know that they have brought Churchill back and given him substantial war powers. We know him from the last war to be a fighter."

Everyone knew that Churchill had been First Lord of the Admiralty in the Great War and had a reputation as a warrior, even serving in a front-line regiment in the trenches while still a member of Parliament. It was only after his colossal failure at Gallipoli that he'd been forced out of government. Now it seemed the man was back, but it did not faze Hitler one bit.

"The British will settle once they realize the futility of their situation," Hitler murmured. He waved a backhand at France. "Once France and the Low Countries are knocked out, they will have no choice but to negotiate. Then.... then we will forge a new alliance with them. Our real enemy lies to the east." His eyes rose sharply up to the head of his navy. "Raeder?"

Grand Admiral Erich Raeder straightened up. "Mein Führer, we currently have ninety-eight U-boats operating in either the North Sea or the Atlantic. Although they have sunk several British and French warships, their main goal is to cut the enemy's supply lines. The bulk of our surface ships are committed to supporting the Norway operation. Our ships that were previously blockading Danzig are now being reassigned to that as well. I am concerned, however. We've taken several losses in Norway, including the heavy cruiser *Blucher* being lost just yesterday. Norwegian shore batteries have inflicted serious damage on our ships. Three destroyers and several transports have also been lost. Transports that we will need later on down the road."

Hitler spared a quick glance at Göring. As Chief of the Air Force, he had underestimated the fighting willingness of the Norwegians and had not assigned an adequate force to help cover the invasion of that country. Knowing of his failure and Hitler's condemnation, he had recently relocated several bombing wings to subdue the resistance.

"Our shipyards in Kiel and Wilhelmshaven are working at capacity and we're currently on schedule to replace those losses and to add substantially to our ships at sea. Six new U-boats will be leaving their pens within a week, nine more by the end of June. *Bismarck* will be rolling out of the yard sometime in August. Our decision to renew our aircraft carrier project also continues. The expansion of our shipyards in Kiel should put us on schedule for a completion of *Graf Zeppelin* sometime in the middle of next year, provided the flow of resources goes uninterrupted. In short, Mein Führer, our current naval resources are adequate in meeting our current commitments. If we were to go beyond these operations, the situation would change drastically."

"How so?" Hitler asked. "What if we need them to subdue the British later?"

There was a slight general sigh from several of the briefers in the room. Raeder hesitated for a moment then answered.

"To meet the English head on, warship for warship would require more power than we currently have. The reason behind our U-boat build up was to cut their overseas supply lines without the necessity of engaging their navy in surface battle. The naval treaty we previously had with them after the Great War, allowed them a substantial lead in surface ships. While many of their ships are older and some even obsolete, the Royal Navy still boasts more ships than any other navy in the world. They've had over a hundred years to build up their naval infrastructure. We WILL cut their supply lines, sink their transports and cargo vessels, starve them into submission. That is how we will subdue the English."

Hitler rubbed his temple as if a sudden headache had come over him. His thumb ran over the scar that he now bore on his face. He had long heard the endless whining of the naval chiefs since he had come to power. The modernization of the German military had been one of the major goals of the Nazi party since the beginning, but it had come at a cost. The army had made huge strides forward in modernizing its equipment and overall strategy and fighting tactics, but the cost had been the abandoning of the traditional Prussian school that had been the pride of the German people. The buildup of the air forces had been the easiest of them all. Stripped of its air force after the previous war, Germany had made huge strides forward under the leadership of Göring. But Germany had never been a seagoing power in comparison with the Allied navies. Its navy had been practically wiped out after the war and Germany had lacked the infrastructure needed to rebuild it. Hitler's near disdain for that service did it no help either. Most of Germany's war resources were allocated elsewhere with the exception of their famed U-boats.

"As for France," Hitler began, turning his attention back to the map before him. "What preparations are being made for our offensive against them?"

Keitel answered. "We are preparing all of our available resources for the French campaign. Speer has submitted his report on our war production. Our training depots are full to capacity with new recruits. We should be very close to our troop strength goals by early 1941. General Brauchitsch here can brief you on our preparations for western operations."

Walther von Brauchitsch was the head of the OKH, Army Command. However, in the confusing apparatus of the Nazi military command structure, the OKH was in nominal charge of the army while the OKW, in theory if not in practice, had been formed to oversee the coordination between all three branches of the military as well as carry out the orders of Hitler himself. There was a not-so-secret rivalry between the two organizations as each vied for control.

General Brauchitsch began his report. "Our border forts are fully manned. The Norway operation is moving along. Twenty-first Corps has secured Oslo and Kristiansand and now move against Narvik. They are well supplied and equipped. I must say, our paratroopers have performed spectacularly, much to their credit. They secured key enemy airfields and landing grounds in vital zones quickly and with few casualties. I expect to be in full control of the country by the end of July.

"As General Keitel has informed you, our troop goals should be reached by early next year ahead of time for a planned offensive in the west. Our plan calls for massive bombardment of the French forts along their Maginot Line by the Luftwaffe as well as launching several feinting attacks against them there. The real assault will go through the Netherlands and Belgium. Once Poland has surrendered, we should have no problem relocating the vast majority of our forces. The French, as we assumed they would, followed a strong defensive doctrine, manning their fortifications along our mutual border. The British have formed army units in the southeast of their country but so far, our intelligence assets have confirmed that only a small number of their troops have landed in France.

"Our plan of attack follows the Manstein Plan. A great single force sweeping westwards through Holland and Belgium and into northern France. General Halder and I agree that our goal should be the capture of Calais and Dunkirk in the initial attack. Once the northern coast ports have been secured, we can turn south towards Paris. Our increased production of motorized units will mean that our infantry units can move faster and keep up with the projected advance of our panzers. I've currently earmarked a total of one hundred sixty-seven divisions for this operation, a total of four million men. We've code named this operation Case Red."

General Keitel opened a small notebook. "If Herr Speer's production estimates are accurate, we should have between three thousand five hundred and three thousand eight hundred tanks, nearly eight thousand heavy guns and six thousand aircraft available for the campaign. Anyways. . . . "

"What date have you set for the campaign?" Hitler cut him off in a hushed tone.

"The exact date has not been set yet, but it will be sometime in the spring of next year," Keitel replied. "Plenty of time for us to consolidate our gains and prepare the necessary forces."

Hitler studied the huge map, hovered over France and nodded. He'd had a fixation with that country and with the city of Paris in particular. Having been a veteran of the Great War of 1914-1918 he'd fought in those trenches, against those soldiers and had come home defeated and disgraced as so many young German men had in that war. The humiliation that so many Germans had felt by that defeat and the treaty terms imposed upon them by the victorious Allies had been resented even deeper by the man who now led the Reich.

"Gentlemen," Hitler began, "I intend to leave for Poland in two days to inspect our victorious soldiers on the front. After that I meet with Mussolini in Vienna. I will be discussing this plan with him at that time. I've been informed by him that British diplomats in Rome have made small overtures of peace. No doubt he will discuss that as well." He put his tongue in his cheek and let out a small laugh. "Perhaps Chamberlain will sue for peace before a single German boot sets foot in France. The British do not want war. They have a global empire to maintain, and war would drain them too much."

"Mein Führer," General Keitel cleared his throat before continuing. "Like you, we all hope for a brief conclusion of any war with England. Perhaps if Case Red goes as planned and with a swift capitulation of France, Prime Minister Chamberlain may indeed accept a formal peace with us. However. . . . as your military planners, we would be remiss if we did not plan for the possibility of a more protracted conflict with them. And so. . . . General Halder and I, along with General Brauchitsch have discussed the need for plans for offensive operations against the British Isles directly. Perhaps these plans will not become necessary in the future, but it would be wiser to have them than to not."

A moment of silence in the room. Hitler appeared to digest the information and then, after a long moment nodded his head up and down.

"Better to have a plan, I agree. Hopefully we shall not need such operations, but we cannot hope for victory, we plan for it! Reich Minister Goebbels, you will continue to use your resources to rally our people. Through your propaganda we shall also reach out to the British people across the channel. Let them know that we do not wish war with them. They are of Saxon blood and heritage. They should know that we are willing to fight them, but we would rather not. If his people do not support a war, Chamberlain will come to us. He is weak and he knows it. He knows that I know it too. I saw it in his eyes in Munich."

Goebbels, the viper-like Minister of Propaganda and the one Hitler trusted most, nodded in agreement with his Führer. Both men knew that given the tools, Goebbels could move mountains. Hell, he'd convinced the German populace that the Poles were the ones who'd started this new war, Hitler knew he could convince the English people that the German people were not their true enemy. Everyone in Europe knew the Bolsheviks in Russia were the real enemy. Any possibility of an Anglo-German alliance would depend greatly upon the speed of next year's campaign and the desire of the British government to sit out the conflict on the continent.

"We shall meet again following our final victory in Poland," Hitler told the group. "As you've been instructed, Reich Minister Himmler will be given authority in certain zones there, including Warsaw. The Wehrmacht is to cede full authority to him there."

The revelation that SS field units would be allowed control over whole swaths of Poland did not come as much of a surprise to many of the regular army officers. However, there had been rumors spreading around Berlin, rumors of a quite distasteful kind regarding the goals of those units. At home in Germany, both the SS and the Gestapo fell directly under Himmler's control and those two forces had become the unnamed terror of the Nazi party. Too many Germans in recent years had been whisked away in the late hours of the night for even discussing the activities of those organizations. Several high-ranking military commanders had been removed for even suggestions of conduct that they had seen as too dishonorable. But Hitler knew that every one of his generals understood better than to disobey this directive. Silence was sometimes the price that had to be paid for victory.

CHAPTER TWELVE

Corporal Ernst Krauss sat atop his Panzer IV and peered through his field binoculars at the town of Sandomierz. The distant outline of its town building and the tall church steeples could just be made out. For two days now the forward units of the 2nd Panzer Division had been relentlessly pushing deeper into central Poland. They had fought six major skirmishes in just as many days prior to that. But for the last two there had been no visible sight of the enemy other than the distant sound of artillery.

This was a welcome reprieve for Ernst and his tank crew. It had been a hard fight since the Poles had attacked Germany and forced the Reich to respond and they'd had precious little time to rest since then, less than three weeks ago. There had been casualties of course and for the first time in his life he'd been exposed to death. The emptiness of it. But he felt that he and his men had weathered it well, better than he'd expected and in the aftermath, he felt pride. Pride in his men, in himself, in his service and most of all, pride in his country.

He had never met any Poles before. Not before the army and not while he was in the army. None, that was, except for the ones that he had the privilege of escorting into prisoner of war pens. He didn't have anything against them, didn't hate them, didn't know them. Truth be told, he could care less one way or the other about Polish people. But having been in their country now for nearly three weeks, he was surprised, shocked even, to discover how their country looked much like his own home. The houses and buildings looked much like they did in Germany. The people themselves may have even been mistaken for Aryans if he didn't know otherwise. You might even think that they were smart, except that every German schoolboy knew just how dumb Polish people were. They weren't animals mind you, but they weren't smart either and every German knew it. That was what they had been taught and he saw no reason to debate that fact.

The midday sun beat down on them, he wiped the sweat off his forehead, let his binoculars hang around his neck, uncapped his canteen and took a nice long drink of cool water. The panzer formation was moving along a dirt road at a modest fifteen kph, the long column stretched for several kilometers in either direction.

Battalion had informed them that there might have been Polish troops in the area to defend the town, but it didn't look that way to Ernst. He hadn't heard so much as a shot fired from that general direction all day long.

"It's fucking hot," Private Nicholas complained. He and Private Albrecht were sitting atop the front of the tank as it rolled forward. "Who would've thought Poland could get this fucking hot."

Albrecht laughed and gave the other a cross look. "It gets hot in Germany too stupid. Do you think that we're in Siberia or something?"

Nicholas, a seventeen-year-old kid, shrugged his shoulders. "It doesn't get this hot back in Rostock. At least not that I can remember."

"Rostock!" Albrecht laughed and rubbed the other kid's head. "That's practically Denmark. Trust me when I tell you that it gets hot. In Munich some summers are unbearable. You have to go swimming three times a day just to stay cool. Munich. . . . those churches over there look like the churches in Munich. Hey corporal, are Poles Catholic or Protestant?"

Krauss screwed the cap back on his canteen and smiled back at his gunner. "Catholic I think."

Albrecht waved a hand in response. "Catholics. . . . too many rules. Take it from me, boys, Lutheranism is the best way to go."

"The Führer is Catholic!" Nicholas retorted. "Are you bad mouthing the Führer?"

Albrecht didn't reply. His eyes drifted across the horizon, at the town buildings that were getting larger as they got closer. "I hope there's a Lutheran Church here. I'd like to go to service this Sunday."

Krauss put his binoculars back into their case and dropped them back inside the tank. "I'm sure there'll be services soon," he told the younger man. "This fighting can't go on forever. Sooner or later Poland will give up. Very soon too, I think. Then the war will be over."

He saw no reason for that statement to not be true.

"I heard some of the men from headquarters say that Britain and France entered the war too," Nicholas stated. He cupped his hands over his eyes and looked up into the cloudless sky. "I wonder if we'll have to fight them too. My father fought in France in the Great War. He said it was hell."

"I heard the same thing," Albrecht told him. "The boys I heard it from said that the French army crossed into Germany and burned a bunch of towns to the ground. I don't believe it though. If it were true, the generals would have told us. Besides, I hear that the French don't like to fight. One of the older sergeants said that they'd rather eat crickets and pastries than fight." He grinned as he said it.

"Don't pay attention to rumors boys," Krauss told them both. "When I know something, I will tell you. Take my word for it, France didn't attack Germany."

The long regimental column passed by a wooden road sign: **Sandomierz 13 kilometers**. Marching towards them in the opposite direction was a line of unarmed Polish troops flanked by German infantrymen and motorcycles. The prisoners, a couple hundred of them at least, wore dark khaki uniforms that were stained throughout with mud and sweat and blood. The officer that led them had a bloodied bandage wrapped around his head. Some Germans watched them as the prisoner column marched passed, others paid them no attention at all.

Polish prisoners of war had become such a common sight lately. Tough fighters though. They'd surrendered only after being shelled relentlessly by German guns, bombed by from the sky, surrounded, cut off and starved of food and ammunition. As the enemy soldiers went by Krauss could see the defeat in their faces, that look of men who did what they could but ultimately failed in their duty as soldiers. As hard as many of them may have fought, they simply were no match for the German forces. Their guns were better, their equipment newer and their tanks were heavier.

Several of the Polish troops looked at their German captors as they marched passed, in good order too Krauss noted. Some of the other panzer crews shouted at the defeated troops, mocked them, one threw an apple core at them and told them to eat what was left. The Poles said nothing, but some returned the stares. One Pole, a sergeant, caught his eye. Krauss looked at the older man for a moment and the sergeant stared back as he kept marching forward. His face was filthy, his hair bloody, his uniform ripped to shreds, a bandage over his left hand where two fingers were missing. Krauss's tank rolled by him and the two exchanged long, hard stares.

Krauss was aware of a small sense of embarrassment as the prisoner stared at him. The Polish sergeant's gaze was piercing, almost hypnotic. He barely felt the small nod of acknowledgment that he offered the other man. In the exchange the young German corporal could see something else in the captured sergeant's eyes and in his face. It wasn't just defeat that he saw, although there was plenty of that, but there was something else too. Hate. The Polish sergeant was practically seething with it.

Ernst lowered his eyes away from the other man's stare and the column continued to pass by the armored vehicles. The Polish sergeant turned his stare away from Krauss then put his hand on the shoulder of a young soldier marching by his side and squeezed, tears running down the other soldier's cheeks.

"Fools," Nicholas said. "What a country of fools. Did they think nothing was going to happen after they attacked us?" The kid shook his head.

The tanks rolled on and on. Just about an hour later the regiment came to a halt just outside of the scenic town of Sandomierz. The town sat on the west bank of the Vistula River with a single stone bridge spanning the river. The old town was built in a double circle, with most of the houses and small buildings forming the outer ring. The inner ring was made up mostly of the larger buildings, a school, some churches and a large open area in the center of town. In the middle of it all was a single block building that served as town hall with a tall watchtower structure attached to it.

Several pillars of smoke rose several miles to the north and north-west. There was a single wide causeway that led straight to the heart of town. The panzers were pulling off that causeway into empty fields and dirt roads, letting the line of smaller staff cars and vehicles go by.

"Shut it down," Krauss ordered Private Schmidt, the driver. The engine shuddered then stalled out.

Groups of the other panzers were huddled together here and there. Their crews gathered chatting away, smoking cigarettes, joking around and laughing. Some had taken to resting under the shade of the trees and catching up on some much-needed sleep. This was one of those times that Ernst had learned where the rank-and-file soldier could sit around while the officers figured out the next step. During his training back in Germany this time would often be marked by hours of intense boredom. But that was before this war had begun. Now these brief interludes were felt by the troops as a welcome relief after days of exhausting movement and fighting.

The other members of his tank crew exited the huge Panzer IV. The engine hissed in relief of the past two days under the hot sun.

Ernst pushed himself up from the cupola of the tank where he'd been standing and dropped down the side of the giant tank to the ground. He pulled his handkerchief out and wiped the sweat from his face. It had been hot these last couple of days, much hotter than he'd been used to back in Dresden. The jet-black uniforms of the panzertruppen did not help with that either.

There were several men of his battalion gathered around a cluster of trees. He gave his men leave to rest then walked over to the group. One of them saw as he approached then smiled at him.

"Herr Krauss, where have you been?" He asked sardonically. "Did you get lost again?" It was Corporal Müller a friend of his from tank school. "How come you're always bringing up the rear?"

Ernst smiled back at his friend. "I have to watch your ass my friend. Always charging in without thinking. You're going to get yourself killed soon."

Sergeant Wagner, another tank commander, offered him a cigarette which Ernst thankfully accepted. He hadn't smoked before the army and even before the fighting began, he'd barely done it at all. But the last few weeks had been strenuous, and he found a little relief in cigarettes.

"Sergeant Wagner was just regaling us all with tales of his mighty heroics," Müller said, and the group laughed out loud. Müller was always a joker and popular with the other men. "First tank into the town. Bravely wrestled bottles of milk right out of the hands of babies!" The group broke into laughter.

Wagner waved his hands. "NO! Not bottles. I drank right from their mothers' tits! And what tits they were too!" He gestured with his hands.

Krauss practically choked in laughter. Sergeant Wagner was a stout man, all of five foot five inches tall and much broader than panzer troops typically were. He was also an awkward fellow, waddled when he walked and animated his arms when he spoke. But he was also damn good at his job.

"So, who knows what's happening?" Krauss asked. "Are we stopped here for good?"

Müller shrugged his shoulders. "Who the hell knows. But it's a nice town to be stuck in for a while."

Most of the townspeople had closed themselves inside their houses, afraid to come outside. Very few civilians were out on the streets, some woman carrying a bag of produce, two old men sitting on a brick wall smoking their pipes, watching the black and gray uniformed Germans now occupying their town, a stray dog sniffing around a boarded-up building. three men close to the town hall were talking with a group of German officers in front of the building, The Polish flag had been taken down and the swastika was now being hoisted up the flagpole.

The scene had become all too familiar these last few weeks. German forces moving through and occupying small towns and cities all over southern Poland were often met with terrified civilians who would lock themselves inside their homes with the hope that a closed door might keep the invading troops at bay.

That first week Ernst had witnessed many of those civilians dragged out of their homes by the Wehrmacht but had little time to pay attention to it. Those people had obviously been troublemakers and the army was simply taking precautions to keep the violence in the cities to a minimum. It was not until a week into the fighting that he'd caught his first glimpse of the families, including women and children, being loaded into trucks and horse drawn carts that he'd started to wonder. . . .

He shook the thought away then took another drag on his cigarette.

A horn blared from the road a few meters away. Ernst turned to look as a single command car drove through the lines of panzers parked on either side of the causeway. The car's driver honked it's horn repeatedly for the troopers to get out of the road. Following behind the command car came a series of half-track vehicles and two of the famed *Opel Blitz* trucks, dozens of troops in the rear of each vehicle.

The small convoy made its way up the causeway. The officers in the car shouting orders at the soldiers at the side of the road. Finally, it came to a stop in the center of the town, the trucks and half-tracks taking up parking positions in the town square. Orders were being barked, the men in the back of the vehicles jumping down and forming up along a row of homes.

Many of the men of the panzer regiment watched the scene, others paid little heed. Two officers emerged from inside the town hall, from the distance Ernst thought one of the officers was Colonel Rohm, the regiment CO. He met with the officers in the command car and there appeared to be a heated exchange between the two groups.

"Who are those men?" Müller asked to no one in particular. The insignia on the command car was too far away for anyone to see.

Sergeant Wagner sneered, and all eyes fell on him. He looked around at the group, took a final drag of his cigarette, let the butt fall to the ground then stomped it out with his boot. "SS," he finally answered quietly.

Krauss spared a quick look at the exchange taking place a hundred meters away between the two groups of officers. "SS?" He turned back to Wagner and cocked an eyebrow. "What are they doing here?"

Wagner eyed the formation of *Waffen-SS* that had formed up in the square and shook his head silently.

Eventually the sun set, and the soldiers were settled down for the night. The town hall had been taken over as the headquarters for the German military. Several town buildings and houses had also been taken over for administrative purposes and to house the officers, the families removed under threat of force.

Corporal Krauss had found himself a nice rocking chair earlier in the day and had placed it next to his tank and rocked back and forth until he'd fallen asleep. His men had sacked out an hour or so earlier and as Friday turned into the very early hours of Saturday the town had gone mostly dark, except for a couple of small lanterns in the center of town. The town square was shielded by two rings of houses and buildings and there was little danger of any Polish troops off in the distance of sighting the lights. The few German sentries awake were going this way and that in the darkness, hardly visible in the moonlight.

It was just before five o'clock in the morning when someone shook him awake. His eyes flickered open, and he jumped slightly at whomever had shaken him out of his dreams. He grabbed instinctively at the wrist of the person and tossed the blanket that he'd had draped over himself. It had been Private Mayer, his radio operator, that had woken him. He inhaled sharply then let go of the other's wrist.

"What is it?" He croaked out, his mouth dry.

"I'm sorry, Corporal. They've ordered us to move out," he inclined his head towards the command staff where Major Zant was standing, hands clasped behind his back. "I got you this?" He extended his left hand and offered a cup of dark black coffee then reached into a small bag and retrieved a small biscuit and a cut of meat.

Ernst took both and nodded his thanks. He stood up from the comfortable rocking chair and bit into his small breakfast. The very first rays of sunlight were beginning to beam over the canopy of tall trees to the east. The battalion began stirring and get themselves together, men taking a few minutes to chow down some breakfast, others shaving and others taking this time to relieve themselves.

Ernst finished his biscuit and slice of ham and began to sip on his lukewarm coffee.

"They've order us out already?" He inquired.

Mayer nodded. "Apparently so. I woke up to take a leak and the sergeant there told me to wake everyone up. Major Zant wants us out of here in an hour."

That doesn't seem right, he thought. He'd been under the impression that the entire regiment was to quarter there. Besides, there wasn't any fighting going on in the area that he'd heard of.

He grabbed his tunic off the back of the rocking chair and put it on. Sergeant Wagner was walking nearby just as he finished buttoning himself up.

"Sergeant," he called, the other man stopped and turned to face him. Wagner seemed to always know what was going on, he was good for that. "We're moving out?"

Wagner nodded and looked pissed. He spit. "They want our asses out of here within an hour, I guess. Who knows why? There was a real spat going on over there earlier," he pointed to the town hall where the commanding officers had quartered last night. The regular army officers were not there anymore, nor was the Colonel's command car. Instead, there were two uniformed guards standing outside the doorway.

"Some SS big shot arrived late last night apparently," the Sergeant continued. "That's all I know. Whatever. Got tired of sitting around anyhow." He stocked off angrily.

Panzer troops were used to moving fast, they'd trained and drilled for that repeatedly. When an officer told them an hour, you could bet it took half that time for the regiment to dress and prep themselves to move out. The *SS* units that had moved into town the evening before didn't waste time either. The first tanks were not even on the bridge over the Vistula River yet before civilians began to be dragged out of their homes.

The tanks began to rev up their engines and one by one they moved onto the single road through Sandomierz and over the stone bridge crossing the Vistula. Tank after tank passed by the row of homes on their right.

"Okay," Krauss said to his driver. "Let's get moving." The tank lurched forward onto the main road passed the town and headed for the bridge.

Rows of townspeople were hurried out of their houses. Families, women, children and the old were among them. Though not the entire town was among those herded into the street, Ernst noticed as he pulled his goggles down over his eyes. He scanned the row of homes as they drove passed them and noticed how many of the homes and businesses were still shuddered up and intact. The men from the *Waffen-SS* unit were taking people out of several of the houses, others were being left strictly alone.

Several of the women were crying hard as they were brought out, children in hand. An old man tripped and fell when an SS trooper shoved him in his back with the butt of his rifle. Ernst's forehead crinkled as he observed, not sure what to make of what he was seeing with his own eyes. What kind of trouble could an old man possibly be to warrant that kind of behavior?

A captain of the SS, dressed in a gray overcoat, stood in the center of the activity, quietly observing as his orders were being carried out.

The stray dog he'd observed yesterday came trotting around the corner from one of the closed businesses and began to bark. More people were brought out of the houses and lined up next to the others in the street. There was more yelling, more barking.

Ernst watched quietly at what was going on. There must have been close to two hundred civilians standing out front of the houses now, many crying, others pleading with the gray clad Germans to no avail. There was a small boy standing alone. The child could only have been maybe three or four years old. His knee stockings were dirty, and his clothes were disheveled. His back was turned to Ernst as the tank rolled past and the child was seemingly oblivious to all the commotion. No parent seemed to be with the little boy. The dog kept barking and barking. The little boy, standing all by himself, turned his head around observing what was happening

He was a good-looking child, like all boys of that age were. His cheeks were rosy and plump, his hands were small and soft, small brown hairs stuck out from under his little cap. The boy turned at the sound of the tanks rolling by, saw Ernst and for a moment their eyes met. He smiled and waved a friendly, sweet little wave and Ernst gave the smallest of smiles back at the boy. There was something pinned to the little boy's coat, and he squinted to see what it was. As the sweet little boy with chubby, rosy cheeks kept waving, he finally made out the shape of a little yellow star pinned to the boy's coat.

The stray dog just kept barking and barking.

Just as Ernst was about to raise his hand and wave back at the little boy, an SS guard grabbed the child and yanked him hard in the opposite direction. Krauss slowly moved his eyes back to the column of tanks ahead as he and his crew marched back to war. The last thing that he heard just as they began crossing the bridge was the echo of a rifle going off and the dog's barking ceased.

Flight Lieutenant Sharp could see a large assembly of tanks, vehicles and ground troops sitting along the Vistula River and in whatever town that was down there. He barely even knew where that was anymore. He glanced over his right shoulder quickly, his wingman was still there. The two Spitfires raced across the sky ten thousand feet above the earth at nearly 350 mph, four Messerschmitt's on their tails.

Sharp and his wingman, a Canadian named Mackie, had sortied just before sunrise to provide cover for some retreating Polish units that had been caught down around Przemysl. The remnant of the Polish Army that had gotten out of the area were now desperately headed east to Lwow, a steady stream of civilian refugees trailing behind them. The Luftwaffe had wasted no time in strafing the long lines of tempting targets now strung across the back country roads unprotected.

Mackie and he had arrived on sight just in time to find a flock of Ju 87's, having just released their bomb loads, heading back to their airfield. Figuring the slower Stukas for easy targets, the two had flown straight in at them only to be surprised by the sudden arrival of a squadron of Bf 109's.

The 109's had come in at them in separate pairs from the southeast and south and had the advantage of altitude and cloud cover. Neither he nor Mackie even knew they were there until the Germans were right on top of them. The two barely had time to break off their pursuit of the Stukas and make a run for it. The chase had been on since then.

Lately the Jerries had gotten better at engaging Allied fighters and rather than meet the faster British planes head on, they'd adjusted their tactics. One group would come straight in at them while a second group would come in from another vector to try and cut them off. The Messerschmitt was a slower fighter one for one with the Spitfire but in a dive, nothing would be faster than four of them sweeping in from two different directions and diving down on them from an additional ten thousand feet.

He pulled his Spitfire into a hard banking turn. A volley of rounds fired from the Germans went wide and missed.

Sharp mentally crossed his fingers that they'd be out of their high-speed turn before the second two Germans could get into an extended firing range. He'd been a fool to not see the situation that he'd led Mackie into and kicked himself for it. He should have kept his eyes peeled for just such a trap.

From his cockpit he could look up and see the second pair of 109's coming down on them. They'd be within firing range in a matter of seconds. With the crossfire coming from the two groups, both he and Mackie would be cut to shreds. He'd have one shot to get them both out of this and that was it.

He closed his eyes and gave the order. "Mackie, go inverted and follow me down!"

"WHAT?!"

"Just do what I do dammit!" He screamed.

With his fighter already half rolled over, his right wing down and his belly exposed Sharp rolled completely over, his underbelly now facing straight upwards and he himself now hanging upside down in midair, be pulled his yoke back and sent his Spitfire hurling towards the ground. Mackie stumbled for a brief second but followed suit.

Their airspeed was picking up and their altitude was falling fast. They'd have less than a minute before hitting the ground.

"Break on my mark!" The ground was rushing up at them, the Germans were still closing on them and picking up speed. On top of that they were approaching from two different directions and Messerschmitt's had a greater firing range. "Hang on Mackie and follow my lead."

The forest was rushing up at them at almost a tenth of a mile per second. His altimeter was winding down fast. 17000.... 16000.... 15000.

His airspeed was now upwards of 360 mph and still increasing.

The second two German fighters now opened fire; a hail of rounds erupted around the two Spitfires as they dove downwards. A series of bullets hit the rear of his fuselage.

"When we break, we break right!" 9000.... 8000.... 7000.... 6000.... 5000. "BREAK BREAK BREAK!"

The two Spitfires broke right almost simultaneously and sped off at 400 mph at just about four thousand five hundred feet. The second pair of Messerschmitt's that had attempted to cut them off had missed their window and sped past their comrades who were now right on Sharp's tail.

"How you doing Mackie?"

"I'm with you, sir," the Canadian replied. "You've got some damage though, sir."

"I see it." Sharp turned his head back and could see the bullet holes in his plane. *Nothing I can do about it right now.*

A spray of additional machine gun fire lanced out from the pursuing 109's. He bopped and weaved in order to evade the gunfire. Despite having the speed advantage British planes lacked the firing range of their German counterparts. In a chase such as this one, that disadvantage was utterly deadly as the Allies were quickly finding out.

"We're going to need to split up, lad," he told Mackie. "We'll break and make a run for it. Try and get to Lwow if you can. If you can't......" His words were cut short by a stream of tracers raining downwards on him.

From the left the second pair of Messerschmitt's were once again descending on them, picking up speed as they descended, firing streams of ammo at the British planes. Sharp instinctively banked his fighter right while Mackie went left, a deadly mistake as it turned out. The right wing of Mackie's fighter lifted and went right into the line of enemy gunfire, a salvo of bullets punching through his wing like paper.

"DAMN!" The Canadian said over his radio. The younger man fought to control his flight and level back out. It was a move that he knew to be both useless and too late.

Sharp looked over his left shoulder and could see his squadron mate, white smoke now trailing behind him. He sighed heavily and spoke into his radio. "Mackie. What's your situation lad?" No answer. "Mackie?"

A strained voice came back. "No good, sir." A world of strain was in the other man's voice. "She's not responding. . . ."

Sharp could almost picture the other fighting hard to get control over his fighter. A scenario every pilot faced but none ever wanted to really think about.

"Hang on laddie. I'm on my way!"

"No need to, sir," Mackie replied, all the tension in his voice was gone. "I'm not going. . . ." The line went dead.

Mackie's Spitfire erupted in a single fireball that now streaked a half a mile above the earth as the enemy machine guns blew his aircraft apart.

Sharp watched in horror as what was left of his mate incinerated in midair. A long exhale later and he brought himself back to flying his own craft. He'd lost pilots and friends before today and he understood the risks that they'd all signed up for each time they lifted off. That didn't make the loss any easier but there was a code that they had chosen to live by, and death was a part of that code.

A few more shots rang out from the pursuers, they were ranging volleys, testing the distance between them and the retreating Spitfire. Each volley fell short. Even the second pair of Germans that had taken out Mackie, having picked up speed in their descent simply couldn't catch up to the faster Spitfire.

He kept the throttle full open, his engine drinking up his fuel as fast as it could. The pursuing Germans kept on him for another ten minutes or so but eventually gave up on it as the distance between him and them became too great.

He had no idea anymore just where he was. Small farms and the squared off pastures of the Polish countryside were all that his eye could see. He throttled his plane down and flew off northeast. If he couldn't get back to the airfield he'd taken off from earlier, perhaps he could spot a flat piece of land in which to land and make it back on foot.

It was nearly thirty minutes later, after no sign of any airfield, that he spotted a convoy of Polish troops off to the right and a couple miles out.

Out of a forest came a steady stream of them, infantry at first but then several trucks appeared out of the woods. He turned his craft sideways, showing off the red, white and blue circular roundel indicating the Royal Air Force, so as not to be mistaken for an incoming German.

He relaxed slightly as he watched the Poles point upwards at him as he flew overhead. As Sharp approached the trees more vehicles made their way out of the woods. Tanks, they were tanks. But not like any tanks that he'd ever seen before. Certainly not the light 7TP models of the Polish army that he'd seen before. These tanks were different, their armor plates were smoother, their turrets were bigger.

He brought his craft lower to the ground, hoping to identify the incoming troops and with luck make radio contact with them. His radio was of course set for Polish Army frequencies. He reached down to grab his radio set when he made a sudden realization. He was headed northeast, and these troops were moving due west. For a moment he couldn't understand, and he hesitated for a moment. If they were German, they certainly wouldn't be headed west, and he hadn't heard of any major Allied advances. He shrugged it off then clicked his radio set on.

Just as he did his aircraft was suddenly being pelted by ground fire coming from the advancing troops. Hundreds of small rifle rounds could be heard striking the underbelly of his plane. The plane sputtered and his cockpit lost electricity as his craft took repeated hits. More hits blew through the fuselage. His gauges went dead just as he passed over the line of trees.

The engine propellers shut off abruptly and the only two things he heard was the warning bell sounding and the wind whipping by him. His altitude was descending, and his speed was falling quickly. He was gliding on momentum only. Sharp pulled back on his yoke to keep the nose of his plane up, below him the treetops were now just meters from the bottom of his plane.

He'd had just enough momentum to clear the line of trees before dropping down hard to the ground. Fighting just to keep the nose of his aircraft up he didn't have time to crank the landing gear down manually. The craft hit the ground hard, the rear of his plane hit first then bounced off the ground before coming back down, the wings skidding along the terrain, the plane plowing along the ground despite the sudden loss of speed upon impact.

A powerful lurch sent Sharp forward, his cockpit controls rushing towards him, only to be yanked back by his safety harness. He instinctively brought his hands up to protect his face from the shattering glass. His head slammed hard against the rear of his cockpit. The plane finally skid to a halt after a few more seconds and the last thing that Sharp heard was the sound of unfamiliar voices growing louder. Then darkness took him.

CHAPTER TWELVE

Churchill puffed away on his cigar as he thumbed through the stack of papers before him, giving each a final signature in turn. The last one signed, he tapped the papers against his office desk and handed them over to the aide waiting for them. He took a generous sip of Scotch, knocked some ash from the burnt end of his cigar and fell back in his leather backed chair.

It had been only three weeks since he'd returned to government to help run what was called the Ministry for Coordination of Defence, which he'd taken to calling the Ministry of Defence. On the surface the ministry appeared to be a tiger with no teeth. It's mission, to coordinate the defense of the nation, fell mostly on the shoulders of the three branches of service, each with their own Cabinet Secretary answerable to the Prime Minister.

This would have made the position that he now filled rather redundant and was no better than a Cabinet member with no portfolio at all. However, he had changed all that upon taking the position. Winston had immediately taken to centralizing the authority of the Minister of Defence in coordinating the actions of all the branches of the services. In other words, no ship, nor aircraft, nor single British soldier would move a foot without his knowledge and tacit approval. This may have not been to the liking of other Cabinet Secretaries, preferring instead to work directly with the PM, but it was a necessary first step in forming a national military machine that fell under a single ministry.

Little by little that vast machinery that was the British military establishment came more and more under Churchill's direct control. The Prime Minister, at first anyway, made politely worded protestations, however when Winston, equally politely, explained that it would be impossible for him to "coordinate the defense" if he had no authority to do so, Chamberlain quietly accepted that logic and remained silent. So, when the first orders came out of his office and made their way down the chain to the cabinet secretaries, they begrudgingly fell in line.

The loudest voice of opposition came from the Secretary of War, a man named Leslie Hore-Belisha, who himself was widely unpopular with the commanders of the Army that he was the political head of. A close friend of the king and with political ties to the Liberal Party in Parliament, he had quietly, and at times not so quietly, attempted to bypass Churchill. Chamberlain seemed willing to allow this dissent between two members of his Cabinet so long as had the virtue of "reigning in Churchill". This too failed as Winston had been one step ahead.

The Liberal and Labour Parties had both approved of and even pushed for Winston's return to the government and with a few calls to some of his Conservative friends in Parliament he had ended Hore-Belisha's hopes of bypassing the Ministry of Defence. Chamberlain knew that his tenure as Prime Minister hung by a thread and had to maintain some sort of coalition between the parties. The message to Hore-Belisha was to shut his mouth and an even more subtle message to Chamberlain was "Churchill stays, or you go". Chamberlain had no choice.

So now Winston was going about doing the job that he had longed for: Preparing his country for war. As much as he'd liked to have resumed his previous post as First Lord of the Admiralty, he found his new position had a far more sweeping agenda and that as Minister of Defence he could do as much for his beloved Navy as he ever could.

It wasn't easy by any means to get the nation geared up for this war, but he knew that he could get it done. That it had to be done. Britain had gone from a state of disarmament in the late twenties and early thirties to a state of halfhearted rearmament after Austria was annexed by Germany and through the invasion of Czechoslovakia. While he and many others had been all too aware of the threat that Hitler and his Nazi thugs had posed to Europe the people in power, including the Prime Minister himself, held out for some illusion of peace.

The country now had to be roused from that illusion and he was determined to do it even if it meant doing it by himself.

He puffed on his cigar and looked up at his chief military aide Commander Charles "Tommy" Thompson, RN, a man he'd met at the Admiralty and quickly came to appreciate. Though he was technically still attached to the Admiralty, Winston had unofficially hijacked the young man to be a principal aide and advisor to him.

"What else do we have?" He asked, letting out a stream of smoke.

"I have the latest production numbers here, sir," he held up a folder. "You'll be able to look them through before your meeting with the Cabinet this afternoon. Also, I've put together the information that you'll need to present regarding naval conflict in the North Sea as well as combating the U-boat threat."

Churchill grumbled. "Should the subject of the war even come up." Some of the other aides smiled and laughed.

Commander Thompson grinned and continued. "I spoke with the Admiralty office again first thing this morning. Forces for Narvik and the Faroe Islands operation are ready to go. Still working out the details for Greenland and Iceland but hopefully we'll have something solid put together in a day or so. No German surface vessels have yet been sighted between Scotland and Iceland. Also, the Canadians reported two more U-boat sightings east of Newfoundland. That brings the total to five."

Churchill took it in. Canada would very soon become Britain's main supplier of grain and staple products and very shortly Canadian units would be crossing the Atlantic in masse. Even a few German submarines could spell potential disaster for Britain if they began sinking ships coming out of Halifax or the St. Lawrence.

"What about Malta and Gibraltar? Did you put through those orders I asked to send out?"

"Yes, sir. They were sent out last night."

Churchill nodded and took another puff of his cigar. "The Mediterranean will become vital to us particularly if Italy should decide to enter the conflict."

"I took care of everything, sir," Tommy replied. "That should cover all new developments, sir."

"Hmmm.... Well carry on then, Tommy." Churchill pushed himself up from his desk with some effort. "Oh, I want you to do something," he reached into his coat pocket and handed over two small, sealed envelopes. "Have this sent out to the Admiralty. It's for the First Sea Lord. Here's one for General Gort in France. Do make sure that they receive this directly."

Commander Thompson cocked an eyebrow as he took the two notes. He didn't open them; he didn't have to. He knew what they contained. It was improper that Churchill, despite being Minister of Defence and a senior Cabinet member, to directly contact the military commanders that served directly under the First Lord of the Admiralty and the Secretary of State for War respectively. Thompson tapped the sealed notes against his hand for a moment, bit his lip and looked at his boss.

Another puff of cigar smoke and a slight grin. "Personal correspondence I assure you," Winston said in a sly tone. "Oh, look at the time. I should be leaving for Ten Downing." He threw his coat on with an assist from another aide.

"Yes, sir. Your car is waiting for you. You'll be...." Thompson looked at his watch... "a few minutes late I fear."

Churchill shook his head. "I'll walk it. It's just around the corner. Besides...." He stepped closer and whispered, "I always like to keep the bugger waiting." He chuckled as he patted the other man on the shoulder.

It was a warm sunny day, and his walk was a mere two blocks to the Prime Minister's residence at 10 Downing Street. His bodyguard, a retired police detective named Walter Thompson or the 'other Tommy', followed behind him as he walked through Westminster London. Churchill puffed away on his cigar and thumbed through the papers that Commander Thompson had given to him.

He'd be late for the cabinet meeting and that was just fine with him. In truth he was finding it hard to keep on schedule for just about anything these days. Heading up and re-forming a government ministry was no easy task and his days began early and often ended late, late at night.

This country had relaxed far too much in the decade leading up to this conflict and it was taking all of his energy and ingenuity to get the nation on its war footing. Having a PM and half a cabinet that was still doing everything that they could to avoid a full-scale war was just making things that much harder.

To his surprise and disappointment, the cabinet meeting had not yet convened. Chamberlain's War Cabinet consisted of eight men not including the Prime Minister himself of course. Present was Leslie Hore-Belisha and Sir Kingsley Wood Secretaries of War and Air respectively, the First Lord of the Admiralty the Earl of Stanhope, Sir's Samuel Hoare and John Simon the Lord of the Privy Seal and Chancellor of the Exchequer and Lord Hankey, who currently held no portfolio and Winston himself, now the head of the newly renamed Ministry of Defence.

The Prime Minister and Foreign Secretary Halifax were notably absent from the room.

Churchill greeted other members of the Cabinet. Leslie Hore-Belisha, who had been speaking with the Secretary of State for Air and grinning, caught Winston's eye. The two men glared at each other across the room. Hore-Belisha's grin faded away and he turned his gaze away from Winston.

The door to an adjacent secretary's room opened and Chamberlain and Halifax emerged, along with two staffers. The Prime Minister greeted his Cabinet as he entered and motioned for all to sit. Churchill pulled out his chair to sit and realized Chamberlain was looking at him oddly. Chamberlain cleared his throat loudly then nodded to the cigar still in Churchill's grasp. He stamped the half-finished cigar out in an ashtray then took his seat.

The Prime Minister was looking gaunter than he had in recent days. His features were pale, his eyes slightly darker and he coughed frequently. Halifax sat to his immediate right, his finger rubbing along his lower lip.

"Gentlemen," Chamberlain began, "thank you all for coming. Before we proceed today with a full briefing for the prosecution of the war, I and the Foreign Secretary here wanted to discuss some recent developments. The Foreign Secretary has been in touch with our friends in Paris where both our governments are helping to establish the new Polish government now in exile in France along with several thousand Polish soldiers and airmen who fled after the fall of their country. Both the French and we are putting pressure on the Soviets to release thousands more soldiers that were taken prisoner when they moved into Eastern Poland."

A general sigh fell across the members of the war cabinet. The Soviet capture of the eastern part of Poland last week had come as a shock to the world. It was generally agreed upon that Moscow had signed some sort of secret agreement with Berlin when they signed their blasted non-aggression pact last year. The Germans had secured their eastern boundary with the Soviet Union with the blood of hundreds of thousands of Poles.

"Additionally, we've received intelligence from our embassies in the Baltic countries. It seems that the agreement between Moscow and Berlin extends into that corner of the continent as well. Lithuania, Latvia and Estonia will fall into a Soviet sphere, if not outright occupation itself. At any rate it's a development that could indicate an alliance between Germany and the Soviet Union." Chamberlain shook his head gravely. "Such a situation would certainly present a dire situation should the two combine their forces. It's no secret that Stalin has no love for the West."

"It would be hard to believe that those two countries could cooperate in such a way," the Earl of Stanhope stated. "The Soviets and the Nazis are ideologically opposed."

"We must assume that position has changed," Lord Halifax replied. "If not an outright alliance than certainly that non-aggression pact between them guarantees vast territorial concessions to the Russians. Either way the situation presents a problem. We already know that Stalin has designs on Finland and would like nothing more than total control of his corner of the Baltic Sea."

Chamberlain continued. "At any rate, we'll continue to keep our eye on that situation and make plans to intervene if we absolutely must. Now. . . . on to business. What is the status of our expeditionary force in France? Winston."

Clearing his throat and adjusting his eyeglasses, Winston leaned forward in his chair. "General Gort currently has somewhere in the area of one hundred and fifty thousand men with him in northern France. We're expecting to ship two additional divisions across the Channel in next few days. Fortifications are being built around the Channel ports and entrenchments along the Franco-Belgian border. Our army will operate on the left flank of the French First Army under Plan D. Although, as you know Prime Minister, I am skeptical of this plan. It assumes too much on a German attack coming straight in from the east. I am dubious of that fact, and I've had plans drawn up. . . ."

"Excuse me, sir," Secretary of War Hore-Belisha interrupted, his fat face craned awkwardly to look at Churchill. "But any attack from Germany would obviously come straight from the east. Our military planners have expected that since the last war and have been planning for it. I myself have been making detailed observations and plans for our defensive lines. I've submitted these plans and I'll soon be making inspections of our lines in France myself."

Hore-Belisha's combative and often contradictory stance with the Imperial General Staff was well known as was the generals professional dislike of the man.

"As I was beginning," Churchill continued, "I've had plans drawn up for a foray into Belgium that would meet any German attack through that country head on. Belgium offers us better opportunity for defense than the French coast."

Chamberlain and Halifax eyed each other briefly then looked back at Winston with patronizing looks.

"Your plans for moving forces into Belgium has been looked at Winston and rejected," Chamberlain told him. "We're not looking to act expansionary or provokingly while a diplomatic solution is still being discussed. We'll continue with our current plan. If the situation calls for changes, we can examine them then. What of the Air Force?" His gaze shifted to Sir Kingsley Wood.

Churchill sank back into his chair and inwardly cursed.

"We currently have seven RAF fighter squadrons operating in France," Sir Kingsley reported. "With plans for four additional squadrons to be posted there in coming weeks. On the home front we're continuing to train additional pilots for both fighter and bomber squadrons. We've had a recent arrival of trained pilots from New Zealand and Canada that should help us fill the ranks but we're still falling short of flight personnel. We lost some very good pilots in Poland and those losses will be felt unfortunately."

"And our bombing campaign?" Chamberlain asked.

The so-called bombing campaign over Germany consisted of dozens of British bombers dropping bomb shells filled with thousands of paper leaflets. The shells were designed to break apart at high altitudes over Germany and rain their leaflets across the landscape. The "leaflet campaign" as some called it, called upon German citizens to not fight and instead seek a negotiated peace agreement. It was another in a long list of futile gestures to avoid a war which was already going on and Winston had once again made his protestations of it known.

"It continues, Prime Minister. We're waiting on more leaflets to be printed up. Seems we've dropped all that we previously had stockpiled."

Churchill sneered inwardly and mentally rolled his eyes. They should have been dropping bombs on those cities and not drowning the Germans in a sea of paper.

Chamberlain nodded his approval, as if such approval somehow brought them closer to victory over Nazi Germany. "Very well. As for the Royal Navy?"

James Stanhope, 7th Earl of Stanhope and First Lord of the Admiralty was the political head of the Royal Navy. It had been Winston's old job in the last war, and he'd been offered it at the outbreak of this new war but had instead refused only to be offered his current position as the head of a coordinated defense of the country. He'd never liked Stanhope, too much of an appeaser and had done little to nothing to modernize the navy in the time between wars. Churchill did not fail to notice that Sir Dudley Pound, the military head of the fleet itself was absent from the cabinet meeting as was anyone from the Imperial Staff itself. A War Cabinet meeting without a single member of the branches of service....

"The fleet is well equipped and provisioned, sir," Stanhope said proudly. "We've engaged several German surface ships and U-boats at sea already. Our blockade of German trade lines is intact. There've been some losses but nothing that will greatly impact us. In fact, I spoke with

Admiral Pound just this morning. Our destroyer's depth charged a U-boat just off the Irish coast and possibly a second one southwest of the Brittany coast over the past couple of days.

"As for our shipyards themselves, we're continuing to bring in all available workers and training them as fast as we can. I feel confidant, as do the admirals of the fleet of course, that we will be in a very strong position to dominate at sea. The Navy's chief concern, however, are these coding machines the Germans are working with, Enigma. As we're all well aware we've had just a devil of a time getting any kind of handle on deciphering those codes. Our crypto analysts have been working themselves mad trying to crack them and I think it could pose a problem for us."

"I thought we'd had that reasonably under control?" Chamberlain asked. "I was under the impression some Polish code breakers had solved that problem. We were able to read some of their military signals before. What happened?"

"Yes, sir, that is true. We were getting a partial read from German Army signals. Their Navy ships, however, they're a bit different. Seem to operate on a slightly different system than the Army does. Apparently, their entire encoding system undergoes a complete set of changes that requires each of their users to change over every so often. So far we haven't been able to pinpoint when those changes happen."

"So, every so often their entire code system undergoes a significant change? Is that what you're saying, James?" Lord Halifax asked.

Lord Stanhope nodded. "Yes. But it's more than that. From what I understand, and I don't pretend to be an expert, the entire set of codes doesn't just change over time, but each machine itself is set to very specific settings so that no two machines can code or decode the same. A message that comes through on one machine could very well be meaningless on another."

"Brilliant buggers," Churchill muttered, wishing he had a cigar.

The PM folded his hands together and gave the matter some thought. "Well, we do have some very good people working on that. Those people over at MI6 seemed to have some success last month. Also, those chaps at Bletchley. Sooner or later, I have to believe they'll have come up with something. Whatever resources are needed we'll make sure they are made available."

"Thank you, Prime Minister," Stanhope replied with a smile.

"Mister Prime Minister, I have a few additional issues," Churchill began, and Chamberlain gestured for him to continue. "This may come as no surprise, but I am not as confidant as others that our defenses have been seen to as best as they could. As of this morning I am told that preparations for the Faroe Islands and Norway operations are ready to go. The landings in Norway should occur sometime before dawn tomorrow. However, I'm of the mind that we should take this opportunity to mine Norwegian waters, around Narvik bay as well as farther south around Bergen, Stavanger and the Danish Straits."

Halifax gave a disapproving look. "Without the Norwegian government's approval or permission? And wouldn't an operation like that bring the fleet perilously close to German airfields?"

"We're at war, my Lord," Churchill answered sternly. "The Norwegian government didn't give the Germans approval to invade their country. And as for the fleet, going into peril is what they do and every sailor of them knows it. I.... I think we can accomplish this within a week. Mining those waters could cost the Germans dearly or, likewise, it would cost us even more dearly if we didn't."

Halifax raised his eyebrows and looked to Chamberlain and nodded, who in turn looked at Winston and nodded an approval.

"Thank you, Prime Minister. Now, I do have several other things that I'd like to discuss." He opened the folder he'd brought with him and began.

CHAPTER FOURTEEN

Mr. Edward Bagshaw gazed around at the crowd that crammed the landing of the Dover Priory railway station. The entire train station was as busy as he'd ever seen it, or at least as busy as he'd seen it in many years. A passenger train was sitting idle at the station preparing to depart with a trainload of young men headed off to the war. Everywhere there were young men dressed in uniform, some wore the dark blue outfits of the Royal Navy, the name of their ship emboldened across their caps, others wore the sky-blue uniforms of the Royal Air Force, but most of the young lads wore the brown trousers, tunics and side caps of the British Army. Pinned to their caps were the distinct badge of whichever regiment the soldier belonged to.

Wives and mothers wept as they saw their sweethearts and sons off, a young child, pinned to his mother's side waved to a young soldier hanging out of the train window, another soldier crouched down petting his beloved dog's head, a one-armed middle-aged man with an eye patch wrapped his one remaining arm around his son. All were seeing the boys off.

Mr. Bagshaw noticed a mustached sergeant pacing back and forth along the landing, his hands clasped behind his back, his features stern and his back ramrod straight. Inwardly Mr. Bagshaw smiled as he recalled a very similar looking man in a sergeant's uniform not that different from this one who paced a similar train station all those years ago, seeing another group of young men off to their own war against the same enemy they were facing once again. But that had been so long ago.

He was now a man in his middle fifties with thinning hair and an expanding waistline. He had dressed in his favorite green trousers, a cream-colored button-down shirt, blue sweater vest, brown tie and of course the brown fedora that he never left the house without, rain or shine. Mr. Bagshaw had always felt that no proper Englishman should leave his home without their fedora.

They'd arrived at the station early that morning, he and Mary, to see their oldest boy off. As they pulled their car into the lot, he recalled an intense feeling of both nostalgia and terror. The terror was for Thomas, his boy, knowing full well of the things that awaited him in France. The nostalgia was for himself and the memory of his own father bringing him to the train depot years earlier, in the Spring of '15, when he and his own mates went off to fight in those damn trenches of the Western Front. He was quite sure it had been the same for his own father who had himself left his home shores of England to go off to South Africa for his own war. A family tradition it seemed.

His son Thomas stood there on the platform, a foolish, boyish grin on his clean-shaven face. He was all of seventeen, tall, slim and handsome. Thomas had joined up straight out of secondary school, even before war had been declared on Germany. He'd been a good student and he and his mother would have liked for him to go to university for future studies, but the army recruiter had gotten in his head. It seemed that the allure of the uniform and adventure was something that lived inside every young man.

"Lots of lads here," Edward said. "Lots of lads."

They're all so young, he thought.

"Are they all with the West Kent?" his wife Mary asked.

"Not all of them, Mum," Tommy answered. "Those right there are with the Buffs. The ones with the Dragon badges. The ones with the Saint George Cross are the Royal Sussex."

Mary shook her head. "Dragons, Stags, Horses.... how do you keep them all straight?"

"We memorize them from boyhood, my dear," Edward told her. "A childhood spent collecting toy soldiers does that to you."

There did seem to be soldiers from all different regiments from all over Southeast England. Each regiment of the British Army had a long and distinguished lineage and tradition. Assignment to any one of them was an honor no matter which regiment you served with. Although some of them, such as the Coldstream or Grenadier Guards, came with a great deal of prestige, very few units of the British Army had failed to distinguish itself in some way, particularly in the last war.

One of those regiments was the Queen's Own Royal West Kent, the 1st battalion of which had been called upon to fight in France once again. The trains were daily carrying men from all over southeast England to the harbor in Folkestone from where the troop transports were carrying men and supplies across the English Channel to Calais in France, where the British Expeditionary Force had been assembled.

Mary put her hand softly on Tommy's shoulder. "Are they going to feed you on the way over?"

Thomas gave her mother a wry look. "Mum. . . . Jesus. I'll be in France by noon."

His mother sobbed then put her head on his shoulder. "I know. . . . I just...worry."

"Dear," Edward began. He knew she was going to be a mess; his own mother had been as well. "There's a whole army over there, dear. There's plenty of food. He won't want for food." *At least not for a while anyhow, but when the fighting begins. . . .*

"I'll be fine, Mum," Tommy told her reassuringly. "Bobby and the boys shipped across the Channel this morning. They're probably over there waiting for me right now. You know how we all are when we get together. Best mates. Safest I've ever been in my life is with them." He smiled at her, that boyish grin that he had.

Edward put his hands on his wife's arms and rubbed her gently. "There's nothing to worry about, dear," he lied.

Mary wiped her tears away and looked at Edward. "That's what you said when you were over there, dear. I remember. I remember the newspapers."

Edward nodded back. "And I came home, didn't I? The whole bloody British Army is over there right now. Must be half a million of them by now. And the Froggies.... well they've got an even larger army. Besides, I think Hitler got what he wanted in Poland."

"Five minutes!" The train conductor's loud voice boomed. He held up five fingers in the air for all to see. "Five minutes!"

Thomas looked at the conductor, then back at his parents. Other servicemen were saying their last goodbyes to their loved ones now and beginning to board the train.

"Well...I guess...." He faked his way through a smile. He was always smiling.

"Photograph folks?" A man asked. He was short and wore a camera around his neck. "Photograph of the family?" He asked holding up his camera. "Only a shilling."

Edward nodded and the three gathered together, Tommy in the middle, his father's arm around him. The bright light bulb flashed, and the signature snap of the camera went off. The photographer smiled and nodded. He reached into his breast pocket and produced a card.

"Call on me by Sunday, I should have it developed. My name's Gibbons." He handed Edward the card. "You can settle with me then."

"Thank you," Edward told him. "Our name is Bagshaw. Five fifty-two Flemish Road."

The photographer wrote the information down then went about his business.

Edward looked at Thomas. "Well, you'd better be getting aboard lad." Mary held in a sob then stepped away to wipe away her tears. "I want you to have something, son." From his pocket he produced his pocket watch and chain and put it in his son's hand.

"Your watch? Father I can't. It belonged to your father."

"And his father before him. Brought it back from India. It's yours now." He closed Thomas's hand around the watch and fought to stifle a tear. "Carry it with you, lad."

Thomas nodded and sighed, a single tear streaming down his cheek, then another. "Dad...."

Edward didn't wait to embrace his son, his boy. He wrapped his arms around the seventeen-year-old and patted him hard on the back. He whispered in Thomas's ear, "Mind yourself, son. Stay safe when the shooting begins."

"Dad, we'll be laying barbed wire and digging trenches. That's about all they're doing over there. Not even a shot fired."

Edward let go of Thomas and stepped back slightly, looked at him in the eye and nodded. "That's how it began for us too." He wiped a tear from the tip of his nose. "Just stay close to your sergeants and do what they tell you. The NCOs are the backbone of the Army. Always have been. They'll know what to do."

"All aboard!" The train conductor bellowed.

Thomas and Edward hugged again, then Mary hugged Thomas for an extremely long moment, not wanting to let go. He kissed his mother goodbye, put the pocket watch in his pocket and nodded. He picked up his bag and stepped up onto the train and disappeared into the passenger car. A moment later the train let out a whistle and began rolling forward. Dozens of soldiers hung out of the train windows, waving their final goodbyes to the sea of loved ones left on the platform.

Edward and Mary stood and watched as car after car of the long train passed by until it had left the station and the boys were off to war.

Field Marshall John Standish Surtees Prendergast Vereker, 6th Viscount Gort could hear the whine of fighter engines as a flight of Hawker Hurricanes flew over his headquarters building in the coastal town of Boulogne-sur-Mer in Pas-de-Calais. He sipped on his cup of tea and watched with a lackluster interest as the man standing in front of the large wall mounted map of the French-Belgian-German border was busy giving all the wrong information regarding the defenses that the British Army had erected along its front line.

The chubby-faced Secretary of State for War, Hore-Belisha was busy pointing at the long series of defenses and the positions of the troops indicated on the map. At times he seemed to just ramble on incoherently, incorrectly stating things that simply were not true and placing the blame for the "complete unacceptability for the defense of northern France" squarely in the laps of the British General Staff and Lord Gort.

At times the passionate Secretary of War seemed to suggest that the only people interested in the defense of France were the French and taking several, not so subtle, punches at the generals of the expeditionary force. He even complimented defenses that he assumed had been built by the French but had been erected by British engineers while at the same time harshly criticizing the placement of the British positions.

Lord Gort and his staff remained politely quiet during the tirade but under the surface the Commanding General was seething mad. He and the Imperial General Staff in London had bumped heads with Secretary Hore-Belisha in the past but in recent weeks it had only gotten worse. His constant interference in day-to-day army matters and his derision for the top commanders was becoming well known among the troops and causing a serious lack of confidence in the officer corps.

"My Lord, did you hear what I said?" Hore-Belisha asked in a low tone.

"I did, sir. Every word."

Hore-Belisha smiled and nodded. "Excellent then. So, I expect that these changes to go into effect immediately." Looking back at the map he pointed at the indicated German Army positions. "I don't expect the Jerries to make much of a move now that they have Poland, but you never know. The French have done a stupendous job with their fortifications, and I would like to see our own brought up to standard."

"Mister Secretary, the defenses in which you praise the French Army for, were in fact built by our own troops, sir. British troops. British engineers designed them, and British backs labored to build them." Lord Gort had attempted as best he could to keep the contempt out of his tone, but he was quite sure he had failed.

Wrinkles creased Hore-Belisha's head for a moment in confusion then shook his head as if what the Commanding General had just said was of no matter. The man had clearly failed to read any of the reports that had been filed with the War Ministry nor, it seemed, did he know how to read a map.

"I've spoken with General Gamelin, sir," the Secretary began. "He has assured me that the defenses of which I speak, can be built much, much faster than we have been building them. Did you know, General Gort, that the French are building pillboxes in three days flat? Hmmm? Why is it that we are taking so much longer?"

Gort's Chief of Staff, General Pownall cleared his throat and spoke up. "I believe you may have misunderstood, General Gamelin, sir. He is French after all and perhaps he used the wrong words. Furthermore, the French have had a number of years to develop their defensive lines. I can quite assure you, Mister Secretary, that it takes a bit longer than three days to build our pillboxes."

Hore-Belisha bit his lower lip and nodded his head gravely. A slightly flushed look came over the man's chubby face and he was awkwardly silent. General Gort could not tell whether he was silent out of embarrassment or if he was contemplating an apologetic word. Previous experience with Britain's Secretary of State for War would suggest that no apology was forthcoming.

"General Gort," Hore-Belisha began in a tone that was both stern but not appearing to be condescending in any way, "the defense of our French allies is absolutely paramount, and I do not take lightly, or kindly, at having my observations at our apparent lack of defense mocked or challenged. I believe that General Gamelin was quite clear when we spoke, and I wish to be quite clear now. Gentlemen, upon my arrival back in England this afternoon I will be assembling quite a list of deficiencies that I see we have here and making serious recommendations for their improvement."

He visibly puffed himself up and clasped his hands behind his back. "The King himself knows that I'm in France today. I am quite sure, gentlemen, that he will personally wish to speak with me at some point regarding our expedition here and I will be very forthcoming with him."

General Lord Gort, Commanding General of the British Expeditionary Force, put down the cup of tea he'd been sipping on, straightened his back with all the discipline that forty-five years in the British Army could muster and nodded an understanding. He understood alright. He understood, as did the rest of his staff and for that matter all the generals back in London, that Hore-Belisha had absolutely no idea about how to run a military. His friendship with the King was well known with the General Staff and the loud and pompous Hore-Belisha would often use this in order to persuade the officers to do things his way. Disregarding the fact that his policies had often been proved wrong.

"Sir, the plans for our defensive lines have been put forth and submitted to the War Office," Gort stated. "My staff and I shall certainly do everything that we can to meet with the changes that you desire. I would and I believe all of us would benefit from your written instructions. If you wish to make substantial changes to our defensive plans, I understand your position. As soon as orders come down through the chain of command, you have my assurances, Mister Secretary, that we will do our best to meet them." He grinned slightly as he spoke the last few words, trying to put a sympathetic twist in his words.

Apparently satisfied with Lord Gort's response, Hore-Belisha smiled and nodded his approval to the general.

"Good. Good. Rest assured I will be putting those changes on paper just as soon as I get back to London, gentlemen. Now," be looked down at his watch. "I was hoping to have a lunch with the boys before my return flight. I like rubbing elbows with the men in the ranks."

Gort smiled. "Of course, sir. Lieutenant Crisley I'm sure will be delighted to escort you to the enlisted mess."

"Will you be joining me today, General?" Hore-Belisha asked politely.

"I'm afraid I cannot, sir. General Pownall and I have a lot of work to do before the French arrive later today.

"Ah. I understand." Hore-Belisha donned his wide brimmed hat. "In that case gentlemen, I shall leave you. I look forward to seeing you again soon, General."

Lord Gort snapped his heels together and extended a hand to the man, Hore-Belisha shook it. General Pownall opened the door for him, and both watched as he left, a sergeant in the hallway escorting him off. General Pownall closed the door behind him and turned back towards Lord Gort and let out a long sigh.

"I don't really appreciate the way that man talks to you, sir," Pownall told him, unprompted. He had acted the good soldier, both had, and bit their tongues when all they wanted to do was give the dandy politician a damn good thrashing. "Doesn't even bother to address you as My Lord."

Gort waved it away. "What did you expect from old Horeb?" An unflattering reference to Hore-Belisha's Jewish heritage. "Throw's that 'friends with the King' thing around quite a bit, doesn't he?" He pulled out a pack of cigarettes from his pocket, offered one to his Chief of Staff.

General Pownall lit them both up. "From what I'm hearing even the King doesn't have much to do with him these days. Not cut out to be Secretary of State for War if you ask me."

Lord Gort blew out a stream of smoke and nodded slightly. "Doesn't matter. Winston's back. For all intents and purposes, Churchill's now in charge at the War Ministry. So. . . . what else do we have? The French are probably on their way now. For a Frenchman, General Blanchard does seem to arrive to scheduled events rather on time."

"Not too much, sir. Disregarding engineering advice on our defensive works from the old Jew, we're right on schedule with everything. Couple of things, however." He produced a small note from his breast pocket and unfolded it. "A Nazi U-boat torpedoed one of our transports crossing the Channel early this morning out of Portsmouth. Only a few casualties from the crew, but the transport was carrying some of our newer model Matilda and Mark Three tanks. It'll take us some time before we receive replacements for them. They were scheduled to be used to train the Polish troops we recently adopted."

"Can't the French train them on their tanks?" Gort asked.

Pownall cocked an eyebrow. "On the Renault, sir? Iron deathtrap. Besides the French don't have enough of them for the Poles to train on. No, we were expecting to train them on our equipment. Also, a shipment of wireless radios that we got last night turned out to be defective. Not sure yet what the problem is, but until we get replacements for those also, we'll be relying on hard lines for our forward communication."

"Splendid." Gort replied sarcastically. "Any other good news?"

"We'll have an additional division ashore by this time tomorrow. The 132nd Infantry Brigade should be in port this evening. Another RAF squadron should be posted here by week's end. That's the good news. Oh, also, your personal case of Johnnie Walker did arrive, you'll be happy to know. I thought it would make your dinner with General Blanchard go a little smoother."

Lord Gort chuckled slightly then took another drag of his cigarette. "Good. If that's all Henry, I'd like to take care of some things before General Blanchard arrives."

"Of course, sir," General Pownall said then graciously left the room.

General Lord Gort sat down behind his desk, took the last drag of his cigarette then put it out. Picking up the phone he double clicked for the switchboard. "Get me the War Office. I want to speak with Churchill."

CHAPTER FOURTEEN

There was something about the sound of boot heels on a hard tile surface in a hallway that further echoed the sound that Rommel always liked. It was a very professional sound. The pure white halls of the OKH (Army Command) were wide with little in the way of furniture or decoration and only reinforced the crisp clap of all the heels from all the men and women who worked in the offices off the main hallway.

The General came to the office that he was headed for, quickly ran his fingers through his hair then opened the door and walked in. The men inside the office quickly stood to attention as he entered the room. Rommel looked at each one, good looking men all, physically fit, hair trim, uniforms pressed, shoes properly shined and hands well-manicured. The look of three young men who'd never seen a day in the field.

The young sergeant sitting behind the desk facing the doorway jumped up to a rigid attention, his eyes focused hard straight ahead.

General Erwin Rommel stared at the young man, perhaps twenty-two or three and held his gaze on the man for a few long, awkward seconds that he made stretch on with his silence. Finally, he put his cap down on the desk.

"At ease," Rommel finally said and the men visibly relaxed. "General Rommel for General Halder."

"The General is waiting for you, sir," the sergeant replied and indicated to the doorway to his right.

Rommel walked into the private office of General Franz Halder, Chief of the General Staff. Halder sat behind his immense desk. Even among other officers of the German Army, Halder stood out. His signature flat-top haircut, dimpled chin and round eyeglasses made him easily recognizable.

He looked up from his work and urged Rommel forward. "Come in Erwin, come in. Just finishing up some business."

Rommel quietly closed the door behind him and made his way across the office. Halder indicated the chair across from him and Rommel dropped into it.

"May I offer you something to drink?" Halder asked, not taking his eyes off his paperwork. "Coffee? Tea?"

"No. Thank you," Rommel replied.

Finally, Halder put the last notes on a paper, put his pen down and leaned back in his chair. From his top desk drawer, he produced a pack of cigarettes, lit one up and looked at Rommel.

"So, you're back from Poland. How was it?"

Rommel grunted. Halder had never been in combat, a staff officer by training. "Bloody. Brutal. I will say this, from what I saw blitzkrieg worked better than anyone thought. Certainly better than the Poles could have planned for. Of course the only view I got was well after the fighting was already over."

He had just returned from Poland after escorting Hitler around the battlefields, touring the destruction that the German blitzkrieg has wrought. It had been a slaughter. In only three weeks' time the Polish army of one million men, had been absolutely decimated. The highly maneuverable and modern Germany Army had rolled right through their country with lightning speed that surprised everyone, including the Germans.

Halder grinned. "Yes, the Poles didn't put up much of a fight did they? They didn't see it coming. Their heads were still stuck in the last war. You remember those trenches, don't you?"

Rommel didn't answer. He had been in those trenches on the Western Front. Fought in Italy as well. He'd been in both the infantry and artillery in that war and had excelled at both. He'd seen more than his fair share of killing and death back then. After that war he'd been rotated through a series of assignments instructing young infantry officers, even helping to train Hitler Youth units, before finally being assigned to the Führer Battalion, Hitler's private front line bodyguard unit.

"The French won't be as easy as the Poles were," Rommel told him straightly.

Halder blew out a stream of smoke. "What makes you think we'll fight the French? Thinking is that they'll sue for peace soon."

Rommel gave Halder an intense stare but did not answer, not wanting to give the other man the satisfaction of insulting his intelligence. Finally, Halder relented. "Perhaps they won't be as easy." He took another drag from his cigarette, let it out. "The Frogs have already settled into a defensive posture. That Maginot Line of theirs is their national redoubt. Their great fortress. They marched into the Saarland a couple weeks ago, burned a few houses down then withdrew. That's been the extent of their operations against us."

"It's still early," Rommel countered. "Everyone likes to mock the French as being soft and weak. I've seen otherwise. I know they can be strong when they need to be."

Halder waved a dismissive hand. "Did you forget your history, Rommel? The War of 1870? Gave the French a good kick between the legs back then. When have the French ever done the same to us, hmmm?"

"Napoleon Bonaparte. I seem to remember reading about him in the history books as well. He turned a second-rate army into a monster. They dominated the whole continent."

"And failed."

Rommel raised his eyebrows and nodded. "Which will only make my point for me. He failed because he was too arrogant. Kept making war on everyone. It didn't help him either that he never subdued the British. The Royal Navy strangled off Napoleon's overseas trade. His failure to knock them out of that war was his undoing."

Halder sighed. "Don't be so cynical, Rommel. That was a different time. Even now Britain's Prime Minister reaches out to us to try and negotiate a peace. The British aren't interested in another war, it would put their great empire at risk. If you haven't heard they are having their own problems in India."

"You say that Franz, but they continue to fight. Chamberlain might be weak but do not underestimate the British people. I hear that man Churchill is back and if he has his way there would be no peace on our terms."

"If Chamberlain can get a treaty and keep the peace and their independence, it is believed he will agree to it. The main thing is to keep the French and British armies from combining their strength. Herr Ribbentrop seems to believe it can happen."

Rommel threw up his hands. "All I am saying is not to underestimate the British."

"Noted. Now, why don't you tell me why it is you are really here. Because it is not to discuss nineteenth century warfare."

"No. It's to discuss future warfare," Rommel replied. "One way or another, whether with British assistance or without it our troops will clash with French troops. I must believe that plans have been drawn up for an assault on France. We've just crushed the Poles and Danes. Our eastern flank with the Russians is now secured. The only logical next step would be to turn on our old adversary."

Halder considered himself before replying. Rommel had been a rising star for years now, seen as one of the most experienced and expert officers in Germany. He had a tactical genius that many older officers lacked, even secretly envied and Rommel's grasp of the greater strategic situation was just as good.

"It wouldn't exactly be a national secret to say that we have a plan for France," Halder told him, trying to dodge. "We have rooms and rooms of plans. Right now, we are in the process of reorganizing following our victories in Poland and Denmark. There's still fighting in Norway. Until that is over with, our plans for the immediate future are uncertain. Since the French do not seem to be in a hurry to fight, the Führer also does not see a reason to hurry."

"But it will come, Franz, and we both know it. Hitler hates France. Hates them with a passion. I've studied them, studied their defenses, their geography, their generals and I understand them. I also know of our great advantage over them. Blitzkrieg. We've shown that it can work, proved it in Denmark and in Poland. France would be the ultimate test of the doctrine."

"How so?"

"The French desire to restrict their movements. To act defensively. Their entire strategy consists of holding key areas and forcing us to try and take them at great cost to us. They're generals are old and still think in terms of the Great War. Lines of trenches and defensive works holding back our forces. Thousands of troops sitting in static positions hoping for us to attack them on their ground and on their terms." His fist was now pounding lightly on the arm of the chair he was sitting in. "Blitzkrieg changes all of that. France would be perfect for that form of warfare."

"You know, Erwin," Halder's tone had changed to a slightly friendly one, "Your talents and your ability to get into another's mind is well known. You've obviously got the Führer's ear and his confidence. It is true we've studied their defenses as well and we agree that the French are most likely to remain fortified behind their own lines. To, as you say, make us pay a heavy price for digging them out of entrenched positions."

Rommel nodded back at him. "Mobility is going to be the key. The army is going to have to achieve an encirclement of the French in a relatively short period of time."

Halder said nothing, just sat back in his chair and listened with suspicious curiosity.

Rommel continued. "A breakthrough between the British and French lines will have to be achieved, followed by a sweeping drive to the coast." Rommel spoke almost as if he were reciting a verse from a well memorized book. "That's a lot of movement over a lot of territory. The panzer divisions in the lead will have to move fast and hard to secure vital bridges and keep ahead of the French and British forces."

"That's a very nice plan, Erwin," Halder said. He carefully considered his next words. Planning for the attack on France had long been in the works but it was kept far from the ears of divisional and corps commanders. Only the top military leadership and planners in Germany knew of the operational plan. "And how did you arrive. . . ."

"I can read a map, Franz," Rommel cut in. "I haven't gotten any information from anyone if that's what you're thinking. I'm in command of the Führer Battalion. That gives me a lot of free time. The Schlieffen Plan was a good plan but had some serious flaws in it. Men on foot can only move so far in a day. We've solved many of those flaws in recent years. Blitzkrieg is proof of that."

The Schlieffen Plan, as it had been called after the Great War of 1914 to 1918, had been the primary military strategy employed by the Kaiser's Germany. It had called for a giant 'swinging door' strategy of attack into France, cutting through Belgium which had been neutral at the start of the conflict. The plan had worked initially but had become quickly bogged down in the mud. The slow-moving infantry had failed to gain the advantage it needed and despite coming within just miles of Paris, the German army had instead settled into four years of arduous trench warfare with the French and British.

Interestingly enough, the few major advances on either side of that war, had come from the use of early armored vehicles and tanks. The Cambrai Offensive of 1917 had shown just how effective tanks could be in coordination with infantry attacks. A lesson that the Allies had seemingly forgotten it seemed.

Halder finished his cigarette and cleared his throat. "The French defenses are much more formidable than the Polish were. They've had twenty years to build them. However. . . ." He let the words trail off.

"However, the French strategy is based on a static defense. You and I both know that. What's going to be required are fast moving units and commanders who can drive them."

"So... you're asking me for...?"

"You know what I am asking for, Franz," Rommel replied, his voice indicating he was tired of this game. "The same thing I have been asking for months now."

"A combat command."

"A panzer command!."

Halder sighed. "The Führer is very fond of you, Erwin. He and I spoke briefly about you before he went to Vienna to meet with that dago bastard. He told me that you've been pressing him for a panzer division. I advised against it, I won't lie." He lit up another cigarette.

That didn't surprise Rommel. He'd been maneuvering for a panzer command for a while, fending away offers to command mountain troops or an infantry division. He'd studied the panzers, memorized every detail about them for years now, followed the development of the blitzkrieg doctrine since its inception. After seeing what they were capable of in Poland, he was desperate for the command of one.

"But it seems my objections have fallen short," Halder continued. "Seems several other generals have also been pushing for you to get your own command." Another drag, another smoke stream. He hesitated to continue for a few moments, but finally said, "The Thirteenth Motorized is being reorganized into a panzer division. General Rothkirch is being reassigned to Manstein's staff."

"The Thirteenth?" Rommel mulled then nodded his head slightly. "Veterans of Poland. Proven men."

"I'll assign it to you effective for the end of July. Should give you more than enough time to finish with your current duties and for us to assemble the tanks necessary to outfit the division."

"Panzer Threes?"

Halder nodded. "And some fours. Speer's done wonders with manufacturing numbers since he took over for war production. You'll have a full panzer regiment as well as some of our newer mechanized vehicles as well." He took another drag on his cigarette then crushed out the last of it in the ashtray. "Will this make you happy, Rommel?"

Rommel remained motionless in his chair, not giving any indication one way or another, not wanting to give Halder more string to toy him with. Halder was a career staffer, never fired so much as a shot in battle. His reputation as an efficient organizer was well known, but so was his twisted wit.

"The end of July is more than enough time," Rommel finally said, not a hint of emotion in his voice. "I thank you for your time today, General."

Halder stood up from behind his desk and extended a professional hand. "Congratulations to you, General Rommel."

Rommel, taken slightly aback by the courtesy, stood up and shook the other man's hand.

The courtesies exchanged, Rommel turned to exit the office and started towards the door.

"Oh, Rommel. One more thing." Rommel turned back to Halder. "If I were you, I'd keep my mouth shut when the subject of future battle plans comes up in casual conversation. Just a word of advice. You may have the Führer's favor right now, but the Gestapo has little sense of humor when it comes to the security of the Reich. We've both seen what happens to people in the late hours of the night."

Having gotten what he'd come for, he nodded slightly to Halder in acknowledgment and thanks, then closed the door behind him as he exited the office. Picking up his cap off the sergeant's desk he strode back down the wide, white hallway he'd come through before, a small grin gracing his features as he walked away.

CHAPTER SIXTEEN

From the conning tower Lieutenant Commander Alistair Chadwick glimpsed through his binoculars at the far-off burning ship that was slowly sinking beneath the waves. The cloud cover was thick, and the rain was coming down hard, despite a calm ocean surface. It was just after noon and they hadn't seen the sun at all that day, only the rain and the burning torch that had been a British merchant ship until just a little while ago.

The distress signal from the merchant vessel *Brother Lucas* had been picked up less than an hour earlier while *Orkney* had just secured from a battle drill. The aging *Odin*-class submarine had been on patrol out of Freetown on the west coast of Africa going on three months now, before hostilities in Europe had even begun. Originally scheduled to return to port a month ago *Orkney* had been ordered by the Admiralty to remain at sea and to patrol the vital sea lanes that British and French convoys were passing through.

With the majority of the Royal Navy and French Fleet operating in the North and Mediterranean Seas, few warships were left to secure the important sea lanes that both countries depended upon so greatly to keep supplied. The Royal Navy operating in West Africa had dwindled down to only a handful of warships, most of which were no larger than light cruisers. The battleships and heavier cruisers were trying to keep the German Navy bottled up in their own waters. Despite their attempt, at least a handful of surface raiders had made their way into the North

Atlantic prior to the outbreak of war, along with God alone knew how many of their terrifying U-boats.

At twenty-seven Alistair had not had the pleasure of encountering one of the notorious German submarines at sea, but he'd heard plenty about their reputation during the First World War. The killer U-boats of that war had very nearly cut off Great Britain from its overseas empire during that conflict and Germany had only had a handful back then. Despite a serious lack of surface vessels, it was rumored that the Nazis had been busy building up their new fleet of U-boats in the last couple of years. A North Atlantic swarming with the nasty buggers was not a thought that appealed to him.

"It couldn't have been that long ago, sir," Sub-Lieutenant Dorsey, Chadwick's exec, stated.

Chadwick nodded gravely, still watching through his binoculars as the ship, still a good dozen kilometers off the bow, slipped beneath the waves, black smoke still trailing skywards marking where the ship had been.

Chadwick finally finished scanning the ocean surface with his binoculars and looked up at the thick, dark sky. If there had been another vessel out there and it's running lights were off it would've been difficult to spot it on the dark gray horizon.

"Maybe it was a Jerry U-boat that got 'em," Dorsey offered but Chadwick shook his head.

"No. Even a merchant ship crew can tell the difference between a torpedo and shell shot. The radio message they got off said they were being shelled."

"Well, they didn't stick around did they, sir?"

"Neither would I," Chadwick replied in a low tone. "A cruiser or battleship could hit a target miles away. Shred a merchant ship to pieces in seconds and be on her way before anyone knew she was ever there."

Dorsey grunted. "Maybe it was a destroyer." Dorsey was a good officer, but he was young and this was his first assignment at sea.

"Too far from any German base. Destroyers don't have that kind of range at sea. No. It was a cruiser or worse." He inhaled and exhaled noisily. There was no sense in guessing about it. "Alright, Tim. Radio in our position and call all available hands-on deck. There's probably survivors."

"Aye, sir." Lieutenant Dorsey replied and went right to work.

The *Orkney* was an O-class, or *Odin*-class, submarine that had been built nearly fifteen years earlier and was a relic and nearly obsolete. Despite that fact, the Royal Navy still employed several of them in the fleet. For all its grandeur and might, the Royal Navy was simply spread too thin across the globe. From the West Indies to the Indian Ocean and the Far East, the British Empire was simply too vast for a cutting-edge navy to maintain and hence the reliance on older ships to take care of the day-to-day tasks of patrolling the seas.

Several of the ship's enlisted ratings emerged from below decks carrying rope, medical supplies and rescue equipment. A single open lifeboat appeared as they approached, followed by another a few moments later. A crewman in one of the boats, having spotted the approaching *Orkney* and identifying it as a Royal Navy vessel, waved his oar around in the air.

The sea around the boats was covered in debris and still burning patches of oil. Several of the merchantman's survivors were still in the water, clinging to life buoys, the rest of them were safely in the two open boats.

"Get a line on those boats!" Lieutenant Dorsey snapped at the enlisted ratings that were swarming around the narrow deck of the sub.

The scene was rather chaotic. Most of the merchant sailors were still in a state of shock, the horrifying events that had destroyed their ship still not having set in for many of them. Some were busy trying to keep a hold of their shipmates that were still in the water, others grabbed furiously for the rope that Petty Officer Stuart had tossed at their boat.

As *Orkney* came to a halt, the two lifeboats bumped up against the hull, more lines were tossed out to the men swimming about. Several bodies, or whatever was left of them, bobbed up and down in the ocean.

The Royal Navy men helped to get the merchant marines out of their boats and went to work getting them tended and cared for. One man, clearly an officer, helped to get his men out of the lifeboat and then stepped aboard the deck. He wore the white shorts and white shirt that were common in the summer months, his shoulder boards indicated he was a midshipman. His uniform was drenched, whether in water or in sweat, Chadwick couldn't tell.

Several of the crew had been injured, one man holding his limp arm with his other hand, another man had used pieces of a day uniform to bandage his bleeding leg. A third man was completely unconscious and had to be delicately removed from the lifeboat and placed on a stretcher.

Some of the crew that were still in the sea were clearly exhausted and desperately flapped about in the water to try and get some momentum.

Chadwick looked down at his men on the deck. "Perkins!"

A young man swung around and looked up at him. "Sir!"

"Perkins, get a line on yourself and go get those men if you please," Chadwick ordered, pointing to the four or five sailors still struggling to stay afloat in the water. Perkins was a skinny young man and an excellent swimmer, and he wasted no time in stripping off his shirt, tying a rope line to himself and jumping headfirst into the water.

Despite the heavy falling rain, the recovery effort was going as smoothly as it possibly could. One by one the crew of the *Brother Lucas* were covered in a blanket and helped make their way below. The crew of the *Orkney* assisted the shell-shocked survivors down the hatch where the boat's medic was seeing to their injuries. The young surviving officer of the sunken merchantman caught Chadwick's eye and the two exchanged a brief salute.

A hundred and fifty yards off the bow the last of the *Brother Lucas* slipped beneath the surface, the sea around the vessel turning white as the last pocket of oxygen in the hull released to the ocean surface.

Chadwick took a quick mental count. Eleven crew had been in the first boat, seven in the second boat and perhaps five more being rescued from the water even now. Twenty-three. A normal merchantman of this size and class would have had a crew of roughly forty.

Beside him, Sub-lieutenant Dorsey barked additional orders to the men on the deck. Two more of the crew tied rope lines to themselves and dove into the water as Perkins made his way back with the first man hooked under his left arm.

It took another fifteen minutes for the last of the survivors to be rescued out of the water, the merchant sailors who had been wearing full rain gear, were utterly exhausted by the time they were pulled aboard having been flailing about in the ocean for the better part of an hour.

"Tim," Chadwick began, "please see to our guests. Radio command and let them know we've recovered survivors and request instructions. I'll be down shortly."

Dorsey acknowledged and climbed down the hatchway ladder.

Lieutenant Commander Chadwick stood on the conning tower with his hands behind his back and continued to look across the dark ocean horizon. The dark skies in the distance thundered.

Admiralty Office, London
12:10 PM GMT

Commander Archibald Norwen sipped at his midday cup of tea and read through a series of reports that had come in that morning. Since his department had been recently folded into the mainstream of British naval intelligence gathering, the floodgates of intel reports had been opened and it didn't take long for Norwen and his staff to realize just how much information had been kept from his office for one reason or another, despite its mandate to disseminate naval intelligence and recommend courses of action to leadership.

In the constant struggles and inter-agency disputes between rival branches of the intelligence community it seemed that not everyone was playing very nicely. Every arm of the Secret Intelligence Service, often called MI6, had a different agenda and each one wanted to take credit for things at the expense of overall efficiency. Information useful to one party could potentially be kept by another arm of the service and that hurt overall performance.

However, since the outbreak of war and with the new Ministry of Defence taking care to reorganize the intelligence services, information was being passed now from one entity to the next with greater frequency and ease.

Commander Norwen read through the last few pages of his daily briefing reports. Not much new to learn, the German Navy was still quite busy with their Norway operation. A few U-boats had reared their heads to the unfortunate end of several British vessels in the North Sea and even the English Channel. A couple of transports sunk between England and France, the destroyer *Lindsey* had been torpedoed and sunk yesterday on patrol around the naval base at Scapa Flow in Scotland, another destroyer torpedoed near the Irish coast, but had managed to not only stay afloat but to depth charge the German in return.

New reports of Kriegsmarine activity had also come in from the French. A German sub had sunk a French light cruiser and a corvette both coming out of port at Bordeaux. There were also the additional losses of merchant ships coming up from Africa and Brazil and from across the Atlantic from North America. The merchant losses taken so far were nothing short of devastating and it had only been six weeks since hostilities began.

Then, there was the last page of the report.

"Hmmm...." Norwen grumbled. "Did you read this?" Daniel Towman turned his head to his superior. "Gibraltar reported picking up transmissions from a Portuguese transport plane out of the Azores that radioed in about spotting a large surface vessel while on a run between the Azores and Cape Verde. That was yesterday morning. I can't think of any of our ships that would have been in that area alone with no escort."

Towman shook his head in agreement. "Perhaps another American?"

"No. The Americans know those waters are hunting grounds for Germans. The American Navy isn't straying into an active war zone." He paused and gave the matter a little thought. "We have been losing quite a bit of our merchant ships in that stretch between the African and Brazilian coasts. A single 'large surface vessel', that could be one of Hitler's pocket battleships."

"*Gneisenau* is uncounted for," Towman told him. "So is *Graf Spee*. But that ship was sighted off Madagascar just a few days ago."

"*Graf Spee* can make over eight hundred kilometers a day at sea. She can move quickly. The Navy has a whole squadron dedicated to hunting that ship down." He lowered the report and stared off into nothingness in mindful thought. "If we could sink her.... that would make the Admiralty very happy indeed. Says here the Portuguese reported the ship moving southwards. If my math is any good and if she was moving at cruising speed, she'd be somewhere just west or southwest of Cape Verde right about now."

Normally it was not the business of Norwen's department to make recommendations on such minute operations such as the hunt for a single navy cruiser or battleship. As a department within the Naval Planning Office, it was their job to assist in coordinating a greater naval effort on a more strategic scale and no doubt his superiors would agree with that policy. However, if one only followed simple logic, one may draw the conclusion that convoy defense was vital to the overall strategy of the war and the threat of a surface raider such as *Gneisenau* or *Admiral Graf Spee* would place said strategy in great danger. It was simple and precise and no officer in the Royal Navy, or any other navy, could ignore such a reasoning of the inner workings of the service.

"We need to keep any eye on this, lad," he told Towman. "Call up Operations. See if they've got any planes passing by Cape Verde or off the west coast of Africa anytime soon. Maybe we'll get lucky."

HMS Orkney
200 Miles SW of Cape Verde
2:42 GMT

Alistair Chadwick was hovering over the charts table when Lieutenant Dorsey placed a steaming cup of earl grey in front of him. Chadwick looked up from the sea charts and nodded his approving thanks. They'd been on patrol in the Atlantic now for three months now, they might be short of proper food rations, clean clothing, fresh water, machine parts and any number of other things that made a sub operate at sea, but one thing they had plenty of was tea. His grandfather used to say that no proper Englishman went to sea without a good supply of tea.

"Thank you, Tim," Chadwick said then took a small sip. "How are our guests doing?"

"They're settling in, sir. Most are still in shock. Steward Davies is looking after them."

Chadwick nodded. The merchantmen had lost nearly half their comrades when their ship went down. During the rescue they'd found half a dozen bodies, or at least what was left of them, floating in pieces in the ocean. The captain and first officer had not been found at all. Having been below decks when the attack commenced it was assumed they'd been killed then or drowned when the *Brother Lucas* capsized. The sole surviving officer, a midshipman named Kennedy, had been on the bridge when she was hit and had led his crew off when the situation became hopeless.

"Make sure they're taken care of, Tim," he told his exec. "We heard from command. We're to rendezvous with the French destroyer *Fougueux* here. We'll offload the merchant crew then and take on some additional supplies from the Frenchman."

Dorsey's forehead creased. "Additional supplies? We're not returning to Freetown?"

Chadwick shook his head. "Afraid not. We're one of the only ships to patrol these waters. Once we resupply with the destroyer, we'll plot a course. . . . here, due west and resume our patrol. I may only be a lowly lieutenant commander, but my guess is that the Admiralty suspects we have a surface raider on our hands."

"It's like you said before, sir. Probably a cruiser."

"Or worse."

Dorsey's eyebrows raised up. "A battleship?"

"Not ruling anything out right now, Tim," Chadwick said and took another sip of his tea.

Tim exhaled. "I wouldn't want to tangle with a heavy cruiser much less a battleship. Not out here alone."

"Imagine the destruction those ships could do to our shipping lanes," Chadwick retorted. "They could cut an entire convoy to pieces. Destroyer escorts would be utterly useless to defend against them. No, no. We continue our patrol, keep our eyes peeled and alert the squadron if we spot anything. We're not the only ones out here. *Ark Royal* is at Freetown, *Hermes* at Dakar. One thing is for sure we can't let raiders like those hunt our supply ships down."

There was a large wide-open sea between the coast of west Africa and Brazil that connected the northern and southern half of the Atlantic and was a vital choke point for transports going back and forth from Britain to India, the Far East and Australia. German U-boats and surface raiders had already taken a toll on those shipping lanes. The so-called Battle of the Atlantic had begun just as soon as the first bombs fell in Europe and the toll it was taking was already high.

Until British shipyards could push out the numbers of cruisers and destroyers that it needed in order to fully secure the Atlantic seas and crush the threat the U-boats posed, it was on the shoulders of older ships and subs like *Orkney* in order to fight the war on the oceans.

Chadwick glanced at the clock. "We'll rendezvous with the French in approximately six hours. Pass the word to the lads and to our passengers."

"Aye, sir."

"I'll be in my cabin, Lieutenant. You have the conn."

SS *Le Belle Mer*
182 miles WSW of Cape Verde
6:49 PM GMT

"Merci," Captain Martin Renard thanked his first officer as the other poured him the first glass of Pinot Noir. The captain of the ship was always served first on any French vessel. The first officer proceeded to top off his own glass and then that of Sub-lieutenant Nicholas Gagné the ship's engineering officer.

Captain Renard held his glass up in a toast. "To France and to victory!"

"Vive la France!" The other two toasted simultaneously. The three officers took a drink of their wine.

The captain grabbed his fork and knife and cut into his roasted duck and took a fork full of the tender meat. It was good meat, much better than a merchant ship captain should have had on board, but he'd had friends in low places. When they'd pulled out of Cayenne the day before yesterday, he'd managed to stow away a half dozen of them as well as a generous supply of reds, whites and bourbons to make the voyage back to France a little more bearable. Of course, it had cost him. Or rather it had cost the good people of France.

Menard was hardly the first merchant ship captain to abuse his clients, in this case the French government. He'd been at sea since he was fourteen, worked his way up from common deckhand until he skippered his own ship, and he'd worked every job in between and knew how to make records reflect what he wanted them to reflect. Besides, there was now a war on, and dockyards were overburdened, and cargo was often misplaced or simply vanished. His career was made living on the in between and he now owned a very nice house in Normandy to prove it.

His first officer, Laval, was cut of the same cloth. Not much younger than Menard, he'd spent most of his career in the merchant service as ship's bookkeeper and quartermaster, brushing off promotion in favor of the anonymity of being what was perceived as a middleman all the while cooking the books of merchant vessels. Some might call it theft or others worse. The French government itself might even consider it piracy, a charge that was punishable by years on the infamous Devil's Island prison. But Laval was too shrewd for that. He never, never took payment in francs, preferring instead the devalued banknotes of the Spanish peseta. They were much easier to hide in overseas accounts. His retirement plans weren't quite as ambitious as others.

However, France was now at war, and it was their patriotic duty to serve their beloved country and the Tricolor flag. But neither man saw any reason why war should not also be good for their personal pocketbook.

Laval held up his glass. "To Herr Hitler! For giving us this opportunity to wet our beaks!"

The three men toasted again and downed some more wine. It was a very good Pinot Noir. Menard was quite surprised that such a good vintage could be had anywhere in French Guiana. The single, small French colony on the northern coast of South America was known as an exporter of coffee and rare minerals, not wine. But the black market there was thriving, and many things could be gotten for a price.

Menard scooped another fork of the tender bird into his mouth and chewed, little dabs of the gravy dripping down his fat chin as he ate. He was not a man known for his table manners.

Behind him the intercom whirled. Menard, frustrated by the intrusion, put down his fork and flipped the speaker switch up.

"What is it?" He said in a tone that denoted his displeasure with whomever disturbed his supper.

"Mon capitaine," a voice replied over the intercom. "We've spotted a ship off the port quarter. Moving on a heading of one eight seven. I put her at six miles out, perhaps closer."

Menard grumbled, the other two spoke between themselves and continued with their own dinner.

"What do you make of her?" Menard asked.

"I... I don't know, sir. From this far out, I it's think a British vessel."

"A British ship," Menard said then burped. "Well...." He left the sentence unfinished.

Laval raised his wine glass once again in toast. "To the Royal Navy!" He said then burst out laughing. Menard waved a hand at him. Laval and Gagné drank their wine down and laughed uncontrollably.

Menard threw his dirty napkin at Laval, "Shut up!"

"Oh capitaine," the voice over the intercom began again. "There are flashes...."

The hull shattered, the bulkhead that had been there just a moment before disappeared in the flicker of an eye. In a heartbeat of a moment the dinner table was turned into a hundred thousand wooden splinters that were sent flying in every direction. The men that were Menard, Laval and Gagné were eviscerated almost instantly and in a matter of seconds so was the *Le Belle Mer*.

CHAPTER SEVENTEEN

"General Marshall to see you, sir," the young petty officer standing in the middle of the door announced. The young man held the door open as Army Chief of Staff General George Marshall walked into the office of Admiral Stark, the Chief of Naval Operations, then closed it behind him.

Admiral Stark stood up and extended his hand, Marshall shook it.

"Good morning, admiral," Marshall told him.

"Won't you sit down, George." Stark indicated to the chair opposite his desk.

Marshall sank into the leather seated chair and crossed his legs, his duty cap dropped in his lap. Admiral Stark offered a cigarette, which Marshall politely declined, then lit one up himself and eased back in his reclining chair.

"Thanks for seeing me on such short notice, Harold," Marshall told him. "I know how busy your schedule is right now."

"No bother at all, George. So, what was it that you needed to see me about?"

"I thought we'd better have a discussion with each other, get on the same page as it were before our next briefing with the President. With the situation in China getting so damned bad and with Europe falling back into chaos...." he shook his head, memories of France in 1918 coming back to him. "Seems like in one direction or another there's a fight brewing up and I'm...well, I'm not sure just how long we can realistically sit out of any conflict."

Admiral Stark nodded his head in agreement. "What did the President say last month about the world appearing to come apart at the seams? I know how you feel about it all, George. Sitting out a fight and watching from the benches isn't easy for men like us."

"I just thought we might be wise to try and come up with a future strategy together. Both the army and the navy have been war gaming scenarios out for twenty years. It seems like a war with Japan or more recently another war with Germany might actually come to fruition."

"We've definitely been playing out the situation with Japan," Stark told him. "Seems almost inevitable from a naval perspective. I mean the Japanese have been sticking to their side of the Pacific now, ever since they beat the hell outta the Russians back in oh five, but with their rate of expansion both in terms of territorial gains and their naval build up, I just don't see how we don't butt heads with them at one point or another."

General Marshall nodded. "And, obviously, we're of the same mind. The army's also been playing out theoretical wars with Japan for several years now. Our entire national defense strategy, in my opinion, however, relies too strongly on old age tactics and strategies that I fear have just recently become obsolete."

The world had just watched in horror as Germany overran Poland in a matter of days and Denmark in just hours and although fighting was still going on in Norway the power of the blitzkrieg, or lightning war, had reshaped warfare overnight. The age old and tested strategies of large armies establishing vast networks of defensive works and entrenchments and "slugging it out" with each other had simply become obsolete. Mobility seemed to now be the king of the battlefield and right now the Germans were the masters of mobile warfare.

"You mean on land or at sea?" Stark inquired.

"I mean both. We're watching as country after country fall is falling like rocks. Having a fast-moving, hard-hitting force that can cut through defensive positions and then slice through into rear areas is proving to be quite effective. Those armored units the Germans have right now.... Jesus.... I'll level with you, Harold, the thought of tangling with those damn things makes me shudder. From reports I've read on them our own M2's wouldn't last five seconds against one of their Panzer Threes or Fours."

"I see your point, George and I tend to agree with you. But you said both land and sea. What did you mean by that?"

General Marshall rubbed his bottom lip and considered the question for a moment. "I'm not one hundred percent sure. I was up late last night going over battlefield reports from Poland and some British Army units fighting in Norway. Reports that don't paint a very rosy picture and it got me into thinking and reevaluating things. If mobility can be so effective on land and for that matter in the air, why not at sea? We've been looking at things from a pretty traditional point of view. I think we need to dispel ourselves of this conventional form of warfare. No offense to you navy guys, Harold, but the days of Trafalgar are in the past."

Stark chuckled. "I'm picking up your heading, George. However, I would like to point out that Jutland wasn't a hundred and thirty years ago. It was nineteen sixteen when that happened. But I do see where you're going with this. If the Germans could muster up a fleet that could hit us across the Atlantic, then be gone before we could respond then that would prove to be very effective indeed. But I haven't seen any intelligence that suggests the Germans even have the capacity to build such a fleet. Hitler isn't too big on naval power."

"I was more worried about the Japanese than the Nazis," Marshall replied, "You said it yourself last month when we were briefing President Roosevelt. The Japs may have as many as ten aircraft carriers and who knows how many more being built. They're nothing more than mobile airstrips at sea. Used in that way and learning from what the Germans just did to Poland I don't see why they couldn't do something similar. If three or four of those big carriers of theirs put to sea loaded with bombers, I could see them doing some real damage."

Stark considered it for a second. "Hmm. We've got some naval planners who have been throwing around just such ideas. Carriers being used for offense I mean. Typical aircraft carrier doctrine is more for fleet protection than for offensive use."

The aircraft carrier, for all it's might and power, was seen as little more than a way to keep the heavy battleships and cruisers of a fleet safe from aerial attack. Conventional naval doctrine of the United States still called for the heavy guns of the battleships to win a fight. Although, there were some who no longer agreed with this there was no significant reason to depart from it either. There simply were no examples of aircraft carriers being used in such a fashion in war.

Marshall put his palms up. "Well, the army didn't see the tank as anything more than an infantry support weapon either, at least not before six weeks ago. We've also had some of our own people pushing for an offensive approach for armored warfare. I've got a colonel of mine that has been writing some rather convincing arguments of his own. I'll admit, he wasn't exactly taken very seriously up until now. But even I've had to admit that he was right about a lot of things."

"That Patterson fella?" Stark asked.

"Patton," Marshall replied. "How'd you know about him?"

"Scuttlebutt travels in these hallways. When you came in here you said something about fighting a war with either Germany or Japan. But I'm starting to get the feeling that you meant war with BOTH Germany and Japan. Isn't that what you came here to discuss, George?"

Marshall nodded gravely. "I can see I can't hide my thoughts from you. I have to wonder, as well as you and I have come to know each other, whether the thought has crossed your mind as well. Those oceans aren't as big as they used to be, Harold. The Germans have submarines that can go from the French coast all the way to Bermuda before needing to be refueled. Hell, we're developing bombers that have an eight-hundred-mile range."

"I have thought about it. We've even put together some plans of dealing with it, should it become necessary. Although, our primary strategy is obviously aimed primarily toward the Japanese." He opened a desk drawer and pulled out a green folder, handed it to General Marshall. "This is something that my staff and I have been working on. They're plays off the old Plan Orange, which some now consider to be defunct. It's a list of alternative policies. It needs some revising, but I was planning on bringing it up to you at next month's joint briefing."

Marshall scanned through the documents. It seemed that the navy had not been sitting idly by either, instead developing plans for singular wars with either the Germans or the Japanese and plans should they have to fight both powers across the Pacific and Atlantic Oceans. The army was also busy developing just such case plans, but those plans were just now in their infancy.

The original strategy for confronting Japan, called War Plan Orange, had been developed in the 1920's and had stressed the need for a "grand battle" between the United States and the Japanese Empire, with an assumed attack and invasion of the Philippine Islands by the Japanese. The American fleet, based on the west coast, was then to sortie in its entirety westwards, engage and destroy the Japanese Navy in some grand battle and rescue the Philippines before it's capture.

"Been holding out on us army guys, Harold?" Marshall said, smiling at the other.

"Just trying to be prepared," Stark replied. He finished his cigarette. "A two front war obviously isn't something any of us would like to see but it is a possibility. All we really did was combine elements of Plan Orange, war with Japan, and those of Plan Black, war with Germany, and this is what we've tentatively come up with. Like I said, George, it's something we're just now putting together."

Marshall handed back the green folder. "We're putting together some of our own plans ourselves. I've got General Arnold pressing me for a full court review. He's of the mind that his air forces can do the job of pounding the enemy into submission with aerial bombing just fine."

General Henry 'Hap' Arnold had been known to be passionate about the buildup of the army air forces and in particular he was a proponent of massive strategic bombing, claiming that the destruction of enemy forces, and for that matter civilians, could best be achieved by vast fleets of high-flying bombers dropping thousands of tons of explosives on the enemy. A strategy endorsed by some but seen by most of the military leadership as far too costly and ineffective. There was an adage in the army about infantry being the only force that could capture an enemy position.

"General Arnold's reputation and theories are well known," Stark said waving his hand away in dismissal. "I think he spends too much time thinking about how best to use just one arm of the fighting forces rather than seeing just how effective the overall military can be when used in coordination and not competition with each other. Bombers can bomb, but they can't liberate a town or capture a bridge can they? Besides, his policies simply wouldn't work in the Pacific."

"Because of the island hopping required?" Marshall asked and Stark nodded. "I agree. Although his tactics do warrant further consideration, I agree with you that his view of operational warfare is far too limited. Believe me I've had this discussion with him in the past. It would be simpler if he hadn't recently been proven somewhat correct. The German air force just obliterated Poland right out of the sky and may have proven his point for him."

Stark shook his head slightly. "I disagree with that. It's true the Nazis did dominate the skies, but they didn't act alone. The whole point of that lightning war strategy of theirs was that both army and air force acted in concert with one another. Their air force provided vital ground support and aerial supremacy while their armies took the ground. General Arnold might be wise to study that aspect. The coordination between air force and ground force was vital for the Germans."

"And I fear it will be again in the future."

"You mean France?"

Marshall only nodded.

Admiral Stark exhaled noisily. "It sure would fit the profile. Blitzkrieg unleashed onto Western Europe...devastating. Maybe it won't come to that but...."

"I think the safe money says it will," Marshall finished for him. "Hitler's simply out of control. Dammit, we should never have allowed this to happen. We should've stepped in after Munich."

The Munich Agreement had been the French and British decision to allow Hitler to gobble up the Sudetenland in Czechoslovakia. The decision had been allowed without even consulting the Czech government and had been widely seen as an abandonment by Britain and France of that country to the Nazis. Roosevelt had felt very strongly against it and had urged both those countries against such an agreement, however, the appeasers in Europe and the isolationists in America had made it impossible for the President to realistically do anything about it.

"Well," Marshall continued, "Ours is not to question why..." He didn't finish. "You know, Harold, I half expected to come in here today and have to argue my point with you."

Stark laughed out loud. "Yeah well, occasionally we blue bellies think ahead. Doesn't happen every day but now and again we do."

Marshall chewed his lip. "I'd like to suggest that we have members of our staff work together in the coming weeks. I think that it would be an extremely good idea if we came up with a doctrine change of our own. I'd like to offer the President a serious set of options if the need should arise."

"Sounds to me like you and I are thinking along the same lines, George. Some sort of combined arms doctrine where all the branches are working in close coordination."

"Well, that's certainly part of it. But I'm also.... I don't know... thinking that we need a complete reevaluation of our defensive strategy. Like I was saying before, if blitzkrieg and mobile warfare can work so well on land, why not at sea? I'm not the navy man, you are, but last night I really got into thinking about whether or not such a thing could even be accomplished at sea. That's when the thought of those damn Japanese carriers hit me. If the Nazis could use air power so overwhelmingly and effectively, then what would stop the Japs?"

Admiral Stark leaned forward in his seat. "I've got a Patton of my own, Bill Halsey, an admiral. He's been making some claims kinda like what you're talking about. Claims carriers can and should be used in such a way. Got himself certified as a pilot a couple years back down in Pensacola and he's intimately involved with carrier tactics. If you listen to him, you'd think the battleship isn't the king of the ocean anymore. Can't say I agree with him on that one, but he does have some pretty good points. I think he'd probably agree with you on this. Blitzkrieg at sea as it were."

"So, you think it's possible then?"

Stark grimaced. "The thing about the open seas, is that you can see your enemy coming miles and miles away. Sometimes hundreds of miles. I don't know, George. I'm not sure I can honestly see a large enemy fleet sneaking up on us, evading our sea and air patrols, then dropping bombs in our backyard. We've got a ring of defenses out in the Pacific that would make such a thing close to impossible. I'd bet more money on a pack of those German U-boats sneaking up on New York or Boston before I could ever see a fleet of Japanese carriers hitting us in San Diego or San Francisco. The logistics alone would be a nightmare."

"This Admiral Halsey of yours, what are his thoughts on the matter? Just curious."

"Like I said, his view is the use of carriers as an offensive force. Halsey's a bit of a maverick mind you."

"Well, it's usually the mavericks that write the book on future wars. That's what they called men like Grant and Sherman and Farragut you know. They changed how conflict was fought from the bottom up."

Stark conceded the point. "You may be right, George. I'm not opposed to new viewpoints, and I don't think I'm too old to still learn a thing or two."

"I thought I recalled the navy doing some war games the year before last out in the Pacific. Didn't you guys play out carrier attacks on Hawaii or some such thing?"

"That was part of it," Stark replied. "Defending Hawaii from an attack by air and sea. But the US Navy played the attacking force and we sortied with enough supply and tanker vessels for the fleet to make the trip from California to Honolulu. That's a lot of ships to have to refuel. If you're suggesting that the Japanese might be able to do the same, well again I'd find it hard to believe. Tokyo is a lot farther away than Honolulu is from the west coast. Sailing their whole fleet across the Pacific Ocean, hit us and then sail back to Japan?" he shook his head. "They just don't have that capability, George. By the time they hit Wake or Midway Island, we'd have adequate warning they were coming. Battle Fleet would sortie from Pearl and any element of surprise would be blown. That was the whole thinking behind moving the Pacific Fleet out there."

General Marshall sat quietly for a moment, his head swimming in thoughts. Finally, he threw up his hands. "Well, like I said, I'm not the navy man. These were just thoughts that I was having last night. The

Germans are really showing us a new kind of fighting and I've got to admit I'm a bit on edge about it. The Polish Army just had its rear handed to them. They fought an unconventional war using conventional thinking. The Norwegians are doing the same right now, fighting the German armored vehicles with rifles. We've seen as the Luftwaffe has dominated the skies over in Europe and I have to think if they can do it over there, surely the Japanese can learn from them. They are allies after all."

"I don't disagree with you," Stark replied. "But we haven't exactly sat around on our hands in the last few years either. We've got those new radar stations that can detect planes for miles away. Got them on our newer ships and we're putting them on our islands in the Pacific. The Poles didn't see where their attackers were coming from, we have that ability. Also, it does help just a bit to have about five thousand miles to see your enemy coming."

"Point taken," Marshall replied to him. "Well at any rate, I think it's still a good idea for both of our staffs to work out some major operational overhauls. Since you've already taken the liberty to draw up some first steps, I'd like to merge some of your people with some of mine. Armies and navies don't win wars independently of each other."

"I agree with that!"

"Good. I've got some people in mind to work on a joint project like this. If it's alright with you, Harold, I'd like to put together a joint staff if it were. Some clever minds, experts who can help develop some new operational plans. If the whole point of observing our potential adversaries is to try and learn new things, different forms of fighting then we've got plenty of examples to look at right now. Plenty."

Admiral Stark nodded his approval. "I'll have my chief of staff get in touch with yours, George. They can collaborate and put something together on that end. In the meanwhile, I'll have this memo done with by our next meeting. I want to discuss some things with our intelligence office before I put the finishing touches on it."

"Well then I look forward to our next joint briefing," Marshall replied. He stood up; Admiral Stark followed suit. "I appreciate you giving me sometime today, Harold."

"No problem at all."

The two men shook hands. General Marshall turned and walked back towards the door, stopped just as his hand grabbed the knob and turned back to Stark.

"By the way. Just an thought, but I'll be speaking with Colonel Patton later this week. He asked for some time to discuss some of his proposals. Might not be a bad idea for you to talk with your own Admiral Halsey. Get his opinion on what we discussed here today."

Admiral Stark smiled back at General Marshall. "As it happens, George, I've got him on my schedule sometime next week." The two men grinned at each other. "I'll let you know how it goes."

CHAPTER EIGHTEEN

"How the hell did a bloody Englishman end up with the bloody Irish Guards?" Corporal Flanagan asked casually in between chews of the same piece of dried meat he'd been gnawing on for almost half an hour now. It was his fifth piece today. Sticks of dried beef and hardened biscuits seemed to be all that anybody had to eat anymore, the supply trucks were only coming in from the port about once every two or three days now.

Private Miles Creech sat in his foxhole, rifle propped up against his shoulder, a cup of cold tea in hand. He shook his head slowly. "I sometimes ask myself that, corp. Just unlucky I guess."

"Bloody fucking hell," Flanagan replied. "Serving in the Irish Guards is the honor of a lifetime, Private. Anybody lucky enough to be posted to a Guards regiment should be bloody honored." The short Irishman was irritated. He always swore a lot when he was irritated about something.

Creech drank down another gulp from his cup of cold tea. "I am half Irish you know. Me mum."

Corporal Flanagan chewed down another chunk of the hateful stick of dried meat, took a swig from his canteen to try and moisten his mouth. "Bugger that! Your name's Creech! That's an Englishman in my book boy! It's not your ma that counts. You got your father's name, it's his heritage you got flowing through your veins. How come you didn't end up in some nice English regiment? Didn't you come from Cheshire?"

"I was born there. Left when I was two. Been in Belfast since I was five." He drank another gulp of cold tea, his eyes staring blankly in front of him. "The army didn't much care where I was born when they sent me my notice, corp. Be at such and such a place on such and such a date they said. That's what the letter Mr. Chamberlain sent me said. So, I went there. Next thing you know they throw a uniform on me that says Irish Guards on the shoulder. I didn't get no say in the matter."

Corporal Flanagan forced down the last of his dried beef and emptied his canteen. He was sick and tired of dried beef. Would've given his left ball for a pot roast right now or fish and chips. "Still.... it's a bloody honor to be in the Guards isn't it private?"

Creech nodded. "Yes, corporal. A real bloody honor."

"And especially the Irish Guards," the corporal continued, all the excitement he could drum up after four of the most unexciting weeks of his life. "Any Irish unit in the whole bloody British Army is an honor to serve in. Ain't that right, private?"

"Yup," Creech answered equally as dull with this conversation as Flanagan was. It was merely a way to pass the time at this point.

The British Army had landed four brigades on the northwestern coast of Norway four weeks earlier, supported by two French brigades. Their job was supposedly to fight the Germans and keep them from taking the whole of the country but thus far they'd done little in the way of fighting and more in the way of retreating and falling back. The Germans were advancing northwards, slowly but surely squeezing the country and the remaining Norwegian army to death. An army of a hundred thousand Germans had been pushing its way up from Oslo for nearly two months now. Their advance had slowed in recent days, but they really didn't have to move too fast, since the Allied force of forty thousand hadn't moved one step forward to try and stop them.

Flanagan continued, "Irish Guards.... Irish Dragoons.....Royal Irish.... the bloody Ulster Rifles.... did I tell you that I served with the Ulster Rifles before?" Creech nodded. "Well, I bloody did. Three years. Had to earn my way to the Irish Guards, private. Earned.... my.... bloody.... way! Now they just hand it out to anybody it seems."

Since landing in Norway nearly a month ago the summer weather had set in. The country suffered from no heatwaves that was for sure.

Creech had found the climate of Norway to be very agreeable, cool and fair, much like Northern Ireland.

The men of the 1st Battalion of the Irish Guards Regiment, assigned to the 24th Guards Brigade had come ashore near the port city of Narvik in the very north of the country. They had been told that their objective was to secure the port so the Germans could not use it as a base against the Royal Navy. Supposedly they were also to keep the German armies in the south half of the country from reaching the precious iron mines of the north but so far, the vast majority of the fighting had been done much farther south.

The Germans were taking their sweet time about moving northwards to take Narvik, the last major town in the far north of Norway. As far as most of the men of the Irish Guards were concerned, they could take as long as they wanted.

Miles finished his cold tea, tossed the metal cup onto the ground next to his gear and stood up in the foxhole then looked around at the countryside around him. Trees were all he saw. Lots and lots of trees. "I don't think they're coming today, corporal."

Corporal Flanagan grunted, looked up at the younger man. "They will," he replied. "Trust me boy, they'll come eventually. Germans don't like to sit still. They like to me on their bloody feet. Do you know who Frederick the Great was?" Creech didn't answer. He found it was best to let Flanagan ramble on rather than interrupt him. Interruptions irritated him too. "Frederick the bloody Great was a king, lad. Fought the French back in the seventeen hundreds or something like that. He was a German, though they called them Prussians back then, not Germans, Prussians. Old Frederick marched his men from one end of Europe to the other. Never stopped marching you know. NEVER! They wore gray back then too.... Buggers. They still wear gray. Not much for fashion but they know how to march and mark my words, Englishman, they're going to march straight through those woods sooner or later. Mark my words."

B Company had been posted to an outlying area to the east of the port city where they were to act as a picket just in case the Germans happened to show up. The whole company, one hundred and fifteen men, had dug foxholes, put up barbed wire fencing and erected earthwork defenses nearly three weeks earlier with orders to "dig in and wait". Well, they'd dug and waited and waited and waited.

The Irish Guards was part of the famed Guards Brigade which included the Scots Guards and the South Wales Borderers regiments, both famous regiments in their own rights. The Irish Guards had only been formed about forty years earlier, compared to the three-hundred-year histories of the other two regiments it was brand new but had proven itself in the previous war with Germany. Most of the men in the regiment, naturally, came from Ireland but here and there one could find a Scotsman or an Englishman in its ranks.

The Allied force had formed a crescent shaped defensive pocket around Narvik. The 1st Battalion of the formed the easternmost part of that pocket. The Welsh were to the north and the Scottish on the southeast while a reinforced French regiment held the positions just south of Narvik.

There were only a few roads that lead there and none of them were wide enough for more than one vehicle at a time to use. This meant that supplies going back and forth along these roads often took a great deal of time in order to reach the outlying pickets. Reinforcements, if they were needed, would be slow in arriving as the vast majority of infantry would have to move by foot. An infantry column moving along one of those roads could potentially take an entire day to get to its destination.

Farther south two additional British and French forces had landed at the towns of Namsos and Andalsnes. They'd been reinforced by the retreating elements of the Norwegian Army which itself had been forced into a full-fledged retreat after the fall of Oslo and Bergen, the advancing German forces in full pursuit and constantly nipping at their heels.

"Bloody supply ships better come in soon," Corporal Flanagan said. "I'm tired of dried beef and stale biscuits." The hefty Irishman pushed himself up off the ground and stood up. He peered up out of the foxhole they were both occupying and scanned the woods ahead.

To the left and right about twenty paces off in either direction, other foxholes were dug, each with two occupants in them. Creech often wondered to himself whether or not those other foxholes had occupants in them just as charming as Corporal Flanagan was.

"What time is it?" Flanagan asked.

Creech checked his wristwatch. "Almost sixteen hundred."

Flanagan grumbled. "The truck should be by shortly. I wonder what they're serving for dinner?"

Creech didn't reply. Knew better not to.

"I'd give my left ball for a roasted chicken," Flanagan said, and Creech barely held in a muffled laugh. "I'd give your whole cock for some mutton and fresh bread. Not that shitte they've been serving us. You'd think that old Mister Chamberlain could have kept us better supplied than he has been. But.... that's about what we Irish expect from an Englishman."

The two soldiers stood there in their chest deep foxhole looking straight out at an empty wood. It was only four o'clock in the afternoon but already the sun was setting, Narvik being far in the north of the country the days were remarkably short. The woods to the east of Narvik were not at thick as anyone thought they'd be but there were certainly more trees here than there were back in Ireland.

Creech, more than once in recent days, had the thought of grabbing his rifle, heading into those woods and shooting a deer for supper. The boys would certainly love some venison for dinner for a change. This idea came up against two opposing facts. First, he had seen no sign of any deer for the past week or so. Apparently, the animal seldom strayed far from the thick of the forest several miles further east. The second problem was that the officers in charge had forbid hunting of any kind. The fear of rifle fire might produce an unwanted result, such as attracting Germans or, worse yet, being fired upon by a soldier's own mates by mistake.

"Well, it's 'bout bloody time," Flanagan muttered.

Miles turned around to see a half dozen trucks make their way up a winding road. The trucks would be picking up the men holding the picket and dropping off their replacements for the evening. Three times a day each platoon changed shifts and another platoon took their place.

"Is this what we're going to be looking forward to, corp?" Creech asked. "Sitting in a hole I mean. I heard this is what they did in the last war down in France. Sat in holes."

Flanagan waved a hand dismissively. "Won't be like that this time boy. Trust me on that. German Army's got themselves all sorts of new toys to play with. New tanks that can drive father in an hour than a man can run in a day. I don't think there's gonna be much sittin' around this time, boy. But hey, you just keep near good ol' Corporal Flanagan, eh. You can't go wrong if you do that."

Creech picked up his rifle, slung it over his shoulder and buckled up his gear. "Lucky charm are you, corporal?"

"Damn right. Nobody's ever gone wrong following the Irish. My dad was lucky too, so was his. Bastards put bullet holes and bayonets in both of them, but they kept on ticking you know."

Creech looked at him. "Really?" Flanagan nodded. "The Germans shot them?"

"Wasn't no Jerry that did it, boy. It was you bloody English. HA!" He laughed out. "I may fight for King and country boy, but under this uniform I'm Irish republican. So was dad." He laughed out again.

Creech smiled at the other man. Flanagan was an acquired taste. He'd drawn the short straw three days in a row now when it came to pairing the men up together in the foxholes. He'd had to sit through three days of the man's never-ending loquaciousness. The Irishman was a very good soldier but when not performing his soldierly duties he became quite melancholic.

As the line of trucks drew closer some of the other men could be seen standing up from their positions and buckling their gear together. Two men that had gone down the hill to what was serving as the latrine were now making their way back up to gather their belongings.

The 1st battalion was a hardy lot and was lucky enough to have a lot of veteran soldiers. The battalion had typically had a hard training schedule back in garrison. Drill and drill were the order of the day and they'd gotten plenty of that. Creech had gotten his mandatory service notice late last year and reported for duty on September 1st. He'd been working in a bookstore in Belfast before that and physical activity had never really been his cup of tea.

He remembered his first few days of training as being extremely arduous. Waking up two hours before sunrise, the rigidity of the day-to-day schedules, learning how to fire a rifle, operate a radio and read a map had been challenging experiences for him and at first he'd rejected it. That first week in barracks had been the most difficult, but it got progressively easier when he'd realized that all the other men there had been something else before being conscripted as well.

By chance his bunk mate, Willoughby, had also been English. He'd gotten to know Willoughby quite well after that first week and after that, things had become much easier. Willoughby, a fisherman by trade, had become one of the best recruits in camp and had helped Miles to learn what he needed to learn. Willoughby took a one step at a time approach to soldiering. "Learn one thing, learn it so well you can do it in your sleep, then learn the next thing and do it again" he would constantly say. An approach to life that apparently, he'd learned working on fishing boats.

"Well, let's get a move on, lad," Flanagan said. He hoisted himself up out of the hole and dropped his hand to help Miles up. Miles took his hand, put a foot up and pushed himself up then brushed the dirt off his backside.

Several dozen yards behind the entrenchments was a wide-open cut and a long dirt road going off in both directions. If you followed the winding road down the hillside you'd eventually come to a small hamlet, several small rural buildings, about twelve kilometers from the town of Narvik itself. The road widened after that until you got to the town itself, which was not much more than a couple of thousand people that made most of their living off fishing. The port of Narvik was a rather small port when compared to ones like Bristol, Portsmouth or Belfast but it was enough to get a single large freighter to make port at a time.

The hamlet along the hill road had been made into an outpost and that was where B Company, 1st Battalion had made its home.

The line of trucks pulled up to the top of the hillside and came to a halt in an open area in the woods. The passenger side door of the first truck opened and a single officer stepped down. The last two trucks were towing something behind them, but Creech couldn't see exactly what they were from his angle.

The platoon leader, Lieutenant Mayshed, made his way over to the first truck followed closely by platoon Sergeant Lowell.

From the rear of the trucks the tailgates dropped and the men in the back hopped down to the ground, unloading their equipment with them, Vickers and Lewis machine guns, crates of ammunition and a couple of 2-inch mortars. The final two vehicles pulled up and Creech finally saw what they were towing behind them.

"Bloody hell," Flanagan muttered. "Where'd they scrounge those up from?"

Two men emerged from either truck and unhitched two 25 mm anti-tank guns from their vehicles. It was a flimsy looking piece, a long and narrow barrel with a rather inadequate looking shield mounted to the carriage to protect the operator behind the gun. He'd never seen this model of gun before, but he'd seen similar ones in the past, small anti-tank guns that looked more like miniature artillery guns but fired a single armor piercing shot rather than an explosive shell. They were meant to disable an enemy armored vehicle. But the ones that he'd seen in the past seldom performed in the way that they were designed to do.

"Are those ours, corp?" Creech asked.

"Nah. Look like Frenchie guns to me. If they're bringing them up here..." He turned his head around all in both directions as if looking for something.

"Never fear, Second Platoon is here!" One of the men from the relieving group called out. There were the repetitious greetings between the two groups with friendly greetings and jests going on between them.

"Alright!" Sergeant Lowell hollered. "First platoon form up." He held his arm up with a closed fisted hand in the air as the men began to file towards the roadside.

Corporal Flanagan gestured towards the men unloading the field pieces and their ammo crates.

"They're expecting something, lad. Mark my words on that."

Creech shrugged. "You don't know that. We've been here a whole damn month and..."

"And what did I say about those god damn Germans?" Flanagan crossed himself as he swore. "I said they was coming, and they are, boy.

Think about it, lad. They've had a whole month to place those there," gesturing towards the anti-tank guns, "but they've waited until now. Cause the generals in charge wanted to see which direction the bloody buggers were going to come from."

Miles thought about what he was saying. Flanagan had been in the army for years now and had been through a lot, had even seen combat out in Burma. As much as he was eccentric he was also looked up to by the men in the company, especially the younger, more inexperienced ones. He knew the ins and outs of soldiering, knew how to talk to his superiors, kept his eyes and ears to the ground. As exhausting as he may have been at times, he was very often proven to be right.

The men of 1st platoon fell into formation, sergeants in front, lower ranks in the rear. Lieutenant Mayshed was the platoon officer, he was standing with Captain Murphy, who was the company commander and had accompanied 2nd Platoon. The two were talking behind one of the parked vehicles. Miles eyed the two officers, looked at Flanagan who looked back at him and nodded. If Captain Murphy had come up for the night watch, then something was indeed happening.

"Alright!" Sergeant Lowell bellowed. Lowell had a deep baritone voice and a long, thick mustache. "At ease, lads. Now listen up carefully. Lieutenant wants us to get these here guns in place before we strut off." He nodded his head towards the two guns being pulled back away from the trucks that had towed them up the hill.

"What the devil are those, sarge?" someone asked from the formation. "Looks like a bloody water gun the fire brigade uses."

"Shut it! I want your bloody opinion, I'll ask you for it!" Lowell roared; the man was a natural sergeant. Probably forty years of age and in better shape than most of the younger men in the platoon. "They're to use on those bloody Jerries." Flanagan was right. "I want one there and the other one over there," the sergeant pointed to two different points on the line. "Get 'em up there, lads and cover 'em up with brush."

"Have we got Nazis coming, sarge?"

"Never you mind what's coming, Higgins!" Lowell snapped back, "I've got your name. When I ask for your input, feel free to give it to me. 'Til then you move when I say move. Now move!"

It didn't take long for the platoon to get to work, but it did take a while to drag the two guns through the soft, muddy ground as the small tires on the gun did not move through wet terrain easily. The guns were of an older French design, smaller than other anti-tank guns that any of them had seen before. They were also lighter than the common British designed QF 2-pounder which was the standard in the British Army.

"What'd I say?" Flanagan began, the thick Irishman pushed the main carriage while Creech, O'Malley, O'Kelly and Toal lifted each of the two legs up. "Jerry's coming right down that there road, lads. Listen to Corporal Flanagan he knows what he's talking 'bout."

"Sweet Christ, I think you're right," Private O'Kelly said, an air of desperation was in his voice. "You heard old Sergeant Lowell. He said it. These are to use on the Jerries when they show up. Jesus. I was starting to think those bastards weren't coming."

They finally towed the gun into place, right in between two foxholes, some barbed wire and a handful of thin trees that overlooked the single long weaving road that came out of the western line of trees where the British defenses were. The second gun was placed about fifty yards to the right, behind a large fallen tree. It struck Creech that if German tanks and armored vehicles were to come this way, chances were the buggers weren't going to come down the road in a single file column but out of the trees and forests that flanked the road. The Germans, after all, weren't stupid and had to know that the British were here.

"O'Malley, gather up some branches and try to give it some cover as best you can," Flanagan ordered. "Toal, Creech, pack some dirt under the legs of this French piece of shitte, otherwise it'll be shooting at the moon when it comes time to use it. Bloody French can't design a proper gun to save their bloody lives."

"Don't need it to save their lives, corp," Toal groaned. "Need it to save ours."

"Ours too," the corporal retorted. "Damn French guns aren't properly balanced. Look at the barrel then look at the legs. The barrel isn't designed to fire at the angle we need it to. Then when she fires off a shot, the damn thing bucks like a horse. On this ground and with those tires, the bloody thing'll roll back three paces after the first shot. Pack that dirt tightly lads. It'll steady the gun if we have to use it."

Creech took his entrenching tool off his pack and began pulling shovelfuls of earth underneath the rear legs of the gun. The ground was moist, and earthworms wiggled around in the disturbed soil. The rear legs were remarkably light and easy to lift to put mounds of earth underneath them. The gun itself was light and that was both an advantage and disadvantage. No doubt they were designed to be easy to move around and use on battlefields in quick time, but by the look of the barrel and the breech, it did not look like it would stop anything as large as any armored vehicle the British had much less anything the Germans did.

"Well, well, getting our hands dirty are we," a voice said from behind.

The group turned to see three soldiers approaching from behind, signature brown uniforms, tan bandoliers draped over the torso, brodie helmets and bayonet fixed Lee-Enfield rifles in their hands.

Corporal Flanagan sneered at the group. "It's you lot who should be getting your damn hands dirty. Us lads have been on this bloody line all day long. If the capt'n wants these damn things ready, he shoulda' got you to do it. I'm bloody hungry."

"We'll have plenty of work to do tonight, corporal," the man on the left of the three told him. He was decently built, around five foot ten inches tall with dark brown hair poking out from underneath his helmet. He ran his fingers down his clean-shaven face. "I'm sure Lieutenant Hastings has plenty on his list for tonight."

"Ah well, the other bloody Englishman!" Flanagan chided the other man. "You know, Willoughby, I was just asking your friend over here earlier how a bloody Englishman ended up in the Irish Guards. They drafted him. What was your story again?" The other men laughed.

Willoughby chuckled. "Well, they asked for the best, Corporal Flanagan. They asked for the best." Willoughby looked over at his friend and old bunk mate. "Did you draw the short straw again, Miles?"

"Aye," Creech replied. "Three days in a row now."

"Why don't you go catch us some fish, Willoughby," Flanagan joked, and Creech laughed.

Private Willoughby laughed at that. "Aye, would if I could. I think we're going to be catching a whole lot of something else soon."

Miles looked at his friend and his smile disappeared. "What do you mean, Benton?"

"Didn't you lads hear?" Nobody said anything. "There's fighting just south of here," Willoughby told them all. "Germans are attacking our boys just down the coast a way. Namsos or something like that. Word came through this morning."

Toal waved it off. "Just another rumor. That's all."

The man standing next to Willoughby shook his head. "No, not this time. The radio operator himself told Sergeant Leary. Lots of radio traffic between headquarters down there and the navy boys off the coast. Couple of ships sailed off to go rescue them lads."

"What kind of ships?" Flanagan asked.

"Hell if I know, Corp. I'm in the army not the navy. But they sailed off south of here."

"It's true," Willoughby said. Benton Willoughby was only in his mid-twenties, but he wasn't like so many other lads in the service. He didn't take to rumors and gossip the way that others did. Army camps had a way of breeding rumors and untruths and there were always stories of this or that floating around. But not with Benton. He'd grown up working on his grandfather's fishing boat, raised in harsh conditions and around men who didn't have time for idle gossip. You worked until you didn't. You got good at what you did or you were off the boat. There were no other options. If he said something, you could bet that what he was telling you was true.

"Bloody hell," Flanagan spat. He looked right at Creech and pointed two fingers at him. "What'd I tell you, lad. Well, better get ready boys. The big show's about to begin."

CHAPTER NINETEEN

There was smoke on the distant horizon and there had been the faint sound of a thunderous explosion a few minutes earlier. No distress signal had been picked up from any vessel in the vicinity but obviously something had occurred. Seagoing ships didn't just explode without a reason and only three ships that had recently passed through the area. Two were British merchants and the third was a Dutch passenger liner that was returning home to Rotterdam.

Captain Rory O'Conor of the Royal Navy stood on the open deck outside of the main bridge of the *Leander*-class light cruiser, his first officer, Commander Paul MacMillan stood just feet from him, the two men scanning the horizon with their binoculars.

Through the wide-eyed lens, the gray-black smoke could be spotted on the ocean as easily as a chimney in wintertime. Although the explosion itself had not been seen by any of the lookouts, it certainly had been heard, there was no mistaking it. There was a distinct way that sound seemed to travel over water that echoed further than it otherwise would travel over land. And there were no storms nearby to cause such a terrible sound.

HMS Neptune had been sailing east parallel to the northern coast of South America on patrol when the explosion happened. The smoke on the horizon was no more than a distant stream, hardly noticeable with the naked eye. The sun was shining brightly and there was barely a cloud in the sky to block out its glare. But that did not stop Commander MacMillan from spotting the distant fire, the captain zeroing in on it after a moment's adjustment.

O'Conor had been in the navy for a quarter of a century now, had served during the Great War, had seen and heard his share of combat during his career and his instincts told him to be alert. Although far from Europe and the North Sea, the oceans themselves had once again become deadly battlefields in the worldwide game of chess that seemed to rear its ugly head once a generation.

The North Atlantic was crawling with the threat of deadly German U-boats that had dispersed to all corners of the ocean. Hitler's prized fleet of submarines were the number one threat to the Royal Navy and Britain's overseas lifeline. Despite their relatively small numbers, they would rear their ugly heads to torpedo Allied shipping. Thus far only single merchantmen and stragglers had fallen victim to them, but it was only a matter of time before the vipers began to target the far richer convoys and Britain had too damn few destroyers to escort them all.

The other threat to the Allies at sea were a pair of surface raiding warships that had escaped the blockade in the North Sea and managed to worm their way out into the open ocean. One was the great battleship *Gneisenau,* and the other was the heavy cruiser *Admiral Graf Spee.* Both ships were incredibly deadly and were more than a match for anything that the British or French fleets had guarding over their supply routes. While it was believed that the *Gneisenau* was still far in the north, Naval Intelligence had a high degree of certainty that *Graf Spee* was raiding along the South American and African coasts and had even managed to sail as far away as French Madagascar.

Captain O'Conor remembered seeing firsthand the bloody carnage caused by Germany's famed submarines in 1916 and '17 and did not relish another conflict, one he knew, after a quarter century in the service, would eclipse the previous one.

After another moment of examining the far away smoke with his binoculars, O'Conor lowered his glasses, cupped his hands over his eyes as he looked up at the hot sun then wiped the sweat from his forehead.

"Alright, Lieutenant," O'Conor started, speaking to young Sub-lieutenant Harper standing just feet behind him, "alter course for that smoke."

Harper nodded his head. "Aye, aye, sir," he replied in his native New Zealand accent. The officer stepped back into the covered bridge. "Helm, bring us thirty-five degrees to port!"

O'Conor let his gaze fall back to the horizon. Commander MacMillan hung his binoculars around his neck and stepped closer to his captain. Like most of the rest of the crew MacMillan had been drawn from the New Zealand Division of the Royal Navy, native New Zealanders serving in the Royal Navy. Although he'd only recently been assigned to *HMS Neptune* his service record was impeccable and he'd proven himself quite a capable first officer.

"What do you think, sir?" MacMillan asked quietly.

"I think it's wartime, Commander," O'Conor told him and sighed. "We'll have a better idea in while, but don't be surprised if we find one of Hitler's U-boats lurking out there. Hell of a time for our scout plane to break down. We could use our eye in the sky right now."

Commander MacMillan nodded his agreement. *HMS Neptune*, as with every other ship in her class carried on board a single catapult launched seaplane for aerial reconnaissance. Last night however, that seaplane had broken down with engine problems and not for the first time either. On a couple of previous occasions the single Fairey Seafox biplane had broken down. Repair crews had rigged up fixes before with hopes of getting new replacement parts, or for that matter a replacement Seafox, but those repairs had only been temporary and had ultimately failed late last night and as of this morning it was out of action completely. A serious setback and tactical disadvantage.

"Well Commander, let's not take any chances shall we. Sound action stations."

"Aye, sir," MacMillan replied, the first officer stepped back through the main bridge hatchway and picked up the ship's intercom mic. "Action stations. Action stations. All hands to your stations." A blaring horn bellowed a couple of seconds later letting the entire crew know to jump to it.

Up and down the length and breadth of the light cruiser the crew ran this way and that, grabbing their helmets and life vests along the way, scrambling to get to their action station. The crew of a *Leander*-class cruiser was just under seven hundred sailors and although most of them had never seen combat before and a good number of them, almost half actually, had been conscripted just months earlier, they had trained tirelessly until their reaction time had been trimmed remarkably well.

O'Conor had previously held the enviable position as first officer of *HMS Hood*, the pride of His Majesty's Navy. *Hood* had been the single largest battlecruiser sized ship ever built and by far the most powerful, only to be surpassed by the heavier battleships which were becoming the new standard in the Royal Navy. While XO on *Hood* he'd honed his skills and mastered the battle readiness drill, a skill that he'd carried with him when it came to his current assignment. Under his command *HMS Neptune* had become one of the shining examples of battle readiness in the entire fleet.

The captain stepped back through the open hatchway onto the bridge, traded his peaked cap for a helmet and fastened a life vest over his navy whites. The bridge officers and crew didn't miss a beat either, each of them quickly changing their headgear and slipping the safety vests over their torsos in fluid motion. The call-to-action stations blaring through the megaphone vibrated throughout the entire ship broken only by the sound of rubber boots squeaking along the deck as sailors rushed to their assigned positions. Sailors passed through narrow bulkheads, secured hatchways behind them, chief petty officers barked orders at the ratings, reminding them to get to their duties and keep their eyes and ears open.

O'Conor took his chair, adjusted his chin strap. He always did hate wearing his helmet. While other parts of his uniform were typically custom fit for him, a helmet's chin strap always seemed to never fit right, either it was too tight or just loose enough to wobble when he wore it.

"Course is zero five five degrees, sir," Sub-lieutenant Harper reported.

O'Conor nodded his acknowledgment. He rolled his sleeve up and checked the time, 1123 hours.

"Rudder amidships, half ahead," he ordered

"Rudder amidships, half ahead, aye, sir," the helm replied.

O'Conor sat quietly, thinking to himself and barely registered the yeoman that stepped beside him and placed a cup of hot tea in his chair cup holder, earl gray with a single lump of sugar and a slice of lemon.

"Thank you," he whispered to the yeoman.

The bridge was quietly professional, the only sounds came from the splashing of waves against the hull, the hushed discussion taking place between the two crewmen at the navigation table and the radio operator reporting in their position over the two-way. The men had been molded into a professional fine-tuned machine since their voyage had begun just weeks earlier. Incessant drilling and top-notch officers could do that to even the greenest of crews.

Typically, *HMS Neptune* patrolled her zone on her own but did have a backup. The French battleship *Strasbourg* had been assigned to the area to assist with the Royal Navy in hunting down German surface raiders. The single French battleship in the western hemisphere was one of two ships that had been built for the purpose of hunting down Nazi commerce raiders on the ocean. Merchant losses were already beginning to show, and the fighting was still early on. Both sides had understood well the benefits and dangers of merchant losses on a grand scale, a lesson the British and French had both learned during the First World War.

Unfortunately for *HMS Neptune*, *Strasbourg* was nowhere in the vicinity, her commander having decided that it was his duty to protect the approaches to French Guiana rather than cooperate with the Royal Navy despite a mutual agreement between the two governments. O'Conor hoped for but did not expect any assistance from the French. But still his standing orders from the Admiralty were to radio in his position regularly. His French counterparts would no doubt become quickly aware of any situation and hopefully, emphasis on hopefully, move to assist if any situation grew out of control.

"All crew is to action stations, sir," Commander MacMillan reported. Two minutes thirty-seven seconds, he mentally noted. The men had gotten good indeed.

"Very good, Commander, Surface contacts?"

MacMillan glanced quickly at Lieutenant Patrick, who shook his head. "No surface contacts, sir."

Neptune had been equipped with a brand-new array of aerial radar and surface detection equipment prior to her current voyage. Although both were untested in combat and rumors about their unreliability were sweeping through the fleet. Many officers still preferred to use the old tried and true method of lookouts scanning the horizon as it was in the days of Nelson, shouting out after spotting an enemy. Captain O'Conor inwardly cursed at the loss of his seaplane. Enemy submarines were nearly impossible to spot at the best of time, but even those damn killers needed to come to at least periscope depth in order to fire off one of its torpedoes. A good pilot in even an old biplane could spot one of those devils kilometers away and radio its location back to the ship.

The minutes ticked by, and the dark, black smoke grew larger and larger in the front window. The trail of smoke rose for hundreds of meters into the sky, a hulking wreck beginning to take form on the ocean surface, half submerged, it's bow still above the waterline but slipping away beneath the waves slowly.

Commander MacMillan stood in front of the large forward window, binoculars up to his eyes, "She's a tanker," MacMillan reported. "Still burning.... I can't see anything in the area that look like lifeboats but it's still too far out."

O'Conor swung half around in his chair. "Lieutenant, radio it in. Find out if we can get an identification on the vessel."

Tankers were notoriously slow ships at sea and were easy prey by enemy submarines. A single torpedo often had the deadliest of results. Tankers, with no armor whatsoever, would instantly burst into flames, hundreds of thousands of gallons of petrol leaking quickly into the seas spreading the fire. Crew members that were fortunate enough to survive the attack itself would often face even worse deaths by burning to death in the middle of a sea of oil.

Captain O'Conor turned his chair back front and he and his exec exchanged quick glances. "If Hitler can get U-boats this far into the Atlantic...." He didn't finish the sentence, just shook his head at the thought. Common military logic was that German U-boats were much more limited in their range than a traditional surface vessel. A pack of the stealthy submarines operating between South America and Africa could spell serious trouble for the Allied convoys.

"Sir," Sub Lieutenant Harper began, he was standing over the radio operator, hand on the young sailor's shoulder. "Georgetown acknowledges our message. They report a tanker, *La Sirene*, out of Bordeaux was scheduled to arrive in Cayenne tonight. It's the only tanker expected for over a week."

Captain O'Conor nodded his affirmation. "Thank you, Lieutenant. We may encounter survivors, let rescue crews and the infirmary know to expect them."

"Aye, sir," Harper replied.

"Helm, increase to full."

"Aye, aye, sir," helm replied.

The propellers revved up and *HMS Neptune* increased her pace, gliding along the ocean surface at near thirty knots. The burning wreck of *La Sirene* grew larger and larger with each passing minute. The tanker's precious cargo of petroleum had indeed caught fire, as had been expected and huge amounts of thick black smokestacks erupted upwards, spreading outwards as more and more of the oil in the hold spilled into the open sea. An enlarging blanket of fire burned on the ocean top just as surely as if it had been a burning forest.

Captain O'Conor peered through his binoculars as the situation became clearer. The bow of the French tanker, or what was left of it, was now sticking straight up into the air, it's forecastle completely out of the water and slowly dropping below the surface.

"Sweet Christ," someone whispered. Sailors hated the sight of a dying ship and her crew.

O'Conor stood up from his chair. "Commander," he said to his exec, "I want you to. . . ."

"Contact, sir!" The voice came from the radar operator. "Aircraft bearing forty degrees starboard! Eight thousand feet!"

O'Conor and MacMillan rushed out onto the starboard lookout deck, binoculars held high scanning the skies.

"There it is, sir!" Commander MacMillan said, pointing his finger.

The captain locked his sights on the single airplane, the glare from the sun kept him from identifying the craft. "Is it one of ours?"

A moment or two passed by. Finally, Commander MacMillan shook his head. "I don't think so, sir. Could be a Heinkel." The Heinkel He 60 was a seagoing recon plane used by the German navy.

"Damn!" O'Conor snapped. He let out a hard sigh. "Damn!"

Commander MacMillan let his binoculars down and looked at his captain. "Sir?"

O'Conor grimaced and looked at the younger executive officer. "U-boats don't carry search planes, Commander."

Commander MacMillan's face paled as he understood the implication.

"Surface contact, sir!" Harper bellowed out of the main bridge, his voice unnaturally thunderous. "Contact bearing zero zero five degrees!"

All eyes turned quickly ahead of the ship as behind the large sheet of smoke from the burning tanker, the unmistakable bow of a heavy warship quickly became clear. It's sword-like frame slicing through the waves at what must've been twenty-five knots. Smoke from the burning French ship having provided the perfect cover for the Nazi raider.

Captain O'Conor's face went quickly pale but his training instinctively kicked in.

"Hard to port!"

Captain Hans Langsdorff allowed himself a slight smile at the view and the sight of the smaller British warship make a hard turn to port just as he'd expected them to. The British ship was cruising along at full speed and its last-minute decision to turn to port was nearly textbook but not without its flaw.

By keeping up at such a high speed the British ship had deprived itself of the ability to maneuver sharply and was now committed to making a wide turn away from the larger German ship.

The thick black smoke from the burning tanker had provided Langsdorff with the perfect cover to close the distance with the enemy ship without detection. Although he had not expected at all to encounter a British warship this far out and with no air cover whatsoever, he nonetheless did not shy away from a chance at a fight when the opportunity presented itself. His own aerial reconnaissance plane having spotted the enemy vessel approaching straight on, probably expecting to rescue any of the tanker's survivors. Instead, they now had walked straight into a slugging match with a much larger foe.

"Guns are ready, sir," First Officer Walter Kay reported.

Langsdorff nodded. "Fire."

From the forward bow three eleven-inch guns ripped out deadly armor piercing rounds in thunderous unison.

The first salvo fell short of hitting *Neptune*, although in O'Conor's mind they hadn't come short enough from hitting their target. *Neptune* was still turning hard to port at full speed, trying to keep the burning hulk between it and the German heavy cruiser which was clearing passed the wreckage.

He swore inwardly at himself for not being more cautious in approaching the burning tanker. Had he kept the speed at half he could have maneuvered *Neptune* quicker and possibly even gotten in the first shot when the German had suddenly appeared. Not having his own aerial plane suddenly seemed like a deadly impediment. The German obviously did not have that problem.

His own guns were now zeroing in on the German cruiser ten thousand meters to starboard. Though the heaviest guns *Neptune* sported were eight six-inch guns and hardly a match for the thick armor of a German heavy cruiser. This was going to be a slugging match and he knew it.

"All batteries fire! Return fire!" Commander MacMillan shouted his order.

Seconds later the light cruiser lit up with return fire. Its mid-sized guns opened fire on the larger German. The six-inch gun barrels belched out streams of fire with each round. A mass of semi-armor piercing rounds took all of sixteen seconds to reach its target, ten thousand meters away. Sprays of water splashed upwards near the *Graf Spee* as five of its six rounds missed the target. A sixth round impacted against the enemy ship's thick armor.

The exchange of fire continued.

There was a loud whomping sound against the forward hull as the enemy shell impacted with little more than a large ding to show for the hit. He'd expected his own first salvo to fall short, it was little more than an attempt to show strength and send the British into a panic, which he guessed he had succeeded at. The enemy light cruiser was now straightening out from its turn and heading perpendicular from *Graf Spee* at high speed, its aft batteries rotating and preparing a second salvo.

Graf Spee was clearing the burning tanker, the second set of it's huge eleven-inch guns bearing down against the British warship, correcting its elevation as the distance between the two vessels began to get shorter.

A second full salvo from the British vessel opened fire. A *Leander*-class light cruiser was equipped with few guns capable of damaging anything larger than a ship its own size. Only eight six-inch guns adorned its deck, hardly capable of piercing the armor of a German heavy cruiser. It's only saving grace was its quicker reload and targeting time.

Of the rounds fired, two impacted against the forecastle of the huge German.

Captain Langsdorff watched through the bridge window and shook his head.

Pathetic, he thought.

"Fire!"

His forward guns, having settled on a firing position, opened fire, sending six huge rounds at the British. It took just under sixteen and a half seconds to see the results. Five rounds missed. The sixth scored a hit. Even at ten thousand meters out the result could be seen in the form of a fireball rising from the enemy cruiser.

HMS Neptune shuddered as the enemy round tore deep into her armor decking and exploded. For a moment the floor fell out beneath them. The huge round cut a three-foot hole into the hull and sent an explosion climbing skywards.

The British guns quickly fired back a reply at the enemy.

"Lieutenant Harper!" O'Conor yelled. "Radio in. Request immediate assistance. Request that French battleship come to our aid!"

Harper acknowledged the order and went to work.

Captain O'Conor turned to his exec. "Commander," he put his hand on MacMillan's arm. "Damage report."

The taller first officer, put down the telephone he had been speaking into. "Direct hit to our number two boiler. Bulkheads are secure. Fire crews on their way."

"Casualties?"

MacMillan shook his head. "No information yet but. . . ." He blinked and sighed. "They're going to be heavy no doubt."

"Can we get the boiler back up?"

"They're working on it now, sir. Chief Crosby needed ten minutes to get a handle on things. I gave him four."

From the rear of the ship came the sound of return fire from *Neptune's* aft batteries. The hit to the boiler could, O'Conor knew, already have been the kill shot. With only one boiler down he'd only be able to make just under twenty knots. The German could very easily close the distance between the two ships in that time.

O'Conor wiped the sweat from his forehead and looked back towards the enemy warship six miles in their rear.

"Four minutes. . . ."

Another whomping sound and then another. The British gunners had indeed adjusted their sights and gotten in two more hits on *Graf Spee* just as the German had turned in on a straight-line course, bearing down on her prey.

The single hit on the British ship had sent a fireball explosion from the midsection of the enemy vessel. The deck lookouts had reported a direct hit on what appeared to be the aft boiler of the light cruiser. For a handful of seconds smoke towered out from the wound he'd inflicted on them, but it lasted only a little while, which meant either his shot hadn't done the damage he'd hoped for or the Royal Navy sailors on board that ship were very good at their damage control.

"Two hits to our bow, sir," Walter Kay reported. "No damage."

Captain Langsdorff stood in the center of the flag bridge as a paragon of cool professionalism. The window armor plates had been half lowered to shield those on the bridge from enemy fire.

"They got lucky," Kay commented.

"No, Commander. We're the ones who got lucky," Captain Langsdorff told him. "We got lucky by spotting them first. They had no air patrol, and we did. Killing that tanker drew them in, but their lack on aerial cover gave us the advantage." He shook his head in disapproval. "Foolish move. One has to wonder what was going through the head of their captain."

From the bow came the deafening sound of *Graf Spee*'s guns firing again.

Captain Rory O'Conor wondered to himself what the hell he could've done differently. His lone seaplane had been down for repairs depriving him of his ability to see exactly what it was that was in front of him.

Damn, he thought to himself. *Damn myself and damn the damned French for not backing me up.*

"Incoming!" One of the enlisted men shouted from the outside deck.

Graf Spee's huge eleven inchers opened up on the escaping *Neptune*, her own guns responding at almost the same instant. No doubt the meager British rounds were passing by the German shells in midair in what seemed like a pathetic attempt at retribution. His own shells were simply no match for the armor of a heavy cruiser. The guns of the French battleship *Strasbourg* could have torn the German to pieces but, alas, the French captain had decided to not act in concert with his Royal Navy counterpart.

"Helm ten degrees to starboard!" O'Conor shouted his command.

HMS Neptune altered heading just half a second before the first enemy shell fell just yards off the port side stern coming dangerously close to the ship's propellers. Secondary enemy shells fell far short in *Neptune's* wake, sending up geysers of water as they came crashing down. His own gun crews fired off their own rounds at the pursuing German.

For each hit that the German got in with her massive guns, the British would have to get in two or three just to call it even and even then they'd have to land on the same spot two or three times. A German heavy gun could blow holes in *Neptune* like Swiss cheese. One well-placed armor piercing round, like the single one already taken, could prove ultimately deciding.

Neptune's only advantage against the superior foe was her speed and maneuverability and, maybe, the twenty-five years of experience of her captain.

Less than ten thousand meters to aft the German was closing, making two knots more than *Neptune* could make right now. *Graf Spee* could reload her forward guns every twenty-four seconds, adding in for adjusting her bearings and flight time of the shell, O'Conor had just about forty seconds before the next rounds came. He mentally noted that fact.

The smaller British guns could reload faster than the German could but lacked the destructive impact of the huge rounds of the enemy.

"Sir!" The captain turned his head toward Sub Lieutenant Harper. "Casualty report from the boiler room."

Captain O'Conor held up his hand. "Not right now, Lieutenant." Harper shut his mouth instantly. "What's the status of repairs?"

"Chief Crosby's still working on it, sir. The damage was more severe than we thought. Crosby and three other men are all that's down there. They're cut off down there, sir. The bulkheads held but damage has barricaded the access points. It's going to take a while to clear it away."

O'Conor scowled. "Damn," he whispered. "Have Lieutenant Stephenson coordinate the damage control efforts himself. They've got to get through down there or those men in the boiler room'll suffocate to death." He patted Harper on the back and sent him on his way without waiting for acknowledgment.

That first hit could not have landed in a worse place, and it was a one in a hundred shot. O'Conor almost half complimented the German gunners who had scored it. The arced shell had come in high and descended right on top of the light cruiser, plowing straight through the thin armor around the rear stack and ripped a hole ten feet deep, exploding just atop the boiler room. Boiler rooms aboard navy vessels were notoriously dangerous under any conditions and could become unbearably hot in very little time. Any crew in that compartment could very well be cooked to death without ventilation or the boiler could well explode and sink the ship.

O'Conor looked over at his first officer who was half standing out the port side lookout hatchway. Commander MacMillan looked back at his captain.

"I don't know who I hate more right now. The German or the French," O'Conor told him and a small grin graced MacMillian's face.

"Before the day is over, I think you'll have made up your mind, sir."

The notoriety of Royal Navy gunners was legendary and every sailor around the world knew of the long tradition to dedication of duty that British sailors were instilled with. Indeed, many of the great naval battles of the last three hundred and fifty years involved them. Starting with the great victory of the English Queen Elizabeth over the Spanish armada followed by their victories at the Nile, Quiberon Bay and Jutland which solidified Britain's control of the seas and of course the crowning achievement against Napoleon at Trafalgar.

Today was no different. The dutiful British gunners, outmatched as they were, had scored more direct hits than his own gunners had. Although unknown to Captain Langsdorff at the time, his single round scored had done more damage than all that the British shells that had found their target.

Langsdorff looked out the forward viewport with displeasure at the scorched deck plating and the sight of the main anchor chain which had taken a direct hit. Fortunately, the anchor had been designed to take such a hit and was holding together but it would not be easy to repair. The German commerce raider was far from a friendly port and retreating all the way back to German territory would be highly dangerous.

Still, he mentally tipped his hat to the British gunners.

He looked quickly over at the clock on the wall. 1157 hours. Only twelve minutes since the first exchange of fire. In previous wars enemy vessels typically passed each other in parallel formations, mirroring each other, firing vast broadsides at the other. Usually in those scenarios it had come down to the simple math of which side had more ships. More ships equaled more firepower. In those instances the British had almost always come out on top, having had the largest navy in the world.

But this was a different kind of war. Now ships of war moved and maneuvered more like the armored units of the army. Moving fast, hitting hard and avoiding the other's shots. Singular cruisers and battleships could now square off on nearly equal footing.

Langsdorff had mastered this art during his interwar service. It was a quality which had landed him his current command. He understood the new rules for battles at sea and he intended to teach this lesson to the British today.

"Keep us on him," he ordered his helmsman. "Be prepared. The Englishman will try to evade us."

"Aye, Captain," the helmsman acknowledged.

The bridge was bustling with activity. The crew had been drilled and drilled at such things and had responded well in the previous weeks when encountering enemy merchantmen. But there was a big difference between the crew of a merchantman or tanker versus a fully armed British warship.

Today the boys were getting a taste of real blood.

The forward turret again adjusted its sights on the enemy vessel.

"She's turning to port, sir!" Lieutenant Wattenberg reported. He looked over at Langsdorff and grinned. "Just as you said, sir."

The main guns fired.

"Ten degrees to port!" Captain O'Conor ordered, the helm quickly acknowledging.

O'Conor began tapping his fingertips against his leg, mentally counting down the seconds in his head.

"Incoming!" The lookouts called out.

HMS Neptune had already begun turning to port. O'Conor had done his utmost best to time it perfectly with just seconds to spare. He knew that the German captain was trying to close the distance between the two ships and with the hit to the rear boiler slowing them down, he was accomplishing just that. The only sensible course of action was to zigzag in order to avoid the enemy's ranging shots. *Neptune* still had the advantage of maneuverability.

The ship cut to port and tried to put more distance between them and their pursuer. The exchange of gun fire continued.

Commander MacMillan stood in the doorway, moving his head back and forth between his captain and the enemy in their rear. Captain O'Conor, stood nearly motionless, his eyes drifted off into nothingness, his mind carefully counting down the seconds.

He stood nearly statuesque in the center of the bridge, his eyes glued straight ahead towards the forward bow. The seconds ticked away and ticked away....

Finally, he snapped his head up and shouted, "HARD TO STAR-BOARD!!"

The helmsman yanked the wheel back in the opposite direction. The sailors on the lookouts retreated back into the protected bridge just as the ship changed its direction yet again and veered back to starboard.

The deck pitched as the ship made its hard turn. Men shifted their body weight to keep straight. The tip of the bow swung to starboard, the hull dragged across the ocean in a high-speed turn.

To port, three shells fell into the empty sea, splashing into the water harmlessly as they missed their target.

Neptune's starboard side began to turn perpendicular to the enemy vessel. Her gun turrets brought themselves to bear on the approaching enemy ship. The starboard side torpedo launchers were loaded and ready, their crews standing by for the launch order. As soon as the light cruiser straightened out of her turn, he'd fire everything he had at the German, turning all her guns towards the giant. She'd be exposing her sides to the *Graf Spee*'s larger guns and giving up some of the distance between them, but they'd also be throwing everything they had back at the German.

Graf Spee was squarely on the horizon. *Neptune's* guns were primed and ready. Its course opened up its maximum firepower at the risk of exposing its own silhouette.

The aft guns let loose, followed a second and a half later by the bow six-inch guns. Her torpedo tubes swung out as far as they could, ready to send out a full spread of the lethal torpedoes just as soon as they got the go ahead.

"Torpedoes in the water!" One of the lookouts hollered out.

Captain O'Conor and Commander MacMillan snapped their heads towards the starboard lookout, his binoculars up against his eyes, his finger pointing out to sea.

"I gave no order to fire!" O'Conor snapped but instantly knew that the lookout was not reporting on an outgoing torpedo, but an incoming one.

Commander MacMillan held up his binoculars to scan the sea. "Torpedo bearing zero five zero, sir!"

O'Conor put his hands up to shade his eyes from the sun.

The incoming torpedo was shooting straight in, only fifteen hundred meters out, running at just under twenty-three meters per second. At that heading and speed the torpedo would hit them square in the starboard beam. There was no way that the shot had been fired from *Graf Spee* she was too far out.

"Reduce speed to half," O'Conor ordered. "Come to heading two niner zero!"

The helmsman again acknowledged the order and began swinging the wheel back in the opposite direction, engines cutting their speed, letting the ship maneuver faster than she otherwise would have.

MacMillan scanned the sea. He couldn't possibly fathom that the torpedo came from *Graf Spee*, it was still too far off.

In the ever-decreasing distance the German heavy cruiser fired off another salvo.

Two more British shells found their target with excellent precision, both striking *Graf Spee* on the forward deck, one shell coming just shy of the forward turret house, sending up a shower of deck plating. Another enemy shell was heard flying by the upper bridge deck with only inches to spare before passing overhead and splashing down into the ocean behind her.

"Enemy vessel is turning to port again, sir," a crewman reported.

U- 35 had reported firing off a single torpedo at the retreating enemy ship. The British must have been turning to avoid that shot. Langsdorff had hoped that the torpedo had found its target of course, saved him the trouble, but in war a good commander must always expect the unexpected. He was sure that the enemy commander had certainly not expected the sudden arrival of a U-boat as he'd turned his ship into the wind in an attempt to get all his guns to bear on Graf Spee.

His failure to foresee that had forced the enemy ship to turn back away from the pursuing heavy cruiser in a vain attempt to try and outrun or outmaneuver him. But the time involved in all this maneuvering had allowed Langsdorff to close the distance down to almost eight thousand five hundred meters.

"Captain, sir," Ensign Gerhardt said. The young man was standing along the bulkhead wall, a radio headset over his right ear. "Forward turret ready."

Langsdorff nodded. "Open fire."

"Fire!" Gerhardt ordered into his microphone.

The gun barrels erupted once again, their trajectory set lower than it had previously been. The Brit had been good at evading the higher angled shots with great success, let them try and evade what was coming for them now. The torpedo had forced him into a course he had not expected to make. Now was the time to push the advantage and end the chase.

Three watermelon sized rounds were unleashed at the British warship. The huge six hundred- and sixty-pound shells traveled at damn near seven hundred meters per second, skimming just feet above the ocean surface at an ever-decreasing angle. By the time they got to their target the huge shells should hit just at or right below the water line of the British light cruiser. Even one good shot could effectively cripple him.

The British bore away. Its direction changed yet again. No doubt its crew was in a state of panicked confusion. The sudden slowdown in the cruiser's speed had let it turn away quicker than she would have if she'd been moving at full. Their commander was obviously experienced but had walked into something that he was not prepared for. How things might have been had the British plane had been airborne.

The German shells fell just seconds later sending up a ball of smoke and fire. The heavy rounds hit the aft quarter. It took just a couple of seconds for the sound wave to reach them. Smoke drifted up and away from the enemy vessel.

"Ensign, order our aerial observer to pass by the British. Report on her damage."

"Yes, sir."

Captain Langsdorff dropped his binoculars down to his chest and donned a wolfish grin.

The entire ship seemed to jump up out of the water as the shells struck. Captain O'Conor had barely enough time to grab a hold of a handlebar to keep from tumbling over. Though he had not yet seen it for himself he needed no help in immediately realizing the damage that had just been inflicted on them,

Twice today he'd walked straight into a fight. The first time he should've known better and been more cautious. The second time was unforeseeable. That torpedo that was closing on them must have come from a Nazi submarine. It must have. He didn't think that any U-boats had made it this far away from continental Europe, but he'd guessed wrong.

Captain O'Conor steadied himself and rushed out to the closest look-out to view the damage to his ship. It was bad. They'd taken at least one direct hit to the aft quarter. Debris was falling away from the ship and smoke trailed away. On deck at least six sailors were down, he couldn't make out whether they were still moving or not through the smoke in the air. A second later the aft ensign came loose, and the flag fell overboard.

"Get me a damage report, dammit!" He turned his head back towards the bridge and ordered.

Harper, who was holding his hand to the right side of his head, nodded. "Aye, sir."

The hard impact suggested that the ship had taken more than one hit. The German's eleven-inch shells could rip through the aft section's thinner armor like a machine gun through plywood. Naval ships had been designed to be better armored at the bow and its sides. The rear of the ship was always the most vulnerable.

Commander MacMillan moved behind O'Conor and shouted for the helmsman to straighten out his course. The tall naval officer turned back towards the approaching torpedo and watched as the stream of bubbles darted through the ocean surface. MacMillan and O'Conor watched together as the torpedo range closed even as *Neptune* turned her bow away from the incoming lance. Both men silently prayed against all hopes that it would miss and for one brief second it almost looked as if it would. But it didn't.

The torpedo slammed into the starboard bow and in one deafening moment sent the forward section of the ship exploding upwards while the rest of the ship sank back beneath the water surface. The explosion from the torpedo impact sent enough force through the main hull to literally break the ship in half. The main bridge broke away from the forward bow in one thunderous moment. The forward deck rose, sending the forward turret skywards and killing any crew that was manning it.

Screams were heard and bodies of sailors were blown in a dozen different directions, splinters of wood and metal shards flew out like porcupine quills ripping other men to pieces. A second of a heartbeat later the bridge erupted sending the men inside flying into the compartment ceiling. The lucky ones wouldn't even feel their skulls crushed by the bulkhead. Anyone not lucky would die slowly of blood loss or the fireball that encompassed the bridge like an oven.

Captain O'Conor, not having enough time to react to the impact, was swept up off his feet. The explosion drove his body six feet into the air before dropping him down onto the observation deck and landing on his back with the force of some god of war. His spine snapped in a millisecond. He tried to call out in pain but was not even sure if he was making a sound. The only thing his ears could hear was the rippling explosion.

The ship was dead.

Next to O'Conor, Commander MacMillan's leg twitched like some pulsating organ, though it was only attached to the younger man by a mass of bloody, entangled sinews, bone and tissue, his leg having been ripped almost completely off by the blast. The rest of his body was lying face down on the deck with his head split open.

O'Conor struggled to lift his head up and look down at his broken legs. He lay there on his broken back and watched as a soundless explosion balled upwards, smoke belching out of every corner of his ship He twisted his head backwards and saw what was left of his first officer. Though the explosion seemed to have robbed him of his hearing before he closed his eyes, he swore he could hear the sounds of screaming.

CHAPTER TWENTY

Everything was coming apart. The policy of appeasing Hitler by granting him whole territories on the continent seemed to be failing. Then there was the delicate government coalition that he had formed by stitching together Conservative, Liberal and Labour party goers that he had agreed to let serve in his government that was now failing. Then there was his grasp on his own Conservative Party that seemed to be slipping away. And now even his health was failing him.

Chamberlain was dying.

The doctors had initially hidden his diagnosis from him, convinced him he was suffering from common stomach ailments, but the pain had persisted for months now until it had become simply unbearable.

His features were gaunt, his skin had lost what little color he ever had, his nights grew shorter, and the days grew longer. He had found sleeping was becoming next to impossible without taking pills. He was eating less and less each day and he'd lost enough weight that his clothing was getting too big for him.

The first person to notice the change in him was, of course, his beloved wife Anne. As all dutiful wives, she began to suspect there was a problem early on and had strongly urged him to go see a doctor, which he had. The doctor had told him it was probably from the stress of his position and had given him some concoction to help settle his stomach. After just a few days the pains had just gotten progressively worse, but he had steadfastly refused to get a second opinion, chalking his symptoms up to nothing more than the strain of governing a country on the brink of war.

But it was not the stress nor strain that had ailed him. After seeing specialists at the hospital and undergoing an exploratory procedure he'd initially been told by those very doctors that they had found cancer in his bowels but that it was not any cause for alarm. They had told him the cancer was not deadly and that his lifelong excellent health would make recovery quick and easy. A follow up procedure in May had removed the cancer and the surgeons told him that he would not have to have any more surgeries and that the matter had been fully resolved.

But that had been a lie. The cancer had been terminal. The doctors knew that six weeks ago but had hidden the truth from him. Now it was only a matter of time.

Chamberlain knew what he had to do. Only his closest friends and family had known about it. He had not told anybody in government about his condition, not yet anyway. But as the Prime Minister of the United Kingdom and as a lifelong servant of that government, he knew that he had a duty to inform at least one more person.

George the Sixth, his Imperial Majesty, King of Great Britain and Emperor of India and all the other titles that he held, stood in his private office in Buckingham Palace, his arms not behind his back as usual but hanging at his side, his fingertips running back and forth along the bottom of his Royal Navy uniform jacket. He gasped for a few moments and his expression was that of total and utter shock. Finally, the King licked his dry lips and found his words.

"How long?"

"Do I have?" The King nodded. Chamberlain shook his head once. "Months perhaps." There was no sadness in his voice. He was a servant of the King and the King needed to know.

"I pray God this is not true," the King told him. He reached into the breast of his jacket and pulled out his silver cigarette case. The King was a notorious chain smoker.

Neville cleared his throat and gave His Majesty a gracious smile. "I thank Your Majesty for his thoughts and prayers. I am afraid the prognosis is quite certain."

King George lit up another of what would be many cigarettes throughout the day. "Can nothing be done? We have some of the best doctors in the world here in London. There must be something that can be done."

"I'm afraid not, Your Majesty. I've been to the very best doctors and the very best hospitals. It is, as they say, written in stone." He let the words sink in for a moment, the King took a long drag of his cigarette. "I'm afraid that we have an unenviable set of decisions that will have to be made in the very near future."

King George nodded at the Prime Minister. There was a job to do and a nation to govern. As King he was the titular head of that nation and his head of government had just informed him of his impending death. "Of course. The government."

"It must survive, Your Majesty. My own mortality aside there must be stability in government."

His Majesty nodded his head in agreement. "You're right of course. Dare I ask what thoughts you've given on this matter?"

Chamberlain's eyebrows furrowed. His Majesty gestured for the two to sit on the sofas across from each other. Chamberlain sat, crossed his hands in his lap.

"Halifax of course should become my replacement," Chamberlain told the King, not a hint of doubt in his voice. "He and I have worked well together, and he sees things very much like how Your Majesty and I see them. He's well respected and the cabinet will support him as Prime Minister."

King George crossed his legs and cupped his left knee in his hand. "But will Parliament? Halifax is seen as being very close to you indeed, Prime Minister. Not to be disrespectful, but your own position in Parliament isn't what it once was."

Chamberlain bit his lower lip for a moment and reluctantly nodded. "That is true, Your Majesty," he conceded. "The government has lost much support from the opposition. No doubt Attlee will come out against him. Halifax is not popular with either Labour or the Liberals."

"Not just the opposition," the King said bluntly. "The Conservatives are not exactly in lock step. My ears tell me that Lord Halifax has grown unpopular with many of them. That might pose a big problem if even a handful oppose him. Governing is difficult enough with the opposing parties, but next to impossible if your own party is splintered on the issue."

"Yes. I've given that matter some thought, Your Majesty. Some in the party may oppose it, but no doubt any new Prime Minister would choose to shake up his cabinet. All new Prime Ministers like to bring in new faces, fresh ideas. Halifax is as conservative a man as you'll find anywhere in London, but he's also a pragmatist. He believes in compromise. He could coax support by offering some cabinet positions here and there, pick up support from the ruling party."

The King hesitated to speak for a moment, gave thought to his words. "Forgive me, Prime Minister, but I doubt very much that simply shaking up the cabinet would solve all of your problems and I doubt your own party would just fall in line behind Lord Halifax should he pick up the baton." He took another long drag on his cigarette, let it out noisily. "Have you spoken about this with him yet?"

Chamberlain instantly shook his head. "My duty compelled me to inform Your Majesty with this information before I spoke with anyone else. Only my wife and a very few of my family knows yet. However, I cannot say that the subject of his becoming PM has not come up in conversation in the past. We have discussed such a possibility before."

"Well, there is a substantial difference between discussing such things over a casual dinner with an old friend and actually having to discuss it as a real possibility." The King's words came out almost like an old schoolteacher educating a young student. The shock of the news of the imminent death of his Prime Minister, having been put aside, both men understood all too well the importance of having a functioning government especially during wartime.

"You're not wrong, Your Majesty." The older Prime Minister hesitated for a moment then said, "I thought we'd have more time."

The King understood the feeling. "Unfortunately, we aren't always afforded the luxury of picking and choosing the time for things. I can tell you that speaking from experience. Getting back to the subject at hand, however, I do fear with the current situation we find our country in and with the friction in both houses of Parliament that any government Halifax attempts to form would be met with resistance. There is a wing of the Conservative Party that does not support the current foreign policy of this government. Lord Halifax has, what do they say in America? Hitched his wagons to yours as far as that goes.

Chamberlain smirked. "As always, Your Majesty, you've quite adeptly deduced the situation. Do you recall what we discussed at our last meeting? About our reaching out to Berlin?" The King nodded. "Well, we've been having some measure of success on that front. Our embassy in Rome has been in direct touch with Signor Mussolini. Halifax has been in direct contact with Ciano, Italy's Foreign Minister. We've been given assurances that our overtures will be discussed with Hitler, if they have not already. Mussolini has been very effective in the past when acting as a go-between. The Swiss have also agreed to mediate on our behalf as well. Both Lord Halifax and I feel very confident about reaching a solution to this entire matter in the near future. Before things get too out of hand."

"I see. Does your friend in Paris agree with you on this?"

Chamberlain grimaced. "Monsieur Daladier and I have a difference of opinion when it comes to dealing with Hitler, I'm afraid. We worked in close concert with each other previously, even before Munich, but the French Prime Minister has come to believe that Hitler has no intention of honoring any agreement we make with him. Honestly. . . . I can't say that I blame him. The history between France and Germany has been fraught with conflict in the last century. I believe the French still live in the shadow of nineteen fourteen."

"Hard to blame them. I supported you when it came to dealing with that man in Berlin in the beginning, supported you through the Munich conference and with Czechoslovakia and through all of that and I support you now, Prime Minister. However, I would be remiss if I did not tell you right now that I have a, I don't know, a reservation about the way we handled it all."

"You mean appeasement?"

"I find myself thinking of the bible about it all. You know, unchaining Lucifer from the pit and all that. Hitler has shown nothing but disdain for diplomacy, no matter what offerings you make."

"I'm not ready to give up on it, Your Majesty. Neither is Edward, uh, Lord Halifax that is. And he's shown that he can do the job just as good as any man. Besides, I can think of no other man in government right now that the House of Commons would get behind. No other man."

An awkward silence fell between the two men and the same thought ran through both of their minds. The opposition parties disliked Halifax intensely seeing him as too closely associated with Chamberlain, both men had supported the foreign policy of appeasing the Nazis. Although the Conservative Party had once supported that policy as well, in recent months a fracture had occurred which threatened the entire government. Chamberlain's once big tent coalition had dwindled down to just a handful now and even that seemed to be threatened.

"There is Churchill," Chamberlain stated offhandedly.

His Majesty's features seemed to indicate that he was not in favor of that idea. He sneered at the suggestion. "Churchill..." The King shook his head at the thought.

"He's the only other one I can think of, Your Majesty," The Prime Minister told him, though the tone of his voice said he was not in favor of that idea. "Although, like you, I think that would not be in the best interests of the nation."

"Not in the best interest of the nation? It would be a disaster for the nation," the King spat. "My personal feelings about that man aside, I just don't trust him to lead us to where we need to go. His policies are all wrong. And with us now at war.... well, the name Gallipoli comes to mind."

"I agree with you, Your Majesty. The wrong man. His only saving grace is that many in the Commons support him. Even Attlee supported him back into government. Gave me very little choice in fact. I had to bring him back or face no confidence. No matter how bad some of his policies may seem, he always seems to have friends in the party who support him. Also, in fairness, Gallipoli was not entirely his fault. His plan was a good one."

"Then there was India and Africa too for that matter," the King retorted. "And the abdication."

The King's personal dislike for Churchill had extended even further when Winston had backed the King's older brother Edward after almost everyone else was calling for Edward to abdicate the throne back in '36. The short reign of King Edward VIII after less than a year had been a political scandal that had rocked Britain and had resulted in his brother's abdication and his own ascension to the crown. Churchill's public support for Edward, and thus not for George, had been an insult and had left the new king with a bad taste in his mouth for the man.

"So, Halifax really is the only choice," Chamberlain replied. "As it is, I'm not proud of it, but Halifax could not do any worse than I could. Perhaps even succeed where I have failed."

The King locked eyes with the older man sitting across from him. There was so much dignity in the Prime Minister that he felt a need to defend the man against himself.

"That will be just about enough of that," His Majesty said, a note of authority in his voice. "You have succeeded in many things where others have not."

For a moment it seemed to the King like Chamberlain had held back some emotion over the words, but then, before he would succumb to them, he composed himself. "Thank you, Your Majesty. Your words are most kind. So, Halifax is our man."

The King nodded. "It seems so. I hate to be so callous about it, but the time has come Prime Minister. There's no avoiding it anymore." He finished the cigarette he was smoking and tossed the butt into the tray on the table next to him. "You'll have to speak with him about it and it'll have to be very soon. Such matters of state cannot be delayed."

Neville nodded his agreement. "Once again, Your Majesty has put it quite adeptly."

Churchill put down the midday cigar that he was smoking in his ashtray and looked out the window of his private office at the War Office in Westminster. He had a stack of reports sitting on his desk that painted a dismal picture on multiple fronts. Although there had been gains made in the past few weeks, the greater situation was not looking good.

In order to deny Germany key operating bases in the North Atlantic and North Sea, the Royal Marines had moved to capture Iceland and the Faroe Islands off the Scottish coast. Likewise, Canada had sent an entire infantry brigade to occupy the Danish possession of Greenland. An initial British plan to occupy Greenland had been abandoned after consultation with the United States indicated that the Americans would not look kindly on a European power grabbing land in the western hemisphere. The operation was quickly changed to have the Royal Canadian Army capture the huge territory. A resolution that did not violate the American's so-called Monroe Doctrine.

These minor victories aside, the momentum of war was still very much on the German side. Despite a few successes at sea the U-boats were taking a terrible toll on British shipping. Tens of thousands of tons of supplies had already been sunk by the German Navy and it was only going to get worse as more and more of the killer submarines streamed into the Atlantic.

On the continent the German Army was now firmly in control of Poland, that country's industrial and natural resources now added to that of the Third Reich and would prove to be quite formidable in the coming months or even years. In France, the huge French Army after a rather brief and unsuccessful foray into Germany, was now sitting still behind their famously built defensive line along the Franco-German border, the British Expeditionary Force holding the northern flank, nobody moving so much as an inch in what was beginning to look like a repeat of the brutal trench warfare waged in the previous conflict. To top it off the situation in Norway was getting worse by the day. Hitler's decision to take that country at the same time as his forces stormed across Poland proved to be a correct one. The speed at which the German forces were now advancing northwards was alarming. The British generals in that country had failed to move with sufficient speed in order to stop the Nazis or even slow them down. Now only two pockets of British troops remained and both, he knew, would be hopelessly lost if not evacuated in the coming days.

And if these developments were not bad enough then there was also the latest diplomatic cable that had come through in the early hours this morning. The Red Army had just launched an invasion into Finland. Stalin had struck at last.

There was a light knock at the door.

"Come in," Winston answered. The door opened, Commander Thompson stepped into the room. He was dressed, as usual, in his Royal Navy dress uniform with gold aiguillette cord hanging around his shoulder.

"Sir, I have General Ironside and Admiral Pound here. They're asking for some of your time."

Winston's forehead creased in confusion. The uniform heads of the army and navy were not just any visitors by any means, but it was not usual for either of the two to just casually drop by the War Office to meet with a senior cabinet official, let alone for both to show up unannounced and without an appointment.

"They're here now?" Winston asked and Commander Thompson gave an affirming reply. Winston blinked in confusion, picked up his cigar and puffed away again. "See them in."

Both men strolled into the Minister's office, caps in hand. General Ironside, head of the Imperial General Staff, was a bear of a man who towered over most people. He had had a long career in the British Army, having commanded British troops in South Africa, France and the Middle East. He'd originally been pegged to take command of the BEF, now occupied by Lord Gort, but had been offered his current position instead. Admiral Dudley Pound by contrast was a much shorter man with a small frame. His health had been rumored to be bad and it showed. His current age of sixty-three would make him eligible to retire from the service, however, other admirals of the same rank and time in service were seen as even more sickly than Admiral Pound was.

"Gentlemen," Winston greeted them in a confused and slightly harsh tone.

"Minister, thank you for taking the time to see us," Admiral Pound said. "I know that this situation is most unusual."

Churchill nodded in stern agreement. "Most unusual. Some may even use the word improper," he put extra emphasis on that last word. Heads of the uniform services answered directly to their respective cabinet secretaries, in this case the Secretary of State for War and the First Lord of the Admiralty. These men had spent their entire careers obeying and respecting a chain of command and their presence here today could be interpreted as a violation of that.

"Yes," Admiral Pound replied in a semi apologetic voice. "We both understand how it must seem and how it could be interpreted, however after carefully thinking the matter through," he spared a quick glance at General Ironside, "we both felt that it was absolutely necessary."

Smoke rings floated up and away from the burning cigar. Churchill was leaning back in his chair, the look on his face did nothing to hide his dissatisfaction with either man.

"Go on," he said.

General Ironside cleared his throat, the bulky general shifted his weight from one foot to the other. Churchill had not offered them a chair to sit and both men knew better than to ask for one.

"First off, Minister both the Admiral and I wish to express our regrets at having so occupied your time and by not giving notice of ourselves before coming here today. As Admiral Pound has said, we did not think that it could be helped. As I'm sure you've surmised, both of us are here today without the knowledge or approval of War Secretary Hore-Belisha or the First Lord of the Admiralty. It is because of them and not despite them that we felt we had to come here today. There have been a number of, shall we say, incidents, that we felt we could no longer look the other way."

"Or keep quiet," Pound added.

Winston plucked his cigar from his mouth. "What are you referring to? If it's more about Leslie Hore-Belisha and his relationship with the General Staff, you've wasted my time and your own, gentlemen. I might also add, you may have very well ended both of your careers with this behind the back escapade."

"Behind the back, sir?" Admiral Pound replied in an innocent tone, His voice sounded almost hurt by the comment. "Certainly not how we would put it, Minister. Believe me when I tell you, that the General's words are heartfelt for the both of us. If either of us thought for one second there was a chance to make our case to either the Secretary or the First Lord, we would do so." He hesitated, his face had gone flush, and his breathing was heavy. "However, neither of our superiors have seemed all that interested in hearing us out."

"Indeed, sir. Secretary Hore-Belisha does not even bother to communicate with me much anymore," the General added to his colleague. "I have not even been invited to any of his briefings with the Prime Minister and I fear my memos and reports on our military readiness have been completely disregarded."

Winston took a slow inhale of his cigars. He had noted on more than one occasion of the lack of uniformed military personnel at war meetings. While the Secretary of War did not know of it, Winston's eyes and ears had informed him of the growing rift between Hore-Belisha and the Imperial Staff and field generals. His own personal correspondence with General Gort in France had reinforced this growing chasm between the Secretary and the army. Churchill had tried the political route in order to cure the problem by centralizing more authority within his department, but it was taking time to put it all together.

"I know of the disagreements between the army and the Secretary of State for War, but I'm a little surprised to see you here, Admiral. I've not heard of any animosity between yourself and the First Lord. Have I heard wrongly?"

Admiral Pound shook his head and ran his bony hand through his wispy gray hair. "You have not, sir. I, well, I must say honestly that I've stayed rather quiet on many things when I wish now I'd spoken out about. While I do not have any personal dislike for the First Lord...." he coughed, "I have found myself in a position where my own counsel to Lord Stanhope has been disregarded or ignored. I'm an old man now, Minister Churchill and I don't have the same strength that I once had, God knows. But I've given this nation and the service a lifetime of devotion, and right now I'm watching as that service and that nation is being put at risk."

Churchill listened to the two men, careful to keep his demeanor calm and neutral. He had served in the army and had served as First Lord of the Admiralty before and he knew both services well, had much respect for those wearing the uniform. But he also had no love for those that side stepped the chain of command no matter what their intentions may be. That being said, he was also brought back into government to bring order from disorder and to clean up the mess that Chamberlain and his ilk had created.

He knew Admiral Pound well and knew him to be a good and honorable man. He also knew that the man was not the type to stick his neck out this far unless there was a very good reason behind it. He was too old and too sickly and had no interest in the game of politics.

"Very well, Admiral Pound, General Ironside, I am listening, however, I must warn the both of you right now that by coming here today and going down this road, you might very well be ending two very long careers. No matter what happens in the end, no matter what may come of this or my own personal feelings, I cannot guarantee that by the end of the day you will still be wearing those uniforms. With that said, you have two choices before you. You may both turn around and walk out now if you wish, in which case this matter will go unspoken. If you stay, well. . . ." he took a long puff of his cigar, "the consequences will be yours to accept."

The room was quiet for several moments. Neither Ironside nor Pound said a word or moved an inch. Churchill shrugged then said, "Very well. Please begin."

CHAPTER TWENTY-ONE

Since departing Freetown in Sierra Leone on the western coast of Africa over three months earlier, the small *Odin*-class submarine had been refueled only once, three weeks earlier by a passing British tanker. The only supplies that they'd taken aboard were from the French destroyer *Fougueux* ten days earlier just after rescuing the survivors of the *Brother Lucas*, a British merchantman that was returning home from India with a hull full of cargo. The rest of the time the *Orkney* and her crew of fifty-two had been on constant patrol between West Africa and the coast of South America.

Being an island nation was both a blessing and a curse. On one hand having command of the seas around your island gave one a great strategic advantage against being attacked. In the long history of Britain only two invasions had ever been successful. The first was by the Anglo-Saxon people which had emigrated there in the fifth century. The other by William the Conqueror and his Norman invasion in the year 1066. The Romans, the Vikings, even Napoleon himself had all failed to conquer the isle.

On the other hand, being an island nation with a sizable population and suffering from a lack of resources and farmland, that country had to import many of its goods in order to survive. Supplies had to come in from all parts of the British Empire, grain and wheat came from Canada, rubber from the East Indies, oil from the Middle East, troops from every corner of the world. For Great Britain to thrive, or for that matter just survive, it required a constant flow of supplies from her overseas territories and trading partners. That required a large merchant fleet, the crews to man those vessels and large investments of money and resources to keep that merchant fleet operating.

In the past seven weeks one German heavy cruiser, *Admiral Graf Spee*, had threatened that vital supply line and run up a rather impressive tally of kills to its credit. The heavy warship turned commerce raider had sunk at least eight British and French merchant vessels since being let loose in the Atlantic. One tanker had also been captured off the coast of West Africa and used to refuel the Nazi cruiser before that ship too was sunk and her crew left adrift. Then news had come in just days ago that the raider had sunk its biggest prize in the war yet, the Royal Navy light cruiser *HMS Neptune* in an action off Dutch Guinea, the sole Dutch colony in South America. The loss of *Neptune* had sent shock waves through the sailors of the Royal Navy assigned to the squadrons that had been tasked with hunting down commerce raiders, in particular the *Admiral Graf Spee*.

HMS Orkney had the distinction of being the only ship in the Royal Navy that had even been in the vicinity of the enemy cruiser, albeit belatedly, and not become a victim of it. The first time was during the rescue of the crew of the downed merchantman *Brother Lucas* nearly two weeks earlier off Cape Verde. The second time came while patrolling the Mid Atlantic Ridge east of Brazil when, from the conning tower the lookouts had spotted a lone reconnaissance plane which had been identified as a Heinkel He 60, *Graf Spee's* lone aircraft, used to conduct long range aerial patrols to identify new victims for the surface raider.

And then there was today.

Lieutenant Commander Alistair Chadwick peered through his periscope sights and knew exactly what it was he had, there was no mistaking it. The sight of the German heavy cruiser dead astern was undeniable. The ship was emerging from out of a heavy storm. Chadwick found it ironic that every time anyone had spotted the *Graf Spee,* she always seemed to have a storm at her back.

A bad omen perhaps?

He wet his dry lips and tried to make out some detail through the periscope lens.

The Nazi looked to be zigzagging, that is shifting its course in a series of sharp turns from port to starboard and back again rather than just sailing in a straight line. Naval ships often did this in wartime in order to avoid torpedoes from submerged enemy submarines. It was costly in terms of burning a lot of fuel, but it greatly reduced the risk of being hit by enemies lurking beneath the ocean waves.

The skies behind the German cruiser lit up in a flash of brilliant lightning. Alistair chewed on the inside of his lip as he gave the horizon a full 360-degree scan. The enemy ship was dead astern and heading this way.

An *Odin*-class sub could only make about fifteen knots when running on the surface, but right now she was submerged at periscope depth and could only make nine, which was only ten miles an hour. Your average Nazi *Deutschland*-class heavy cruiser, which *Graf Spee* was, had a top speed of just about twenty-eight knots. Outrunning her was not even an option.

"Our ghost is back," Alistair said in a hushed tone, speaking to no one in particular, but he kicked himself instantly knowing that the entire control room was as silent as a graveyard waiting to hear what he had to say. He stepped back from the periscope and folded up its arms. "But she's zigzagging," he quickly added, "so she hasn't spotted us."

Sub-lieutenant Tim Dorsey was standing just feet behind him, arms folded across his chest. The young man, Alistair could see, was holding his breath in anticipation. He finally released and let out a long and quiet sigh of relief. None of the *Orkney's* crew had any experience in combat including her officers.

Alistair looked around the control room, all eyes were on him, even those who pretended to look away were giving him sideways glances.

"I put her at about fifteen kilometers out," he told his exec but made sure he was loud enough to put the others at ease. "Coming out of a storm front from the look of it so I doubt she's launched her scout plane," although he had no proof of that. This German raider was incredibly astute at naval navigation and chasing down her prey.

Rumor among the naval officer corps was that the commander of the *Graf Spee* was one of the most revered naval officers in the entire Kriegsmarine, a genius in seagoing warfare and a hero of the famed Battle of Jutland in 1916. A veteran officer with nearly three decades of experience at sea and a deadly warship in his arsenal. Chadwick had been commissioned an officer in back in '33 and although he had enough experience and seniority to merit a seagoing command, he had never seen battle and had no great wish to test himself against such a man. In addition to that his one sub was no match for a heavily armed and armored German cruiser.

"Down periscope," he ordered.

"Aye, sir," the enlisted chief, CPO MacDonnell copied. "Down periscope."

Alistair turned to MacDonnell, his chief enlisted sailor. "Chief, make our depth fifty meters. Ten degrees down bubble."

"Aye, sir. Helm, bring us to fifty meters, ten degrees down bubble!" Chief MacDonnell ordered in his thick Scottish voice.

Alistair wiped the sweat off his brow, felt the deck shift under his feet as the sub dived down further underwater. If he had been the captain of a German cruiser, the first thing he'd do, and for that matter the first thing the book would call for, is a recon patrol of the surrounding seas to get a 180 view of his front and flanks. No doubt a man such as the revered Captain Hans Langsdorff would have followed that bit of military logic.

Alistair tapped his exec on the chest with his knuckle and the two walked across the cramped control room to the small map table. He lifted the wooden lid and pulled out a stack of charts, found the one he wanted and grabbed a pencil.

"We're here," he marked the chart where their current position was, northeast of the Port of Natal on the eastern tip of Brazil, then drew a line down the coastline, ran through some numbers in his head. "At her current speed....and.... on this course she should be about here tomorrow morning." He glanced at his wristwatch. "About sixteen hours." He marked another X on the chart. "Now.... *Ark Royal* is somewhere around here, off Ascension Island. If they sail due west, their planes can be in attack range of *Graf Spee* about that same time. Give or take an hour or two." In his head that made sense, but he knew as he said it that it depended upon an accurate location of the sole British aircraft carrier operating in the South Atlantic and that was information, he could not be one hundred percent sure of.

"That's if they continue on at their same speed," Dorsey commented. "The book says the German can make twenty-eight knots at top speed."

Chadwick nodded. "And right now, she's probably cruising along at around twenty. If she goes to top speed, that would bring her to about.... about here. About seven hundred and sixty kilometers. Still within the range of *Ark Royal's* planes. But they'd have to move now."

"With all respects, sir," Dorsey began, he hesitated but Chadwick nodded for him to continue. "It's a big ocean, sir. *Graf Spee* could change course, swing northwards back towards Cape Verde or even turn west again, into the Caribbean." He tried to keep his voice down, so the men wouldn't hear them, but the control room of any sub was a small space.

"I agree he could very well do just that," Chadwick replied. "But consider this, if he was going to swing west, he'd have done so under cover of that storm. That ship's been spotted one too many times in the past couple of weeks in this area," he ran his pencil around the African coast. "A surface ship that size would be hard to miss if you had every plane and ship in the Allied fleet out looking for one there. Besides, Hitler's U-boats have enough range to cover this area, but one thing they can't do, at least not yet is reach down into the southern oceans. Think about it, Tim. A Nazi heavy cruiser prowling around off the coast of South Africa or sailing into the Indian Ocean. The sight of the swastika off India or the Spice Islands would send panic throughout the entire region. The psychological impact alone would be worth it. Now that she's been fully refueled.... Hmmm." He chewed his lip and shook his head at the repercussions of what he'd just said. "No. No he's heading south again."

Lieutenant Dorsey nodded in agreement of this. The farther south an enemy ship like that sailed, the harder it would be for any Allied warship to catch her. In fact, orders that had come in from the Admiralty at the start of the war that emphasized the need to keep the war out of the Indian and Pacific Oceans where the Royal Navy was spread even thinner than it was in the Atlantic.

Lieutenant Commander Chadwick studied his chart for a few silent moments, his fingers ran over the fine paper map as he silently planned his next move. The worst thing that could happen, he knew, was for the raider to make it south past the Cape of Good Hope and around the southern tip of Africa, free to raid like a wolf on a wide-open plain with no hunter to kill him.

There was only a single course of action.

"Radio this in, Lieutenant," he ordered Dorsey. "Give her position and heading, south by southwest at twenty knots." He lifted his head to look at his exec and the younger officer nodded.

"Aye, sir."

Chadwick looked back down at his charts. He knew that the Nazi might very well be listening for a transmission of any kind in the local area and that the chances of not having their transmission picked up on were slim to none and normal operating procedures would call for strict radio silence in almost all situations with one exception being to radio in the sighting of enemy surface ships of strategic importance. This certainly qualified as strategically important and their duty was clear, warn the fleet and call in the rest of the squadron.

He stood hunched over the chart table, his left forearm rested on the small table, the fingers of his right hand ran back and forth along his brow. There were only a few convoy routes that hugged the South American coast, imported food from Argentina mostly. The vast majority of Britain's supplies flowed from Africa, India and the Far East and went around the southern bend of Africa. Many of those convoys converged on Cape Town before sailing either east or west and that made the entire region as ripe a hunting ground for enemy activity as there could be.

There was a Royal Navy squadron that patrolled those waters, but he knew they were older cruisers and would be individually outmatched against the German warship if it came to blows. The same was true of the squadron which patrol the waters between Buenos Aires and the Falkland Islands. Most ships typically patrolled apart from each other, then radioed in to the others if an enemy was sighted. In the case of the two heavy cruisers off Cape Town. *HMS Sussex and HMS Shropshire* usually patrolled many miles apart and there was no guarantee that they were in mutual support range of each other.

But the *Graf Spee* and her skipper had not made names for themselves by sinking Allied warships. She was a commerce raider that was operating under orders to do just that, send Allied merchant vessels to the bottom of the ocean and move on and not to get sucked into surface battles with enemy ships. If the ship were to sail around the Cape no doubt she'd try to avoid Allied warships, just as she had before, but this time, fully refueled the ship could make it all the way to Japanese territory and Japan and Germany were allies, technically speaking. If the ship were to operate in the Indian Ocean out of Japanese held territory, there would be little that the Royal Navy could do about it.

Chadwick straightened back up. "Chief."

"Sir?"

"Come to port fifteen degrees please. Let's give our friend a wide berth."

"Aye, aye, sir."

Moments later *Orkney* began shifting her course. They'd let the huge warship have plenty of space to continue on its journey and to hopefully avoid detection by her. If Captain Langsdorff followed the book, then he'd get his seaplane airborne and get a good pair of eyes on the seas around him then straighten out his course shortly afterwards and make for the mid-Atlantic to save her fuel for hunting. In the meantime, *Osprey* would keep its eyes and ears on the enemy for as long as she could.

Chadwick mentally crossed his fingers and hoped to the Almighty that they could get a message to the fleet. *Ark Royal*'s air group could be the difference between stopping the enemy cruiser or allowing it to continue on its rampage. The Royal Navy listening station in Freetown should receive their transmission and provided there wasn't any politicking back at base, they'd relay the enemy vessel's heading to the carrier group.

In the meantime, *Orkney* would just lurk in the shadows and try to keep the warship within sight.

Lieutenant Dorsey came back up to Chadwick's side. "Freetown acknowledges the message was received, sir."

Alistair nodded. "Good. Rig us for silent running, Lieutenant. We'll let our friend go by us and continue her way south. When she's past this point, call it ninety-five minutes from now, we'll turn south on a course of one seven zero. If the man sticks to zig-zagging and closer to the Brazilian coast, we should be able to keep him in our sights for a while."

"If we follow that bearing don't we risk losing him, sir?"

"It's a risk, Tim. But he has nothing to hunt for along the South American coast. Eventually he's going to have to swing east into the wide Atlantic. I mean to meet him when he does. Everything's going to depend upon our squadron being in the right place at the right time."

Captain Langsdorff had just taken his first bite of the tender lamb shanks that his steward had prepared for his dinner when the yeoman arrived bearing the message folded up in his hand. Walter Kay sat across from his captain at the small cabin table. He scooped some boiled carrots up and took a sip of his Riesling. Outside the ship had finished clearing the ocean storm that had been their cover for the past six hours and the evening sunlight was setting in the western sky.

Captain Langsdorff took the folded-up paper and chewed on his lamb as he read the message.

"Mmmm." He dabbed his napkin at the edges of his mouth. A local coded transmission with no bearing had been picked up. Spotters had not seen anything on the surface or in the skies. He finished reading the note and passed it to his first officer.

"Has our seaplane launched?" He asked the yeoman.

"It's in the water now, sir."

Langsdorff finished his chewing and looked over at Walter Kay who read the note and looked back over at his captain.

He shrugged. "Could have been a weather plane flying above the storm."

"At the same time we were emerging from it? Weather planes don't encode their transmissions."

"No surface contacts spotted," Kay stated then grunted. "Enemy sub?"

"Must be," the captain replied. "We have to assume it is anyhow. And if it sent out a coded transmission, we must assume that it was sending our location and heading to its base."

Kay ran his tongue around the inside of his cheek. He was smart enough to come to the exact same conclusion. The storm had been a particularly rough one and launching their scout plane had been ruled out due to the high frequency of lightning and the high velocity winds. The decision had been made that they could not risk losing their eye in the sky and so instead sailed through the maelstrom without knowing what lay ahead of them.

"Orders, sir?" the yeoman asked.

Captain Langsdorff thought carefully for a moment. The fingers of his right hand ran up and down the stem of his wine glass.

"Have Lieutenant Ascher continue on our previously set course," he told the young sailor. "It'll be dark in an hour. We have a friend out there. Let's play his game for a minute or two."

The message had been received by the radio operator in Freetown. The young seaman manning the tower had taken the information down word for word.

Urgent. Confirmed Nazi cruiser Admiral Graf Spee spotted two hundred-forty miles east of tip of Brazil. Heading: SSW at twenty knots. 1841 GMT. Orkney out.

The young eighteen-year-old tore the message paper off its pad and handed it directly to Midshipman Pelham, his CO. Pelham read the note and went immediately to the telephone on his desk.

"Operations. Yes, sir. Midshipman Pelham here in communications. We have a high priority message from one of patrol subs. Well, sir the message reports they've sighted *Graf Spee* off the Brazilian coast. It gave a location and a heading for the ship. East southeast at twenty knots. Yes, sir. I understand, sir."

He hung up the telephone and put the note in his breast pocket. An officer from Operations would be by shortly to view the dispatch. Operations would know what to do.

CHAPTER TWENTY-TWO

The horizon was dark and cloudy and under cover of darkness and total blackout conditions it was easier for *Graf Spee* to make alterations to its original course that would hopefully go unobserved by enemy eyes. The crew was exceptionally well trained at evasion tactics, and they'd been at sea long enough and drilled enough times to know exactly what to do before the captain even needed to give the order.

Radio intercepts had detected that transmission almost four hours earlier and had not picked up another one since then. Not that Langsdorff had expected to pick anything else up. If it was an enemy submarine that had sent it, and he knew in his gut that it had been, then the odds were good that the British would send whatever ships they could to cut him off from the Argentina coast.

But rather than going in search of the enemy beneath the waves, which would have proved to be a waste of time as the cruiser was not equipped for anti-submarine warfare anyway, he'd decided to use the opportunity to pull a deception of his own and kept the ship on course southwest. The enemy expected them to be moving along the South American coast and he intended to keep them thinking that was still the plan.

Langsdorff and Kay had devised a different course of action. Under cover of darkness the zig-zagging course the ship had been maneuvering on had gradually straightened out and her heading would soon change to take them further and further away from the coast. Within hours she'd be sailing towards the middle of the South Atlantic. The great gap between continents where no Allied warship patrolled.

Once there they could break east and hunt the Allied merchant convoys making their way around the Cape of Good Hope. The ship had plenty of fuel and *Graf Spee* was the fastest and most heavily armed warship sailing the southern oceans and could be off the coast of South Africa in mere days.

Walter Kay took his peaked cap off, poured them both a cup of steaming black coffee and handed the first to Langsdorff who nodded his head in thanks. The captain unbuttoned his tunic. In the presence of the rest of the crew he would never allow such an informality, but he was in his private mess, a small compartment where he and his senior officers would dine together and discuss ship operations. It was separate from the officer's mess, where he would dine with all the officers on board ship. But once a week or under certain circumstances the two top officers alone would use the room out of earshot of all others.

Captain Langsdorff was hunched over the small dining table, unrolled charts spilled out over its sides. Condiment shakers were used to mark their location on the chart and the estimated locations of Allied squadrons off South America and Africa. At least two squadrons were known to be patrolling these waters to hunt down German ships.

"It is a shame that we've had to change our plans over a game of cat and mouse," Kay commented. "The men were looking forward to putting ashore in Buenos Aires."

Langsdorff grunted his acknowledgment but never looked up from his charts. The truth was he had not been that crazy about putting into port to begin with. His ship had been refueled, courtesy of an Allied tanker and after the previous engagement last week with that Royal Navy cruiser he was quite ready to get back to commerce raiding. The mission they'd been sent out to perform.

"They'll get past it," the captain replied. "Our mission isn't to make the crew happy, Walter. We've had a good run of success sinking enemy merchants out here. We're loaded with supplies and ammunition and our tanks are nearly full. Other than mere diplomatic courtesies we really had nothing for us there. The Führer demands all of us do our duty. Sinking Allied freighters is ours. Besides, military logic should explain our change in plans. There's a Royal Navy squadron between Rio de Janeiro and the Falklands that we could have very well run into. After last week's enemy encounter and the hits we took from one light cruiser, I'm not so sure I want to run into two or three."

The British vessel they'd traded fire with off the coast of Guinea had landed several hits on his ship before *U-35*'s torpedo ended the confrontation and sent the Royal Navy ship to the bottom of the ocean with all hands. They'd just finished with making repairs to their forward gun turret and anchor chain at sea and nobody in Buenos Aires could have done any better. Other than the courtesy check in with Germany's diplomatic office they simply had no good reason to sail there. Since international law forbade warships from remaining in neutral ports for more than twenty-four hours, one might rightly claim that such a stop was actually tactically unwise since there was a Royal Navy squadron less than one day away.

"I agree with you, sir. In fact, when you decided on this change of course I thought the maneuver was brilliant. Sailing between two continents at their widest point instead of the more traditional routes is not something I think that Headquarters would have approved of." He dropped down in his chair and threw his left leg across his right knee.

"And if Berlin wouldn't have approved of it, what do you think the British would think? A little something I borrowed from an Englishman actually. Do you know anything about the Arab uprisings?" Kay shook his head. "An Englishman named Lawrence led an Arab army across a desolate stretch of desert in order to attack a Turkish coastal position from behind. The Turks were so concentrated on defending from an attack by sea that they never saw Lawrence coming across the wastelands." He circled his finger over the charts. "This is our wasteland. When we cross it nobody will see us coming."

"So, what happened to this Lawrence?"

"He went on to great glory. Survived the war. Many say that because of him the Ottoman Empire collapsed. I'm not suggesting we'll go down in history like Lawrence, but the tactic was sound, and it worked for him."

"Well, I just hope that the English won't see this little trick. Since we are borrowing from one of their own."

"This will probably be a onetime thing. Enough Allied convoys pass between Cape Town and French West Africa, we should be busy for quite some time." He exhaled and straightened back up. "I admit, I would have liked the chance to sneak around the Cape and press on into the Indian Ocean again, but..." He shrugged and left the rest of his thought unsaid.

Kay took another sip of his coffee. "Perhaps we still will. The war is just getting started."

"Hmmm. That is my secret fear. I would not look forward to a long and protracted war at sea. We're far from home and we don't have any bases this far from Germany from which to operate. In the last war we did but they were stripped from us. Now we are like wanderers at sea. Highwaymen." He chuckled and Kay looked confused. "An old English phrase. Highwaymen were robbers that hid in the forests. When carriages passed by, they would come out and rob them at gunpoint."

"Ah," Kay laughed. "Like the American westerns. Well, put like that I can see your point. But this war will end differently than the last one did, I think. There is something.... different. More confidant. Hitler has given us a purpose."

"We felt confidant back then too. Whether it's today's navy or the old Imperial Navy I joined as a boy we all do our duty. The Fatherland expects no less from any of us."

"Well then we should make the Fatherland proud, sir. We have the best ship with the best officers and the best crew. Though I admit that I had my doubts when we first left port, excited as I was. So much of our crew being made up of boys still wet behind the ears."

"The men have performed admirably," Langsdorff commented in a soft, tired sounding voice.

"I agree," Kay replied, repressing a sudden shock. Captain Langsdorff was the type who demanded that the men under his command did their duty. NO EXCEPTIONS. He was hardly the type to give praise of any sort, even in private.

Langsdorff remained silent, sipping away on his cup of coffee and reading his charts, tracing his left index finger along the top of the map. The man had a long and well-earned reputation for being a stickler for devotion to duty. He expected much from the men under his command, and he drilled them mercilessly. In return he gave them victory. He also ran as tight a navy ship as sailed. Things that most sailors in most navies were accustomed to doing, such as gambling and alcohol, weren't tolerated at all aboard his ship. Sailors caught since leaving port had already suffered corporal punishment and officers who the captain even suspected of knowing of such activities were berated by him in full view of the crew. No punishment could be more severe for a junior officer, both looking for the respect of his men and to climb the ladder of navy ranks.

"Do you have any concerns regarding our change in plans?" Langsdorff inquired and Kay shook his head.

"No, sir. Berlin probably won't be pleased with the failure to check in with the embassy though."

"No, they probably won't. But our goal is to sink enemy merchants. The Führer wants enemy shipping to suffer. We accomplish that and it'll satisfy Hitler. The shipping lanes running along the African coast are virtually undefended." He took another sip, looked at the clock on the wall and sighed. "We'll split the night shift. You take the first shift. I'll relieve you at zero two hundred."

"Understood," Kay nodded.

"And Commander," Langsdorff began as he took another sip. "Keep a sharp eye out."

HMS Ark Royal
84 Miles West of Ascension Island

Captain Cedric Holland sat relaxed in his chair on the main bridge of the aircraft carrier HMS Ark Royal, sipping slowly on his evening cup of Earl Grey as he read through tomorrow's dispatches before turning in for the evening. He'd been up since before dawn and today had been a long one. The crew conducted a series of battle readiness drills that had taken up the better part of the day. All of them had gone well and it reinforced the high esteem that he held his officers and crew in. The section officers had all reported better than average response times and a significant improvement over previous drills.

He'd passed along his congratulations to the crew afterwards and made a note for the morning watch to give the boys some down time tomorrow as a result. Their latest cruise had been rather uneventful so far, even though there was a war going on. The air patrols had seen no sight of an enemy vessel since encountering a German Q-ship, a warship disguised as a merchant vessel, late last week. The crew of which were right now cooling their heels in an Allied POW camp in South Africa.

He took another sip of his tea and closed the dispatch book. It was getting late, and he was tired. Tomorrow was another day. The night shift had come on just a half hour earlier and Holland was ready to call it a day.

"I think I'll turn in," he told the officer of the watch, Lieutenant Commander Ross.

"Yes, sir. Have a pleasant evening, sir," Ross replied.

He downed the last of his drink and grinned in acknowledgment and started off for the aft hatch. He hadn't made it two paces when a junior officer, paper in hand, approached him with a look of seriousness on his face.

"Excuse me, sir," Sub-lieutenant Green began. Green was senior officer in the radio department this evening. Any messages that came in over the radio were his responsibility to deliver to the bridge. "This just came in over the wireless. Scrambled."

Holland took the paper and frowned as he read the decoded message. His brow furrowed. One of their subs had a confirmed sighting of *Graf Spee* moving along the Brazilian coastline and command wasn't about to miss any chance to sink the enemy raider. Coordinates and heading had put the ship just about two hundred nautical miles east of South America and headed southwards at twenty knots.

"Eighteen forty-one hours," Holland whispered. *It was damn near 2200 now.* "You confirmed this?"

Green nodded. "Yes, sir."

Three and a half hours old, he thought.

He tapped his finger against the paper and did a quick calculation in his mind. *Ark Royal* was the lone British aircraft carrier in the South Atlantic and had been assigned to assist in hunting down German surface raiders. Earlier today they'd turned on an easterly course along the equatorial coast of Africa. Now headquarters was instructing him to turn the ship around and move as quickly as possible in order to catch the German before she sailed out of range. Captain Holland mentally sighed that it had taken three and a half hours for the bigwigs in Freetown to relay this information. But that was the navy for you.

"*All possible haste,*" he read off the last few words to no one in particular. "Commander Ross."

"Sir?" Ross turned and stepped in.

"Commander, bring our course around on a heading of two seven zero. Inform our escorts we'll be moving to full speed."

Aye, sir. Also, I've just been given this meteorology report."

"Oh?"

"Yes, sir. Heavy weather reported northwest of here and moving south. Might be the makings of a hurricane."

"I see." Holland considered his next actions for a moment then nodded at Ross. "Very well. Keep us away from it, Commander. If it looks like it's pushing toward us, adjust course as you see fit. Also, leave instructions to have our planes ready for a pre-dawn launch."

"Sir?"

"That's right, Commander. I want all our birds up and looking for an enemy surface vessel."

"Aye, sir."

Orders were relayed and the helm began turning the ship around on a course due west. The bridge crew responded with the professionalism that Captain Holland had come to expect of them. It was truly unfortunate that he'd be canceling tomorrows scheduled down time but there was a Nazi warship on the move.

HMS Orkney
0032 Hours

Alistair was asleep in his bunk, a halfway decent novel someone had loaned him lay open and resting on his chest, rising and falling with every breath he took. He'd retired for the night just an hour earlier and had tried to relax a bit by reading but he'd found the novel to not be the distraction that he'd hoped for and had dozed off right after the beginning of the first chapter. The mattress he was forced to sleep on was nothing more than a worn-down old thing which he'd had to stitch together himself and typically provided little comfort at all, which was why he spent so little time in bed. Old newspapers were rolled up and placed under the head of his bunk just to provide a bit more cushion to it when he did sleep. But it was never a long, deep sleep.

The intercom chirped once, then again a few moments later. His eyes popped open, and he jerked his head up suddenly. He sat up, nearly banged his head on the ceiling above his bunk, then hit the switch.

"Go ahead," he said and rubbed his tired eyes. He'd only squeaked out an hour's worth of rest after another long day.

"Captain, it's Midshipman Talbert, sir. Message just received from Freetown. You'll want to see this."

He exhaled noisily and ran his fingers through his wavy hair. "I'll be right there," he replied and closed the intercom circuit. One quick look at himself in the small mirror bolted to the wall and he decided to take five minutes and groom himself first. A cold-water shave wasn't ideal but aboard a sub that housed fifty sailors it was all that could be spared. He put on a fresh day uniform and stepped through the hatchway.

There were only three men on duty when Chadwick arrived in the control room. Midshipman Talbert had the watch and PO Davis stood at the conn. Chadwick nodded at the Petty Officer as he walked by to the main plot. Talbert straightened his back at Chadwick's approach.

"Sir."

"What do we have, Talbert?"

"This just came in over the wireless, sir," the young officer produced a transcribed message.

Chadwick took it and read over the message. Freetown had indeed gotten their earlier message concerning sighting *Graf Spee* sailing along the Brazilian coast, but it had taken them over two hours to work the report up the chain of command and then a further hour and a half for them to decide on a course of action. He shook his head slightly at the time delay. It was sometimes difficult to rely on a headquarters that was over a thousand miles and three time zones away.

HMS Ark Royal was being dispatched westwards to help pen in the German. That was a relief to him. At least *something* was happening. But the message went on to read that the carrier's position was still well northeast of his current position. *HMS Orkney* was to shadow the enemy heavy cruiser as best as possible.

Alistair looked up from the message and half crumpled it in his hand.

How the hell are we to shadow a ship that can outpace us by a good ten knots? He thought.

Just after sighting the enemy ship yesterday, he'd purposely changed course just to avoid being detected. Now command was set on his chasing the heavily armored vessel down. *Ark Royal* had enough attack planes aboard to sink the warship three times over, but *Orkney* was armed with a mere dozen torpedoes with an effective firing range of roughly five thousand yards. Chadwick personally had no desire to get that close.

"Thank you. You were right to wake me."

"Yes, sir."

Chadwick bit his lip and took a few moments to consider the situation. The main chart showed their current position, a hundred miles east of Recife Brazil. The German had passed by their position just seven hours earlier and had been following the Brazil coastline. Nobody had any reason to believe the ship was going anywhere except southwest. However, the famed Captain Langsdorff was anything but a typical naval commander and if they'd picked up *Orkney's* earlier transmission, which Chadwick had to assume that he had, then it was entirely possible that the man had ordered a change of course to avoid Allied warships that were posted further south towards the Falklands.

Alistair had been in the Royal Navy for only 5 years now and had limited experience when compared to a man like Langsdorff. But he'd also been a submariner for his entire career thus far and had been trained to conduct war at sea under more nontraditional methods. There was no way in the world that his boat could outrun a *Deutschland*-class cruiser. He was going to be forced to come up with an alternative course of action and considered the situation carefully for a minute.

"Check the logbook. What time did we lose visual sighting of *Graf Spee*?" Talbert grabbed the leather-bound book and flipped through its pages. "Conn, what's our course?"

Petty Officer Davis craned his head around. "One seven zero, sir."

"Visual sighting lost at twenty fifty-eight hours GMT, sir," Talbert said, holding up the log. The enemy ship was still moving southwest then and would have gone completely dark shortly after sunset. Lieutenant Dorsey had been in the conning tower yesterday and would have kept the German in his sights right up until the last minute. Langsdorff was also no fool. He'd sunk a dozen enemy ships at sea, including a British light cruiser, in just about three months' time. The man's unpredictability was undoubtedly his most useful asset. With that thought in mind Alistair was pegging his bet that his opponent was no longer heading south and that the ship was going to break out into the Atlantic. There would be bloody hell to pay if he were wrong.

For better or for worse, his money was now riding on that and there was damn little hope of catching him out there, but it was better than none at all. But he had a decision to make.

"Conn," he said and gave his next orders the slightest hesitancy, "bring us another ten degrees to port. Full speed."

It was just before 0200 hours ship's time when Captain Langsdorff stepped onto the main bridge. Every shutter on the ship was closed at night and every blind drawn. The only lights on were the dull red lights of the night shift or the regular operating lights that could run in the parts of the ship that were under the waterline. It was a moonless sky, and the oceans were calm. Her hull cut across the surface of the water like a sword through the air.

The men on the bridge stiffened a bit as Langsdorff made his way onto the center of the command deck. He motioned his hand, and they went about their business as usual.

Walter Kay stood in the center of the room, his hat hanging off a hook on the back of his chair. He looked over as Langsdorff approached him, glanced at the clock, then back at his Captain.

"Sir," he greeted Langsdorff. "Good morning."

"Good morning, Commander. How did your watch go?"

Kay shook his head and put the watch book he was writing in back in its place. "Uneventful, sir. We're just about to make our last course adjustment here shortly and after that we'll be on an easterly course. Heading straight into the heart of the open ocean."

Langsdorff nodded lightly. It was humid in the cramped space and what little air there was came from tiny little vents at the top of the bulkheads. Even at night the humid air of Earth's equator was grimacing, made even more uncomfortable by the ship being closed with little movement of air.

He looked down and ran his fingertip around the compass's brass housing.

"Our speed is eighteen knots," Kay continued. "By daybreak we should be six hundred kilometers east of Brazil and out of the prying eyes of any enemy patrol planes."

"We hope so anyways," Langsdorff commented dryly. "I've been going over intelligence dispatches and reported convoy activities. I think that if we move swiftly enough, we can catch a northbound convoy off the Angolan coast. There's a sizable gap in convoy protection between South Africa and the Ivory Coast. We come in from the north, we should run straight into one. If British intelligence believes we're heading for Argentina, they'll never see us coming."

Kay nodded in agreement. "Doubtful there'd be more than a couple of destroyer escorts in a convoy like that."

"Exactly. And we'd finally get a chance to hit a target larger than some stray merchant ship," Langsdorff replied optimistically. Even a small convoy would have at least a dozen merchantmen, slow moving and lightly protected that would be cut to ribbons by a ship like his. "Ninety-six hours from now if we hold our course, we'll be in prime hunting position."

"So long as we don't run into any enemy ships or planes along the way. Are you worried about our friend from yesterday?"

Langsdorff shook his head at the question. The chances of a British submarine keeping pace with them, with the greater surface speed and with their course changes, would have been impossible. No Royal Navy sub was that fast and his own radio operators had picked up no indication of any further transmissions nearby. Though there was a danger, as there always was in war, of running into the unexpected, the sheer statistics of happening upon that sub again were slim to none. No, he was quite sure that he'd lost them. Chances were that sub would continue thinking *Graf Spee* was sailing southwestwards towards Argentina. Only the most adept commander in the world would even imagine, against all proof to the contrary, that Langsdorff would have turned due east and headed away from the coast. The British Admiralty didn't give command of subs to captains like that. Those men were reserved for the great surface battleships and carriers.

"No," Langsdorff muttered. "I think we've lost our shadow. There's one chance in a million of bumping into him again."

The morning sun was just breaking in the east and the first glimmer of light began to illuminate the wide-open horizon. From the conning tower of *HMS Orkney* eighteen-year-old Able Rating Percival wiped the salt water off his face with his handkerchief. The boat was cruising along the ocean top and the morning breeze was already warm. Not as warm as the waters off Africa had been mind you, but certainly warmer than his native Coventry, England.

He'd been in the Navy for eight months now and volunteered for submarine duty right out of training and right before the war broke out. His father had wanted him to be assigned to one of the big battleships that Britain was so proud of. But service was service, and Percival had found that he'd had a quality that the Royal Navy looked for in its submariners: size.

Put simply, he was small framed. He'd resented it his entire life, what boy wouldn't? Being five foot three inches tall and weighing a mere eight stones, three pounds was hardly the dream of any eighteen-year-old. But when asked to volunteer for service aboard a Royal Navy submarine, along with the incentive of increased pay and a quick promotion, he'd taken it. It was either that or a shore side assignment working the radios in Singapore.

The promised promotion, however, had still yet to come through.

Peering through his binoculars, he slowly scanned the horizon ahead. The seas were calm, and this was the hour when visibility was at its best. He might not have had height on his side, but his eyesight was perfect.

He moved his binoculars clockwise at a 180-degree arc across the sea. Looking for something...anything. They were so far off the coast and away from any of the major shipping lanes it was doubtful that anything besides the most daring fishing boat would even venture out this far. Why in the world they were out here was anybody's guess but scuttlebutt below decks was that the captain was executing some secret orders direct from the Admiralty. Maybe even Churchill himself.

God that would be nice. A mission come directly from the Prime Minister himself! He dared to think it.

After several minutes of scanning the horizon, he lowered his glasses and arched his back in a stretch. From behind him came the sound of the rusty hinge of the access hatch squeaking open.

"Morning," Seaman Harris greeted as he propped his feet up under him. Percival nodded back. "Pot of hot coffee ready for you mate."

"Coffee, really?" He asked with surprise. "Bloody hell that sounds good." His voice was full of excitement. It had been weeks since he'd last had a cup. But when he looked back at Harris and saw the other boy laughing at him. "Oh shitte. You bastard."

"Had to do it mate," Harris said then tagged him on the back. "Ain't no damned coffee on this tub. 'less the Capin's got some stashed away.

Anyway, I'm relieving ya'."

Percival sighed and shook his head at his own naivete. He un-slung the binoculars from around his neck and handed them to him. He was tired and wanted to get to his bunk.

"Alright. Well enjoy your nap. Don't play with yourself too hard," Harris joked, and Percival patted the other man on his face.

"Keep telling your jokes, Harris and I'll piss on your bunk."

Harris laughed at him and took the glasses as he began his watch. Percival had been up since 0200 and was looking forward to getting back to his bunk. The sun had almost completely broken in the east now and day watch had officially begun. Harris already had the binoculars up to his eyes was sweeping his gaze from side to side. Percival bent over, grabbed the hatch handle and pulled it open. He put one foot down on the first rung of the ladder down and started to descend when he suddenly stopped.

"Eh!" Harris called out and Percival looked up at him. "Come 'ere. Have a looksie." He waved his right hand at Percival who looked at the back of the man with an expression on his face that said he wasn't amused. Harris was going to try and sucker him again and he knew it and wasn't going to get caught by it again.

"Look!" Harris said. He shot a quick look back down at Percival who only shook his own head in dismay. "Look!"

"God dammit," Percival muttered under his breath as he pushed his foot off the ladder and stepped in beside Harris. "You better not be foolin'." He snatched the binoculars angrily away from him and muttered under his breath as he gazed out in the direction Harris had been viewing. "I don't see anything!"

"Right there," Harris said impatiently, pointing his fingers off to the distance. "Sixty degrees off the starboard bow. Right below those small clouds."

Percival, exasperated, focused in, moved his lens slowly around in that area, squinted slightly. "I don't see —" He adjusted his sights again and inhaled sharply. "Holy shit!"

The sound of the ship's bell rang twice then once more. Navy tradition in fleets all around the world marked their operating shifts that way. One ding of the bell for each half hour of a shift. The ringing was a comforting one to Hans Langsdorff. Like the Navy itself Langsdorff was a man of tradition. The first thing he always would notice when he returned home to Germany would be the absence of the bell's ring.

He inhaled the sea air sharply as the bridge shutters opened and the first gleam of morning sunshine just barely shone across the ocean. He graciously accepted the mug of hot coffee that his yeoman had offered him and nodded his thanks to the young man.

Lookouts were posted at all points of the ship, radar was clear, and their seaplane was being prepped for a recon patrol. They'd had to come to a complete stop in order to drop the seaplane into the water and he didn't like to be sitting idle in the middle of the ocean for any prolonged amount of time. Doubtful that there was anything within fifty miles of their position, he still didn't like to chance things. They'd already bumped into one British warship on this cruise unexpectedly and he didn't want to get caught exposed.

It was a new day, and the ship was on a new course. It wasn't the one he'd been ordered on, and command would most likely not care for the fact that he'd disregarded his orders. But victory was all that really mattered in war, and he'd planned on delivering a victory to them that would shake off any irritation this inconvenience may have caused to the diplomatic corps.

"Captain, sir." Langsdorff turned to Lieutenant Wattenberg, "Seaplane is in the water, sir and we're ready to get back underway."

"Very well. Bring us to eighteen knots, Lieutenant. Get us back underway."

From outside came the faint sound of a plane's propeller whining to life and a few moments later there was a gentle lurch forward as the propellers spun back up.

"Depth is now one zero meters, sir," Chief Petty Officer MacDonnell reported from the conn. The older non-com had a reassuring hand on the young helmsman's shoulder.

Alistair gazed through the periscope at the image of the far-off ship. It was still a good distance out of range for any of his torpedoes and although the ship did appear to be stationary for several minutes, it was now inching forward once again.

"She's moving again, sir," the sonar tech reported, his right forefingers were pressed up against his headset, listening in as the sounds of the enemy's propellers echoed out underwater.

"Yes, I see that," Chadwick replied gently, his eyes still glued at the image in his sights. *Orkney*'s bearing would put it at a three-hundred-and-ten-degree angle to the *Graf Spee*'s bow and moving just under the surface at a steady eight knots. "Percival, I'm going to make sure you get that promotion the navy promised you," he said and that made Percival grin.

"He appears...to be...moving back on a straight course," Chadwick stated, pausing occasionally as he observed his quarry through the sights. He folded up the periscope arms and pulled the sightings back down to the floor. Midshipman Talbert and Sub-Lieutenant Dorsey were also present in the control room. Talbert was nervously biting away on his fingernails and Dorsey stood like a rock, with his arms crossed across his bulky torso.

"You were right, sir," Dorsey commented, astonishing himself with the words. "You were right. They weren't pulling into port. They're heading right out to sea."

"We need to alert the squadron to their new heading," Chadwick said. He looked at young Midshipman Talbert, still chomping away. "Harry, radio it in. Make sure we get a reply." He patted the young officer on the shoulder and sent him on his way.

"They'll pick up our signal, sir," Dorsey told him. "There's no way they won't."

Alistair shrugged. "Nothing we can do about that now. That ship will be sailing beyond our range in a very short time. Maybe there's a cruiser or...I don't know, something within range that can catch up with her." He produced a handkerchief from his pocket and wiped away the sweat that had formed on his forehead. "This time tomorrow it'll be seven hundred miles away and good luck finding her again afterwards."

"Even if *Ark Royal* had sailed straight west, they're still going to come up short," Dorsey replied. "Nothing but empty seas where they're heading now."

Alistair gave a disparaging nod. "That's why we've got to radio it in. It's all we've got. Chief MacDonnell, pass the word along to wake everyone up and go to battle stations."

"Aye, aye, sir," MacDonnell replied and went about passing along the word.

This was as close to an enemy vessel as they'd ever been and the fact that nobody on *Orkney* had any combat experience whatsoever, was not lost on Alistair. Also not lost on him was the fact that the officers and crew of *Graf Spee* had, since the war began, been running around the Atlantic Ocean sinking vessel after vessel, even sending a Royal Navy cruiser to the bottom along with one of the best trained crews in the entire fleet and a captain with thirty years at sea. Against such a ship *Orkney* was little more than an annoying fly buzzing about.

"We'll hold this bearing," he said to Dorsey. "If we stay on course, we'll have him dead amidships in less than an hour. If we're still within range of our carrier's air patrol-"

"Excuse me, sir," Talbert interrupted the conversation. "I'm sorry, sir. But can I have a minute of your time."

Alistair nodded. "Very well." He looked back at Dorsey. "Load the torpedo tubes. I want to be ready just in case."

"We have a bit of a problem, sir," Talbert whispered to Alistair as he led him to the tiny radio closet. The radio operator, who had been tapping out his message, stopped and looked up at the two officers. "Radio, sir," Talbert began, his head turning back and forth between Chadwick and the radio operator. "Ummm. . ." He stammered.

"What's the problem?" Chadwick asked sternly then turned his gaze on the radioman.

"It's the VLF, sir," the radioman reported, taking off his headset. "It's not transmitting. I tried switching channels but..." He shook his head gravely.

Alistair eyeballed the machine for a brief second, the connections running under the bolted down metal desk into a closed locker, then brought his attention back to the kid manning the equipment.

"You've checked the connection?"

"Yes, sir," the kid replied and gulped visibly. "It's not the transmitter equipment, sir. I think..."

"Try it again!" Chadwick snapped.

"We've tried sending out a message three times, sir," Talbert informed him. "We'll try again. But I believe the problem is in the antenna."

Chadwick blinked back at him. "Oh, for God's sake. Try it again!"

The radioman put his headset back on and nervously tried to punch out another message through his system. He repeated the message again and again. Finally, he exhaled and shook his head.

"I'm sorry, sir." The boy's voice was genuine.

Chadwick's eyes widened in disbelief, and he looked down at the mass of radio equipment and endless intertwined wires that connected it all together then brought his gaze back up to Talbert.

"Figure it out, Harry," he ordered him. "Rip it apart and put it back together if you must but get that damn thing working. Understood?"

"Yes, sir."

Alistair walked away, exasperated. The men in the control room glanced at him as he walked past. No doubt some had heard what had just transpired. Alistair kept his gaze straight, but he could feel their eyes on him as he strode past. He'd been in the Navy long enough to know that fear was one step away from total disaster. And no officer had the right to allow fear to take control. Though he was getting close.

Captain Langsdorff was stooped over the charts on the wardroom table when an intense ringing in his ear began. It was a mild ringing at first, but the irritation grew steadily. Soon it had grown to be outright debilitating. So much so that he hardly noticed the time go by or his senior aide speaking to him.

"Sir?" A soft voice said over his shoulder. Langsdorff straightened back up and turned his head. Lieutenant Wattenberg looked at him, a concerned expression on his face. "Are you feeling alright?"

He rubbed the bridge of his nose and tried his best to grin through the discomfort. He nodded his head gently.

"I'm fine, Lieutenant," was his reply but it wasn't the truth. In truth the ringing was close to unbearable. He'd had encounters like this before, but they usually preceded tense situations. He couldn't shake the feeling that something felt out of place somehow.

Something's not right, he thought.

Suddenly the ringing in his ear was replaced by the wail of an alarm klaxon blaring throughout the ship. The piercing pain was overridden by his training and years of experience at sea. He put his pain aside and immediately started for the door. The two officers exited the wardroom and made their way down the passageway towards the bridge. He could hear boots hurrying down corridors as the crew headed to battle stations. He walked briskly, Wattenberg closely behind, then sprinted up the flight of steps onto the main bridge deck.

Under his feet he could feel the ship pulling a hard move to starboard and knew that it was an evasion tactic.

A voice was just calling his name through the intercom when he stepped onto the bridge. Commander Kay was standing at the port side window, binoculars in hand when the captain arrived.

"Report!"

"Incoming torpedo attack, sir," Kay replied. "Two thousand meters and closing."

"Increase to flank!" He shouted but Kay was already ahead of him.

"Already done," Kay answered.

Graf Spee's propellers sped up and the ship rolled to her right, the deck beneath them tilting as the huge vessel turned away from the incoming torpedo attack. There was a series of overlapping orders shouted but Langsdorff's voice bellowed over all of them.

"Get me a bearing on that enemy ship, Commander!"

Kay acknowledged and finished buckling up his headgear just as he stepped out onto the port bridge wing. The compass ball at the front center of the bridge was rolling quickly, the ship breaking fast, her engines speeding up as she turned. With luck they'd miss those torpedoes by a wide margin and be out of range of any enemy ship in just a matter of minutes.

"Torpedoes bearing, two four zero!" Kay's voice boomed.

"Target all guns at that bearing," Langsdorff ordered. He finally grabbed his headgear. "Fire everything!"

From outside there came the mechanical sound of the gun turrets rotating into firing position, each 28- and 15-centimeter gun trained themselves in the direction those torpedoes were coming from. Kay and the lookouts with him just stepped back inside and shut the hatch behind them. Outside the air went deadly silent for a fraction of a second and then, with the percussion of a train crash, the guns opened fire.

Dorsey stood next to Alistair, the stopwatch in his hand ticking was the only sound in the room. Alistair tracked the action being played out above the surface. *Graf Spee* was veering away now, having spotted the incoming torpedoes she was now trying to evade. Alistair inwardly cursed. He'd hoped he'd get another few seconds out of those torpedoes before they were spotted. Best of all worlds would have been three hull shots, but that was doubtful from the beginning. The sailors on that ship were well trained veterans. They were perhaps the best crew in the German Navy.

The range of the cruiser was just about two and a half miles out. A lot of distance for those torpedoes to cover. They'd gotten lucky at all to even get those shots fired. Had the cruiser not stopped to drop its seaplane in the water before getting moving again they would have already been out of range.

"Time?" Alistair asked.

"One minute, eight seconds," Dorsey replied.

"Ready tubes two, three and six," Alistair said. The seconds ticked by as the attack unfolded. They'd adjusted their heading just seconds after firing off that first spread and now the waiting was on. "Ready... ready. . . . NOW!"

A second spread fired off, their deadly payloads propelling through the water. They accelerated away at a fast twenty meters per second but there was a lot of ocean to cover and for each second that ticked by *Graf Spee* turned a little bit farther away from them and the odds of catching her became desperately lower.

The torpedoes streamed forward, backwash trailing behind in their wakes. Alistair watched them go. Off in the distance he could catch glimpses of flashes of light from the cruiser.

The ship vibrated as each of its big gun fired, one after another, streams of fire spilling out of their barrels after every shell. The seas in the direction of the incoming attack erupted in geysers of water as each round splashed down into the ocean. The hope was to take out those torpedoes long before they struck the ship's hull. If they got even one the odds of surviving swing heavily in their favor.

Captain Langsdorff stood like a statue on the center of the bridge, unflinchingly calm. Half the sailors on the bridge were barely older than teens, but already they were men, veterans of combat and his composure reverberated and gave them strength. Despite the attack underway he was completely cool. His thoughts were clear and his mind focused.

And most importantly, the ringing in his ear was gone.

"Now at flank speed, Captain!" The helm reported but he gave it no reply.

He gazed back down as the compass ball continued rotating clockwise. Five degrees, then eight, ten, twelve...The ship was listing now, it's stern swinging out towards the direction of the incoming torpedoes. In just a matter of seconds those torpedoes would reach their mark and Langsdorff intended to offer them the narrowest of targets.

Outside the machine guns roared to life. Hundreds of tracer rounds discharged from a dozen different points. The seas between the torpedoes and the ship became saturated with bullet rounds.

. . . . fifteen degrees, eighteen, twenty. . . .

"Time?"

"One minute forty-seven...forty-eight...forty-nine."

Alistair watched anxiously the enemy shells began falling into the sea. *Graf Spee* was turning away from the incoming attack; no doubt trying to narrow its own silhouette and offer the smallest target to an incoming torpedo attack. Alistair had fired both his torpedo salvos at different angles and if his geometry was accurate, they'd see the results of the attack in less than a minute and a half.

The second attack was away, running on a negative bearing to the first. As *Graf Spee* increased its speed it also moved into direct line of the second torpedo wave. In the distance the German guns continued to thunder away, flashes of bright light marking each shell that went off. Those shells were covering an impressive amount of ocean area. A compliment to the ship's designers.

The next three minutes might well be the longest three minutes of his life.

Dorsey continued counting softly. "...fifty-seven...fifty-eight..."

There were audible sighs of relief as the news relayed that one of the incoming torpedoes had exploded far short of the ship. One down, two to go. The ship was now thirty-five degrees on its turn, the bow cutting into the choppy ocean waves. But its speed was forcing the ship to make a wide turn.

Kay stood staring through the porthole at the incoming attack. The torpedoes were so close he hardly even needed his binoculars at this point.

"Ten seconds, sir," he announced.

"Brace for impact!" Langsdorff ordered and the men gripped anything they could to keep steady. The ship was well armored, but any impact was going to have horrendous consequences.

The torpedo wakes were visibly clear as they raced towards their target. The first was closing in aft, the second closed in amidships. Guns ceased their firing. Men took cover and braced themselves as the first torpedo closed in on the aft rudder, expecting any second to be lifted off their feet.

Seconds ticked by and men waited, expecting an explosion at any moment. When no explosion came a single sailor raced to the edge of the ship just in time to watch the torpedo cut barely across the cruiser's wake.

The second torpedo's air wake came right up to the ship's hull then disappeared.

"Impact..." Walter Kay started then his words trailed off. Seconds ticked by.

Again nothing.

Perched on the upper starboard deck a single lookout spotted pockets of compressed air emerging on the opposite side of the ship and moving away.

"Sir, I think... I think the second torpedo..." Wattenberg stuttered but Langsdorff cut him off with a finger. He could already guess what happened. The torpedo must have gone too deep to impact the hull and passed right beneath the ship.

"Captain," a second voice spoke up. "Sir, air patrol has eyes on a submarine periscope." Langsdorff shot his gaze back to the radio operator. "Bearing two one two! Distance four thousand meters!"

The captain spun around, grabbed a stunned Lieutenant Wattenberg by the arm and squeezed tight.

"You have your target bearing. Sink that boat now!"

The order was relayed, gun turrets ceased their fire and shifted their sights. The sailors inside reloaded shells, checked then double checked their elevation, adjusted as needed. A perfectly choreographed series of actions that had been executed time and again.

A few moments of silent respite were broken as the guns opened up once again. In the distance three more unseen torpedoes closed in on their target.

For just a few moments Alistair thought that *Graf Spee* had finished with its senseless shelling of empty ocean. He thought after the flashes in the distance had ceased perhaps her Captain had decided to simply make his escape into the vast ocean and save himself the trouble of trying to sink a single enemy sub. He also thought – hoped really – that his first torpedo attack might bear some fruit. But he'd been wrong.

The second attack was still underway, a good eighty-eight seconds from even reaching the range of the ever-narrowing target. Then the flashes reappeared again off in the distance and for several heartbeats of time Alistair felt time come to a standstill. Their pause in firing was just long enough to adjust their sights and train their fire on a different location. HIS.

Through his sights he saw the first shells begin to land just a dozen meters away. In seconds more of them splashed down around the boat and suddenly *HMS Orkney* found itself at the epicenter of a storm of falling artillery shells. Each round splashing down into the ocean and sending a geyser into the air. One could hear the splashing from the shells above.

Alistair slapped the periscope handlebars upward and screamed out, "Dive! Dive!"

Chief MacDonnell urgently repeated the order. The helmsman forcefully pushed the wheel down hard and the Chief clapped his own hands over his as if the two men would only make the sub dive that much faster. But nothing could dive that fast.

Suddenly there was a hard and violent crash up against the hull. The deck fell out below them and took the men off their feet. The front of the boat buckled and shook furiously before abruptly leveling back up again. The lights flickered and there was a high pitched shrill that pierced the eardrums.

Dorsey caught Alistair by the arm as he lost his balance. Chief Mac-Donnell took a tumble onto the deck and the helmsman's face slammed into the wheel. Alistair put his hand on the XO's huge shoulder, using the bigger man to balance himself then nodded that he was okay. The comm buzzed and Dorsey snatched the mic.

"Go ahead."

"Torpedo room, sir," the voice came back, panic strewn. "We're taking on water." There was a brief break and what sounded like someone shouting, then the voice came back. "It's bad, sir. I think we've...goddammit..." The line went dead.

"Torpedo room. Torpedo room!" Dorsey called. He looked at Alistair who gave him a curt nod and took off through the hatch and down the passageway.

"Straighten us out, MacDonnell," Alistair called out. "What's our depth?"

"Only twenty-five meters, sir."

"Keep us there, Chief. Ninety degrees to port!"

"Aye, sir!"

Alistair wiped his face with the back of his hand. Suddenly it was awful damn hot in here. He could feel his heart beating right out of his chest and the adrenaline flowing through his veins. He also felt a sudden awareness that he was, in fact, still living and breathing and was silently thankful for that. If he could just get out of the line of fire, hope for the best, he might save his crew and maybe even the boat but without that damned radio working, calling for help was going to be impossible.

It seemed to all that *Graf Spee* couldn't bear away fast enough. It was now fifty degrees into its turn and still tacking. Any gun with an angle on the target was firing away They'd escaped the torpedo attack, though just barely and out of sheer luck. One had missed them by mere feet, the other, which would have been a dead-on hit, had sunk too far underwater to be effective. Though nobody on board would ever know just how close that one had come. Perhaps nobody really wanted to know either.

Langsdorff and Kay looked at each other, both men gave affirmative nods to the other, both thinking the same thoughts. The crew had acted with lightning-fast reflexes and the pilot had been sharp and alert. One thing was for sure, there would be many commendations given out for today. He would see to it that the Führer himself heard about their bravery.

"Captain!" the radio operator began. From his headset a frantic voice screamed into his ear.

"What is it?" Hans demanded.

"Sir. . ." the man didn't finish his statement.

The ship convulsed violently, and it felt as if the entire rear hull seemed to upend. The sound of the explosion was absolutely deafening. Everywhere men were tossed around like dolls, and in one instant the deck dropped out from under them. On the bridge the explosion sounded like a tidal wave crashing against a beach. The slow and terrible seconds that followed felt like forever to those aboard.

Hans body hit the deck with enough force to knock the wind out of him, but he barely registered it. The shock of the impact had caught him completely by surprise and it took his brain several seconds to comprehend what happened. But he guessed just what that was by the time he found the strength to push himself up off the floor.

The high-pitched sound of the alarm wailing was the first noise that he could hear, then the un-mistakable sound of confusion and half panic from the men on the bridge. His eyes locked onto to Walter Kay, himself half kneeling on one leg. Hans got back on his feet, grabbed the sailor next to him, his eyes blank from shock, and shook the kid then smacked his face hard enough to get his attention focused back on the here and now.

He took three feeble steps towards the port hatchway. Walter was back on his feet and had his hand already on the latch when Hans put his own down on top of his and together both men pushed the door open. A blast of warm air rushed instantly into the bridge compartment, when they both stepped through the hatch, Kay looked over the railing at the men running along the length of the ship, Langsdorff scanned the rear of the ship where the impact had been felt. He gazed up at the mushrooming fireball that was rising and away from the cruiser. It must've been fifty feet high. His mouth gaped open at the sight of the chaos on the rear deck.

Fire crews were already racing towards the site of the explosion, hoses in hand. Bodies were lying near the impact, uniforms and skin burnt and melted together. The wailing of the alarm dug deeper and deeper into his brain as he watched the scene unfolding before him. His eyes were fixed on the stacks of smoke trailing behind them. It was thick and jet black and that could only mean one thing.

"Sir!" the excited voice came from his copilot.

"I see it," Commander Broyles replied before the other could say another word. His head was perched over his left shoulder and his eyes were fixed on a distant, almost imperceptible, point on the horizon off at their eight o'clock. There was a dark cloud rising off in the distance and it was getting thicker fast.

Broyles looked down at his fuel gauge and gave it a stern tap with his finger. Fuel supply was right at the halfway point. He looked at his watch and chalked the time next to the gauge. The flight would have just enough fuel to go and check out whatever that was out there before having to turn around and head back to *Ark Royal*. It was going to be close.

He squeezed his throat mic.

"Eight Oh One Flight, one my wing. Tallyho!"

Alistair was conferring with Chief MacDonnell when Tim Dorsey stepped back into the control room. His shoes squished as he walked, and the bottom of his trousers were soaked. Behind him were Seaman Greene and Petty Officer Wood, their uniforms drenched and dripping water.

Alistair gave the other man a look of dire urgency.

"What's to report?" He asked.

Dorsey gave a disapproving shake of his head. "Not good, sir. We're punctured in at least three places in the forward compartment and taking on water fast. Shell must've perforated through the outer hull. I've sealed it off but..." He again shook his head hopelessly, exhaling noisily. "Sir, we're not going to have long."

He stared blank face at the other man. Alistair understood just what the XO was telling him. It wouldn't take the entire forward third of the boat to flood before they sank. In only a matter of minutes it will have taken on enough water to make surfacing impossible, a short time after that the sub would slowly descend into the darkness, all the while the crew would listen in horror to the sounds of the hull collapsing before finally imploding at around two hundred meters. It took Alistair a minute to get beyond the shock he was feeling.

Perhaps it was too much to hope that *Orkney* could be saved.

His sight fell to the floor and for a second his face was strangely emotionless. The mission, HIS mission, had failed and he knew it. The boat was going down quickly and there was nothing he could do about that either. So, it was the men.

Save the crew, he thought.

"Chief MacDonnell," he began slowly. "Blow the ballast tanks," he couldn't believe he was going to say this, "prepare to abandon the ship."

"Aye, aye, sir," MacDonnell replied somberly.

Alistair put his left hand on Tim Dorsey's shoulder. "Get the boys above deck," he said. Dorsey made a short move then stopped when Alistair squeezed his shoulder. "And Tim, grab the Jack." He let go and the first officer made his way down the corridor only after giving a sharp nod.

"Blow all tanks on my mark," MacDonnell ordered. "On three... two... one, mark!" His voice boomed. Air bled the ballast tanks until they were empty, and *Orkney* slowly began to surface. Men hurried to grab whatever they could and started evacuating the control room. The dial on the depth gauge ran counterclockwise as the boat headed for the surface. It was a one-way trip though. Never again would the ship be able to dive and, in fact, when enough of the ship was flooded it would begin to sink again and that would be the end of her.

The sound of the wailing alarm cut through the air. Thick, black smoke rose thicker than it had been just moments ago. The torpedo impact had hit the exposed fuel tank at just the right angle. The enemy shot had come in from nearly dead astern and had struck right between the propeller screws and the armored hull of the port quarter and only inches below the water line. The impact punched through the ship's outer skin and ignited the fuel in the tank which was now gushing into the ocean as it burned.

From the elevated deck Hans stood overlooking the damage control effort playing out below him. Officers on deck shouted orders, their voices bellowed over the chaos. There was no way in the world that his ship was going to sneak away as he'd planned. Not now. They were lit up like a chimney on the sea and if, by some miracle, he managed to elude enemy ships then they were going to be berthed for some time while the damage was repaired. He felt a swell of consternation.

On the aft deck fire crews fought to try and put out the flames that were licking up the side of the ship. The explosion had created a fireball that had risen a good hundred feet into the air and burned hot enough to have instantly killed two sailors who had the misfortune of being too close. Their bodies, both burnt to a crisp, were right now being wrapped up in canvas and hauled away.

"Sir," Walter's voice came up from behind, but Hans didn't bother turning around. "Sir, I've had the port fuel pumps shut down," he reported as he stepped up beside Langsdorff. His face was blackened, and his eyes were bloodshot and watery. "Patrol plane reports sighting an enemy submarine surfacing about three miles out. The pilot seems to think it's been damag. . ."

Hans held up a single hand and Walter fell silent.

"It doesn't matter," he cut him off. "As soon as damage control efforts have been completed, we'll have no choice but to head to port. It's still early in the day and we'll be lucky if someone doesn't spot that smoke." He balled up a fist and pumped the railing with it, swearing to himself. His position had been compromised and the ship would be forced to limp away.

Even with only one fuel pump he could still outpace any submarine. And if that sub had indeed been hit by even one shell it would be in even worse shape than *Graf Spee* was.

"Break radio silence. Inform command that we'll be checking into Buenos Aires." They both turned and began walking towards the bridge. "Also, inform them that..." He let his words trail off. There was an excited flurry of activity on the bow deck. The sight of officers and sailors alike running from the forward section confused him. For a moment Hans thought that maybe a fire had broken out forward. He spotted one of his officers, Lieutenant Klepp, shouting in his direction, both arms waving around in the air. Klepp's fingers were pointing up and his view turned skywards again, at what was fast approaching from the heavens. Like vultures they were diving downward in a staggered formation, one after another. Kay saw them too and rushed forward, ordering the men to mount the anti-aircraft guns. The men instantly reacted to the incoming threat. It was almost not surreal. Almost dreamlike.

Hans adjusted his helmet chin strap before dashing back into the bridge. He had just enough time to order another evasive course change before the first enemy plane came screaming down upon them.

Machine gun bullets strafed the cruiser's bow. Hundreds of rounds ricocheted against the steel hull. Bullets broke apart and sent bits of shrapnel spraying across the deck. Sailors ran for their very lives as the enemy fighter dove down on them. Anti-aircraft guns rolled into firing position and began pumping out streams of ammo. Only second later the entire ship lit up with the sight of tracer rounds firing.

"Watch that flak fire," Broyles said into his mic. His aircraft was third in line on the attack run. He watched with wide eyes as the lead plane went plummeting toward the cruiser, machine guns firing madly. The warship had suddenly erupted with anti-aircraft fire and hundreds of small bursts exploded in the skies above. When the lead plane hit fifteen hundred feet, he released his payload, and the pilot pulled his plane out of the dive.

A single five-hundred-pound bomb came dropping down at an angle and splashed into the empty ocean, exploding meters away from its intended target. In the seas below, *Graf Spee* made another sharp turn, and the ship began another evasive maneuver as the next plane lined up on the moving target.

Behind him Alistair could hear a large booming sound in the distance. He lowered his hands down to help the next crewman making his way up the long ladder and shot a glance back in the direction of the far-off action taking place out there. He'd gotten up to the conning tower in time to see a giant trail of smoke off in the distance. He wasn't sure exactly how it had happened but assumed that one of the torpedoes he'd fired had found its mark. Astonishing really but what hadn't been on this patrol.

Midshipman Talbert had been the first officer on deck and had two inflatable rafts already in the water by the time Alistair climbed out of the sub. He'd grabbed what he could, what he thought a good captain would take: a compass, charts and a flare gun. The radio operator had failed to get his equipment back into working order so getting out an SOS had been impossible. Being this far out at sea it might well be a while before any rescue was forthcoming. But there was always a chance.

From a distance away there had come the sound of an explosion as well as what had faintly sounded like heavy gunfire. He could barely see anything with his naked eye and the glare of the sun off the ocean surface was too bright.

He climbed down from the conning tower and caught up with Mid-shipman Talbert who was overseeing the inflation of a third raft.

"Do you have your binoculars?" He asked. Talbert reached into a side pouch and handed them over. Alistair wiped around his eyes and uncapped the lens. He scoured the southward horizon. The *Graf Spee* was maneuvering away in an evasion pattern. He refocused the lens and could make out what he thought looked like fighter planes swarming in on the huge warship. But why...?

No not fighter planes, he thought. *Dive bombers.*

The motion of the hull being rocked gently by the waves brought him back to what was going on around him. His men were loading into the rafts, each man carrying only a single blanket and whatever water and rations they could stuff into their pockets. Anything beyond what they'd need to survive for the next few hours was a luxury they couldn't afford.

Sub-lieutenant Dorsey descended the last rung of the ladder from the tower, more men still following behind. The hefty first officer exhaled noisily as he touched down.

"MacDonnell's bringing up the last of the boys, sir," he announced. "They're grabbing any medical supplies they can. And I got this, sir." He held up a folded Union Jack and handed it to Alistair.

Alistair took it then looked back towards the fight going on out there.

There was a very brief cheer from the men around him at the news that the gunners had hit one of the British planes. A bright fireball erupted in the skies above them and a single dive bomber literally blew apart, it's broken wing and main fuselage tumbling through the air. Captain Langsdorff didn't applaud but he certainly didn't blame the crew for celebrating the minor victory either. In a deadly game like this one, every kill was a win no matter how small it may seem.

"Thirty degrees to starboard!" He called out.

He rolled up his sleeve and looked at his watch again then pouted.

"Please God," he prayed silently.

"Jesus Christ!" his copilot cried out as the plane ahead of them burst into flames. It's wing flew off in an instant and the fuselage exploded. There was zero chance that the crew had survived that.

Broyles cringed at the loss and the thought that two of his men had just lost their lives. He was momentarily grateful, however, that their deaths had been quick.

The German ship was dead in his sights now, still trying to weave its way through the seas. Bits and pieces of the exploded plane pelted up against his like small rocks. His craft was descending rapidly, and his speed was better than two hundred mph. Below him the great ship was making another hard turn to starboard, but she wasn't moving as fast as she otherwise would have. Smoke drifted up of the aft quarter. Whatever it was that had hit them it had been what had alerted the squadron to the *Graf Spee's* presence. Without that smokestack rising like a banner it was very likely it would have sailed away unnoticed.

Altitude was now at three thousand two hundred feet, and he opened up with his own double machine guns. Useless against such a target but it would give those men operating the deck guns a little something to worry about. Behind him there were five more bombers lined up on an attack approach.

His altimeter was running counterclockwise rapidly and at the speed he was going he literally only had seconds before either pulling out or hitting that hard surface.

Twenty-five hundred...twenty-two...eighteen...The nose of his plane was aimed directly amidships, and the distance was closing fast, the ship was getting bigger in his sights with every second. His wing guns were blazing. Fifteen hundred feet...twelve hundred...bits of shrapnel pelted against the outer skin of his plane. He was determined to take his plane in as close as possible. At his current descent speed, it was going to be close.

"Sir," his co warned. Broyles ignored him. He could see it.

Nine hundred feet...eight...seven...six...he pulled back hard on the yoke with both hands, sparing only a brief second to yank the bomb release then used all his strength to pull his plane out of its dive. He could almost smell the salty air as his craft hit just under five hundred feet altitude. It certainly wasn't a by the book maneuver, but it was a sight to behold and if Broyles lived through it, he told himself he'd never do it again.

"Madness," Walter Kay whispered as he watched the plane descend. No dive bomber would have ever gotten this close to their target. Not if the pilot wished to live through it. But this one did. Machine gun rounds saturated the air above the ship and for a second it looked as if the small plane might have taken a hit, but it just kept coming. He could almost see the propeller blades; it was that close.

His mouth dropped open as he stared out the forward window. The enemy plane's wing flaps were fully exposed, and the pilot was pulling his nose up. From its belly a single 500-pound bomb released and dropped nearly vertically. The pilot pulled his plane up and away with just seconds to spare.

The armor piercing bomb struck the forward deck just ahead of the main turret. The ensuing explosion ripped through the hull and into the decks below. Chunks of metal and human flesh blew up and out from the impact and the ship rocked forcefully. The anchor chain went whipping through the air and over the side. Contained by the bulkheads the force of the explosion blew back upwards, wrenching the huge turret up from its support girder.

The floor jumped up under his feet. Bits and pieces of metal rained down and human flesh and blood spattered across the forward deck. Hans stumbled to view the damage. His mouth gasped at the sight of it. The bomb had ripped open a wide breach in the bow and fire and smoke were spewing up, men lie dead or dying on the deck. In a matter of minutes he'd been struck at either end of his ship, and it wasn't over yet.

The sound of a large boom reverberated across the ocean surface, and it was clear to Alistair that the enemy ship had taken some kind of hit. In a way he genuinely felt pity for those German bastards getting hammered right now. It was not an end that any sailor would truly wish upon another. But that ship and that crew had certainly sent their fair share of mariners to the bottom of the sea. Including the entire crew of *HMS Neptune*.

"Sir," Dorsey said in a hushed tone. He was standing right behind Alistair. The last two men still aboard the sinking sub. It was eerily silent, except for the fight still waging in the distance. Three rubber boats full of men bobbed up and down on the waves. The boat was now pulling underwater, each wave came closer and closer to blanketing the fore deck.

"Yes, I know," Alistair said back to his XO. He didn't want to be reminded of it.

Two of the life rafts were already detached and drifting away, the third still tied down, the men waiting on him. To his surprise and joy, he'd counted each and every member of his crew. Despite the loss of his boat, he hadn't lost a single sailor under his charge. Unfortunately, however, the loss of one's command was typically viewed negatively by the Admiralty, and he would no doubt be called to account for it when they got home.

IF they got home.

In his right hand he held out his binoculars to a man in the raft. In his left was the folded flag. He motioned for Dorsey to get into the boat first. He had to be the last man off. That's what the captain was supposed to do. He set one foot into the raft and as he pushed off with his other, he felt a surge of guilt swell up in him. This boat had been home for half a year now and it had served them well. She deserved better.

He thumped down in between two sailors and gave a nod to push off. Seaman Bowman untied the line and with a gentle push of his oar sent the raft floating away. Each man sat respectively quiet and as the minutes ticked by inch by inch, foot by foot, the ocean waves devoured the sub. The conning tower was the last to disappear beneath the waves and then the boat sank bow first into the depths, a last pocket of air bubbling upward as it did.

Alistair sat soberly watching where the ship used to be. He knew the men were all doing the same and he knew what they must be feeling because it was the same thing he was feeling. But those feelings were inconsequential right now and his duty as a Royal Navy officer could not afford them. His obligation was clear: the survival of his crew was the mission.

Broyles circled his plane high above the smoking cruiser and watched apprehensively as another of his pilots took a direct hit by flak. White smoke trailed behind the plane and its pilot pulled his aircraft out of its dive he'd been in. The pilot, Michaels, straightened out his trajectory, kept the nose up as the plane lost altitude. The man had time to get off a last radio message before ditching into the water well over a kilometer away.

The last two of the bombers still armed, swooped down like a pair of birds-of-prey. *Graf Spee* continued to fire away desperately into the air toward them. Had he not lost his own men he might feel some respect for the crew of that ship. But he didn't. Jackson and his copilot were dead, Michaels was down, God only knew if he and his copilot were still alive, and three other planes had taken hits.

Peters and Hill were the last two pilots left with bombs under their carriages. Hill sped in first, his guns blasting away. He lined the nose of the plane up with the ship's main tower, moving only to match the cruiser's sharp turn.

"C'mon, c'mon," Broyles repeated over and over to himself as he watched Hill go in, Peters literally only seconds behind him.

The two planes bopped and weaved their way around enemy fire. Even with the damage the ship had already taken she was still maneuvering evasively, and her deck crews were still putting up one hell of a fight. The bombers were down to the last two thousand feet. One took a small hit to its wing but pressed onward.

"Please God. . . " he prayed as he watched.

Hill let go of his bomb first then pulled his craft up and away followed a few seconds later by Peters, who took a series of bullet holes along his fuselage as he rolled his own plane over. Two 500-pound bombs plunged down and Broyles held his breath. All they needed was one good hit.

Peter's bomb missed by only feet, dropping into the ocean and exploding just below the ship's waterline. Hill's bomb landed just behind the upended turret, pierced through the deck plating and exploded almost simultaneously with its counterpart. From his position Broyles caught sight of a bright red flare and an enormous fireball rose from dead center. It could not have been any better a shot.

He watched for a few more moments as secondary explosions went off then turned his craft away and made off towards Michaels downed position. As he passed by the crippled cruiser, he still encountered some enemy fire, but his quick flyby gave him a good view. The ship was smoking heavily, fires on deck were now raging out of control and whatever was left of her crew were racing away from the rippling explosions.

Michaels had ditched into the water intact and as Broyles approached, he could see the canopy slide open and both pilot and copilot climb out of the cockpit. He grinned as the two waved their arms up at him. Fuel supply was down to a third and he was just about to order his group back into formation when he spotted something from out of the corner of his eye that he did not expect to see. Out there, floating around in the ocean, were three large lifeboats just about a mile out.

"What the hell?" He mused and banked his plane in their direction. The last thing in the world he'd expected to see in the middle of nowhere, other than a German heavy cruiser, was the sight of thirty or forty men packed into flimsy rubber rafts and one of them was waving an unfolded Union Jack at him as he passed overhead.

Hans couldn't move. His body was in shock. He was bleeding from the side of his neck, but he was pretty sure that the medic who had patched his wound had told him that the injury wasn't life threatening. At least that's what he thought he heard him say. He couldn't really be sure, everything seemed so surreal. Other wounded men were being cared for and the dead had their faces covered. The pathetic wailing emanating from the klaxon was now broken and the siren seemed distant, almost like the ship was sending out one last death cry.

"...is dead...getting the boats...Sir? Captain?" The voice was distant and incoherent, but Langsdorff could clearly recognize Lieutenant Ascher kneeling down next to him, his hand on the captain's shoulder. His mouth moved but his words were barely audible.

Hans strained to push his torso up off the floor. There was a sharp pain from the wound on his neck and he moaned as Ascher put his hand behind his back and helped straighten him up.

"Lieutenant?" Hans muttered out. He rested for a few moments. "What...?"

"Sir, we're sinking," Ascher told him sadly. "I've ordered the crew to abandon ship. Sir, do you understand me?" Captain Langsdorff closed his eyes and nodded slowly.

"Kay? Where is he?" His voice was barely much more than a whisper.

"Commander Kay is dead, Captain," Ascher told him. "Lieutenant Wattenberg is unconscious. We're putting him into a lifeboat right now. Sir...Captain Langsdorff, we need to get you off the bridge, sir." There was a pleading tone in the young officer's voice.

Hans looked around at what was left of the bridge, at the smoke that seemed to be everywhere, at the dead men whose bodies lay sprawling on the deck. Death was everywhere. Even the ship itself was dying. He could feel it.

He looked up at the young Lieutenant. Ascher was a good officer and a good man, and he didn't deserve to die out here in the center of nowhere. Hans knew that the British planes that had hit them would no doubt radio in that there were survivors and within a day a Royal Navy squadron would be in the area to rescue, and likewise intern, the crew. Hans couldn't help himself from smirking at the irony of that. In the time since the war had begun, he'd ordered more than a dozen ships to be sunk, some of which went down with their entire crews. But he knew that the British were not that way. The Royal Navy had a tradition of honor to uphold and for a long heartbeat he felt guilt.

"No," he finally told Ascher, his voice was gargled and broken. "Take command. I'm not leaving." He placed his hand on the other man's shoulder and squeezed. "Get the crew off. Get them home."

"But sir..." Ascher's words trailed off and there was a lump in his throat.

"It's okay. Be the captain. The men, take care of the men."

Ascher and Langsdorff locked eyes for a minute and finally the younger man nodded. Hans pleaded with him to help prop him up against the helmsman's station. He groaned in pain as his lay against the cold, flat surface. He smiled back at Ascher and nodded as if giving the man permission to leave him and go.

The Lieutenant remained for a second or two then snapped off a perfect salute. He turned and joined the last of the wounded as they left the bridge. And with that Hans was now alone with the dead and the ship that would soon sink beneath the waves. But at least most of the crew would survive and he could go to the depths knowing they were safe.

With nothing more than the crackling alarm going off he sat peacefully. There was only one thing left to do. He unsnapped the holster on his waist and took out the small handgun. It was his final duty to perform, and he didn't want to waste time. He chambered a round, brought the pistol up to the side of his head and squeezed the trigger.

CHAPTER TWENTY-THREE

The nights in the far north of Norway were very pleasant this time of year, General Eduard Dietl, commander of the German 3rd Mountain Division thought to himself as he stood on the side of the dark road, observing as his troops filed passed him in the early morning hours before sunset. Even at the height of summertime the climate barely rose above sixteen degrees Celsius, and the nights were cool and invigorating. Being so far north the sun set early and away from any major cities the night skies were clear and full of stars.

He rolled up his sleeve and checked the time. It was still another two hours before dawn, the column had been on the march since two o'clock this morning and had made a reasonably good pace for a light infantry division that had not been equipped with many vehicles and marched through the narrow and winding pathways that served as roads in the Norwegian wilderness. Most of his troopers still marched on foot, the vehicles were used to move supplies and equipment on the narrow roadways that ran through the thick wooded mountainous terrain.

His division was marching northwards roads through the thick Norwegian forest, finally moving against the last port town in the country, Narvik. The Allies had landed an expeditionary force there nearly a month and a half ago, but they hadn't moved an inch southwards to fight the German Army.

Now, after weeks of fighting against the disorganized remnants of the Norwegian Army and a few scattered French units in the south, the commanding general of the entire campaign, General Falkenhorst, had given orders to Dietl to take his division northwards, capture the town in the far north and drive out the Anglo-French force. In addition to his own troops Falkenhorst had detached a light grenadier battalion and a single artillery battery to reinforce him.

Intelligence had reported that the British troops around Narvik had no armored units at all and very few field guns, if any. Dietl wasn't so sure. He trusted Intelligence, they had done their jobs well in Poland, but he tried never to underestimate an enemy in the field. In six weeks, it was impossible to think that the Allies had not brought ashore any artillery whatsoever. No good general with weeks of preparation time would garrison such a strategically important town without field artillery to back him up.

However, word was that with the engagements along the coasts further south the attacking German units had also not encountered any enemy artillery either. So perhaps intelligence was correct after all, despite all logical military thinking to the contrary.

From behind him, General Dietl could hear his staff officers at work around the makeshift command tent propped between three thick trees. He remained silent as he watched the men of his division march by, not one of them breaking discipline whenever they noticed him standing there. Most of his men had been in the army for a while now, either volunteering or being conscripted into the service in previous years. But the mountain divisions were considered to be an elite force and all that came here came voluntarily and once they arrived, they were drilled mercilessly. No soldier in his division was a boy, no matter what age they were. They were soldiers, professional soldiers.

The thick forest of the country meant that any vehicle of command car size or larger had to move slowly through the winding roads. Foot-born infantry, of course, didn't have that issue and could march through the woods in company long columns. At this pace he reasoned that his advance units should hit the mountainside east of Narvik by mid-morning tomorrow.

Dietl turned back to the tent with the single large table under it and the cadre of officers working over that table with the light from a single lantern illuminating their workspace. A cup of coffee was waiting for him as he stepped under the canvas, handed to him by a young lieutenant.

His chief of staff, Colonel Kraft, looked up from his maps as the general stood by him, he wore his signature blue scarf around his neck and sipped on a cup of tea.

"We're making good time, General," Kraft told him, Dietl grunted a reply.

"What word from our forward patrols?"

Kraft shook his head. "Nothing yet, sir. No patrol we've sent out has returned yet, sir. It's still early though. I wasn't expecting to get anything for at least another hour."

General Dietl took a sip of his piping hot coffee "Hmm. The fog of war, Colonel. The mortal enemy of armies. I don't like moving this far north without a good sense of what's waiting for us. I don't like it at all. These fucking maps command gave to us could've been drawn by a school child." He threw a disdainful look at the stack of maps layered across the table. "The topography is wrong! That creek we passed yesterday wasn't even on any of them."

Colonel Kraft nodded in reluctant agreement. They'd had to dispatch half a dozen scouting parties just to get regular updates on the topography of the area and to act as first line skirmishers. Even now those forward parties were spread out along a two-kilometer-wide cone shaped area north of the advancing column. They were good mountain troops, intensely trained in light infantry tactics and pioneering techniques, but the general was right, command should have had a better idea of the lay of the land.

"Communications did get a brief report from Corps Headquarters," Kraft informed him. "Looks like the British position at Namsos has been abandoned during the night. The Royal Navy pulled them out under the cover of darkness. The Tommy's are getting good at retreating."

Dietl took another sip of his coffee, let out a sigh. "Don't underestimate them, Hardy. The British can retreat and fall back but when they turn and fight, they fight like furies. For four years in France, we kept telling ourselves that they were ready to break every time we overran their lines and every time they kept on fighting."

"I'm just trying to be optimistic about the situation, General. I meant no offense."

"And you gave none, Colonel." The general put his hand on the other man's arm and squeezed lightly in friendship. "But we are outnumbered going into this fight. Even if intelligence is right and the enemy have no field guns or armor, we're still going up against a superior force and with little idea of the land. We cannot afford to be careless. We cannot afford to underestimate our enemy. What I wouldn't give for a few accurate maps or a couple of reconnaissance planes."

Colonel Kraft sighed slightly then shook his head. "Damn Luftwaffe. You'd think they could've spared a dozen dive bombers or something for this operation. Reich Marshal Göring poured everything on Poland so effectively and in all the numbers that were needed and then some. Leftovers for us I guess."

"Hmm. Seems we're not as important. Besides, the airfields in the south are too far away for Stukas. A flock of Heinkel's would do nicely though."

Dietl looked around the table at the men working quietly in the lamp light. For a light division that barely numbered five thousand men he had managed to pull together some very good officers for his command staff. The elite mountain divisions were often craved after by young men eager to prove themselves and middle-aged men like he and Kraft who had already proven themselves. His staff was one of the best that he'd ever put together in any unit he'd ever commanded.

But no matter how good a staff he might have had, none of them could make up for the lack of air support that they'd have when they encountered the enemy. This was a side operation compared to the entire Norwegian Campaign. No matter how important the capture of Narvik was to secure the country, Dietl knew that he and his men were being sent on little more than what was seen as a milk run.

He looked around the group of officers, found who he was looking for. "Captain Dietrich." The division intelligence officer had been hunched over the table studying some reports but straightened up as his name was called. "Remind me again what the latest enemy force estimates are."

Dietrich didn't miss a beat, didn't even need to check his notes. "At least two brigades, sir, one British, one French. The French force consists mostly of their Foreign Legion elements. We can expect that their position has been reinforced by units from the Norwegian Sixth Division that escaped the fighting in the south."

Dietl nodded, looked back at his chief of staff. "So, we can expect what? Twenty thousand enemy troops dug in and waiting?"

"Maybe twenty-five thousand," Dietrich suggested.

"Twenty-five thousand," Dietl repeated dryly. "Thank you, Captain. Five times our number, Hardy." He sipped again on his coffee. "Well. . . . maybe we'll get lucky."

Colonel Kraft tapped the map splayed out on the table. "General, if we don't have a clear picture of the enemy position, then the same is true for them as well. Six weeks ago, we landed in Norway with over a hundred thousand men, they've had plenty of time to verify that intelligence. We've been nipping at the heels of the Norwegian forces for a month now, chasing them all over the country. As far as those British generals sitting in Narvik, or for that matter London, are concerned, all one hundred thousand of us are moving north." General Dietl listened and said nothing, Kraft had a point. "Those people haven't moved an inch since they landed in Norway, and they just evacuated their other positions along the coast."

"And for all we know, those troops they evacuated are right now reinforcing the enemy in the north," Dietl retorted. "This only reinforces my point, Colonel. The problem is we have no information on enemy positions that we can call reliable. We're marching into the dark with no light to see our way."

"Well, we do know one thing, General," Kraft told him. Dietl looked at him and waited. "We know the Allies have done nothing to move south to stop us. They could have moved forward days ago and set ambushes for us, but they didn't. What does that tell us, sir? Either they don't know we're coming their way, or they think we have a much larger force."

General Dietl took another sip of his hot coffee, shrugged in possible agreement with his chief of staff. He was going to retort with Kraft about the fact that there was no real need for the French and British to leave their positions to attack his force. The farther north the 3rd Division went, the longer its supply lines had to stretch, whereas the Allies could just sit and wait and not concern itself with diminishing supplies. On the other hand, he knew Kraft was right about the enemy setting up ambushes. No doubt if the British leadership knew there was a German force on its way, they could have sent out parties to make its way north as difficult as possible. Ambushes in this terrain would not have been hard and would have cost the German forces dearly.

"The fog of war works both ways, General," Colonel Kraft continued. "Let's see what our scouts have to report, sir. Another hour or two and we should be able to start painting a better picture of the situation."

Dietl pursed his lips and shrugged. "Like I said, Colonel. Maybe we'll get lucky."

Beisfjord Norway
0700 Hours

Narvik was a town that lay on the southeastern shore of the Ofotfjord, a deep-water inlet that led out to the North Sea. From the town there were three roads, one that led northeast, one that led eastwards and another that ran due south. The French held the southern road with a brigade of their famous Foreign Legionaries, foreigners who fought for France. The northeastern road was held by the Welshmen of the 24th Regiment of Foot. The eastern road ran east for seven or eight kilometers then forked, one fork ran southeast and the other ran east. The Irish Guards held the eastern road and the highlands that the road ran through, while the Scots Guards held their southern flank and were entrenched along some mountain foothills that overlooked mostly farmland.

In the weeks since landing in the north of the country the entire Allied force had done little, very little in fact, to meet the threat of the German invasion. In fact, the other two landing sites along the western coast had been abandoned at the first indication of approaching German forces. The Allied force at Andalsnes had been evacuated after only a few hours of skirmishing with German advanced units. Similarly, the force at Namsos had likewise been evacuated when it appeared that German panzers were on their way. The Royal Navy had pulled the British troops off the beach under the cover of darkness, leaving behind only a few stragglers who had quickly surrendered to the enemy.

Now it appeared that the German armies aimed to finish the job, push the entire Allied force into the sea and complete its invasion of the Nordic country.

As it was morale among the Allied troops was pitiful. They'd sat around on their hands for six weeks now, failing in any way to stop the loss of the Scandinavian nation to the Germans, waiting for an attack that never seemed to be coming. Supply problems back in Britain were also causing issues. There was nearly a thousand miles of sea between the port at Narvik and the British naval bases in northern Scotland and every day the German submarines that roamed the seas were cutting the supply lines.

Who the hell knew just what the generals in charge of this operation thought or had in mind but from the perspective of the average British soldier on the ground, things could not be going worse. Most soldiers were natural doers, that is, they were given a task to perform, and they completed it to the best of their abilities. But when said soldiers are not given anything to do, nothing to work on they became lax and lazy and there was nothing more deadly to a soldier than idleness.

Private Angus O'Shaughnessy gripped his Lee-Enfield No. 4 rifle and tried to breath calmly as he shuffled his feet through the tall thick grass under the canopy of trees. He was nervous and he fought not to show it. He'd only been in the army for six months now, having gotten his draft notice like so many of the other lads. He'd been in shock that day. He'd just finished secondary school and had plans for college. But Mister Chamberlain had other plans.

His company must've been a good five or six kilometers beyond the pickets at Beisfjord which itself sat about fifteen kilometers southeast of Narvik itself. He was eighteen and farther from home as he'd ever been before. Likewise, he was five or six kilometers beyond the safety of fixed defenses as he'd ever been.

His platoon had left for patrol just before five this morning. There were forty-two men in his platoon including six corporals, four sergeants and a platoon leader, Lieutenant Collins.

Private O'Shaughnessy tried his very best to breathe normally but he found his nervousness overrode any clear thought. At one point he was breathing so hard he didn't know if the other men could hear him or not.

To his left and his right, about ten paces each, were the men of 3rd platoon. The corporals and sergeants were a few paces ahead of the advancing line which was moving at a cautious pace. Patrol was a highly deadly battlefield assignment that no one ever relished getting. This was O'Shaughnessy's first.

Angus looked to his front, his eyes moved but his head stayed straight. He kept thinking that any movement, no matter how small, might get him killed. He could clearly hear wind whipping through the tree leaves, of birds chirping and somewhere a red squirrel was cracking an acorn against a tree.

Breath damn you, he thought to himself, *just breath.*

The fingers of his right hand lightly grazed the trigger of his rifle, his palms were sweaty, his left hand was gripping the rifle stock so tightly that he thought he was going to break his fingers. He could feel the pounding of his heart beating in his chest like a drum. All he could hear were the deep breaths he exhaled through his nose.

It all happened so fast after that.

He didn't hear anything only felt it. He froze in place, his legs simply couldn't move.

That moment seemed to stretch out into eternity. Whatever it was that had hit him it had gotten him in his shoulder. He'd barely felt it but knew that it had happened. He'd heard of men going into shock when they were hit, sometimes taking minutes to realize what was wrong. He slowly glanced over at his left shoulder, at where he was hit and let out a long exhausting, relieving sigh.

The acorn had hit him on his shoulder and fell harmlessly to the ground.

"Jesus Christ, O'Shaughnessy," Corporal Doyle said to him, as loud as he could whisper. "Loosen up, man. You're wound so damned tight, you're gonna explode."

O'Shaughnessy let out another hard exhale and looked back at Corporal Doyle who was standing about eight paces ahead of him. Doyle looked back at the teen and shook his head with disappointment on his face. Angus blinked then blinked again, finally reality set in. He knew he was fine and that an acorn had simply fallen off a tree.

Doyle continued to stare at him. Angus grinned awkwardly and nodded at the other man. The corporal nodded back. The two men locked eyes.

And then Doyle's head erupted in a bloody explosion half a second later. The sound of the kill shot echoed through the trees a moment after that and then the sound of hell breaking loose followed.

"GET DOWN!"

A cacophony of machine gun fire erupted. Several of the men didn't move in time and at least half a dozen men fell in the first seconds.

Angus dropped to the ground, put his hand over his helmet as a splattering of blood and mud kicked up over his face. He dropped his head so that his helmet covered his horizontal body. It was an incessant firing, but he couldn't tell where it was coming from, the left or the right. Rifles opened fire but they weren't British rifles, he knew that much.

Another man was hit, then another. There were the sounds of panicked screams and men in pain. The machine gun kept firing.

"To the right! To the right!" A voice screamed over the loud machine gun.

One brown clad British soldier, lying in prone position, lifted his rifle and began firing off to the right, another one followed and another after that. Then he could see it, the movement from the right of his eye. He could barely make it out but there were at least two figures wearing helmets crouched behind a fallen tree

"Germans on the right!"

The platoon scrambled to put down rifle fire on the attackers. Additional German rifle fire started up on the left of the enemy machine gun position and another of the boys got hit. The man rolled over, gripping his left arm in pain. His mouth was wide open, but Angus could not hear above the sound of the ripping machine gun.

Lieutenant Collins shouted for those on the left of the line to follow him, urging them forward. The men on the left flank of the platoon crawled their way forward to join up with the lieutenant, who'd taken to the ground along with the NCOs around him.

Angus lifted his rifle up and fired off two shots in the general direction of the incoming fire. There was about fifty yards and a hundred trees between himself and the Germans and getting a clear shot was nearly impossible from where he was. But he fired anyway because there was nothing else he could do. He fired a third shot, then a fourth.

Then the first grenade exploded, a German. It went off about eight paces to his front, just where Corporal Doyle had been standing a few seconds earlier. The explosion sent dirt flying a dozen feet up and hundreds of pieces of small metal bits going in all directions. Then another grenade and another went up along the right of the British line.

A quick look to his right and he could see at least half of the men who had been on the end of the line before were either dead or lying on the ground bleeding. One man gripped his stomach, dark blood seeping through his fingers. One man took a hit to his left bicep but kept firing using only his right arm.

Another grenade exploded just feet ahead of him, small bits of shrapnel pinged against his steel helmet. Angus exhaled and looked back up at the German position. The gray-clad bastards were huddled up behind a pair of fallen trees, good cover for an ambush. He aimed his sights right at one of the Nazi shits, looked like he had a good line, instinctively exhaled then squeezed the last round in his magazine.

He couldn't be sure, but he swore he could see the outline of the German, saw the man grab his hand and fall backwards.

"Holy shit!" He exclaimed, thinking, hoping he'd gotten the bastard.

"Cover fire!" Lieutenant Collins hollered. "Cover fire!"

Collins and the men to his right, about twenty, opened fire on the attacker's position. It was nothing more than an exercise in futility and Collins knew it. The six men to his left, led by Sergeant O'Malley, crouched their way around the flank. The trees gave them some cover to the half dozen men who tried to make their way out of the enemy's sight.

On the left of the British line, to the German's right, there was a depression about fifty yards out that dropped down to shoulder height. From there it looked like it ran northwest to southeast about a hundred feet before emerging about thirty yards from the German flank. From there the British could get at the German's right, if lucky, before the enemy could do anything about it.

The machine gun fire slackened, but the enemy rifles kept going. Another grenade exploded but fell far too short to effectively do anything.

Private Daniel Murphy got hit, the shot went through his left eye as he aimed his rifle. A German got hit too, Angus could see him in the distance, slumping to the ground in between two trees and then lying still.

One soldier, Cleary, ran forward, pulled the pin on a grenade then launched the thing through the air before diving to the ground again. The exploding grenades went back and forth but the attackers had the advantage, that much was certain.

Angus changed out the magazine of his rifle, five shots were the limit. The German Mauser bolt action rifle was a good rifle and in the hands of a well-trained German soldier, it was utterly deadly. If there was one drawback to the rifle it was that after each shot the user had to quickly release the bolt, eject the spent cartridge and then allow for another round to chamber before finally re-locking the bolt again. A good man could do this in one fluid motion, but there was a price to be paid. A long-lasting fire fight could wear down even the best, most conditioned man.

The British Lee-Enfield by contrast, used five shot magazines that, once exhausted popped out of the rifle and allowed the soldier to simply pop a new magazine back in.

Sergeant O'Malley and his men had made it to the depression and were crouching down as they moved forward. In another minute and a half, they'd emerge on the other end of the shallow trench to the chagrin of the German attackers. They'd be facing attack on two sides, the group on their right flank and the thirty or so British soldiers in front of them. If they ran now, they'd probably save themselves and have done terrible hurt to the British patrol, killing no less than eight and wounding five more.

From the other side Angus could make out the shouts of German soldiers yelling to their comrades. The rifles kept firing and the machine gunner did what he could to keep the British pinned down.

He raised his rifle again, fired off a round then slithered forward a few feet. The British line was slowly crawling ahead, putting down return fire. Lieutenant Collins had dropped his rifle and was now holding his service model revolver in one hand, his whistle in the other.

Another grenade exploded, this one quite a bit closer. Somebody on the other side had an arm. The earth erupted upwards then came showering down again.

Lieutenant Collins held the whistle up to his mouth and blew. From the southeast end of the depression Sergeant O'Malley and his men charged out from out of the earthwork cover and ran straight for the German right flank, nothing but trees standing in their way. Collins blew his whistle a second time.

Through the wood Angus saw Sergeant O'Malley leading his men forward, their rifles held up across their bodies as they ran forward, their bayonets fixed. They made a good pace moving between the trees. The group would close in on the Germans in a matter of seconds. Lieutenant Collins and the men gathered around him, affixed their own bayonets to the tips of their rifles, ready to charge into the enemy as soon as O'Malley made contact.

More rounds crisscrossed in the air, another German took a hit, fell, then crawled behind a tree for cover.

O'Malley's squad barreled down on the German flank, only then did he notice the shadowy figures hiding behind a group of thick trees. The man behind O'Malley took the first hit, right to the chest, as the closest German stepped out and fired his rifle at near point-blank range. A second German stepped out from his hiding place, leveled his gun and fired, the third man in O'Malley's group dropped from a stomach shot.

The Irish sergeant, clearly startled by what had just taken place, realized the trap he'd walked into and barreled straight into the first German before the man could reload and took him right off his feet.

Lieutenant Collins stared in disbelief as Sergeant O'Malley's squad ran straight into the Germans that he hadn't even noticed were there.

A knot of trees had obstructed their presence and instead of the British troops rolling up the German position, they were being cut down. Another British soldier got hit, another chest shot, the fourth man in line had just enough time to raise his own rifle and fire a shot into the side of one of the Germans, sending the gray-clad Nazi to the ground.

The whistle fell away from Lieutenant Collins' mouth, and he watched in horror from a distance at what was happening to his men. O'Malley had knocked the first German down and gave him a hard hit on the jaw with the butt of his rifle before making his way forward again. Half a dozen more of the German bastards emerged from the clump of trees, two fired their rifles, both missed.

O'Malley rushed forward another ten feet, aimed his rifle and fired off a shot, dropping one of them before the man could aim his rifle at the fast-moving Irishman. The fifth and sixth man in the attacking group were still on their feet but they'd made the mistake of stopping rather than charging onward and giving up their momentum. The rest of the hiding Germans rushed forward, one aimed and put a round right through Private Lewis's throat.

From his position, Angus could see from the distance of a hundred yards as the flanking attack fell apart. He could also clearly see Lieutenant Collins, the shocked officer trying to gather his faculties and rally the men around him.

"Bloody bastards!" He heard Corporal Kenzie scream a few feet to his right. The short corporal fired off his entire magazine in quick succession.

What was left of the platoon was not looking good. A t least a third of the group was down, dead or wounded. The rest of the men were occupying a stretch of forest ground close to a hundred meters long with enemy machine gun fire strafing this way and that. Around the Lieutenant there were perhaps seven men still able to lift a rifle. Sergeant O'Malley only had three men from the looks of things. The rest were either dead or badly wounded.

Corporal Kenzie rolled over the ground, right into O'Shaughnessy and reloaded a new magazine.

"This ain't good! Ain't good at all," he said out of breath. "Lieutenant's gotta call a retreat otherwise. . . ." He trailed off.

"What about Sergeant O'Malley?" Angus asked the other man.

Kenzie looked and shook his head but didn't answer the question. "We walked right into it! Lieutenant's gotta call a retreat or we'll all be feeding buzzards."

The German machine gun fire ramped back up again, the gunner swinging his weapon back and forth along the entire line of British troops. Another whistle blow loudly. The two men looked over at Collins and his group, but to his surprise Collins had not blown his whistle, wasn't even holding it anymore.

From out of the trees three or four of the attacking Germans charged out, each one holding a single grenade in their hands. They flung them towards the British line, then dropped down to the ground. Just before the explosions erupted, he could see more of the Germans charging forward towards the British.

The grenades exploded almost in unison, sending hundreds of bits of shrapnel outwards, one man caught a spray of hot metal across his face and screamed out in agony. But they had also sent a succession of erupting soil and earth upwards, blocking the ability of the British to see the German infantrymen before they came plowing right through the trees.

The first Nazi ran through the falling earth towards Collins and his men. There was barely enough time to get off the shots that put the hefty man down. But the second and third Nazi got close enough to get their own shots in. Sergeant McLaughlin got hit in the thigh and Private Reynolds took a shot to the head. Collins raised his revolver and shot the first German down but couldn't quite get the second one before being hit by an unseen shooter himself.

The lieutenant grabbed his chest in panic, his eyes turned bloodshot red, and he dropped to his knees before falling forward. It was pure chaos after that.

Two dozen German troops stormed across the distance between the two lines. The machine gun fired one last salvo at the British before going quiet. At first Angus didn't understand why, but Corporal Kenzie sure did. He elbowed Angus in his side and leapt upwards.

"Get up dammit!" He almost pulled the teen up to his feet with one arm.

Angus got his feet under himself just in time to see one of the bastards charging right at him, rifle at the ready. Two shots from Corporal Kenzie ended him but there were plenty more behind that one. Some of the platoon managed to get to their feet before contact was made with the enemy. The Germans fired at near point-blank range. Men on both sides dropped, Private Lancing took a bayonet to his ribs but managed to lift his rifle and put a bullet through the leg of his killer.

Angus, adrenaline flowing through him, aimed his rifle and fired at whichever German he could get his sights on, though he was far too panicked to know if he'd hit the man. Kenzie stood next to him firing off round after round then switching out again after five shots.

"Bastard Collins!" Kenzie cursed, he knelt to reload his rifle. Angus was pretty sure Lieutenant Collins was dead. He was sure that a lot of men were dead. Everywhere he looked men on both sides were fighting for their lives with rifles, bayonets, even knives. He'd never seen anything like this, never dreamed he'd ever see it. Not at eighteen anyhow.

Kenzie grabbed him with his powerful left arm and pulled him backwards, through the trees and tall grass. Corporal Jenkins and two men were off to the left, another man at their feet holding his hand over a bloody eye. A pair of German troops were crouched down in the grass, taking shots at Jenkins and his men. Everywhere there was chaos and death.

Kenzie yanked Angus behind and tree and threw him to the ground then knelt beside him.

"Listen to me, lad. We're getting out of here now! Somebody's gotta warn battalion. We've gotta get back and give them the warning."

Angus stared at him, despite his shock at all the horror, his ears couldn't believe what he was hearing. He was eighteen, Corporal Kenzie was at least twenty-five and what he was saying now sounded a lot like cowardice. His eyes were wide when he stared back at the corporal. He shook his head viciously.

"No. No!"

"Listen to me! Listen! Someone's gotta know what happ..." Angus angrily pushed Kenzie backwards, away from him and the tree. He grabbed his rifle off the ground and struggled to get back up.

Corporal Kenzie stared at the young teenager, shock in his eyes, then screamed out in pain as he collapsed backwards off his feet. Angus was too shocked to completely realize what had just happened. Kenzie tore away at his side, ripped off the buttons of his uniform. His hands were bloody, and he writhed around on the ground in pain.

"Corporal!" Angus shouted in horror. "I'm sorry." He dropped to his knees over Corporal Kenzie and placed his hand of the man's rib cage near where the blood was spreading out.

Kenzie looked at the kid, for a moment he looked like he hated the boy, looked like he was going to take this opportunity to get his revenge on him for getting him shot. But that faded away and Kenzie put one hand on the kid's face and nodded.

"Go! Go now! Don't die here, boy."

Angus just stared at him for a handful of seconds, oblivious to all else taking place around him.

"Okay," he finally got out of his throat. "I'm sorry for pushing you, corporal."

"Go dammit!" Kenzie yelled. "Go now!"

Angus got one foot under him, then the other, gripped his rifle and started off as fast as he could go, running away from the sounds of killing, away from the corporal who had tried to save his life and was now going to die for his effort. He just ran and ran....

.... until his leg kicked out from under him, and he fell flat faced on the ground. His rifle fell away from him, and a stab of pain ran through him.

A bullet had passed straight through his right thigh and sent agonizing waves of pain throughout his body. He instinctively gripped the wound as tight as he possibly could and looked down at his leg. His brown trousers were filling up with blood. He tried to kick his leg out, to get his foot to move and get back up. He pushed his upper body up, moved his left leg underneath him and put his weight on it, then moved his right leg and fell back down. The pain was too much.

He laid there for a moment, his hands clasped over the wound, tears running down his cheeks. He didn't even hear the shooting stop as he tried to crawl on the ground. Didn't hear Corporal Kenzie calling out his name. And he certainly didn't see the dirty faced German mountain trooper walk up behind him as he lie there bleeding. But he definitely heard the bolt from the German's rifle as he chambered a round.

He slowly turned over onto his back, looked up at the other man in utter terror and raised his hands up.

"Please!" he cried.

The hulking German soldier stood over the kid and pointed his rifle straight at the boy's head. *"Dummer junge,"* the German said to him, and his finger squeezed the trigger.

CHAPTER TWENTY-FOUR

Hitler took the pills offered to him, tossed them into his mouth then swallowed them down with a large gulp of water. He sank back into his large, cushioned chair as Doctor Morell stood over him, two fingers gripping the Führer's wrist and his eyes on his watch. The overweight doctor had on an eerie smile that Hitler found slightly uncomfortable, and he hummed softly to himself as he took the Führer's pulse. Finally, he let go and Hitler rubbed the bridge of his nose with his now free hand.

He had suffered from debilitating headaches for years, made worse by air travel. He disliked flying and he had made a point of avoiding it as often as he could. After coming to power in 1933 he'd had several personal trains built for him that allowed him to move around the country without having to fly. The trains also allowed him to be seen by the people. His people. He felt that it was important for a leader to be seen by the people.

His personal trains had been designed to be comfortable but also give him the space that he needed to be able to conduct work. Fully equipped with encrypted radios, briefing rooms, small offices and guarded by a battalion of his SS bodyguards, the trains allowed Hitler to be mobile while still run the nation's affairs.

It also allowed him to avoid the splitting headaches that even short flights always gave him.

The Führer moaned as he massaged the bridge of his nose and eyelids.

"The headache will go away in a little while," Doctor Morell said to him in his usual soft, feminine voice. "Your blood pressure is a little high though. A little tea with dinner would do some good. Please try and relax, Mein Führer. You have traveled a lot lately and you need some rest."

Hitler only grunted at the comment. He opened his eyes and looked up at the pudgy faced doctor.

"Thank you, Doctor Morell. That will be all."

Morell smiled back and nodded. Collecting his bag, he looked at the others gathered around the great room and nodded graciously. "Gentlemen."

The others in the room returned the gesture and watched as the man left the room. A personal attendant offered to refill Hitler's water, but the Führer waved it away. He put the half empty glass of water on the small table next to him.

"Bring us some tea," he ordered the young man. "Iced."

The young man in his pure white tunic nodded, picked up the water glass and then made his presence scarce. Hitler waited a moment before beginning.

Sitting around the large great room of the mountaintop villa, apart from Hitler, sat Joseph Goebbels, the effective Minister of Propaganda and Hitler's most trusted confidant, Joachim von Ribbentrop, Minister of Foreign Affairs, and General Wilhelm Keitel, Chief of the Armed Forces.

The Berghof had been built almost twenty-five years earlier as a simple mountain cabin house. Hitler had purchased the mountaintop villa just seven years ago and had the original home expanded upon and its name changed. It had become his favorite private residence outside of Berlin and he would often spend as much time there as his demanding schedule would allow, bringing his staff and high-ranking members of the Nazi party and government along with him so that he may, as he called it, "hold court" while away from the capital. He'd even entertained high ranking foreign dignitaries at the resort. Chamberlain and he had met here just two weeks before signing the Munich Agreement back in '38. Inwardly Hitler chuckled at the memory. He'd had the British Prime Minister so desperate for peace back then that he'd convinced the man to give away half of Czechoslovakia just to avoid a fight.

Hitler let out a long sigh of relief. "What news out of Hungary?" He asked softly.

Ribbentrop, ever the image of Aryan culture, sat with his left leg thrown over his right knee.

"I've personally been in touch with Horthy," the Foreign Minister replied. "We'd been going through normal diplomatic channels for a couple of months, but the Regent is now in direct talks with us. Now that the Poland operation is over, he seems much more amiable to signing the pact with us. There are some minor details that need to be worked out of course, but they are trivial, and I feel that before the month is out the Hungarian government will declare themselves to be openly on our side."

The Führer, chewed the inside of his lip, looked at Ribbentrop and nodded ever so slightly.

Ribbentrop continued. "The British and French are already sending warnings to our friends in Budapest about siding with us though. The expected threatening language diplomats use. The British ambassador there is apparently being subtle about it. The French, as usual, are not so subtle." He shrugged slightly. "My counterpart in Hungary, Csáky, has made his country's policies quite clear to them."

Hitler scoffed at the news. "Neither can do much, if anything, about it. Hungary is too far away from them and right in our own backyard. The British are not in a position to do anything and the French...." he chuckled. "They're not the warriors that they used to be. Hard to believe the people that gave us Charlemagne and Bonaparte can think only of eating pastries and licking young girls than fighting." The others laughed at the joke.

"I agree with you of course, Mein Führer," Ribbentrop continued. "Once we iron out some last little details the Hungarians will no doubt choose to throw in with us. Budapest understands in which direction the wind is currently blowing. It's neither the British nor the French that has me concerned, however. It's the Soviets. Or more indirectly, Romania. The Hungarian-"

The door to the large parlor opened again and the white clad attendant reappeared and made his way into the large great room with a tray of drinks in his hands. The young man put the tray down on the large circular glass table sitting in the center of the lounge, poured a glass of iced tea for everyone and left swiftly and silently. Hitler reached over for his glass.

"Go on," Hitler told him, then took a sip of his cold tea.

"Yes. As I was saying, the Hungarians are laying claim to parts of Transylvania. They do have some legitimate claims of course, but the Romanians are already viewing Hungary as an aggressive neighbor. With the Soviets on their eastern borders already, they may see our acceptance of Hungary carving out a large swath of Romanian territory as potentially an act of war."

The Führer sank back further into his chair and took it in silent thought. He often would say very little during meetings such as this, especially if he was not feeling well.

Goebbels broke the silence. "The Romanians are quickly becoming isolated in their corner of Europe. We've triumphed over Poland in just weeks, Denmark and Norway are in our hands. They've seen who the true master of the continent is. A little pressure on them and they'll have no choice but to accept Budapest's demands. As it is they already know how displeased we are with them for allowing the Polish army to flee through their country. Thousands of Polish troops were allowed passage to escape when their country fell."

"Perhaps so, Joseph, but consider this, Romania's strategic oil fields are the largest in Europe," Ribbentrop told him. "If we are perceived as siding with Hungary over Transylvania, the Romanians could very well be pushed into the Soviet camp. The last thing we need is for that to happen. We rely heavily on oil imports from Romania. Or, likewise, if we were to remain neutral the Soviets could easily interpret that as a concession that we have no intentions in the region. A war between Romania and Hungary could be all the reason that Stalin needs to invade from the east, once again costing us that oil."

"Hungary might very well find invading northern Romania to not be as easy as they would have hoped," General Keitel offered. He leaned forward, took his glass of iced tea and sipped on it. He looked at Hitler. "The reports from our military advisors to Hungary do not paint a very rosy picture. Their army is poorly equipped and trained. They've got very few units that are up to our own standards. In some units they're still using pack mules to pull artillery. However, the situation for the Romanians is even worse from what we know. And with large segments of their own population made up of ethnic Hungarians and Bulgarians they can hardly be trusted to fight." He took another sip of tea.

"Agreed," Ribbentrop replied. "However, again the bigger picture are those oil fields. Mein Führer, I cannot stress it enough that the loss of Romanian oil could be disastrous for us. Bucharest knows that they have options. Despite the animosity they hold for the Hungarians, they hate the communists even more and Stalin wants their eastern territories. But out of necessity they could find themselves becoming allied with him just to fight the Hungarians in the west. Or they could ally with London and Paris in which case we could find ourselves fighting on two separate fronts."

Hitler let out a snort. Since coming to power in 1933 Hitler had gone to extra lengths in order to court his increasingly fascist neighbors. Italy had been first of course. Mussolini was already in power by '33 and the two countries, enemies in the previous war, had suddenly found themselves as the closest of allies. After Germany annexed Austria and Czechoslovakia in 1938, Hungary seemed like the next likeliest country to join the alliance and Germany had wasted no effort in urging their neighbor along.

But Hungarian politics and the desire to reclaim old lands previously lost to it had moved them closer to conflict with their eastern neighbor Romania. Hitler's promise of mutual assistance and military aid, however, did not extend to starting new wars in the east. Such a thing would have cut Germany off from the precious oil supplies that Romania was selling to them. Without that oil the German economy and its mighty war machine might very well grind to a halt.

"Well, we obviously need to rein them in," Hitler told them. "We'll arrange a meeting with Horthy. Have him come to Berlin so that we can iron out any issues and bring the Hungarians into the fold. We can force him to back down from his claims for now. A year down the road. . . . who knows what will happen?"

Keitel and Goebbels both nodded in agreement.

Ribbentrop shifted in his chair. "If I may offer a suggestion." Hitler nodded. "I have been giving this situation a great deal of thought and I think we may be able to use the entire situation to our advantage. Obviously, Budapest is ready to openly ally with us. Well.... there are a few details yet to work out, but I am sure that will not stop Horthy's government from signing the agreement. But as I said earlier, we cannot afford to risk losing our pipeline with the Romanians. Stalin has his eye on that country. He wants it, or at least a good part of it and has already occupied some eastern territories."

He paused for a moment, rubbed his lower lip.

"My sources in Romania have informed me of disgruntled elements in their government and military. There are those who believe they should cut their ties with Britain and France. They see better opportunities with new allies. Stronger allies. I don't mean the Bolsheviks either."

"An opportunity?" Hitler said. He swished his glass of iced tea around in his hand. "Tell us about your idea, Herr Ribbentrop."

"Well, Mein Führer, the Romanians are desperately trying to avoid a war, either in the east or the west. Although obviously they are more afraid of the Soviets than they are of the Hungarians. However, they also do not wish to lose their lucrative trade with us. They know that Britain and France cannot truly guarantee their independence from the communists. They knew after Poland fell that they were on their own. If Stalin invades, then it's over for them. That's the greater threat for them."

Goebbels nodded his head in understanding. "A diplomatic intervention then. Is that what you are proposing, Joachim?"

"It is. If we act as a neutral third party, negotiate an agreement between Hungary and Romania then we can make a separate agreement with the Romanians for their protection and their oil."

"And will their king accept such an agreement to arbitrate?" Hitler asked.

"He'll have little choice," Ribbentrop replied. "If he doesn't, he risks diplomatic isolation and possibly conflict. As it is his government stands on a blade's edge. He's an autocrat whose country supports the Allies but is the target of two neighboring countries. His only prosperous relationship right now is with us. We can position ourselves with the Hungarians, offer to arbitrate the situation. They'll accept and under those conditions I am quite certain the Romanians will too."

Hitler nodded and made an accepting face. "Sounds masterful. So, Hungary will take possession of Transylvania and Romania will fall under our protection. The loss of territory mostly inhabited by foreigners anyway for the guarantee of protection from the Russians." He smirked and slapped his knee at the idea.

"And their oil," Ribbentrop added. Both he and Goebbels smiled at the Führer's excitement.

"Sounds absolutely masterful, Herr Ribbentrop. I'll leave it to you to put together the details. It'll be proposed when Horthy arrives." Hitler sipped again on his iced tea. "That should take care of that. Now, as for the Allies....my meeting with Mussolini was insightful if not boring, as usual. The dago thinks far too highly of himself. But he's proven himself to be a reliable outlet between us and the Allies."

Goebbels chuckled and nodded. Ribbentrop had dealt with Mussolini and had established a good working relationship with the Italian that his countrymen had nicknamed Il Duce, the Leader. Despite the relationship he had with the man in private circles around Berlin Mussolini was certainly seen as the over inflated junior partner of the German-Italian alliance. Though the man in Rome was certainly good at playing the part that Berlin wished him to play, he too often took diplomatic privileges that were seen as contrary to German interests.

"Mussolini is again acting as an intermediary between us and the British and French," Hitler went on. He took another sip of his iced tea, the pain killers the doctor had given him were slowly beginning to kick in. "As I suspected Chamberlain is not interested in a real fight. There are back-channel discussions going on between London and Rome. They claim they're trying to head off things before it all goes too far. The Italians think they can work out some kind of a deal between us and them."

"Leaving the French out of the talks?" Goebbels inquired.

"The French are not as timid as the British are right now," Ribbentrop interjected. "Monsieur Daladier has made his position quite clear. He is not interested in any negotiated settlement at this time. We all know that he was not happy about Munich anyhow. He didn't want to give in to us like Chamberlain did." He chewed the inside of his lip for a moment. "The Frenchman has more spine than the Englishman does."

Hitler looked at Ribbentrop and shook his head. "The French are nothing without their friends in London. Negotiate a peace with Chamberlain and end the war with Britain and the French will not be able to fight on alone. We can take back the lands that are rightfully ours and undue the stains of the last war." His face grimaced slightly. "Nothing would please me more than to watch the Toads be forced to sign away half their country, the same way we were forced to do."

Keitel cleared his throat. "Well, both the British and French armies seem intent on fighting a defensive war. They've both taken up positions in the west and apart from the failed Saar occupation, which they promptly retreated from, they've taken no action against us. On land that is. Perhaps the British Prime Minister really is hoping for a diplomatic resolution after all." He picked up his glass of iced tea and raised it to Hitler. "You had his cowardice spotted at Munich, Mein Führer." He took a long sip.

"No spine," Hitler quietly commented and shook his head.

"If we can come to some kind of settlement with Chamberlain," Ribbentrop began, "and quickly, I think we'll see the French eventually come to the table as well. It may take a while longer, but alone the French cannot win."

"Well, I can assure you that they have nothing that will stand up to our modern army," Keitel told the group of men. "We've invested heavily in rearming ourselves. We've seen firsthand just how well trained our forces are. The French don't have anything much better than what the Poles had and look at what we did to them. When the time comes, we'll steamroll right through Northern France!" He pumped his fist in the air. "And right on to Paris!"

Hitler grinned at the other man's enthusiasm. "Those plans are for another day, Keitel. We must consolidate our gains first. Poland is ours. Denmark is ours. Soon Norway will be ours and the British are already suing for peace. We have accomplished much together in these few short years. We've shown the real strength of National Socialism. Let us have our talks with the Tommy's. Mister Chamberlain will get the peace he hopes for, but it will be on our terms."

He finished the last of the tea in his glass then placed it back on the table then sank back into his chair. The pain killer he'd taken was making him tired now.

"The truth is, gentlemen, Chamberlain and his appeasers might well be the best ally we could have. He'll settle. He wants peace at any cost."

CHAPTER TWENTY-FIVE

The sound of the first artillery shell shrieking overhead sent the entire company of British soldiers diving into the dirt. The shell landed just twenty feet ahead of the line and exploded, followed a few seconds later by a second then a third a few seconds after that. Sporadic shells fell here and there but nobody had been hit yet.

The Germans only had a few pieces of light field artillery with them but the British forces by comparison had none. The generals in charge of the defense, for whatever reason, had not seen fit to bring any heavy guns over from Britain and that decision was costing them now. Even a few 7.5 cm German guns could push back whatever defending troops were ahead of them on their march to the port at Narvik.

For days now the German mountain troops had slugged their way forward along the narrow roads of northern Norway, until now only a mere two kilometers remained between them and the last port in the country and the one the Allies were now forced into evacuating their forces from. Despite having been outnumbered by five to one the more experienced and highly trained German mountaineers had made a very impressive march through the wooded terrain of Norway and were now close to driving their enemy into the sea.

In contrast the Allied force of British and French troops had begun the process of evacuating almost as soon as the first shots had been fired just days earlier. As soon as the advance elements of the German 3rd Mountain Division had made contact with British patrols, the commanding general had ordered a withdraw from the area, giving up their last foothold in Norway. Despite outnumbering the Germans and the heroism of some of the Allied units, the army was falling back.

In the distance Miles could hear another German howitzer firing followed a few seconds later by the exploding shell and chunks of earth erupting from the ground. The men of 1st Battalion had taken up positions along the road just north of the village of Fagernes on the way to Narvik. The small village had been the home to farmers and fishermen just days ago and now lie burned and ruined. What was left of the small village was little more than a few standing stone walls and wooden barns that had turned to splinters. Here and there dead livestock littered the landscape and empty carts sat along the dirt road. The people who had lived here had fled days earlier.

Miles, his hand on his helmet, looked up at the sight of enemy troops, clad in gray camouflage, running here and there on the opposite side of the village. It was the first time he had actually seen a German soldier since the war had begun. B Company was holding the road just north of the village that the Germans were now moving into. They were coming through the woods in platoon strength, and they weren't trying very hard to conceal themselves either. Probably knowing that they had nothing to fear from the British soldiers that lacked any artillery. Short of a couple of good snipers in their ranks the Brits simply had been able to do very little to halt the Germans.

"Incoming!" A voice shouted.

The high pitch shriek of a mortar shell forced everyone to lie flat and bury their faces into the dirt. There was an explosion and the sound of a man dying. Creech didn't look. He was afraid to.

"Keep down boys! Keep down!" The same voice bellowed.

Miles eyeballed the Germans for a moment then shifted his gaze down to his rifle and for what must have been the twentieth time made sure there was a round in the chamber. He'd only fired off one so far. Or was it two? He'd forgotten already. In the two days of straight retreat and with little or no sleep it was hard to keep one's thoughts in order. He couldn't even recall exactly what it was he'd shot those two rounds at.

On the opposite side of the ruined village lay a thinly wooded area, flanked on the north by the mountains and on the south by shores of the fjord that flowed westward and eventually emptied out into the North Sea. Between the mountains and the water ran the coastal road that went from Beisfjord, which sat at the cove of the fjord, westwards to the small, now destroyed village they now were fighting a rearguard action in. From here the road bent north and ran straight to the harbor where the remnants of the Franco-British-Norwegian force were now escaping from.

The 2nd Battalion of the South Wales Borderers had been evacuated on that first day as had most of the 3rd King's Own Hussars, an armored unit that, strangely enough, had not brought a single tank with them to Norway. On the second day of fighting the pocket around Narvik began to shrink. The French alpine units had been boarded aboard the Royal Navy destroyers just off the coast and evacuated just as the main body of German forces began to engage the right wing of the Irish Guards along the coast road.

The order of the day was to "hold the line" until all Allied troops were safely away.

Major General Carl Gustav Fleischer, commander of all Norwegian forces in Northern Norway, paced back and forth in front of the small house that had served as his headquarters for the past three days. He puffed away on his smoking pipe as he muttered away to himself and ran through the mass of thoughts in his head. His aides stood just feet away, quietly speaking to one another, knowing enough to leave the general to his thoughts.

The King was late and that worried Fleischer. He'd been in Narvik now for three days and had been forced to part with King Haakon the VII on the roads of the north four days earlier. He'd detached a company of his best rifleman to supplement the King's personal guard and escort His Majesty, the Royal Family and what was left of the government to Narvik, having made the difficult decision to go on ahead and to rally what was left of the Norwegian Army in the hopes of driving back the invaders.

The general had expected to be heartily supported by the Allies upon arriving in Narvik only to find that the Anglo-French force had absolutely no intention of engaging with the Germans head on and were in fact already preparing to evacuate. Fleischer, in a display indignant of his rank, told his new "allies" just what he'd thought of them when he'd accused both the army and navy leaders of betraying all of Norway by refusing to aid the Norwegians in a coordinated counterattack. He'd been forced to issue an apology after calming down and concluding that if he wanted his own men and the King rescued, he'd have to do so by boarding the boats of the Royal Navy.

As it was the first of his battalions were already busy loading in the harbor at this very moment and more would be boarding transports in the coming hours.

Smoke rings drifted up and away from his pipe. The general looked up at the dreary overcast sky. It was dark but not raining. Hopefully it would stay that way. *Good,* he thought. *Rain may only slow the evacuation process down.*

From the Ofotfjord came the sound of a ship's horn blowing as it came into the harbor. It was close to seven in the morning now. Hopefully soon...

"Sir!" Said one of his junior aides.

General Fleischer broke out of his reverie and looked over at young Lt. Blix. The lieutenant was pointing down the southward end of the street. From around the corner General Fleischer saw a single horse mounted trooper emerge. The trooper wore the bluish-green uniform of the army of Norway. The man looked in one direction and then the other. He spotted General Fleischer then motioned behind him and gave a quick nod. Several moments later four armed riflemen appeared followed by a single officer in a drab olive colored uniform, brown chest strap and holstered pistol.

The General snatched the pipe out of his mouth as the growing group of men, and now civilians too, began to emerge from the side street.

The officer in charge walked briskly toward him flanked by two riflemen. Their eyes scanned each building as they approached.

Finally, the officer stopped and snapped off a salute to the General which was returned.

"Major Karlsen," Fleischer greeted the other man. Karlsen was the head of the King's Royal detail and had overseen escorting King Haakon to Narvik.

"Sir."

"Where is the King?"

Major Karlsen nodded politely. "He is coming, sir. He is safe." Fleischer exhaled a relieving breath. "We had to take a longer route than we had planned for. The Germans have taken most of the eastern roads and we were forced take the route from Hergot instead. It was not easy either. We left there late last night and marched under darkness."

"Did you have any problems?"

"A few, sir." Karlsen replied then shook his head. "Some snipers gave us trouble. Two of my men killed as was one of the members of Parliament we were escorting. I'm sorry, sir."

The General sighed then shook his head at the major. "Not your fault, Major. Not your fault. You had a difficult duty to perform. The main thing is that you accomplished your mission. The King and his family are safe. The government survives."

More and more soldiers emerged from down the side roads followed by handfuls of civilians, mostly government workers, members of Parliament and their aides and families. At the beginning of the war, when the Germans began landing troops near Oslo, the capital had been swiftly evacuated of most of the high-ranking government officials and their families. Many hundreds of civil servants went with them along with important documents, the royal family and the nation's gold reserves, lest it be shipped off to Berlin.

King Haakon had been forced to take a train into the north of the country, moving from place to place along the way in order to evade German aircraft. When the Allies had landed their own forces on the western shores of Norway it was thought and hoped that they would be combined with the Norwegian Army and drive south to fight the invaders. To Fleischer's dismay that had not materialized.

Now Norway's only hope was to evacuate what was left of its government to Britain and keep the fight going from there.

"Let's go, Major," Fleischer told the man. "The King must be greeted."

General Dietl glanced at his watch and ran his left hand down his cheek and rubbed his jaw. It was nearly 0900. Up in the distance his artillery was even now pounding away at the British positions with not so much as a rock thrown back in response. The pocket around Narvik was growing smaller and smaller by the hour. Dietl had just less than five thousand men with him, and he'd gone up against nearly five times that number.

Sheep, he thought and scoffed.

From his elevated position he could observe the river road and how it curved north at the tiny village up ahead. His men were fighting down there, if you could call it fighting. More like hunting. The mountains around Narvik were steep and forested but that was what his men were trained for. He'd ordered four companies of mountaineers to traverse those mountains and come down upon the enemy from the north side. It would be absolutely impossible to haul any field pieces up there, but his men had some light mortars with them. A few dozen mortar rounds dropping down on the Tommy's head around Narvik would make them think hard about surrender.

In about four hours those mortar shells should begin falling.

Several feet behind him his command staff was busy working out operational details, studying maps and discussing the tactical situation. Just minutes ago he'd been handed a report from one of the forward observation posts that a large group of Norwegians had been seen entering the beleaguered town just to the north of the mountain hills. Military and civilians both. The officer who'd made the dispatch also reported seeing many small boats in the waters north of the city carrying what appeared to be additional soldiers. He noted that the boats were civilian.

Dietl would have to make an example of some of these native fishermen after this operation was over.

He took out a pack of cigarettes from his tunic pocket and lit one up then turned back around to his staff.

"Where are we?" He asked aloud and took a drag of his cigarette.

Colonel Kraft looked up. He had in his hand a small hand drawn map on a folded sheet of paper. "General. We have three companies pushing forward along the road and should be now right in that burnt village." He pointed out the positions on his map. "There's at least one company of British holding the bend, maybe even two. Our artillery has kept them at bay so far but that'll have to stop soon."

General Dietl nodded. The 3rd had been assigned a single battery of artillery at the start of this campaign. But the long lines of supply and communication with the main army down south made keeping those field guns supplied with enough shells nearly impossible. Not because of any enemy forces that may ambush the supply trucks but simply because of the nearly four hundred kilometers distance between him and his supply depot. So Dietl had as many artillery shells as possible loaded up into the few trucks they had brought north with them. Once those shells were gone, he knew the gig would be up.

"Well, Colonel, they shouldn't have to fire that much longer," Dietl replied. "Just long enough to get our infantry in place. But still, make sure we keep enough ammunition in reserve just in case we need it."

"Yes, sir," Kraft responded but Dietl knew that Kraft had already given the order. His chief of staff was always on the same page as he was. "Our second regiment is holding in place just behind the tree line. As soon as our engaging troops break through the British line, here, they'll rush through the opening. Colonel Radl is clear what his objectives are, and I personally told him not to play glory-hound."

"Good. It's nearly nine now. The companies I sent over the hilltops should be in position in another four hours. Until then we can keep most of the men stood down and rested. What word from the navy?"

"Hmmm." Kraft's expression turned sour. "*Scharnhorst* is steaming up the coast. At least ten hours away."

Dietl spit. "Ten? Their last message said eight."

"Yes, general. They're having some sort of problem with their boiler or some such thing. They reported that their pace is slowed. Honestly, sir, who knows. The navy always seems to get a bug in their arse when it comes to cooperation with the army."

"Ten hours," Dietl muttered, aggravation in his voice. "It'll be dark by then. The whole point was to cut the Allies of from their retreat." He smoked more of his cigarette and mentally ran through some figures in his head. The coordinated plan had been for the battleship *Scharnhorst* and her escorts to steam north along the long Norwegian coastline to the very mouth of the Ofotfjord and to cut the Allied ships off from escape. By 1900 hours the sun will have set and the Allies might have very well made off before the navy was in position.

Either way the enemy force will have been driven into the sea and Narvik would be in German hands by night, he thought to himself. He didn't much care what happened after his troops were in town.

Over the past week his forces had steadily driven the enemy backwards through the hills, mountains and woodlands and it had been no easy task either. Mountain warfare never was. But his troops had been trained and prepared for it. Even the detached forces that General Falkenhorst had given him had performed markedly well despite not being trained for this type of terrain. But the campaign had been an exhausting one and his troops would need the rest following it. His orders, his written orders that was, said to move north and capture Narvik and its port and that was exactly what he planned to do. There was nothing in those orders that said he had to give a damn whether the navy did their job or for that matter every Allied soldier and the King of Norway himself escaped to Britain.

The general finished his cigarette and dropped it to the ground, stamping it out with his foot.

"You may wish to get some rest, sir," Colonel Kraft suggested. "Nothing much is going to happen for at least a couple of hours, and you've been up all night. The boys are stood down anyway. As soon as anything happens, I'll alert you."

Dietl hesitated for a moment, the soldier in him didn't care for sleeping while his command was engaged but Kraft was right, he was exhausted, and an exhausted field commander would be no use to his troops.

"Two hours, Colonel. No more." He unsnapped the top two buttons of his tunic and walked off to find a tree to lie under for a couple of hours.

King Haakon VII of Norway was a man in his late sixties and right now he looked and felt every bit of his age. He'd been a lean man all his life but these last few weeks it seemed had made him even more so. His features were gaunt, and his color was bloodless white. But even in his present condition he still commanded the room. Wearing his crisp military uniform with three stars he stood ramrod straight as he walked slowly into a small-town office building that was serving as General Fleischer's headquarters. Even when it appeared that the old king was about to stumble, he quickly recovered his footing and waved away the attempts by his aides and his son, Prince Olav, to help him up the front steps.

The building was little more than a clerk's office with a large front room with three small wooden desks and a chalk board that had been removed from a local boy's school. Through a door and down a short hallway there were three more very small offices that some of the town officials worked out of.

King Haakon took off his hat as he entered the room. Gathered in the room, aside from General Fleischer and the King's retainers, were several senior officers from the army, Admiral Diesen, the Command Admiral of the Norwegian Navy and the single naval officer in the room, Major Karlsen, the head of the King's protective detail, three British officers and two civilians, both appeared to be civil servants.

The King stomped his feet and ran his fingers through his gray hair.

"Your Majesty," General Fleischer began, "I wish your welcome to Narvik could be under better circumstances."

Haakon nodded and smiled. "Give me the straight of it, General. I fear we won't have much time."

"Your Majesty, as you know we are completely surrounded by land." The general indicated to the chalk board which someone had drawn a rather rudimentary map of the area. "The details of which I know you are aware. Your Highness, this is General Auchinleck, commander of the British and French forces here. He and I have been coordinating the defenses of the area as well as the evacuation." General Auchinleck bowed his head slightly to the king. "Our main goal now is to remove you, the Royal Family and the rest of the government to Britain. The Royal Navy has a force off the coast that is covering our retreat."

Haakon shuddered slightly at the word retreat.

General Auchinleck took one step forward. "Your Majesty. First off on behalf of his Britannic Majesty King George the Sixth, I greet you and will do all in my power to make this as painless as possible for yourself and your family." He said through the assistance of an interpreter. The King nodded back graciously. "As the senior commander in the area I have the honor of escorting you to the harbor. *HMS Hostile* is offshore and is ready to receive you."

General Fleischer winced and tried to keep his anger from flaring up. General Auchinleck called himself senior officer, which technically he was as far as the foreign soldiers were concerned. But Fleischer was equal in rank to him and half of the friendly troops around Narvik were Norwegian. On top of these facts, this was Norwegian soil, and nobody was higher in rank than the king was.

King Haakon smiled faintly to the British commander. "Thank you, General. However, I do prefer to leave aboard a Norwegian seacraft. It sends a better signal."

"Ummm," Auchinleck began but Admiral Diesen then stepped forward.

"Your Majesty, as the head of your navy I am indeed honored by your request and your trust in the sailors under my command. However, I must regrettably suggest that you heed the general's suggestion. General Fleischer and I have had this discussion and we both agree. The conclusion among us is that the British warship is much better armored than any of our own motorboats. With enemy U-boats off the coast already, the situation is precarious. After reviewing the dire situation, I must highly suggest *Hostile* transport the Royal Family to Britain."

Haakon chewed his cheek for a moment, looked at Fleischer, who remained silent and offered no objection, then finally he reluctantly nodded.

"Very well," he conceded. "Tell me how the evacuation goes."

General Fleischer answered. "Over half of the Sixteenth Regiment is loaded and should be embarking within the hour. Many of our government functionaries will be boated out to a British cruiser as soon as possible along with our national treasures. It is... just after nine o'clock now. We'll have half our own loaded onto transports by eleven. The Fifteenth is deployed to the east of town to cover our retreat and the British are covering us from the south. The Germans are moving up the southern road now, artillery covering them."

"Yes, we could hear their guns as we approached."

"Yes, Your Majesty. Well, to move things along we also have dozens of small civilian boats shuttling our people out to Royal Navy vessels. With God on our side, we'll have the evacuation complete before sundown."

King Haakon smiled at his General. He inhaled deeply and looked down at his boots, covered with mud then let out his breath. He hated the idea of running, though it wasn't really running. He was leaving his country in the hands of a foreign invader and the armies of a madman. But if history had taught anything it was that a living, breathing symbol of national unity was better than no symbol at all, even though that person may be in exile in another country. The Germans would no doubt set up a puppet government, but he knew it would be looked on by the people of Norway as illegitimate.

His son Olav put his hand on his father's shoulder to give the older man strength.

"Well. I suppose that we should be moving," Haakon stated, not a bit of emotion in his voice. He was king and the king could not be emotional, especially at a time like this.

—•◇✕◇•—

"Bloody, goddamn bastards," Corporal Flanagan swore out loud. Creech was sure he wasn't referring to the advancing German soldiers but rather the British officers barking the orders.

The artillery shells had stopped firing almost half an hour earlier, but the gray-camouflaged enemy infantry was now pushing forward with all their strength. There had to be an entire enemy battalion now spread out in a sweeping line coming up the road. Machine guns on all sides blared as both sides exchanged fire. This wasn't the light sniping that had been going on for most of the morning either, this was a full-on exchange, the kind that the old timers of the last war spoke about. The machine guns firing thousands of bullets at advancing lines of enemy troops. But in this case the Germans had brought along their own machine guns as well and they were just as good, if not better, than what the British had.

"Bastards," Flanagan swore again. He was crouched behind an over-turned four wheeled cart, rifle at the ready. "Bloody officers should've gotten us out of here by now."

Just a few hundred meters behind the line of British troops were the outermost houses and buildings of Narvik proper. A and B companies had been given the task of holding back the enemy attackers while a small force of Norwegian troops was off to the left of the British line just in case the Germans had tried to come down over the hilltops.

"I heard from a sergeant that we had to wait on that Norwegian King," Private Toal replied. He was lying belly down in a side ditch, rifle perched towards the approaching enemy, a few hundred yards ahead and moving forward. "Or something like that."

Flanagan spit. "Fuck their bloody king. I'll bet he hasn't fired a single damned shot." He spit again. "I'm risking my Irish arse to keep his safe. Bet he ain't even in no hurry. Bugger's probably sitting in a nice safe room in town playing cards. Bastard."

The platoon was wedged in between the foothills and a partially de-molished blacksmith's forge. The southern half of the house had caved in. To the right of them the rest of company was spread out across half a kilometer of elevated road. They'd held this position for the better part of an hour now, pushed back to the very outskirts of town by the enemy. B company had one hundred forty-two fit for duty three days ago. As of this morning there were ninety-seven. Twenty-eight had been wounded and carted off in stretchers, seventeen others dead including his friend O'Kelly, shot in the chest yesterday afternoon just feet away from him. Miles had never seen a man die before in his life up until Norway. He was halfway afraid that he was becoming used to it now.

In exchange for the seventeen dead and for being pushed up the narrow roadway he was sure that they'd given the Germans a decent run for their money. He'd personally seen no less than two dozen of them get hit, two by his own rifle. His first kill was only two days earlier and it came as a surprise to him when he'd felt a sense of relief right after. That must be how it is in war. Kill or be killed. His grandfather, a veteran of the Zulu War in South Africa had told him that repeatedly before Miles had shipped off.

Kill or be killed, boy. It's that simple.

Grandfather had been correct.

Miles reached down without looking and grabbed his canteen, still half full and took a swig of warm water. He was kneeling next to a small pile of lumber beside the smithery. He'd learned in the last few days the best cover. Wood was a great place to hide behind, as was entrenched earth like Toal was lying in. Anything that could stop a bullet cold was the best. Hiding behind large rocks, of which there were plenty, was not as good as some of the lads had found out. Bullets hitting the rock tended to ricochet or worse yet split apart when they hit the hard surface. A couple of other men found out the hard way that a bullet spray, while not as deadly as a direct shot, could still maim a man who got caught the wrong way.

"Jerries coming this way, boys." Lieutenant Mayshed yelled as he crouchingly made his way down his line of men. "Don't dilly. Don't be heroes. For God's sake don't waste your ammo!"

"Now he bloody tells us," Flanagan muttered after Mayshed was out of earshot.

A single company of enemy soldiers was moving towards them from along the road all moving in a covering fire formation. Each man making three or four paces then dropping to the ground while the man behind him ran another three or four paces then did the same. Still at least three hundred yards off they were making impressive time. It was said that the German Gebrigsjager literally meant 'Mountain Hunter' and that they were considered some of the best soldiers in the German Army. Nobody could deny just how impressive they were either. They fought with a terrifying efficiency. It was rumored that they'd caught a British patrol in the woods and cut the poor devils to pieces just days earlier. Only a couple of British soldiers had managed to make it back to their lines and the story they told was that of total butchery.

But the 1st Battalion Irish Guards, mostly raw recruits, had been good too. They'd given the Germans a good fight these last four days despite the losses.

Behind the Irish Guards was a full company from the Scots Guards in reserve, ready to push forward to plug any gap in the British line. Behind the Scots were two companies of Norwegian riflemen and some scattering of French Legionaries, pieced together from several units. The Legionaries were made up of non-Frenchmen and were a wicked lot. Tough fighters with a history of standing their ground. It seemed to bother them when they'd been pulled off the line.

The first bullet hit the ground just feet away from Flanagan and kicked up some dirt. A second shot went wild. Creech spun around to see three enemy soldiers lying belly down on the road, rifles popping away. Two Brits returned fire, then a third, just enough to keep the Germans at bay and let them know that they weren't just going to be kicked from their positions so easily.

Miles wiped the sweat from his forehead, adjusted his brodie helmet strap and raised his rifle up towards the enemy. A dozen more were moving their way forward now, with more behind them. One German dropped to the ground as another moved up behind him. Miles waited for the third man to stand up and move, zeroed his sights in on where he thought the man would be then squeezed the trigger as soon as he saw the third German move. He wasn't sure if he got him or if the other man just dropped to the ground for cover but a half second later the bullets started to fly.

It was just after 1100 hours when an aide had woken General Dietl up. The general had discovered a shaded tree to lie under and fallen asleep rather quickly and found himself pleasantly well rested afterward. He'd become accustomed to marching through the dark night and sleeping very little. But he had come to the end of his rope and even a mere two hours could make a world of difference to an exhausted soldier.

Upon returning to his makeshift command post, which was set up under a knot of trees and consisted of nothing more than his command car and a couple of upturned buckets for his staff to sit on while they relayed orders.

"Ah, General," Colonel Kraft greeted him. "Well rested?"

Dietl grunted and nodded and pulled out a cigarette from his breast pocket.

"Good. Not much new to report to you, sir. Skirmish line has moved the enemy up the road several hundred yards. Colonel Radl has managed to push all the way to here." He indicated an area on a map that had been clipped to a piece of cardboard. "Three of his companies are moving forward with his fourth held in reserve. The road is narrow just ahead, between the water and the mountains but as soon as he pushes past this choke point, we can send 1st Regiment to storm into the town. By then our troops in the hills should be in position. We can attack from two sides and envelope them."

Dietl studied and map and took a long inhale from his Turkish cigarette. He knew that maps told one story, but the front line told something different. It was never as easy as that.

"Do we know what's ahead of us closer to town?"

"Our lookouts on the hilltop reported several platoons of Norwegian reinforcements gathering on the south side of town. Another unit was observed behind the British lines. About. . . . here I think. Observers could not identify. Company strength."

The general ran through some basic arithmetic. Colonel Radl had roughly six hundred and fifty men in his 2nd Regiment fit for duty as of that morning. British strength would be closer to two hundred. But the defenders were holding a single choke point with at least another hundred behind them in reserve plus whatever the Norwegians had put into the fray. The mountaineers he'd dispatched over the mountain consisted of a full regiment minus one company. Roughly seven hundred more men equipped with mortars. Once they were in position they'd hit the enemy from both sides, including an elevated position, all the time dropping mortar shells on their victims. Even five thousand men wouldn't be able to stand that for very long.

Still, he was uncomfortable with the lack of naval power. A squadron of German warships showing up on the British backdoor might very be enough to end this action without much additional fighting. The Allies were retreating on ships as fast as they could, but a trapped animal was usually the most dangerous type.

"Where's our artillery?" Dietl asked.

"I had them moved here, sir. Close enough to the fighting but out of the sight of prying eyes."

"Hmmm. Very well. I was hoping that we wouldn't need to put them back into action so soon. But..." He checked his watch again. "Without naval support.... Order Captain Walter to move his battery to here. Right along the waterway. From there he should have a direct sight on the British line as well as the town if we need to shell it."

Kraft looked at his commanding officer. "Yes, sir. But I should point out that we've exhausted most of our shells. He won't have more than thirty minutes worth of ammunition left to shell them with, sir."

"Noted, colonel. We're only going to get one good shot anyways."

The Royal Navy destroyers parked off the coast had a dual part job. The first was to provide escape for friendly forces evacuating from the falling city. The second, and more dangerous job, was to patrol the waters seeking enemy U-boats. At least two had been spotted in the area and one destroyer had already been torpedoed, although it did limp out of harbor and had sailed back for Britain. It was a constant reminder of unseen dangerous lurking below the surface.

For *HMS Hostile* the task had just gotten even harder. She'd been tasked with transporting the King, Crown Prince and Royal Family of

Norway across the North Sea. To add to this, the most senior military and civilian leadership would also be on board as were the crown jewels and several metric tons of gold bullion stored away in the ship's hull. For Commander John Piachaud Wright the very weight of the world was now put on his shoulders. Hunting U-boats wasn't even an option. Just evading them and getting out of harbor and across the North Sea may prove to be the biggest challenge of his career and his life.

King Haakon's escort slowly made their way up the gang plank. The monarch would not set foot aboard the ship himself until his entire family was safely aboard and even then, it seemed to take a great deal of time for the military escorts and civilians to make their way up the narrow walkway.

Commander Wright had greeted King Haakon on the deck with full honors. A typical visit by a head of state, much less a royal, usually involved some sort of splendid ceremony with fifes and pipes and a twenty-one-gun salute. However, under these conditions the captain, first and second officers and a small honor guard of four would have to suffice. To his surprise King Haakon had offered Commander Wright his hand upon boarding the ship. For all his education Wright could not recall an instance in modern history where a monarch and head of state was being forced to flee his country on the naval vessel of another country and no instance whatsoever where such a monarch shook the hand of someone whom some may have considered a lowly peasant.

"Honored, Your Majesty," Commander Wright said as he gripped the older man's hand, not sure if he'd broken some kind of protocol.

"How long for the crossing, Captain?" Haakon asked in accented English.

"We'll be in Scotland by this time tomorrow, Majesty."

Haakon padded the other man's hand and stepped away. He had forced himself to not become emotional during the entire flight from Oslo until now. But he felt as he'd made his way up the gangway a highly emotional tug that got worse with each step he took. Though he'd been born in Denmark, Norway was his home, they were his people, and he was their sovereign.

The king turned and stood with his hands clasped behind his back as slowly but surely his large entourage made their way aboard. Major Karlsen's troop was aboard, as were all members of the King's family. The members of Parliament were shuffling up now, belongings in tow. Military leaders would be the last to leave.

From his view Haakon could see for kilometers in all directions. There was the constant popping sound of distant gunfire. Although he couldn't see them, he knew that there was fighting on the outskirts already and that foreign troops were fighting and dying so that he and his people could make their escape.

The old King stood there and refused to be taken below decks until all were safely aboard. It would later be said that his eyes were filled with tears as the ship disembarked.

Benton Willoughby didn't even pause to register the fact that he'd just killed a man for the first and only time in his life. Put a single shot straight through the charging man's chest. He'd seen him coming, bayonet thrust outwards as he charged across the short distance between the two lines and fired. The German thumped to the ground and lay motionless. Benton put a second round through the man's head just to be sure. That was that.

There must've been four or five hundred of the elite mountain troops pushing forward and pushing hard. Machine gunners on both sides were firing away in long streams, one side trying desperately to punch a hole through the line, the defending side fighting like hell to keep the line together and neither side looking like they were giving.

Willoughby was knelt down behind a bundle of sod that some town's person had piled up next to his outhouse. Obviously, the man had decided it was best to leave it where it was and run for his life rather than lay the sod in his field. Right now, Benton was grateful the man had. It was providing decent cover.

He was smack in the middle of B Company's position facing off with at least two enemy companies. A Company was holding the right flank and a platoon of Frenchmen had just been thrown into the fray. The Nazis were coming in good formation, every third or fourth man would lob one of their famous 'potato smasher' grenades at the British as he advanced. Three MG 30 machine guns were ripping through ammo, keeping the British heads down while the riflemen advanced on them. The Brits, by contrast, had two of the older Browning machine guns firing back.

Benton carefully eyeballed the scene playing out before him. The enemy troops were good at their job and picking them off was not easy to do. A third of the company was down at least. He didn't know how many Germans had been killed, but there were plenty still coming.

From the side of his eye he caught movement and in one quick re-action brought his rifle left, put the man in his sights and squeezed the trigger. The Nazi grabbed his shoulder and dropped his rifle as he fell to the earth.

Lieutenant Mayshed, a bloodied bandage wrapped around his right hand had witnessed the shot and shouted an approval to Willoughby. That was two. Another round chambered in his Lee-Enfield.

His breathing was remarkably steady, and he'd barely broken so much as a sweat despite the heat of battle and the fact that the early afternoon sun was right above them. Before the army he'd only ever picked up the small hunting rifles his grandfather had taught him to use. Before today he'd never shot anything larger than a rabbit.

"On the right!"

His eyes shifted right. Half a dozen Germans had just charged forward then slammed hard to the ground, firing away as fast as they could with their bolt action Mauser 98's. Behind them seven or eight more charged past their comrades. They were perhaps thirty paces off but running quick. Willoughby aimed and fired but missed the moving target. He'd fired too soon as he knew it. Letting out a deep breath he fired again at the same man and nabbed him right in the thigh.

An eruption of earth went upwards as a grenade exploded and he knew enough to know what to expect. Four enemy troops lunged forward through the smoke and came to within just feet of two British soldiers who were holding position behind a low stone wall. The first German took a hit and dropped but the second man hurled himself over the small wall and crashed right into the two defenders, knocking them both to the ground. Two more men from B Company saw this and ran forward, bayonets down, trying to keep the line intact.

Benton inched himself a little higher, raised his rifle to his eyes and fired into the approaching attackers. He lined up his shot and squeezed the trigger. There was the snap of a simple click and no bullet. Empty cartridge.

Damn!

He swung his arm around to grab another clip and realized, too late, the man coming straight at him, no more than two paces away. He'd barely had time to prepare himself as he threw his right hand back on the barrel of his rifle and deflected the bayonet that barely missed him. The chiseled German soldier tried to bring the butt of his rifle down on Benton but a quick step to his right allowed him to miss the attempted blow. He used his own rifle butt to try and clip the other man's chin but missed and caught him in the shoulder instead. The German grabbed Willoughby's uniform as he fell to the ground and pulled him down with him.

Rifles out of hand the two clawed away at each other with fists and open hands. Benton's left forearm was pressing the other's man's right elbow down to the ground as each of their free hands tried desperately to land punches on the other.

Benton Willoughby weighed perhaps twelve stones, or one hundred seventy pounds and was not considered to be overly muscular by any means. The German by contrast weighed closer to two hundred pounds and was as strong as an ox. He smashed his left fist against Benton's cheek then rolled over on top of him. Now the situation was reversed with the heavier German above him. The German tried to hold his arms down but Benton's constant fighting and moving was making it difficult. The bigger man quickly raised his fist and brought his elbow down onto Benton's chest sending an agonizing pain through his body and for an instant sent him into shock from the blow. His body seemed to go still for just a second or two.

To his horror he actually saw the German grinning. The man crossed his thick forearm against Benton's neck and pushed down hard trying to choke the life out of him. He could feel the heat of the German's breath on his face and flecks of spittle dripped out of the other man's mouth as he pressed harder and harder. Benton was running out of breath and after a few seconds his vision was beginning to get dark.

He could feel himself beginning to slip and was barely conscious of how much he was trying to fight back. He could smell the other man on him, felt his breath, saw the pure whites of the other man's eyes as he was trying to choke him to death. His right wrist began to go limp from the pressure of the other's hand. He closed his eyes and with all the strength he had left in him drove his right knee upwards in a desperate move. It was just enough.

The German flinched from the pain he felt between his legs, and he released his grip on Benton's right hand. He wasted no time in bringing his right hand around and slapped the man in the face. The heavy German raised his head upwards to avoid the slap and in that single moment an instinct for survival ran through Willoughby that he didn't know he had. With the German's neck exposed Benton wrapped his right hand around the other man's head and brought his neck down right over his mouth.

The German screamed in pain as he sank his teeth right into the man's throat and tore a chunk of flesh right out of him. Thick red blood ran out of his mouth and down his cheeks. The scream was inhuman. The German released his hold and scrambled backward, his hands gripping desperately at his throat, blood gushing out of the bite sized hole in his neck. Willoughby wasted no opportunity to reach down to his hip and in one movement pulled out his knife and jammed it right into the other man's throat. Blood poured out of his throat like a stream. Willoughby watched the man gag for a moment, choking on his own blood, then his eyes went still, and the life went out of him.

He spit out the blood and chunks of flesh still in his mouth then recovered his knife. He kicked the other man off him and used the dead man's uniform to wipe the blade clean. Picking up his rifle he let his helmet fell off and ran back into the fight.

Mortar rounds were now dropping behind the line. From the mountainside the Germans were now dropping shells right onto the town itself. The Norwegian troops that had been moving up to meet the enemy in the mountains were now falling back in haste. Small arms fire was coming down from the hills. What few towns people that were left were either shuddering themselves in basements or chaotically making their way for the harbor. A British transport ship was docked there and was taking aboard the last of the Scots Guards and as many of the Norwegian 6th Division as they could.

Two dozen small civilian boats and two small boats from the Royal Navy were hurriedly transporting troops and civilians alike out to the destroyers and cruisers still out in the bay. Though orders had been given not to take on any additional civilians, someone was apparently disobeying those orders.

A dirty faced Miles Creech clenched his rifle to his chest and tried to slow his breathing. He was leaning with his back up against a brick wall, his uniform drenched in sweat and somewhere along the way a bullet had grazed his left shoulder and he hadn't even felt it. He was tired. Exhausted in fact.

What remained of 1st Battalion had fallen back into town. The line had retreated in surprisingly good order. The French Foreign Legionaries had put up a ferocious defense against the German forces but in the end had simply been overwhelmed but gave the Brits the time they needed to pull back.

2nd Battalion was falling back and heading for the loading docks. The Norwegian forces on the left were holding as best as they could but they were simply no match for the enemy mortars and machine guns. It was looking like 1st Battalion was going to hold a rearguard by itself.

Corporal Flanagan ran up beside him and dropped down behind a mail drop box for cover. The Germans had pushed them further and further back until both sides had become simply exhausted. Now they were content to sniping and skirmishing with each other.

But already another column of the bastards could be seen forming up. With mortars coming down from behind and the enemy attacking down from the mountainside, it was logical to assume they'd throw everything they had left at the front door and batter it down.

Several uniformed men ran around between buildings handing out fresh ammo clips to whomever needed them. The boys gratefully took what they could get. Some of the lads were fighting wounded. One private had been hit in his calf but was lying prone on the ground rifle at the ready, another man had a tourniquet wrapped around his left arm to stop the blood loss from a bullet he'd taken in the arm, a cocked revolver in his hand.

Sergeant Lowell was moving around the platoon, rather what was left of it, giving orders and words of encouragement. Only twenty men were still fit out of the forty-eight that mustered just three days ago.

"Keep steady, lads," Lowell would say as he moved past. "Steady now."

Miles turned his head around the corner of the brick building he was hidden behind. A platoon of enemy riflemen was taking up position behind a half wall that intersected a road that ran right through town. Another platoon could be made out moving into the shrubs on the opposite side of the road. Everywhere they seemed to be readying themselves to come storming in. Two narrow dirt roads branched off from the main road, one ran northeast and the other northwest right into town. The German infantry were keeping clear of those roadways.

There was the feint sound of engines revving and then the sight of clouds of dust and dirt from down those roadways. In the center road came a large red truck that looked like a civilian vehicle racing forward. On either of the dirt paths the sight of two smaller, armored vehicles could be seen getting closer and closer, one driver and a single machine gunner in each. Three vehicles on three separate roads were going to smash right into the British defenses.

And they didn't have to wait long for the attack to come either. Men hastily put up whatever they could to barricade the roads and the spaces between buildings, wheel barrels, sandbags, an upturned cart, a stack of bicycles, anything that would slow the enemy, even for just a few seconds.

Two anti-tank rifle positions had been set up, one on the right flank and the other in the center. Normally these guns would be utterly useless against enemy tanks, but the lighter armor of the wheeled cars was much weaker, and the guns stood a decent chance of stopping them. The position in front of Miles was exposed, except for a makeshift barricade of home furniture and some sacks of barley that had been quickly thrown up in between two buildings.

More explosions went off blocks behind them. He didn't have the first clue what was going on, all he knew was what was coming in front of him.

The men on the right flank opened fire followed a couple of seconds later by the men holding the center roadway.

Sergeant Lowell fired the first shot at the oncoming vehicle, half a second later a dozen others followed, firing from the road and from inside the buildings. From atop of the vehicle the German machine gunner opened fire as the armored vehicle sped forward, the infantry from the fields rose up and followed the car in, firing as they advanced.

Miles, perched behind the corner of a brick building aimed his rifle at those approaching infantrymen and began firing. The German machine gunner unloaded on them, firing long volleys as it approached. British riflemen fired desperately at the fast-approaching car, shooting at its tires, trying to get it to stop, but it didn't stop. The car slammed hard into the makeshift barricade, its right wheels climbing over the debris, but at one point the car lost its traction and got stuck atop of the roadblock.

British troops running back from the scene were hit by the still firing machine gunner. The driver floored the vehicle then realized he wasn't going further and put it in reverse. The car rolled backwards. Sergeant Lowell took the opportunity to toss a grenade at the vehicle but over pitched it and exploded behind the vehicle. The driver in the car put it back into drive and slammed on the gas pedal.

Sergeant Lowell saw it coming and attempted to run but not before the German gunner saw him move and fired on him. Lowell fell to the ground as a bullet pierced straight through his shoulder.

Miles saw the sergeant take the hit, saw him trying to crawl away but he was too far away to help. He popped off more rounds at the incoming infantry storming through the opening the armored car had created. He killed the first man on the scene, fired on the second but missed by an inch. The British defenders were firing like the possessed. Overlapping rifles shot down as many of the attackers as they could, but they couldn't stop that damn armored car and its gun that seemed to have no end of bullets.

From out of the corner of his eye Miles caught a brilliant bright object fly through the air and then crash down in front of the enemy vehicle, a pool of fire igniting in the middle of the street. Half a dozen more followed. Molotov cocktails. The flammable petrol bombs ignited the street across the path of the approaching car.

"Get out of the damn way!" A voice hollered out.

From behind them several men rolled three heavy metal barrels down the road. He was stunned to see his friend Benton Willoughby among them. The barrels were huge fifty-gallon monsters, usually the ones used for gasoline.

The first barrel stopped, the two men unscrewed the cap and stuffed a long piece of cloth into it. One man lit it with his cigarette lighter than the two men pushed the large drum as hard as they could. One by one the barrels were uncapped, a rag stuffed into it, lit and pushed forward with burning cloth sticking out their sides. The first barrel rolled forward, right through the Molotov cocktail fire and kept on going. The second one caught afire as it rolled right into the advancing armored car. It hit the vehicle square in the front, keeping the car from moving forward anymore, the fire from the Molotov cocktails igniting the gas and the front of the car exploded in a red-hot fireball. The third barrel crashed into the explosion, caught fire and exploded in between the wrecked car and the town's funeral home.

The advancing enemy infantry saw what had happened and began to slowly pull back. The British firing at them as they did.

Willoughby ran into the street, no rifle in his hand and no helmet on his head. He stopped where Sergeant Lowell was lying, injured but still alive. He turned the sergeant over and with all his strength lifted him up and threw the old veteran over his shoulder. With Sergeant Lowell slung over his shoulder he ran as fast as he could towards the harbor.

The men of 1st platoon watched in astonishment as a single soldier from 2nd platoon had rushed into a burning wreck and a firefight to save the life of their platoon sergeant. Man after man followed and made their way to the harbor as mortar shells continued to fall.

Militærhistorisk Samling Gausdal

CHAPTER TWENTY-SIX

Luxembourg had fallen. The German Army had sent in two full divisions in the early morning hours yesterday under the same justification that they had used in 1938 when they sent an army into Czechoslovakia. Their claim that Luxembourg was inhabited by Germanic people and that its potential occupation by French forces, that could be hostile towards the native population being totally unacceptable to Berlin, had been universally dismissed by the Western Powers. Even neutral Belgium and the Netherlands had openly condemned the invasion. The Americans too had voiced their outrage at the hostility towards the tiny Central European country.

But there was nothing that any of them could do about it. The battle lines along the front had been unchanged. Partially because no one had been prepared for the invasion and secondly, and more importantly, because the British and French political leadership could not come to an agreement concerning action. Though the French government had argued weeks earlier of the possibility of a counterattack should Germany invade the Duchy of Luxembourg, Chamberlain and his government had insisted upon caution.

Churchill had quietly sided with the French on this argument and had not been afraid to say so in the dark corners of Parliament and even to certain cabinet members. Churchill had even gone so far as to have plans drawn up for the British Expeditionary Forces in France to move into Belgium and seize vital waterways and bridges should the Germans invade through that country but had, once again, been reined in by the Prime Minister and Lord Halifax.

But now the situation had indeed changed. As Luxembourg now lie as the Nazis latest conquest, Prime Minister Chamberlain had now been laid upon the sacrificial alter himself. Parliament was in an uproar. Labour and Liberals alike had called for Chamberlain's immediate resignation upon the latest folly of what people had taken to calling the Phony War that he was seen more and more as having gotten the nation into. Even members of the Conservative Party had joined with Attlee in calling for a change in government.

Mister Attlee had let loose with a torrent of accusations against the Prime Minister, calling his management, or rather mismanagement, of the war up until this date as completely neglectful and to some extent contrary to the security of the nation. As was usual in the House of Commons the Luxembourg debate had devolved to a shouting match between the two factions. With Chamberlain and Halifax and a few staunch allies on one side and what seemed like everyone else on the other.

Chamberlain had spent a lifetime in the chamber and had become used to taking criticism from his political opponents. He'd become especially used to it in the past few years as his policy of appeasement on the continent had become increasingly unpopular at home. But today's session had struck a particularly sensitive nerve with him. He wasn't sure why. Was it because he was Prime Minister now and his leadership had been called into question? Or was it vanity? Perhaps the thought of King George and the nation watching as his government was imploding.

Or was it that his policies had truly been wrong? He wasn't sure anymore.

In a side conference room off the main hallway, he'd dropped his hat and gloves onto the long table then thudded down in one of the chairs and rubbed his hands together in front of his face.

In the room with him was Lord Halifax, of course, Sirs John Simon, Samuel Hoare, Kingsley Wood and Alec Douglas-Home the Lord Dunglass, one of Chamberlain's closest allies in Parliament. The House had adjourned for the day and would reconvene only one more time on this issue. Tomorrow morning would decide the fate of Neville Chamberlain's premiership of this country and in many ways his entire political life.

Sir John poured himself a drink from the local supply he knew to be in a cabinet against the wall opposite the door. Hoare and Wood huddled close near the end of the conference table, quietly discussing the events of the last two days.

It was Lord Dunglass who broke the silence in the room. "I think that our position is rather strong," he stated in a remarkably reaffirming voice. "All things considered I believe that we fared rather well today. Prime Minister I do believe that the government will weather this vote and survive."

Chamberlain said nothing. He barely glanced down at Lord Dunglass.

The debate had been a vigorous one, God knew. All the opposition combined with several conservative defectors had been quite vocal about his removal as Prime Minister. Although his resignation had been called for on the floor, it was only a matter of hours now when the Commons would return with a vote of no confidence. A part of Chamberlain did not blame them either.

More than one member of his own party had given the longest and most strenuous speeches on the floor.

"If this had come a month ago perhaps, I could agree with that, Lord Dunglass," Sir John Simon, who was the Lord High Chancellor said. "Even after all the. . . . the diplomatic defeats we've taken in the last couple of years, we could possibly survive it. After Czechoslovakia, after the rearming, after Poland and Denmark and even after Norway. But every day we are looking weaker and weaker in the eyes of the nation and with those men out there deciding the fate of this government. Hell. Even in the eyes of the world!" He downed his Scotch in one shot and poured another then sat down at the conference table across from Chamberlain.

"I disagree," Lord Dunglass retorted. "Other PM's have been through worse and survived. The majority of our party is still with us. We made a good case on the floor today. Even Churchill put up a valiant defense of the government. With our situation in France strong, good news from the war at sea and in a few weeks the autumn weather will have begun to set in, limiting the chances of Hitler going on the offensive again,

I believe we will survive the vote and then we will be in a better position politically to find a diplomatic solution and finish this war. Hitler can't go any farther than he's already gone."

Lord Halifax muffled a grunt. "I don't know about that. However, I do think that you are right. Prime Minister," he sat down next to Chamberlain and looked into the other man's eyes. "I agree with My Lord Dunglass that we will still have a governing majority come tomorrow afternoon. This vote will. . . . well set us back, but in the end we'll still have the support of the majority and of the King."

Prime Minister Chamberlain sat; his lower lip pouted slightly. He could feel the rhythmic beating of his heart and was almost surprised to discover that it was not beating out of his chest but rather calmly. He smiled slightly back at Lord Halifax then let his eyes drift around the room at the other men present.

"Gentlemen," he began, all the strength that his body could muster in his voice. "Tomorrow I shall go see the King." Halifax rested backward in his seat, knowing full well what that statement meant. "I shall offer him my resignation and my recommendation for," his eyes turned back to Halifax, and he gave a slight nod, "Lord Halifax to become my replacement."

There were rumbles from the others, except for Sir John, and the men were shaking their heads in discouragement. Sir Kingsley Wood made mention of the King refusing the resignation, Alec Douglas-Home Lord Dunglass replied that the political situation was salvageable and said resignation was acknowledgment that the appeasement policy was folly. Lord Halifax gave the strongest words against resignation and that he was with Chamberlain sink or swim.

The vocal disagreement went on for another few seconds before Chamberlain held up his hand for silence. The group fell quiet.

"Gentlemen," he began but faltered. He knew that he needed to tell them as he had told the King weeks ago. "Gentlemen. I have cancer." He struggled to get those words out. "Terminal. I'm dying." He stared straight at Halifax who looked back in stunned disbelief. "The King already knows."

No one else spoke. Lord Dunglass blinked away his shock at the news and Sir John downed his second glass of Scotch and let out a sigh.

"Beg pardon," Sir Samuel Hoare said in a soft voice, "but how long have you known?"

"Since early May," Chamberlain answered. "I had the responsibility of informing His Majesty a few weeks ago. We discussed such a possibility of my resignation then. He asked me for my recommendation for a new Prime Minister and I informed him that Lord Halifax should replace me."

Halifax, stunned enough by the news of his friend's imminent death, was even more blindsided by the news that he'd already discussed him becoming Prime Minister with the King and had not informed him of this until now. His face went strangely inert, and he rubbed his jaw just to see if he could feel it.

"I.... I.... Prime Minister. First off let me say how deeply sad this news makes me," Halifax told Chamberlain. He was trying desperately to find his words. "I shall pray for your recovery, sir. However, I find myself now thinking of the good of the nation at this time." He was breathing heavier now and was certain that it had less to do with the fact that Neville was dying and more with the fact that he and King George had already seemingly hand picked him as successor. "I am honored that I have the respect of yourself and of the King. However, I must reluctantly refuse."

Chamberlain's forehead creased in confusion. He and Halifax had walked hand in hand now for years and had been friends for years longer. He had always just assumed that the man would accept the position and carry on the policies that both men had fought so hard for. It's not as though the subject had never come up between them in conversation.

"Refuse? My Lord Halifax.... Edward. I don't understand." Chamberlain's voice creaked as he said it. "You do understand the situation? I have limited time left. I thought there'd be more but there just isn't. Now, with this vote I fear we risk letting the situation get away from us. The government needs a steady hand."

Still reeling from the shocking news of the Prime Minister's health, Lord Dunglass shook it off and nodded his agreement with him at his suggestion of Lord Halifax.

"We'll still have a majority in both Houses," Dunglass told him. "They'd support you, Edward. You have their respect."

"I'm not so sure," Halifax replied bluntly.

"This may sound cold, but how long do you expect to have, sir?" Sir Samuel inquired. "I ask only out of the responsibility we have to the nation. There must be government."

Chamberlain nodded lightly in agreement. "Months perhaps. No one can be sure of course."

"Sir," Lord Halifax began. He crossed his arms. "Right now, the MP's have divided. Tomorrow they will reconvene, and they will either have come back with a vote of no confidence in which case my proximity to you will have sunk us both. Or they will return without the vote. However, enough of our own have crossed the bench on this issue to make this government's position precarious at best. Every day we lose more and more support. Even those who once supported us openly have either crossed the bench or have silenced their support for us. Their abstention will itself be a vote of no confidence. Either way gentlemen, Prime Minister, our ground is daily falling away beneath us."

"Lord Halifax, I believe, is correct," Sir John told them. "The opposition will never accept him I'm afraid and too many Conservatives have now switched their position on the issue to agree to it as well. A governing majority will be next to impossible." Sir Kingsley shook his head in disagreement and was ready to challenge until Sir John preempted him. "We need to keep this coalition together. I'm sorry but Edward cannot do that. We're at war, Sirs. This nation must have a government that includes crossbenchers and as fond as I am of Edward, the majority of Parliament will not accept him. There it is."

The Prime Minister remained hopefully silent. He'd had this discussion with King George weeks earlier and the King had come to the same conclusion. Halifax was seen as the logical choice and natural successor for Chamberlain, but he was also seen as too much like the man who Parliament was now turning against. Without the support of even half the Conservatives there was no hope to gain the approval of Parliament and thus a ruling majority.

"If not Lord Halifax, then whom?" Sir Kingsley asked.

"It would have to be someone that the Parliament will support whole-heartedly," Lord Dunglass stated. He shook his head in thought. "I can't think of too many people. Maybe. . . ."

"There's only one," Chamberlain finished for him. He raised his hands to his face and rubbed the bridge of his nose with his thumbs. "There's one person that the opposition will get behind and is respected by enough Conservatives." He fought against saying the name aloud.

There was an awkward moment of silence that fell across the large conference room.

"My God," Dunglass said rather depressingly. "Have we come to this?"

Sir Samuel understood and shook his head. "The King will not accept it. He'll refuse to allow a new government to be formed."

"Are you mad?" Halifax questioned him. "Our nation is at war with the most powerful dictator in Europe since Bonaparte. We've been handed defeat in Norway and the world's largest army sits right across the Channel. The King doesn't have the luxury of refusing to form a government."

Chamberlain grunted an acknowledgment. "Correct. Despite all the bluster and self-adulation, I do know that enough Conservatives have and will back him. Attlee as well in fact. If for no other reason than just to see me off."

Though everyone knew Churchill, knew he'd been in government his whole adult life and had at times held important positions, he'd often been thought of as not much more than a vocal front man. Someone who could be counted upon to push the Conservative agenda loudly from the House floor, but his name did not conjure up the image of a Prime Minister of the United Kingdom.

"Has this been made clear to His Majesty?" Sir John asked.

"It has," Chamberlain replied. "Needless to say, the king's predisposition towards Winston is not a good one. Winston's support for the King's brother during the abdication had left a foul taste in many mouths."

"Churchill has never been popular with the Royals," Lord Dunglass put in. "Remember the old King George?"

"Regardless," Chamberlain said and followed with a moment of silence. "There are two things that I am sure of tonight. Well, three actually. The first is that I will resign my premiership. Secondly, the majority of Parliament will back him in a new coalition government." He stopped and remained silent.

"What is the third thing?" Lord Halifax inquired.

Chamberlain stared off into nothingness. He inhaled and let out a noisy exhale. "Winston Churchill will be the next Prime Minister."

Churchill puffed away on his cigar and took a drink of his Scotch and soda as he flipped through the pages of the book he'd been reading. He sat in the study of his home Chartwell, in Kent, his feet propped up on a stool, his evening robe on over his clothes. He'd been thoroughly immersed in his book on the history of the Hundred Years War and had barely noticed the time or heard the faint buzz of the front door.

He'd found precious little time lately to return home to Chartwell, the country house he'd bought almost twenty years earlier, since returning to government at the beginning of this new war. But he'd found sitting in his study, alone, even for only an evening was a welcome diversion from his day-to-day schedule in London. The diversion also gave him the opportunity to avoid being a part of the dismemberment taking place back in Westminster. The less he was seen there right now the better as far as he was concerned. He never found it necessary to be at the spot of a political scandal if he could just hear about it later. Which he would of course. He still had ears in Westminster.

He had reached the part in his book concerning the Siege of Orléans when the door creaked open. He continued reading, not wishing to give the room's additional occupant the satisfaction. He sat there for a minute, thumbing through the sentences of his book, pretending to read. After a few long moments more he began to wonder.

"Dear," the voice came from behind. Winston feigned surprise. "I know you heard the door open."

"Is that you, my dear?" Winston said, putting the book down in his lap and turning his head around.

"Of course it is," Clementine replied. "Who else do you think it would be?"

"I thought maybe an intruder," he replied in jest.

"An intruder that calls you dear?"

Winston swallowed a cough. "That Buckley woman down the road perhaps. I think she has her eye on me."

Clementine laughed and strode forward, he took her hand and kissed it. He looked up at her standing over him and shaking her head in that motherly way she always did.

"Incorrigible."

"I'm afraid so," he agreed with her. "My mother said the same, you know."

"Yes. I know. Are you coming to bed, or do you intend to stay up all night long? It's nearly ten now and we've spent so little time together." She smiled her sweet smile. He kissed her hand again and smiled back.

"Yes, my love. Of course. I was just so taken with this book," he waved the book he'd been reading. "But.... Ummm, yes. Just let me have one more drink."

She looked down at the drink sitting on the table next to him, it was nearly full.

"Oh, I see." She said teasingly. "Your book. What is your book on, dear?"

"The Hundred Years War. Joan of Arc and all that. You know."

"Joan of Arc, you said? I do remember. Yes. Didn't she believe herself to be a messenger of God?"

"Well, yes, she did," he nodded.

"Uh, huh. My love, you were not reading your book and your drink is nearly full." She touched his thin hair with her left hand and with her right reached into her nightgown pocket and produced a folded paper.

"What's this?" He asked.

"I'm a bit like Joan of Arc don't you think, dear? A messenger of God. It's a telegram that arrived a few minutes ago. It's from Eden." She held out her hand with the folded note.

"Anthony?" He took the offered paper, unfolded it and read. "Hmmm. Perhaps I should turn in now my love. I may be expecting another telegram in the morning from the Palace."

She put her soft hand on his cheek. "From Westminster?"

He shook his head slightly. "From Buckingham."

CHAPTER TWENTY-SEVEN

In the skies above Berlin wave after wave of bombers flew overhead of the jam-packed streets below. Junkers Ju 88's, Dornier Do 17's and Heinkel He 111's all flew in staggered formations high above the city, like flocks of eagles that filled the skies. After the bombers squadrons of smaller fighter craft flew by to the cheer of thousands on the ground. The Messerschmitt 109 fighters buzzed around like hornets in the sky, formations of four weaving passed each other in midair. The last wing flew in a giant swastika formation across the city.

On the streets below hundreds of thousands of German citizens had turned out to watch the parade. The crowd lined either side of the street watching and screaming as their victorious armies rolled by. The 9th Infantry Division, veterans of the Polish Campaign, marched by first. Ten thousand men, eight wide, goose stepped through the packed street, motorcycles, trucks towing artillery and armored vehicles brought up the rear.

The 3rd Infantry Division followed afterwards. Long lines of vehicles passed by the screaming crowd of people cheering them on. Truck after truck, car after car drove through the streets. In the rear of the half-track's soldiers sat thumping their rifle butts on the floor as they smiled at the masses of humanity. The only thing between the parade and the thousands and thousands of people were a thin black line of SS guards and policemen keeping the jubilant crowd back. One small boy who managed to squirm his way under the guard's interlocked arms and run out into the road nearly got crushed by a passing vehicle before being snagged away by a police officer who'd spotted the kid.

After the 3rd Infantry had passed there were hundreds of teenage boys and girls dressed in the black pants or skirts with brown long sleeve shirts and swastika armbands of the Hitler Youth strode down the streets, flags waving, drums beating, extending the Nazi party salute. The crowd cheered them on. School children, some only five or six years of age dressed in Hitler Youth getup threw flower petals on the pavement. Women in the crowd shouted at how cute the had children looked, especially the young black-haired child whose mother had painted a tiny mustache on his face.

Behind the school children came the Führer's car with his line of SS guards mounted on horseback on either side of the moving vehicle. Hitler stood up in his open top automobile, smiling and laughing, arm extended outwards in the righteous Nazi party salute which the people returned as his car drove by.

"SIEG HAIL! SIEG HAIL!" The crowd roared in deafening unison.

In the car with Hitler sat Admiral Horthy, Regent of Hungary and the de facto ruler of that country. The old admiral of the former Austro-Hungarian Navy wore his best navy-blue uniform, complete with red-white sash and flurry of medals. He held up his hand as the car rolled down the street, though he was quite sure no one was looking at him but rather the Führer who was standing up beside him. But Horthy waved anyway.

The excited crowd cheered so loudly that it was impossible to hear just about anything else. Everyone clamored just to get a glimpse of the Führer, Adolf Hitler. Fathers put their children on their shoulders so that the young kids could get a glimpse of the Führer and remember for the rest of their lives the sight of the man who had brought so much glory and greatness back to Germany.

The car carrying Hitler and Horthy passed by, Hitler smiled brightly at the crowd before dropping back into the car seat. Behind his auto was a second with Deputy Führer of the Nazi Party Rudolf Hess. Next to him sat the Italian Dictator and Prime Minister Benito Mussolini. The two men chatted closely as their car followed meters behind Hitler's. Mussolini could not have looked anymore unhappy, it seemed to Hess. The bald headed Italian dictator sat with his hands folded in his lap and he held a scowl on his face. Hess knew the man had come from Rome with the understanding he would be discussing the peace negotiations he was quietly conducting with the British government with Hitler and Horthy. But he did not expect to be playing second fiddle to the Hungarian.

The cars passed and the horses galloped by. Behind them were the heros of Norway. Troops recently returned from the fighting in that country. The camoflouged alpine troops marched by, rifles slung over their shoulders and white summer flowers stuck in their helmets. Men of the 2nd Mountain Division waved and smiled at the girls in the crowd. Their guidons were held high and fluttered in the breeze with inscriptions emblazoned on them of all the places the unit had fought in Norway.

The last in the long parade line was the famous 2nd Panzer Division. The heavy tanks rolled down the roadway two abreast. The men in their crisp black uniforms rode atop the moving beasts. Panzer III's and IV's drove slowly down the road with the smaller Panzer II's bringing up the rear. Officer cars behind them. The sight of General Heinz Guderian, victor of Poland, sitting in the back of his command car sent up another wave of cheers from the wild crowd. The light haired general looked every bit the heroic and professional soldier they had pictured. An image of German superiority and Aryan purity. General Guderian smiled at the crowd and shook his fists up in the air as he passed down the street.

"SIEG HAIL!" The crowd screamed over and over and over again. "SIEG HAIL! SIEG HAIL!"

The excitement of the parade and the heat from the sun had made Hitler sweat. He dabbed his handkerchief around on his face as he entered through the main doors of the Reich Chancellery. The cool air felt refreshing after all that. He always enjoyed showing himself to his people, but it took a lot out of him also. He passed an aide his hat and the SS bodyguard escorted him, Horthy, Mussolini and their large entourage through the hallways of the large government building.

The huge cabinet room was waiting for them. An enormous wooden table sat in the center and elaborate tapestries and works of art adorned on the walls as well as a large map of Europe. A huge bronze spread winged eagle clutching a wreath with the symbol of Nazism in the center of it on the far wall.

Dozens of aides, military leaders and diplomatic staff filed into the huge room behind the heads of the three governments. Rudolf Hess had been excused from this meeting, his role of entertaining Signor Mussolini having been complete, and he was needed no more. Hitler accepted a glass of water from an aide and combed his black hair across his scalp with his fingers. He sat in the center position at the table, Horthy sat to his right and Mussolini to his left. Beside Mussolini sat Ciano, Italy's Foreign Minister as well as some military aides the dictator had brought from Rome. With Admiral Horthy came István Csáky, Hungary's Foreign Minister, as well as General Henrik Werth, the Chief of the Army Staff, Keitel's direct counterpart. Across from Hitler sat Foreign Minister Ribbentrop, Albert Speer and General Keitel as well as a score of German military aides.

The foreign delegates had been placed opposite the wall with the large map of the continent deliberately. A large reminder that the Soviet Union sat dominating the map of Europe could be a useful tool in these diplomatic negotiations.

"I hope that you all enjoyed our parade display today," Hitler remarked and laughed. "The troops needed to be lauded. Poland, Denmark and Norway all in the past four months. Luxembourg in a single morning." He was playfully joyous.

"It was quite impressive," Horthy told him. The mood around the table was seemingly casual for such a formal meeting.

"The gains that Germany has made in the last few years have been impressive also," General Werth added. Werth was an outspoken pro-German military leader in Hungary. Of German descent himself, he found Germany's transformation since National Socialism took over to be utterly remarkable and took every opportunity he could get to praise it vocally. Sometimes to the chagrin of his own government.

A series of agreements went around the table for a minute with some German officers present spouting off about the victory over the Poles, the bombers over Warsaw and the fighting in Norway and the Allied force there being driven into the seas.

"As you can see, gentlemen," Ribbentrop started in a casual tone, "the political situation in Europe has changed so drastically in such a short period of time. The winds and the Gods must be on Germany's side. Think of what we can accomplish in the future together."

"Indeed," Hitler added. "We have the Valkyries on our side. Who can stand against us? Our industrial power has increased fivefold since the end of the disastrous Weimar government. Our country and our people have not been as strong and united as they are now. We all saw a demonstration of our power."

Admiral Horthy nodded. "Yes, Herr Hitler. Quite impressive I grant you. Your armies have made you master of Central Europe and of course Hungary is grateful for all the assistance Germany has given us. We see much to gain by joining ourselves with your country. But we also wish to restore to us the lands that were stripped from us by the treaty we were forced to sign. Germany lost territories in the Great War, and you have since regained them. Hungary demands the same."

"Yes. Of course you do," Hitler told Horthy. "We have undone the injustice of Versailles. Most of it anyway. Our brethren in Austria and the Sudetenland have been joined back to us. The Fatherland has been restored to us. It's only natural for people of the same culture to want to live together and we all know how important it is that Hungary is restored to its former greatness like it was in the days of Attila."

"We want those things too," Ribbentrop added in.

"And we have made sure that certain lands have been restored to you," Hitler continued. "I had the Slovaks return Ruthenia to you. That was just a start Regent. We have important plans for Hungary."

Carpathian Ruthenia had been 'awarded' back to Hungary by German decree in 1938. It had been made part of that fake country of Czechoslovakia two decades earlier and had become a contentious point of disagreement between that country and Hungary. Hitler's decision to back the Hungarian claim to the region had been very popular in Hungary and had all but assured him of Budapest's alliance. The Slovaks, however, had been furious about the decision and anti-Hungarian sentiment was still very strong. Now Hungary wanted a restoration of its former Transylvanian lands. Lands that had been given to Romania in 1918.

Csáky leaned into the conversation on Horthy's behalf. "Our country is quite prepared to sign our pact with Germany and to openly ally ourselves together. The last remaining question really must be the Romanian one. What do we do about the Romanians? Our border is a tinderbox ready to catch fire. If they reject our claims to Transylvania, then we do not see much hope in negotiation."

"The Romanians will come to the table. That I can assure you," Hitler replied. "Things take time, Minister Csáky. Herr Ribbentrop has already been in contact with their own foreign minister. We will address the situation, but we must do so in a position of strength."

"If I may, I believe that this Romanian question as you call it, Minister Csáky, is not the question that you should be asking," Ribbentrop interjected. "No. The real question that we must all ask is the Soviet question. It is ultimately the Communists that you fear, isn't it?"

Csáky shrugged. "Well of course it is. We make no secret about it. The Communists are nipping away at European territories left and right. They've brought the Baltic under their thumb. Some say the Greeks also. Now they are fighting in Finland. Stalin has his eye on Eastern Europe."

"Exactly," Ribbentrop nodded in agreement. "And who is closer to him? Hungary or Romania? The Romanians fear Stalin even more than you do because he is already on their border. The Red Army daily exercises within sight of Romania because they know the Romanians will cave if they must fight on two fronts. Let's be honest here," he glanced around at the military men around the conference table, both German and Hungarian, "the military situation you are in is not a good one. Let's just admit that. If your two countries end up fighting each other, you could very well find fighting in the mountain country a very costly endeavor and it may not end the way you wish it to.

"That being said, Bucharest does not want a war either. With you on their western border and the Soviets to their east it would be unwise of them to provoke conflict. Stalin will invade that country in a heartbeat if the opportunity presents itself. That would leave the buffer between you and the Communists either gone or very much reduced. Then, in exchange for some Transylvanian territory that you might gain you would then have Stalin on your own doorstep. Is that an exchange that you really want or can afford?" Ribbentrop was looking at the Hungarian Foreign Minister, but his words were aimed at Horthy.

Csáky and Horthy gave each other concerned glances but neither said anything. They didn't have to.

"Nobody wants to see the Bolsheviks on European soil," Hitler said. "In truth nobody wants to see them anywhere. Communism is a disease that we've allowed to spread too far for too long. Everywhere it goes chaos follows and look at what they've already done to neighboring countries. They came within a hair of bringing their flawed system to Spain. France, as always, hangs by a thread of having the Marxists in power. If they can get into Western Europe think of what they will do in the east!"

"It would only take one domino to fall, and the rest of Europe would go with it," Ribbentrop said, and General Werth nodded his head furiously.

Horthy exchanged brief looks with his Foreign Minister who then whispered a few words into the Regent's ear. Horthy nodded in silent agreement. His eyes shifted around the table at the same time and rested for a moment on the huge map on the wall across from him. The USSR colored in bright red. . . .

"Herr Hitler, both Minister Csáky and I are in full agreement. The threat of communism is far too great for such border disputes. And, we would much rather have Romania on our border than the Red Army. But I can tell you right now that to leave such an issue as this unresolved would be very unpopular among our people. We would need a definite guarantee that will reinforce the previous Vienna Award and give us back our sovereign territory."

Hitler looked at Ribbentrop and nodded. "You will have our guarantee, Regent. Transylvania will be restored to you. I can promise you that. We are already speaking with the Romanians, and we are working out details on this and other things. Once we reach an arrangement with Bucharest, we will make them give you what you want, your lands in the north. They will agree to it. Italy will agree to recognize the exchange. That will give it legitimacy."

Mussolini, quiet until now, nodded his head in agreement.

"How can you be sure that the Romanian government will agree?" Csáky asked.

"Our relationship with them is the best thing that they have going for them right now," Ribbentrop answered. "They can't depend upon the British or French coming to their aid against the Russians and right now their largest trading partner is Germany. Along with some other considerations you can be assured of getting what you want. Just be patient and put your trust in us. You've trusted Germany so far and look at what it's gotten you."

"I agree," Horthy said and looked straight at Hitler. "I'm satisfied with that. So long as it's clear that Romania will hand over Transylvania to us. Whatever agreement you reach with them will be fine so long as it does not threaten our territorial integrity."

"It will not," Hitler assured him and patted the other man on the back of the shoulder. "We have an interest in your country's security. We want allies who are strong and can defend themselves. We can help you to do that just as we've already done here and in Austria. In Italy too."

"That is what we want as well," Horthy replied. "That brings us to our next point of concern. The British and French. Your armies have performed exceptionally Herr Hitler. With Poland out of the way and now the Allies have been kicked from Norway. But there does not seem to be any appetite for ending the conflict in either Paris or London. We all know that Mister Chamberlain has been removed. This Churchill has made it clear that he's willing to fight it out."

Hitler bristled at the very sound of Churchill's name. Churchill had taken the reins of government just ten days earlier after the resignation of Neville Chamberlain who was quite prepared to resume diplomatic talks through Italy. Churchill had dumbed that down. Talks were still going on in circles around Europe, but they weren't at the level that they had previously been. In France too, Prime Minister Daladier was now in danger of losing his premiership over his own apparent lack of action against Germany.

"The British will return to the negotiating table," Ribbentrop said. "Churchill may be more blusterous but he's no fool politically. His allies in their Parliament are with him now but eventually he'll be forced to seek peace and he knows he'll have to do it or lose his position. His predecessor still sits in his cabinet and Foreign Minister Halifax still occupies that post. Both are still maneuvering for a parlay."

Hitler dismissed the talk. "Churchill is of no consequence! He's nothing more than an amateur at making war. Remember his disaster at Gallipoli? Let him lead them. He'll send his soldiers into one Gallipoli after another and then we'll let him come back to us asking for terms. That man gives wonderful speeches, but he cannot win, and he knows it. Signor Mussolini here is hosting negotiations with his government quietly even now. Their Foreign Minister and Minister Ciano here even now speak with each other. Do you think that people interested in making war would have their Foreign Minister in direct talks with an Axis partner nation? HA!"

"It's true," Mussolini finally spoke, almost gleeful his name had finally been invoked. "Their diplomats and ours have been having very constructive talks. Both Ciano and I feel that we should have an arrangement soon. All those British people really want is to keep their empire. Their territories in Africa and India are what matters most to them." He shrugged. "We let them keep those and we will have secured ourselves peace with the Anglo-Saxons."

"And who knows what happens later. Once we secure peace with Great Britain the French will have no choice but to seek terms," Hitler said. "Remember, Regent, our real enemy is not in the west but the east. It's no secret to anyone that Churchill dislikes those Bolsheviks in Moscow even more than he dislikes us. It wouldn't be hard to imagine the British on our side in a war with the Russians. Should it come to that of course." He smiled gamely.

Csáky leaned over again and whispered something into Horthy's ear. The two seeming to come to an agreement.

"I believe that we have an understanding, Herr Hitler," Csáky told him, and Horthy nodded enthusiastically. "We look forward to signing our pact with Germany and joining our fates together with yours."

Hitler and Horthy stood up, followed almost instantly by everyone else. The two men shook hands and smiled at each other. Even Mussolini managed a grin.

"Excellent! Then we should look forward to that!" Hitler said. "I will have my chauffeur personally drive you back to the embassy. You will not regret the day that Hungary took its rightful place at Germany's side."

The Italian dictator and his foreign minister joined with Hitler and the Hungarians in a friendly gathering. Mussolini and Horthy struck up a conversation and Ciano with Csáky. Hitler excused himself and met with Ribbentrop at the end of the conference table while his new Hungarian and Italian allies made small talk.

"Congratulations, Mein Führer, on your diplomatic victory."

"The victory was ours together, Joachim.," Hitler replied. He put his hand on the other man's shoulder and squeezed warmly. "You made all the right overtures to Budapest. This would not have been possible without your service. Now I must ask you to do another one."

"I am here to serve."

Hitler glanced back at his guests. Mussolini was deep in conversation with Horthy. "The Hungarian matter must be resolved with Romania. We have to accomplish this as quickly as possible. The Romanians need to have assurances of their own or they may consider this pact as an act of aggression against them." Ribbentrop nodded in agreement. "I want you to go there yourself. It will send a message that we take Romania's independence seriously. Not only that but you've been working tirelessly to keep our relations with them good. You can make them see the light. That little parade out there today was more than just a victory celebration you know."

"I agree with you, Mein Führer and of course I'll go immediately. I also think that this meeting with them is at the right time. With Horthy on our side now King Carol may very well wish to invoke national pride."

Hitler looked at him somewhat confused. "What do you mean?"

"The two countries are bitter rivals," Ribbentrop explained. "We strike a deal with Bucharest, one that guarantees them protection from Stalin and continued oil exports to us, I strongly believe that we can have another ally with them. If he knows that the Hungarians are going to sign the Tripartite Pact first, it may motivate him to try and beat them to it."

"I do not like their king," Hitler stated. "I do not trust him. I know how you see things but his history with the French and British concerns me. But I will give you a free hand with dealing with him, Joachim. If you believe that some sort of arrangement can be worked out that is beneficial than you have my permission to proceed."

"I have some thoughts on that. As well as some on Spain and Franco that I think you'll wish to hear about."

"Franco can wait. He's on my list to meet with also. But I put less faith in Spain than I do in Romania. But we must have Romania on our side. That's why you must go. Make arrangements to leave as soon as is possible. They won't be happy about the loss of territory, but matters could be much worse for them and that is what you must impress upon them. Better to lose some lands in their north than their country to the Russians."

"Yes, Mein Führer."

Hitler grinned then turned back to his foreign guests.

CHAPTER TWENTY-EIGHT

His steward rolled President Roosevelt into the conference room that sat opposite the hallway from the Oval Office. As usual FDR was smoking on one of his cigarettes from his famous cigarette holder, which had become a part of his public image, and had a bundle of papers in his lap as he was pushed up against the end of the table. The military advisors and cabinet members stood up from their seats as the President entered the room. It had become informally known as his war cabinet; a group of men who had been charged with the steep challenge of meeting head on what many saw as an inevitable upcoming war. The only real question was who the United States was going to be fighting. Most saw the Japanese as the most likely culprits to start a conflict.

"Please sit down, gentlemen," the President said as he locked the brake. He placed the stack of papers on the table, smoke piping up from the end of his cigarette.

The group took their seats. They had begun these meetings weeks earlier as signs of potential conflict in either the Atlantic or Pacific were growing increasingly visible. It had been no secret around Washington of Roosevelt's deep concern around the growing threats of Nazi Germany and Imperial Japan. With the long list of Japanese atrocities in China growing longer every day and now with Germany's sudden takeover of Central Europe complete, those threats began to manifest themselves. Before, the American public had been rigidly isolationist in their views.

Now they began to see the potential dangers of having such threats, no matter how big the oceans were between them.

"Well, gentlemen," Roosevelt began, "it's been one hell of a last couple of months. Four European countries have fallen to the Nazis in that time. Millions are now living under occupation and hundreds of thousands more are dead. In China, the Japanese are pushing further and further inland since the Chinese offensive has ended in failure. Seems there's very little good news these days."

The news out of Europe was getting worse and worse every day. Hitler's surprise blitz attacks had changed the global political situation nearly overnight. Luxembourg had just become his latest victim. The small duchy had been occupied in a single morning and its monarch, Grand Duchess Charlotte, was now residing in a countryside castle under arrest and guarded by the German Army. Norway had finally fallen nearly two months earlier, its own king lucky enough to flee the country with some ten thousand soldiers. Everyday Germany was proving to the world that it had become the preeminent military power of the day.

The President tapped the stack of papers in front of him. "I have here communiques from foreign dignitaries, ambassadors, heads of states and even everyday American citizens of all descents decrying the happenings in Europe. We knew that Poland was going to go. That was inevitable. But the speed and manner in which it fell was incredible. Then Denmark and Norway too. Luxembourg." He shook his head vigorously. "I think that everyone here knows well where this is heading. My God, I wish we'd stepped in at Munich. Once Hitler had been allowed to take Czechoslovakia, he got it into his mind that he could do anything he wanted and get away with it."

"There really wasn't much that we could do about it, sir," Secretary of State Cordell Hull stated. "The American public just wasn't ready for it. We knew that -"

"The American public wasn't ready for a lot of things, Cordell," Roosevelt cut him off. "But they've placed their faith in me and followed me down the road to recovery every step of the way. Do you know why they did that?" He looked around the room and into the faces of all around the table. "They followed me because I shot it straight from the shoulder with them. Gave them the hard news and I didn't hide anything from them. They followed me because they believed in us, and I believed in the spirit of the American people. I see now that my decision in thirty-eight was wrong. But we can't undo it now. Best we can do is get ourselves ready. Well, I'm going to shoot from the shoulder with all of you here, just as I think I always have. I'm tired. I'm tired of waking up day after day and hearing that some people somewhere have just become the latest victim of this fanaticism that seems to have overtaken the world. Be it in China or in Europe. I'm making it the policy of this government, and indeed this nation, to meet these threats head on."

There were a series of nods and approving looks from most of his people, especially General Marshall and Admiral Stark. Roosevelt let his words hang out there for a moment. He smoked again on his cigarette.

"So," he continued, "let's get down to work. The Neutrality Act revision looks like it's going to pass through Congress with a wide margin. It'll take some of the limitations off foreign arms sales. That alone will be a good first step. Neutrality in a global conflict is no longer an option."

"Once that gets signed off on, we'll be able to sell arms outright," Hull told them. "It'll have to be by cash only, no credit can be issued. But at least the Brits and French can buy weapons directly from our industries. And they'll have to transport it themselves. The US cannot ship it. But it's a good start."

"If I may, sir," General Marshall began, and Roosevelt looked to him. "I agree the new law is a good first step. But, well, it's a small step. Both Admiral Stark here and I have discussed this at length between us and with our staffs. Mister President, the Nazis have had seven and a half years to rearm and modernize themselves into the fighting force we've seen them become. Part of the reason for their success is because most of the rest of the world has simply not kept up with the times. Not the Polish, nor the British nor the French. And quite frankly, neither have we. If Germany turns west, and let's be frank they will, then there's little to nothing the French or British armies can do about it."

Roosevelt listened to the general's words and gave them serious thought. He knew what Marshall was saying was absolutely true. The last war had been the end of a long era. He remembered well the sight of the miles and miles of long trenches and defensive works stretched across eastern France back in 1918. He recalled visiting American and British soldiers in those trenches and hospitals who day after agonizing day had slugged it out with the Kaiser's armies. Only winning final victory through bare attrition. That war had simply starved Germany to death. This conflict was something else entirely. The weapons of war had advanced considerably in just the last few years alone. Germany had quite literally radically redefined how conflicts were being waged and had mastered a new form of tactical warfare. The rest of the world had stood by, watched and done virtually nothing while the Nazis transformed their country into a world class military power.

"I understand what you're saying, general and I agree with you. I know your mind about Hitler and his ilk, and Admiral Stark I know your feelings too on the Japanese. Our sitting on the sidelines is only making things worse. I've had two conversations with Churchill since he's taken the wheel. He's impressed upon me the direness of the situation that they're currently facing. I told him, guaranteed him in fact, that I'd do everything I possibly could to assist them in their present situation. I realize that my hands are tied in many ways but I'm sick and tired of sitting here and watching the world fall apart." He pounded a fist on the side of his wheelchair as he said the last few words.

A few reflective moments of silence fell over the room with some of the gathered offering nothing but half silent grunts and the slightest of nods to the President. The ticktock of the clock on the wall was the only sound in that time. Roosevelt put his elbows on the table and rubbed the bridge of his nose, trying to rid himself of the frustration.

Finally, General Marshall spoke up. "Mister President, sir I've brought with me today a proposal outlining an action plan by our military forces." He flipped open a folder and slid some clipped papers towards the President who took them and glanced through the pages. "Admiral Stark here has been putting together a memo on American defense strategies. I thought we'd have more time to assess the situation, but things in Europe have unfolded more quickly than anyone could have imagined."

Roosevelt fingered through the pages and shifted his gaze to Admiral Stark. "I understand. Admiral Stark?"

Stark cleared his throat. "Well, sir, as the general said the global situation has unfolded so quickly that we're finding ourselves in a more and more precarious situation every day. I'll have the plan formally proposed in next month's defense report, but it basically breaks down this way. Our national defense strategy should be based upon several factors and propose several options. These would effectively replace the old colored war plans were drew up in the twenties. As you know, sir, the navy has been anticipating some kind of conflict now for the last couple of years. Up until very recently it's been assumed that we'd be at war with the Japanese Empire and that the Pacific would be our battlefield. Japan's belligerence is almost certain to bring us into conflict with them. However, we also now must consider the very real possibility of a war with Germany as well. The thought that Germany could ever launch any kind of strike against us directly is slim to none, however, and any conflict we engage in would probably begin one of two ways. The first is that France and Britain have fallen, and the German Navy begins unrestricted attacks against our shipping. It's possible that they could theoretically attack some of our South American neighbors in which case we'd have to engage them under the Monroe Doctrine. But that's also unlikely."

"And the second possibility?" Roosevelt asked.

"That Germany supports Japan in which case they would openly declare war against us following some kind of Japanese attack on us," Stark went on. "The general and I have discussed this possibility at length. While we have differences of opinion concerning the details of such an attack, both the army and navy feel it is likely to come eventually."

No surprise there, Roosevelt and everyone else in the room knew. The entire point behind moving the Pacific Fleet from California to Hawaii had been to respond quickly to any Japanese aggression that would surely come and most likely be focused on the American possessions in the South Pacific and the Philippines. Frank Knox, the Secretary of the Navy, was also attending this meeting and joined in his agreement with Admiral Stark. Both he and the President had approved of the move to Pearl Harbor just months earlier.

Stark continued. "The first scenario that I outline in my report would have the US. and Japan at war without foreign support on either side.

In this case we'd be fighting in the Pacific with the decisive battles being fought in and around the Philippine Islands. A second scenario would pit Japan against us and the British Empire in which case New Zealand and Australia would no doubt also be a part of any conflict. Either of these scenarios would seem to be most likely, sir."

"Most likely, but by no means the only possible likelihoods, sir," Marshall quickly added.

"You're referring to a two front war aren't you general?" Secretary of War Harry Woodring asked. The man was a devout isolationist and there was more than a hint of exasperation in his voice. He'd continually advocated for the United States to stay away from foreign entanglements and get involved in world affairs only under the direst of circumstances. His relationship with the military and civilians working under him had been always tenuous. "War with both Germany and Japan?"

General Marshall nodded. "Yes, sir. That is correct. Under the circumstances we have to consider it a very distinct possibility."

Secretary Woodring grimaced. "I'm not sure that I agree."

"Well," President Roosevelt began before that conversation could go any further. "There's no harm in making plans for all contingencies. Go Admiral Stark. I was listening."

Stark adjusted his eyeglasses. "Well, my next point runs right into what the general just stated. We have to consider a two front war a very real possibility. Not one that any of us would like to see of course but based on what's happened in Europe, we need to be prepared. So, this brings me to the third scenario. This by my reckoning is the nightmare scenario. This nation finds itself at war with both powers only after any possible allies are toppled. Japan is victorious in China and Germany occupies both Britain and France and has control of their combined naval fleet. In this situation the United States, even with adequate preparation time, will find itself outgunned on the high seas."

"Hmm. Not a very attractive picture," Roosevelt stated. "Not one that I'd like to see anyway."

"Nor I, sir. But... well, the map of Europe just changed practically overnight. As you said there's no harm in making plans for all contingencies. The fourth option is a situation in where the United States finds itself drawn into a two-front war in which Great Britain is an active ally. Europe is overrun and China has capitulated. It's in this case that I believe we'll find ourselves sooner or later if not the third option that I spelled out."

"Either way, Mister President, the survival of the British Empire is paramount to our national defense," Marshall added in.

President Roosevelt blew out a stream of cigarette smoke, adjusted his eyeglasses and processed what he'd just been told. Ironic that the fate and continued existence of the British Empire would depend upon the country renown for breaking away from that empire two centuries earlier. Now the defense on this country and very possibly the fate of the free world depended upon Britain's survival.

"If I may, Mister President," Secretary of War Woodring began. He leaned forward in his chair and gave a couple of doubtful glances at Marshall and Stark across the table before turning to Roosevelt. "I'm as outraged as anyone here about what's happening in Europe and Asia. It's a travesty. But I, like a large majority of the American public, am still opposed to intervening in their affairs. I know that my opinion is not shared in this room, particularly by the men in uniform. But beyond those doors you'd be hard pressed to find thirty percent of the American public who would support a conflict with either Germany or Japan let alone both of them."

General Marshall cleared his throat. "That's not exactly what we said, Mister Secretary," his tone was professional but stern. "Nobody in uniform wants a war. Not with anyone. We're here today to brief on options for our national defense. Nothing further. The unfolding situation has forced us to reassess our policy."

Woodring sighed. "Our policy? Peace is our policy, General Marshall. I can understand if there were a German battleship off the coast shelling one of our cities. But Americans are not at risk. American businesses conduct trade with those countries all the time. American commerce is as dependent upon those nations as any other. And, put succinctly, the United States itself is not in any danger. There are two great big oceans between us and them. Let Europe handle its own. American families have no wish to send their young men off to die on some distant battlefield on the other side of the globe."

"Well with all respects, sir, I disagree with your assessment that the United States is in no danger," Marshall replied to the secretary then turned back towards President Roosevelt. "Americans are at risk, sir. Especially the longer any war goes on. What's happening in Europe right now, Mister President, isn't going to stay isolated." He quickly turned back to the Secretary of War. "Just like it didn't in the last war. Eventually German ships will begin openly targeting our ships and that will be the beginning. I was in those trenches, Mister Secretary. I led those men and I saw the rows of dead. Hitler talks up a great game about only taking back what belongs to them, but it's all... well...bullshit. Sir."

Roosevelt stifled a sigh and coughed slightly. It was well known around Washington of the less than friendly disagreements between the top military brass and the man who oversaw their department. Perhaps the unavoidable outcome you got when you have a man whose personal and professional policy was to keep his country strictly isolationist and military leadership who saw what was happening around the world, understood better than most the global strategic situation and made-up national defense strategy based upon those threats. The unfortunate side of this argument, however, was that no matter what the facts may be, that these belligerent nations did indeed pose a threat to the United States, Secretary Woodring was correct that most ordinary people in the country still wanted absolutely nothing to do with another war overseas. No matter how appalling they may find the actions of those countries, they simply were not willing to go off to what most they saw as somebody else's fight. Not again. FDR knew that and knew that attitude was going to constrain him more than he otherwise would have liked to be.

"Gentlemen," he began, hoping to cut off any potential disagreement between the Secretary of War and his own military leaders. He pulled the cigarette out of his mouth and gestured his hand in a short chopping motion. "Nobody here is a fool. I think we all know where this is heading. I don't like things any more than any of you, but I don't have the luxury of burying my head in the sand and hoping for the best. We can pray for peace, but we can also be prepared for the worst." He exhaled noisily.

Secretary Woodring sat back in his chair, his face was nearly expressionless, but Roosevelt knew that just under the skin the other man would be seething. His reputation as an isolationist firebrand was widely unpopular with the leaders of the Democratic Party and behind tightly closed doors other members of Roosevelt's own cabinet had impressed upon him the need for him to resign. He could call for his resignation of course but found that simply keeping him around gained him some support from both Republicans and more conservative members of his own party. However, the man's outspokenness was becoming more of a problem to the administration and eventually would have to be addressed by the President himself.

"As I said, sir, I'll have the formal report done by next month," Admiral Stark finished.

Roosevelt nodded and tapped the pages Marshall had handed him. He'd read through the rest later. "What about Finland? How's the situation there?"

Marshall sighed. "The Finns have put up a heck of a fight. Since the Soviet invasion at the end of June we estimate that there's something in the vicinity of thirty Red Army divisions fighting in Finland to their nine. It's a three to one superiority. Fortunately for Finland, they'd managed to get their Mannerheim Line put together right when the Russians launched their attack. As impossible as it may seem, they've been able to hold the Red Army to surprisingly little gains. Now with winter setting in," he tossed up his hands, "it's anybody's game. Many of those Soviet divisions come from Southern Russia and aren't used to that cold arctic weather and four-foot-high snow."

"They're receiving our humanitarian aid?" Roosevelt asked Cordell Hull.

"They are, Mister President. Mostly unmolested. A couple of our ships have been stopped by the Soviet Navy, but their crews have never been interned. Thank God. I'd hate to think of good American merchant sailors being interned at some Siberian prison camp."

"Stalin isn't pushing his luck," Roosevelt replied. "He knows we're only sending food for the civilian population, nothing more. He doesn't want to elevate things any further. Well... I suppose that only time will tell what happens there." He shook his head slightly in disapproval. "You'd think Stalin has all the land he could possibly need. He hardly needs to go invading new ones. But I suppose that's the nature of despots. Taking what isn't theirs." The clock on the wall chimed and Roosevelt glanced at it then back to the men sitting around him. "Gentlemen, I'm going to have to leave soon, and I'd like to go with the knowledge that we're doing everything absolutely possible to secure the lives and liberty of American citizens. They're counting on us and I'm counting on all of you."

"We'll have something tangible put together for your review at next month's meeting, sir," General Marshall told him flatly. "There is one last thing that we'd like to discuss before we call this meeting." The general hesitated a moment. He leaned forward and crossed his hands together. "One of the biggest problems that we currently suffer from, sir, is a serious lack of manpower in our own armed services. The admiral's staff and my own have run some projections, which I've included in that report there. Our conclusions are that if EVER we are to engage in a global conflict, we'd be woefully behind in terms of trained personnel, particularly officers. If the worst were to happen and we were forced to fight, even on only one front, we'd need anywhere from a million to a million and a half men in uniform in just the first year.

"On the last couple of pages on that report I gave to you, Mister President, I outline this deficiency. It's our strong belief that an expansion of our armed forces is urgently needed. We have entire units at less than fifty percent strength right now. During a war we'd need tens of thousands more just to fill administrative, logistical and medical support posts and that's not to mention pilots, tankers, infantrymen or any other fighting unit. Right now, we rank right behind Portugal in terms of military preparedness."

"So, what are you suggesting?" Roosevelt inquired and Marshall hesitated to use the word.

"I think that the general is referring to some kind of draft," Secretary Woodring answered, unprompted. "Isn't that correct general?"

Marshall nodded. "Yes, sir. It is."

"A peacetime military draft?" Woodring replied, his tone scornful. "Never before has the United States ever implemented a peacetime conscription, Mister President, and I don't think that we should start now. Frankly, I'm shocked to hear this suggestion and a little perturbed that I was not informed of it prior to this meeting." His eyes widened and he gave Marshall a resentful gaze.

Anyone in the room could feel the tension across the table. Marshall sat in his chair, still as a statue and as calm as a breeze, all the professionalism that thirty-eight years in the army had taught him had clearly paid off. Roosevelt thought about the secretary's words for a moment as well as the man's disposition but gave it almost no credence. Even had the Army Chief of Staff included such a recommendation in a report to Woodring it was doubtful that the man would even read such a report and if he had then it was almost assured that such a report would never have reached the President's desk anyhow.

"Alright, here's what I'll do," the President began, he paused in order to craft his words properly. While he might have agreed with Marshall's suggestion on putting the country on a better war footing, he also couldn't out-rightly dismiss his own Secretary of War in front of the others. "I'll read through this report this evening. We'll discuss it at our next meeting. In the meantime," he tapped the pages against the table and pushed his wheelchair away, "I'm afraid I have a meeting scheduled with the Mexican Ambassador that I can't be late for. So, unless there were any more pressing matters. . ."

The group stood up as Roosevelt backed away from the table, nobody speaking forth.

"Then I shall look forward to next month." His steward wheeled him around and towards the door. He left there feeling that there were two wars he was going to have to contend with, one of them being the war between some of the men in that room and he knew that it was going to have to be sorted out sooner rather than later.

CHAPTER TWENTY-NINE

All over London church bells still tolled out in remembrance of the deceased former Prime Minister. Chamberlain's funeral service had been attended by the Royal Family, including the King's brother the Duke of Windsor. The ever-brief king had been recalled from his post as Governor General of the Bahamas in order to attend the funeral. Most of the Conservative members of Parliament as well as the opposition leadership had also attended. In fact, there were even a few heartfelt moments when his political opponents actually spoke with respect of their former colleague whom they had often clashed with on the floor of the House of Commons. Churchill, himself an outspoken opponent of his fellow Conservative, had given what many attendees had said were the warmest and most flattering words of the man. Though others were calling the eulogy faint praise for the person who many saw as leading Great Britain into a most dire situation.

Outside the closed windows of the Prime Minister's office, the feint ringing of the bells of Westminster Abbey could still be heard.

Great Britain's wartime situation under Chamberlain had remained almost static and in desperate shape. Czechoslovakia, Poland, Luxembourg and Denmark had been overrun by the German Army. Despite a valiant defense in the north of Norway, the Allies had lost that country as well at great cost. Over two thousand British and French casualties had been taken during the Narvik expedition and the Royal Navy had lost three destroyers and two armored cruisers covering the evacuation there. It was by the grace of God that the aircraft carrier *HMS Glorious* had narrowly avoided being sunk by a German U-boat.

In Northern France, neither the British Expeditionary Force nor the French Army had made any real attempt at any offensive. While Daladier's opinion of taking action was certainly more in line with fighting a war, too often Chamberlain held out for some forlorn hope of peace. Any opportunity for the BEF to take ground on the continent was therefore stymied.

At sea the news had been little better. A few minor successes by the Royal Navy mirrored those of the German Kriegsmarine. Merchant losses were abysmal and only a handful of German U-boats had yet been sunk in retaliation. But more than these things had been the demoralized mood and manner of the British people. The nation had been outraged as Hitler had taken country after country in Europe, but the swiftness of the conquest had been what was most shocking. Then there was the government's watered-down response that had not helped either and in fact further precipitated the current state of affairs. Dropping leaflets when they should have been dropping bombs.

Churchill shook his head at the thought of it. *Like watching amateur's child playing at war.*

Ironic that the foreign policy that Chamberlain had championed so hard for so long to achieve, that he had pinned his entire political future on, that had ultimately failed anyhow, succeeded in pushing enough members of his own party to force his resignation and be replaced by the very man who opposed his policy so vigorously.

10 Downing Street felt like quite a different place these days. The Prime Minister's residence and executive offices were bustling with a different kind of activity than in the past. The mood was also different. Many of the staff were the same, Churchill had decided not to get rid of everyone who had served Chamberlain so well, but many of them were new people that Winston had known and brought in from various other departments. There was a pronounced sense of optimism in the government that had not been present before.

Winston inwardly reveled in it a little bit.

He struck a match and puffed his half-finished cigar back to life sending rings of smoke upward. It had been hoped by some that his elevation to Prime Minister might end his constant use of cigars, at least during working sessions, but it seemed that was not to be. Winston sank back in his chair and watched the new First Sea Lord, Admiral Cunningham, proceed with his briefing on naval activities.

"...confirmed one light cruiser and one destroyer were sunk..."

In the weeks since taking office he'd held a dozen cabinet meetings. They'd taken on a strikingly different tone from his predecessor's, such as including uniformed service members to war meetings. Several members from Chamberlain's cabinet also remained on with the new government. Despite his own strong desires, he could hardly replace all of them without facing serious opposition within his own political party. Halifax for instance was still in his post as Foreign Secretary, Kingsley Wood had remained as Chancellor of the Exchequer. Halifax was still the 'golden boy' of the Conservative Party and his position within the government was secure, barring some great calamity.

Other men, such as Leslie Hore-Belisha, had been removed as Secretary of War. A man of no consequence around the halls of Parliament, his removal had been seen as long overdue, despite his friendliness with the King. His presence had not been missed, particularly by the General Staff who he'd often clashed with and by Churchill who saw the man as an obstacle to victory. Anthony Eden, a long time Churchill ally, had replaced him.

Across the table from him was Albert Victor Alexander, A.V. to those who knew him, the new First Lord of the Admiralty. A Labour party member, he was one of the opposition leaders who had openly favored Churchill over Halifax as PM. Once again, the Royal Navy was running on a better footing ever since his arrival there.

"...German U-boat activity in the Western Approaches have sunk upwards of one and a half million tons of shipping..." Admiral Cunningham continued, and Churchill listened.

Next to him sat the Foreign Secretary reclined back in his chair with his hands clasped over his chest as Admiral Cunningham went on. Churchill could see him from the periphery of his eye, sitting as still as a rock. The two men had continued to hash it out in the time since Chamberlain's resignation. Despite having been driven from power, both Halifax and Chamberlain, still the leader of the Conservative Party up until his death, had argued vigorously in support of peace with Germany. Though Chamberlain may now be gone Halifax remained and his views on negotiating an end to the war hadn't changed.

"Until our shipyards can replace the losses we've taken, particularly in small escort and screening vessels, we'll be forced to either provide fewer escorts for our convoys or simply have fewer convoys," Cunningham reported thereby finishing his briefing.

Churchill grumbled. "Thank you, Admiral Cunningham. I'll be discussing this with you at a further date. Thank you."

Winston typically had one foot in these briefings and another in the intricate political waltz that he was forced to dance, in part due to the machinations of some still in government. His government. The one he'd stitched together from a coalition of different parties and involved persons whom he disagreed with all his being. Truth be told he'd have asked for Halifax's resignation in a heartbeat if he didn't know for a fact that he'd be facing his own internal crisis if he did. The nation couldn't afford that. Not right now.

"General Dill," Winston motioned to the new Chief of the Imperial General Staff.

Dill had replaced Ironside after that man's professional indiscretion. Ironside had been a good man and a good officer and morally speaking both he and Admiral Pound had tried to do what they thought had been the right thing when they had mutually decided to sound the alarm on the disastrous policies of their superiors in the cabinet. But for those in uniform there was no excuse for sidestepping the chain of command.

Both men had quietly taken retirement and Winston couldn't say that it hadn't been the best for everyone that they had. Military leadership in the last government had often been excluded from the decision-making process and too many of the former cabinet members and ministers held those in uniform in low regard. Churchill shook the thought away and brought himself out of his little mental reverie.

"Thank you, sir." Dill was a medium built man pushing sixty. In many ways he was the opposite of the type of officer that Ironside had been. A staff officer for most of his career he'd earned his position almost by being the most unoffensive man in the room. "I've spoken with General Gort in France, and I intend to depart for his headquarters first thing tomorrow. Upon consulting with the French Army leadership, we both agree that launching any kind of offensive into Germany would be unwise with the onset of winter so close now. General Gamelin is also of the mind that France would need more time to mobilize additional troops. Earliest we would be looking at would be after the spring thaw."

Winston groaned at the news. He knew fully well the difficulty involved in moving large armies in wintertime. The clear-thinking part of him understood the military position but the more hawkish part of him wanted to have the combined Allied armies charge across the border and take the war into Germany.

"That could be a blessing in disguise," Lord Halifax commented indifferently. Both Churchill and Eden threw a stunned glance at the Foreign Secretary. "It'll give us some additional time to work out a diplomatic solution to all of this."

"Diplomatic solution, My Lord?" Eden asked, shock in his voice.

Halifax nodded. "Diplomacy doesn't end when the fighting begins. If we can find common ground with Hitler, work out a sort of mutual agreement, we can still end this conflict before it goes any further."

Eden cleared his throat and sat forward in his chair. "Surely, My Lord, you cannot mean to suggest that we abandon our allies on the continent, do you? Leave a good portion of Europe under occupation?"

"That is not what I'm saying at all," he replied chidingly. "As a matter of fact, I'm as sickened by anyone at the state of affairs and as Foreign Secretary I'm trying to keep the same thing from happening to the British Isles."

There was a short pause at the cabinet table. Churchill remained silent for a few moments but then motioned for General Dill to continue. He knew it was senseless trying to disagree with Halifax on this issue and did not wish to do so in front of the rest of the cabinet. Privately though his patience was wearing thin.

"Ummm, yes," Dill awkwardly began. "Well. . . we now have upwards of four hundred thirty thousand men in France, including RAF personnel, along with most of our heavy guns and equipment, though there were some losses in the Channel from German submarines. We'll continue to reinforce our positions there throughout winter. There's little indication that the German Army is taking up offensive positions. In fact, our intelligence sources report that the units which have been redeployed from Poland to the western front are staying well behind their lines. Unfortunately, Prime Minister, our window for offensive action has effectively closed for the year. Though I would have wished for some sort of demonstration, it simply is not feasible at this point. Had we exploited the Saar offensive with the French...well. . . " He shrugged uselessly at the suggestion.

"On a brighter note, we've had some decent success recently in cracking more German codes. Those chaps over at Bletchley are busy decoding more intercepts as we speak, and they've identified several older communications from Berlin to various military commands around Germany last year that seems to confirm suspicions that Hitler was aggressively pushing his commanders for an earlier war. Prior to his incapacitation."

There had been some of speculation on this subject. Some mid-level officers had tried to sound the alarm last year of an impending war, an alarm that fell on the deaf ears of the previous government. Though the situation by mid-1939 had looked like war was just on the horizon, Hitler's automobile accident had changed all of that. When no conflict materialized the governments of Britain, France and Poland had continued to pursue diplomatic efforts to ease the tension. Germany, meanwhile, had continued to pursue an expansive military buildup. Winston sometimes wondered how things might have turned out had Germany gone down that road an earlier war.

Hitler had been known to be a notorious meddler who had often intervened directly with military and production matters. One of the things that had happened after his accident was that the Reich was governed bilaterally between Himmler and Göring who had allowed the military and political systems to play out with a much freer hand. German industrial capacity had expanded rapidly under the new Armament Minister, Albert Speer, in the time since then and Hitler's recovery. Only time would tell how things would play out now that the dictator was back in total control.

"That is some good news," Winston replied, referring to the code breaking. "God knows we need some. Our own situation offers us few rays of sunshine."

General Dill nodded agreeingly. "However, not all news is good news I'm afraid and I must conclude my report with a rather dismal outlook for our supply situation. We're still well behind the Germans in war production and equipping our new forces is going to take us quite some time. We're also desperately low on any number of things from tanks and motorized vehicles to planes, munitions, spare parts and the list goes on. We'll be able to keep our forces in France supplied through winter but getting more of our industry geared up for a full-scale war is going to be vital if we're forced to fight on other fronts."

"What about our defenses in the Mediterranean or North Africa and the Near East?" Eden asked.

"Hmmm. Good question," Dill replied. "We're fortifying Gibraltar and Malta as quickly as we can. North Africa...well we're still planning that one out. Should Italy intervene today we'd be hard pressed to keep control. The Australian and New Zealand forces would be the logical choice to reinforce us there but we're also considering shifting a division or two from India if we must. There's over a quarter of a million Italian soldiers in Libya now. If they became hostile, they could very well push us all the way to Cairo before we could stop them."

"That would be a worst-case scenario, diplomatically speaking," Lord Halifax put in. "If Italy entered the war against us, we'd have very little hope of negotiating a peace with reasonably good terms. No one has Hitler's ear like Mussolini."

Churchill and Eden exchanged glances with each other and Winston bit down on his cigar. The Foreign Secretary was the chief negotiator for the country, and he'd long ago staked his career and reputation to a policy that time and again had failed and really should have died with Chamberlain. But the man had stuck to his beliefs fervently and had gone from appeasement to acquiescence. Still trying to bring what he saw as a 'reasonable peace' to the situation, he'd quietly been approaching many like-minded members of Parliament. His presence at the cabinet meetings was becoming almost obtrusive.

"Securing Egypt is a strategic necessity, General," Churchill told him. "We'll want that to be a top priority on your list of to do's. Tomorrow, gentlemen, I leave for France to meet with Monsieur Daladier. Among other things we'll be discussing our common strategy and hopefully we can broach this business that we're hearing out of our embassy in Paris regarding his government." Halifax raised his eyebrows as the Prime Minister spoke and his head bobbed up and down in a rare sign of agreement.

For the past two weeks there were accounts of division and conflict within the French government, accounts that had gotten louder in recent days, outside of the typical politicking that went on behind doors. Prime Minister Daladier's popularity among the French citizenry had dropped in recent weeks due to what many there saw as a war of inaction. The man's contentious relationship with Chamberlain and his low opinion of the British had not helped him either. With the Hungarian announcement that they were openly allying with Germany, Daladier's legs were being kicked out from under him now and it maybe he was suffering the same fate that Chamberlain had.

"Well," Churchill continued, "unless there's more good news from anybody," he scanned the faces of the men in the room, some chuckling back at him, "then I declare this cabinet meeting over." He pushed his heavy frame up from the table and the members stood up after him, he half turned to the Foreign Secretary. "May I have a word with you, My Lord. You as well Anthony."

Winston looked like an American gangster in his pin striped suit. He stood with a single hand on his hip, puffing on the last remnants of his cigar as the rest of the cabinet filed out the door. After the last of them exited and the door closed, he stood silent for a while, wishing to carefully craft his next words. Halifax stood next to him, hands across his chest, Eden just steps behind him, neither man uttering a single word. Winston exhaled the last puff of smoke.

"My Lord," he started then rubbed the bridge of his nose. He was feeling vexed. "I understand you and Mister Chamberlain were very close and that the foreign policy of his premiership was crafted by the both of you. I also understand that you and I will forever disagree on that policy. But you knew well this government's position and understood that the policies would be greatly different than the previous one. God man, MUST you wave your politics out there so damn defiantly?"

Halifax's eyes widened and his arms fell down his sides in stunned reaction to the Prime Minister's words. His mouth dangled open, and it took him a long moment to find his words.

"Defiantly?" He puffed noisily. "Fervently perhaps but certainly not defiantly." Churchill sneered at his response. "I agreed to remain at my post after being asked, by you, to do so. My mind of negotiation has never changed, Mister Prime Minister. Never. I am committed to whatever course of action that brings a swift end to this war, sir."

"Your mind on appeasement is well known as is my opposition to it. The course of action of this government is what I deem it to be, My Lord. Right now, my imperative is to ready ourselves for what is to come. The war cabinet must be focused on that. I would ask you to constrain your opinions on negotiations to private meetings."

Halifax crossed his arms and bit into his lower lip. The two men locked eyes for seconds before he relented and gave a nod.

"I understand. For the sake of war cabinet meetings, I shall stay silent on the topic. But I wish to go on the record by saying that I firmly believe that we can still arrange an agreement with Berlin."

"So noted."

"Would you care to hear of the progress we're making?" Halifax asked, then added, "Now that we're alone I mean." Churchill's eyelids narrowed slightly, and he nodded. "Minister Ciano and I have had several positive discussions in recent days. He believes as I do that we have a real opportunity to meet with Ribbentrop in the near future. Perhaps in the next few days."

"Intelligence reports put Ribbentrop in Bucharest," Eden told them both. "Presumably to meet with the Romanian king."

Halifax's brow furrowed at the unexpected news.

"Well, regardless, the Italian minister is of the mind that Mussolini is in a strong position to mediate on the matter. He is Hitler's closest ally."

Winston sighed loudly. Ally perhaps but no friend by any means. Dictators rarely had friends and two of them in the same room often clashed more than they cooperated. Everyone knew that Mussolini was a distant second fiddle to Hitler and it was suspected that Hitler held the Italian in very low regard. How much pull anyone in Rome could possibly have with Hitler was anybody's guess.

"I was planning to send out a diplomatic cable to Ciano after we return from France. Something that your predecessor and I had agreed to. It outlines a series of concessions we were willing to make to ensure peace."

Ensure peace... Winston thought. *How can you ensure anything with people like those Nazis? With a man like Hitler?*

He was tempted to put the burnt-out cigar stub back into his mouth, just to have something to bite down on. He was instinctively against such a move, against such a thought. Any possible concessions Chamberlain could have offered to Hitler to satisfy the man had surely been done already. It always came back to the Munich Agreement. Or the Munich Betrayal as he thought of it.

He gave the Foreign Minister a single, grudging nod.

"Very well," he muttered. "But I wish to review this cable before you send it."

"I understand," Halifax replied. "Was there something else, sir?"

"No, My Lord. No there is not."

Halifax nodded to either man in a polite gesture. He turned and walked away, stopping only long enough to grab his fedora off the hat stand near the door. The double doors quietly closed behind him, and Eden and Churchill were left alone.

"Ready to throw in the towel, isn't he?" Eden commented and instantly regretted it. Churchill snorted.

"He's stuck in the past, Anthony. Still pandering to a man who's deceased. But we must accept that there are still elements of Parliament who support him and what he's trying to accomplish. Unfortunately, I need some of those MP's." He shook the thought away in dismay. "Well...it's about time for a drink."

The two men started towards the single door to an adjoining ante-room.

"Why did you want to see the diplomatic cable before the Foreign Office sends it out?" Eden inquired.

"Sentimentality, my friend. Should I arrive at the gates of Hell, I'll know exactly what it was that I sold my soul for."

The door closed behind them.

CHAPTER THIRTY

The marine guard at the small wooden desk in the main hallway of the Admiralty Building took Alistair's military identification, looked at it then back up at him and scribbled his information down into his roster book. As usual the great building was a centerpiece of activity and was bustling with men and women coming and going. Security was always high and everyone who entered that building was heavily scrutinized. No exceptions.

"Thank you, sir," the marine's voice was crisp and professional. He handed him back his ID and turned his logbook around so that Alistair could sign his name.

"Yes and, umm, where would I find room Ten B?" He asked the sentry.

"Of course, sir," the corporal pointed down the corridor. "Right down the hallway there, down the small stairwell two levels. It'll be on your right, sir. Can't miss it."

Alistair grimaced imperceptibly of being directed to a sub-level office. He'd assumed his destination was one of the higher floor offices, but he nodded his thanks and the corporal's thick, bushy mustache straightened up as he smiled back at him. The floor of the main corridor was made of old oak wood and the echo of the sound of every foot heel from all the bodies made it seem as though an army was on the march. Behind all the closed office doors throughout the building were hundreds of people at work.

Despite having been in the Royal Navy now for going on six years this was the very first time he'd been to the old building. His own time in the service had all been spent on ships at sea with brief duties in Gibraltar and Malta. But he would not have wanted it any other way. He didn't look down at the sailors and officers who worked in offices such as these, certainly not, but he'd joined the navy for a reason and sitting behind a desk wasn't that reason.

But he also couldn't help but marvel a bit at the traditional nerve center of the navy. Even the stairwells here were ostentatious. It had been built over two hundred years earlier as a model of British architecture. Its outward appearance was deeply rooted in the traditions and prestige that Britain had establish generations ago. The building had been designed with a certain pretentiousness in mind rather than practicality. He preferred the simplicity of a submarine over the showy surroundings that had defined British military society for over two centuries now. It was far too aristocratic for his working-class tastes.

But that was Britannia for you. The nation and its people were steeped in centuries long traditions and social customs. Customs that had made the empire what it was today, kept that empire running and had spread British culture to every corner of the globe. But there was another concept that Britons had perfected over the years as well: theater. Knowing the effectiveness of keeping up outward appearances was a true British virtue.

The sub-levels of the Admiralty contained a network of mostly unused corridors and storerooms. What use the rooms on this floor were was mainly to store those things that were of little importance to the navy. When Chadwick had received his orders two days earlier to report to the so-called Naval Planning Office he'd assumed that he was being sent to meet with someone of reasonable position. Now, standing in front of the door in what was little more than a sub-level basement, his first thought was that perhaps this was either a practical joke someone was playing on him or that some sort of mistake had been made. He turned the knob and opened the door.

As soon as he entered the room, he was instantly struck by that unmistakable characteristic that seemed to define government offices everywhere, cigarette smoke. Inside the working staff was made up of a mix of uniformed military officials and civilians. It was a sight that he was unused to seeing and the atmosphere looked much more casual and informal than what he'd experienced while at sea with the fleet where everything was a bit more reserved, at least among the officers.

"Good morning, sir," the voice came from a young brown-haired man sitting nearest the door. His desk was overflowing with stacks of paperwork. The man stood up from behind the pile and ran his hands down his sweater vest.

"Good morning," Chadwick replied giving the young man a once over. He was trim and clean cut. His clothing was modest, obviously freshly pressed and he wore a simple green bow tie. His face was closely shaven, and his hair was neatly groomed. A thin line of hair graced his upper lip. "I'm Lieutenant Commander Chadwick, looking for Commander Norwen. I believe that he's expecting me." He reached into his jacket pocket and presented his credentials and orders.

"Ah. Commander Chadwick. It's a pleasure, sir," the other man greeted warmly and took the papers. "We've been expecting you. My name is Daniel Towman, sir."

"Pleasure. And what is your position here Mister Towman?" Alistair inquired equally as polite.

"Well, officially speaking I'm simply the office clerk. But I suppose I'm a bit of a jack of many trades, sir. I support everyone here in some form or another and I make sure the whole office is running as smoothly as possible."

"I see. Thank you," he said as Towman gave him back his paperwork and tucked it back into his pocket. He took note of Towman's respectful tone and the fact that he took to addressing him as sir and judged him to be a very duteous type of person. A trait, he was sure, that came in handily when working in an office like this.

"Well, let me show you to Captain Norwen," Towman said.

"Captain?"

"Yes, sir. Captain. A recent promotion and between you and I it's long overdue. This way please."

It wasn't as large an office as Alistair had expected. Given the title he'd expected to find no less than an entire floor dedicated to the department. There weren't more than a dozen people working in here today. A single large world map adorned the far wall with dozens of small pins fixed to positions all over the globe. Near the center of the room sat a large table covered in folders, files and stacks of papers of all sizes in a shuffled, disorderly fashion. In a lone recess a teletype machine ticked away endlessly. Everywhere there were file drawers and small desks sitting front to front, half empty cups of tea and cigarettes burning in ashtrays.

Then there was the man sitting behind the desk in an alcove in a far corner of the office, behind a row of file drawers. He was a middle-aged man whose thick, dark hair was mottled with gray. Built thickly around the midsection Alistair pegged him as a man who may have been a wrestler or some other athlete in his younger years. He had the telephone up to his ear when Towman and Chadwick stopped in front of his desk.

Alistair's eyes shifted around at the workspace. It might have been the only workspace in the entire office that was not an unkempt mess. Only a pair of green folders, a full ashtray, a single photograph of a woman, his wife perhaps, and a Chinese bone lighter decorated the desktop. Against the wall behind him were a plethora of paper rolls, like the charts aboard naval vessels, boxes upon boxes with dates marked on them were stacked up and a single poster taped to the wall reminding everyone that the walls have ears.

"Yes, sir," the man said over the phone, looking up at Chadwick and nodding just slightly enough to be noticed. "I'll have it worked up tonight and hopefully we'll have something for you tomorrow. Yes. I understand. Thank you, sir. Goodbye." He hung up and stood up from his chair, the wheels squeaking a little as it rolled back.

"Captain Norwen, this is Lieutenant Commander Chadwick, sir," Towman introduced. "Commander, Captain Archibald Norwen."

Norwen extended his hand and Alistair shook it.

"Please sit, Commander." Norwen indicated to the chair across from him. "Daniel, could I trouble you for some tea please. Commander?"

"Yes, please. Thank you," he graciously accepted before dropping down into the chair and laid his cap on his lap.

Daniel smiled and nodded then went off. Captain Norwen sat back down, pulled open his top drawer and produced a pack of cigarettes. He offered one to Alistair, who politely declined, then lit one up with his Chinese lighter. His chair croaked again as he relaxed back.

"Allow me to offer you my congratulations, sir," Alistair complimented and Norwen's face became confused.

"Congratulations?"

"On your promotion, sir," he replied nodding to Norwen's shoulder insignia. "I was told you were recently advanced."

"Oh. Yes." He shrugged slightly as if he'd completely forgotten about the matter. "Down here in the dungeons rank doesn't mean as much as it might upstairs. Or with the fleet." He took a drag then realized he might have just inadvertently offended the other man. "Not that I mean to suggest that those with the fleet are just chasing rank, Chadwick," he said apologetically.

"No offense taken, sir," Alistair replied smoothly and grinned lightly. Norwen chuckled gently.

"You'll find that we're wound a little tight down here, Commander Chadwick. It's not personal we just don't get many fresh faces that come down that stairwell. Certainly, no war heroes."

"Hardly a war hero, sir," Chadwick replied self-consciously, and his mind briefly flashed back to the memory of his old command sinking into the ocean. "We didn't do anything that any other crew in the Royal Navy wouldn't have also done."

Norwen studied him for a few moments but decided against probing further on that subject.

"Well," he began, exhaling a puff of smoke. "You'll find that around here some of our own battles are fought over weeks or months. Sadly, many of them can be lost and it's no less deadly than any battle at sea." As he said that Daniel returned with a tray of tea with a pot and two cups. He poured a cup each and left without so much as a single word.

"Well, I must tell you, sir, that I'm not entirely sure what exactly it is that I'm here for." He took a sip from his cup of tea.

Caught off guard by the comment Norwen swallowed his own hot drink a little too quickly causing him to cough as it went down his throat.

"You did receive your orders, didn't you? He asked perplexed. "You don't mean to tell me that you weren't informed as to the details, do you?"

"I received my orders two days ago to report here to you, sir, but they didn't include any clarification as to why though. I've been sitting around NB Portsmouth since my board of inquiry in August. I'd assumed that this was simply just another debriefing."

Norwen sighed and shook his head in reply.

"It's not another debriefing I assure you. I asked specifically for you. We had a minor part to play in tracking *Admiral Graf Spee* and when she went down, I followed your career a bit after that. I'd heard that you'd been posted shore side since then and I made a request for assignment here." He shrugged innocently. "Most officers would welcome the chance to get back into the fight."

Alistair's features flushed slightly by the news that he specifically had been requested by anyone here at the Admiralty. After *Admiral Graf Spee* had been sunk and *Orkney* lost, he'd been picked apart by a naval board at Gibraltar, as was customary by the navy when a ship was lost at sea. The loss of a single sub was hardly any great disaster for the service, and it was difficult for him to believe that anyone at all was that interested in him or had been following his career.

"I'm at a loss, sir. I'm not sure what to say. The loss of *Orkney* was well documented by the captain's board. I'm not sure..."

"I think you misunderstand me, Commander," Norwen said and smiled. "I didn't request you because of the loss of your sub. Though I understand what emotions you would place on it. Thankfully your entire crew was saved. No, my interest in your career was a little more atypical. I was handed a copy of your personnel file back in July. I understand that you've been in the service for only a few short years and that you went straight from officer school into submarine service. You're only what, twenty-six?"

"Twenty-seven, sir."

"Twenty-seven," Norwen repeated back. "Risen through the ranks rather quickly don't you think? Most officers your age haven't advanced as fast as you have. Doubtful very many of them have been given charge of a vessel of any type let alone a long-range patrol sub."

Alistair shrugged and said, "Most officers don't sign up for long range patrols like that either, sir. Sub patrol is...well, not for most sailors."

"No of course not," Norwen said with a facetious tone in his voice. "Not when all the glory is to be made on the decks of great battleships right?" He dragged on the last bit of his cigarette. "I know well the fascination that most men have with those huge ships, bustling with guns, rushing headlong into battles." He shook his head dismissively. "I started my own career on destroyers. But the point that I'm making is that your career choices have sent you down a road that few have traveled. Your own modesty aside, Commander, you had a decisive role to play in the sinking of an enemy heavy cruiser. The pride of the German Navy in fact. And by all accounts you did it by outwitting the more conventional. By thinking out of the box in other words. You weren't going to chase a cruiser all over the oceans, were you? No. Of course you weren't. Well, that's what we do around here. Think outside of the box."

Alistair sipped slowly on his hot tea, his own natural inclinations tended towards the decks of those very battleships and cruisers that Captain Norwen spoke of. Though his experience was solely in submarines up until this point, he was still young and had given serious thought to assignment with one of those cruiser squadrons. Any one of them were badly in need of qualified and experienced officers and now that he'd been cleared by the captain's board, he was quite sure that he could get a posting with the fleet again. With that said, Norwen was correct. Sub duty was certainly an unconventional branch of service, one that most in the navy had no wish to be a part of. The command of one of His Majesty's submarines came with a great deal of unconventional training and as already noted, an ability to think out of the box.

"So, am I to assume that my assignment here is not temporary, sir?"

"Listen, Commander, I have the utmost respect for you. I'll make you a deal. After you hear what I have to say, if you decide that this type of work isn't for you then I'll request your immediate reassignment back to the fleet. But I firmly believe, given your tract record, that you would be a tremendous asset here."

"Thank you, sir. May I speak freely?" Norwen nodded. "I really have no clue what goes on here. The Naval Planning Office, sir? I . . ." He simply shook his head.

"Never heard of us?" Norwen asked. There was more than a hint of good humor in his voice. "Not surprised. What you see is what you get. With perhaps one or two more heads not present today. You'll get quite the education but to put it succinctly we're a division of Operations. Our job here is to disseminate information on a strategic level, then pass along recommendations to the Admiralty."

"Intelligence gathering?" Alistair asked.

"Partly."

"Isn't that the purview of Naval Intelligence, sir?"

Norwen shrugged slightly and nodded. "It is. At least that's the navy's primary intelligence gathering apparatus. NPO is something a bit different. We gather intel from less conventional methods then they do. Our information comes from a wider range of sources, we then disseminate it at the operational level. Our primary mission is to provide the Admiralty with a more strategic view of naval affairs. I won't lie either, up until recently we've been a rather devalued little corner of the service. Recent events have changed of course and we're a bit more relevant nowadays."

"If you've become familiar with my file, sir, you know I have absolutely no experience in intelligence work."

"Neither did I, until I did," he chuckled as he smothered the butt of the finished cigarette into the ashtray. "Requirements of the service and all that. But what you do have is a good eye for predicting the unpredictable. Any other man in the position you'd been in would never have gone in the direction you did. That says something about you. About your character. And it's the reason why I requested your assignment here. What we do here in this office requires much the same skills. That ability to plan for the things that others don't plan for and see the things that others miss. We need people who do that here. You see, Commander, if we lost a whole army corps in battle, we'd be hurt but we could still fight on. We could suffer losing half the air force and still fight. But one battle that we cannot afford to lose is the one at sea. We're dependent upon our overseas lifeline and if we lose that battle, we're done.

Being an island nation has its advantages as well as it's disadvantages. We could use a set of eyes here that can see the whole picture and who understands the greater strategic situation. It also doesn't hurt to have a man who's got experience in a sea battle. One who can identify with the men on those ships." He sipped again on his tea and relaxed back a bit in his chair.

Alistair's eyebrows raised up slightly and he pressed his tongue into his lower lip. He still felt hesitant, but it was hard to argue with the captain's point. The disconnect between the those serving in forward positions and the intelligence gathering services and the administrators who ran them from some rear area was as old as the navy itself. As good as many of those officers were most of them had no experience at sea or in combat where the result of their decision making was played out and men died.

Add that on top of the fact that Norwen was his superior officer and he had specifically requested Alistair's reassignment because he thought highly enough to believe that maybe Alistair might actually contribute something of value to this operation here.

"Hmm. Well, I do see your point, sir. I can't help but to agree with you." He rubbed his chin as he said that then his eyes snapped upwards to meet Norwen's and his back stiffened a bit. "What is my assignment, sir?" He asked.

Norwen grinned enthusiastically. "So does this mean that my little talk convinced you to join us here, Commander Chadwick?"

"I'm an officer in the navy and I've been given my orders, sir. I go where the service requires me to go," he replied and Norwen chuckled in response.

"Well glad to hear it, Commander. I'll admit that for a minute or two I thought that perhaps I'd been a little too presumptuous."

"Not at all, sir. Though I'd like to better understand my duties. Going from a serving line officer to a desk position...no offense, is a bit of a change and into a position which I have no experience. What position am I to fill?"

"You'd be my number two," Norwen informed him. "For the time being your job will be to learn the business inside and out. A lot of your daily grind will be normal administrative functions. I'll show you the ropes. Eventually you'll take an active part in strategic operations and now and again we'll have to brief the admirals upstairs. I'll have Daniel find you a place to set up." He scanned around the cramped office as if the thought of giving Chadwick a desk hadn't been considered before now. "Perhaps we'll give him a day or two for that. It'll take at least that long for the paperwork to upgrade your security clearance to come through. In the meantime, however," he put down his cup and pushed himself up from his chair, Alistair followed suit. Norwen held out his hand and Alistair gripped it. "Welcome to the Closet, Commander Chadwick."

CHAPTER THIRTY-ONE

There was a round of laughter in the room and the clinking together of glasses. Ernst smiled happily as he toasted. The usually spacious living room of the family apartment seemed cramped today with all his aunts, uncles and cousins gathered together. Both couches were full and every chair in the house taken. Near the large bay window, the little children played, and the older boys stood respectfully by their parents and occasionally threw playful smiles at their younger cousins.

Ernst smiled and laughed as his uncle finished telling a dirty joke concerning an experience he'd once had with a girl in Munich. Riesling dripped out of Uncle Alfred's mouth as he broke out laughing uncontrollably after he got to the part about the girl having more parts than what he'd bargained for. The ladies in the room gave disapproving looks at each other and simply shook their heads as Uncle lost his composure. One of Ernst's aunts covered the ears of her twelve-year-old son as Alfred told the raunchy story.

His father, Karl, threw his arm around his son proudly and shook him as the three men laugh hysterically. Ernst took another sip of his wine and decided he needed to sit down. The gathering had been a celebration of both Ernst's visit home from the army and the Lutheran Day of Repentance and Prayer. He'd been fortunate enough to get time away from the army on this important day. He'd arrived only yesterday, and it had felt good to be home, even if for only a few days. Mother had been so emotional when he stepped off the train that she'd almost completely broken-down sobbing at the station depot. Papa had also been overcome but held back the tears and settled for a hardy hug and a handshake.

Ernst watched and rolled his eyes when his uncle continued his drinking and storytelling.

"Oh, oh wait," Uncle Alfred began, still laughing uncontrollably. "I remember this time I was traveling through Bavaria and this young girl on a farm..."

Karl waved his hands at his brother's attempt at another joke as the ladies in the room were showing visible signs of tiring of the vulgarity. Some of the younger kids too were looking up at their inebriated relative in curiosity, one even repeating to himself one or two of the dirty words repeatedly. Ernst saw the child, laughed and shook his head at his little cousin Willy, who was a tiny two-year-old with overly chubby cheeks and curly blonde hair. God help the boy to be born to such a boisterous family. The gathering had reminded Ernst of his own youth growing up in this household when such a get-together had been more common.

"Okay, okay, Alfred," Karl told his brother. "I think you should take a rest from your story telling."

"Yes," Aunt Ada seconded. Ada was his wife. "Because that's all they are, stories." She said it and everyone laughed. Uncle Alfred was about to rebuke that statement, but Ada put her hand over his mouth.

Gathering like this had been something that the family had not done for a while. Mama organized it days earlier, hoping that perhaps two or three might well attend, but they now boasted nearly twenty at their third-floor apartment, children included. News of Ernst's imminent return home only made it that much better. She had spent the better part of the last few days cooking and getting ready. It felt almost like an early Christmas.

Ernst leaned back in the sofa and eyed the half-eaten chocolate cake on his plate. It had been months since he'd eaten chocolate and Mama always made the best cake.

"Uschi," Papa said to Mama, "Uschi, we need more wine!" He held up his empty glass. "And some of that Limburger too my dear. Don't hold back now. This is a happy day." He turned to his son. "My boy has come home a man. Son, I can't tell you just how proud I am of you. Doing what you are doing..." He started to become emotional, wiped a single tear from his eye and Ernst looked at him curiously. Papa had had too much wine to drink, and he could tell. "Serving the Fatherland like you are. Well, I only wish that I had served when I was your age." He shook his head and tipped his empty glass up to his lips to swallow the last few drops.

"How do you like the army, Ernst?" Cousin Manuela asked. She coddled her baby in her arms.

"Yes, Ernst," Aunt Eunice quickly followed up. "Is it nice there? Are they feeding you?" Eunice was a nice old lady, but always had been a bit clueless about things.

"Ummm...Yes, I do like it. Ummm...and yes, they feed us. Thank you."

"Well, it's not enough that's for sure," Eunice replied and nodded to the cake sitting on the table between sofas. "You should eat young man. You need to put on some weight."

Ernst drank down a generous gulp of wine and simply nodded his head. Coming home had its drawbacks too. His two younger brothers had been hanging off him, begging for stories from his army time. Mama's chief concern was on his comfort, and she'd hardly stopped baking since his arrival. Papa and he had gone for a long walk just this morning after breakfast where he'd proudly shown off his eighteen-year-old son to all the shoppe and business owners up and down their street, stopping for a while at the store of one of his competitors in the shoe business just to let the other man know how many medals Ernst had won since joining the army.

"He's going to get more than enough to eat before he has to go back," Karl told everyone as Uschi emerged from the kitchen with a round of Limburger cheese and another bottle of Riesling. "Mother will be putting a few kilos on him before he leaves. They'll have to run him more to get it off him. Ha ha ha."

"Do you do a lot of marching in the army, Ernst?" Eunice asked him.

"Not very much, Auntie. I mostly ride in tanks."

Uschi handed Karl the bottle, who uncorked it and began filling glasses again. Mama took a knife and cut into the cheese round. He knew that he'd be forced to answer some rather silly questions when

he returned but he'd held out some hope he could avoid the more out-
landish. He knew some members of his extended family could be rather
ignorant about some things and outspoken about others.

"Well, we're happy to have you back, Ernst," Manuela told him.
"I know that I've been concerned about you. What with the war and
all."

"Bah! Fool Poles started this war," Alfred stated, waving his hands
around in the air. "You know who's really to blame, don't you? The
Jews. Those people have manipulated things for far too long. They've
controlled the money supply for generations now. Well, they're getting
what they deserve now." Alfred sighed then drank half his glass in a single, large gulp.

Ernst blinked at the statement, remembering the images of Poland.
He'd certainly seen plenty of Polish people clogging the roads there, running from the Germans, carrying all that they had along with them in
whatever they could move it with. He didn't know how many of them
were Jewish though. Then the memory of Sandomierz hit him. The small
town, the SS rounding up those people. That little boy...

He pushed it out of his mind and took another gulp of his wine then
let his father refill the glass.

"I do feel a little bit bad for those Jewish people," Uschi said. She put
some cheese and a sliver of chocolate cake on a plate and sat back down
in her chair. "The children I mean. They didn't know what their parents
and grandparents were doing. They can't be held to blame, can they?"

"Oh well, they're all the same, aren't they?" Old Aunt Eunice asked.
"Children or not. I'm sorry but they don't really belong in this country.
They're all immigrants and we don't need those. And that religion of
theirs..." She made a disgusted face and took a drink.

"Exactly!" Alfred agreed heartily. "I for one trust the Führer. He's trying to make Germany great again and moving these Jews out is a good
first step." He sank back in his chair and muttered under his breath, "Ver-
min."

Karl held up his hand. "Now, now. My son didn't come home just to
hear us talk politics." He put his hand back on Ernst's shoulder, his thick
mustache curled as he smiled at him. "Before you know it the French

will be beaten, and the war will be over. We're just so happy that Ernst has chosen to serve the Fatherland. You've made your mother and I very proud of you."

Glasses were raised and Ernst nodded his head self-consciously. He didn't care for the attention that much. He'd even made it a point to change out of his army uniform and into his old clothes just as soon he'd arrived yesterday. As it was Papa had already told everyone he knew, and even a few he didn't, about his 'hero son returning from the war'. Not that he wasn't proud of his army service, he was, he just didn't like to make a big fuss. That and he knew his family well enough to know some of their feelings towards those people that Germany was at war with. Views that he didn't necessarily agree with.

"I'll bet you didn't get anything as good as this in Poland." It was Papa's cousin, Gustav. He was raising his glass of wine and his enormous belly shook like jelly when he laughed. "Although Ernst, when you get to France, be sure to grab a few bottles of the good French stuff for your old cousin." He laughed again then helped himself to a generous cut of chocolate cake.

"Seems like you're going everywhere these days, young man," Alfred said. "Poland, then Luxembourg. Your father told me you even marched in Berlin in the Führer's parade. That must have been exciting! To have been so close to Hitler like that. Hmmm. That is something I would have liked." He sipped again generously on his glass. "Did you get to meet him?" Ernst only shook his head. "Pity."

"So, Cousin Ernst, what was Poland like?" Manuela asked.

He shrugged. "A lot like Germany really. The towns look the same. The churches, houses, even their clothes. I wish I could say it was nice when I was there. But..." He left the thought unsaid and felt a need to change the subject. "On the other hand, I did have some news that I was waiting to share with you. I thought I'd do it tomorrow, but I guess it's as good a time now. I found out that my promotion has come through. When I get back, I'll be a full corporal." There was a collective sharp inhale from the adults at the news and happy congratulations came from everyone. Papa stood up, pulled Ernst up with him and threw his arms around his son.

"A corporal? My boy." He rubbed the back of Ernst's head. "Two years in and he already will be a leader. Ha, ha! Hitler never made corporal, Alfred." Karl took his glass and raised it. "To my son. My oldest. May he continue to make us all proud of him." They toasted and drank.

"Congratulations," Alfred said and winked. "Does this mean that you have a gift for him, Karl?"

Karl looked at his brother and for a moment was confused by the comment. "Oh. Oh yes. I do have something for you, Son. I was going to wait but, well, now is as good a time as any. Come with me. Come." He tapped Ernst's chest and curled his finger at him. Uschi looked confused and was about to say something, but Karl waved his hand at her. "It's a father and son moment. We'll be right back."

Ernst shrugged at his mother but put down his glass and followed Papa into his bedroom. Karl closed the door behind him and urged Ernst to sit on the end of the bed. He giggled like a child as he opened his closet door and sifted through some boxes before pulling out a small, old, black wooden box and ran his hand over it, cleaning away any dust.

"I had something that I wanted to give to you," he said with a big grin. "I was going to give it to you later, but I think the time is right. This was my father's." He opened the small box and offered it to Ernst. "Now it's yours."

Ernst's mouth gaped open, and his eyes blinked in awe. *This was his grandfather's?*

"An Iron Cross?" It was beautiful. The medal was wonderfully crafted, the sheen had dulled around its edges, the year *1871* etched into it, the old Imperial eagle emblem in its center. A single black and silver ribbon fastened to it that was only slightly faded. "I never knew Grandfather had this." The Iron Cross was the ultimate award, given only to the bravest soldiers.

"Yes. Served in the old Kaiser's army. The first Kaiser. I didn't get to serve, and Alfred never had any children. So now this heirloom will go to you."

Ernst took the box and stared at the medal sitting on a bed of cotton, its ribbon folded over perfectly. It looked nearly new though it was seventy years old. The Iron Cross had been passed down from the days of the old Prussian Kings. Created to award soldiers for the highest levels of bravery and to have it was considered the greatest military honor one could have.

"Papa," he began then stammered his words. "I don't know what to say to this. I... I..."

"You don't have to say anything, Son. This is yours. I was merely a caretaker until you were ready. Just remember what it means when you look at it. Remember what it stands for."

"Honor," Ernst told him quietly as he sat gawking at the medal. He couldn't take his eyes of it. "It stands for honor." He thought about all the officers that wore the venerable trophy around their necks back in camp. Every common soldier knew about the symbolism that went with having one, and every one of them wanted one. It meant that you acted with honor in everything that you did.

In that moment he wanted to tell Papa about everything he felt, everything he'd seen and experienced. Most of all he wanted to tell Papa what was in his heart. His real heart not just the facade that most people put on. But he couldn't. He was overcome with emotion and when he looked back up at his father, he could see in his eyes that Papa and knew would not have understood.

The train let out a long, loud double whistle as it slowed it's approached. It had been on the move throughout the night and the people packed into the cattle cars had endured a cold and sleepless night. They'd come for them yesterday morning. The Nazis had. Dozens of soldiers had come in the early morning hours and taken them out of their homes. There had been no warning, no chance of getting out of the ghetto before they came and no choice but to go. The soldiers had taken the people, men, women, even the children, and packed them tightly onto the train. There had been no food or water since they left yesterday and the stench inside was unbearable. The train had obviously recently been used to transport livestock and cow droppings had been left inside. One man, an older gentleman, had complained and been beaten by a soldier for his trouble.

The train whistled again, then came the sound of metal grinding against metal as the brakes applied and the feeling of the train slowing. The people inside who had been sitting began to get up as it did. Most of the occupants were older, all were exhausted and hungry after the long train ride. Kara was one of them. She'd stood up at the first sound of the whistle blowing, her white and yellow dress stained and torn. Her hair felt disgusting, and she'd put it up in a bun. She hadn't washed in three days now, her underwear still soaked from urinating herself during the night. A small corner of the car was used as a lavatory, but she'd been too frightened to use it. Frightened by the soldiers at first then frightened by some of the people in the train car. A man had stared at her throughout the night. She'd been frightened of him too. Frightened to move. Frightened of everything. Most of all she was frightened of this train coming to a stop.

Then there was her daughter, lying in her lap all night long, her little arms wrapped around her mother's neck. Kara had rocked her and sang to her in a low, whispered tone. Hannah. Her name was Hannah, her sweet little, blonde-haired daughter with the green eyes. Kara had hardly moved all night, even when the pain in her leg where Hannah lay became too much. After Hannah had fallen asleep the singing had turned to sobbing and her tears ran down her cheeks and into Hannah's golden, blonde hair.

The train whistled once again and Kara shook Hannah just a little, enough to get her up and on her little feet. The people inside who had remained sitting stood up now, wiping the dust and dried cow shit off their clothing. Kara stood little Hannah up and ran her fingers through her hair then brushed her off her little coat, the yellow star pinned to it and her shirt.

"I'm so tired," Hannah whimpered to her mother, and she blinked heavily. Kara licked the inside of her fingers and cleaned around Hannah's face and cheeks. "I'm hungry," her voice was barely a whisper.

"I know," Kara whispered back and tried to smile at her little girl.

The car jolted as the train finally came to a stop. Some of the others looked around at each other, terror in their eyes. An elderly couple held each other close, a husband touched his wife's face, an infant cried, and families huddled together. Outside the train came loud voices shouting out at each other and bodies walked by the car, their shadows fell across the sunlight coming through the slatted wooden doors. Then the shouting ceased, and it seemed for several moments that went by there was silence and no voice could be heard. This went on for thirty seconds then a minute. Still nothing. It became so silent that the only thing Kara could hear was her own breathing.

Then someone stepped in front of the train door. The jingling of the rusted lock being removed was terrifying. Suddenly each of the doors slid open with great force and the shouting began.

Hannah clung to her mother's leg tightly and Kara looked down at her. "Be brave," she whispered to her. "Be brave my love."

The train door was yanked open with a hard crash and the guards outdoors began shouting at them in harsh, angry tones. The sunshine was blinding, and people reflexively covered their eyes.

"GET OUT! GET OUT NOW!"

Soldiers stood outside of the cattle car, shouting at the people inside, pointing fingers, grabbing and pulling people down. People were taken out violently, pushed, shoved, kicked, prodded with rifles. It was horrific. One after another they jumped or fell onto the outside platform as quickly as they could. Kara stood at the edge of the car, holding Hannah's little hand and dangled a foot off as if she were about to leap down, then a hand grabbed her leg, tore her pantyhose as she was yanked down from the raised car. She slammed to the ground hard then curled up to avoid being hit by the guard.

"Get off the train," the guard called out. "NOW!"

Kara slowly stood back up as the soldier put his hand on her shoulder as if to drag her away.

"Wait!" She cried out. "Please. My daughter!" Her arms were stretched out towards little Hannah who was still up on the car, crying out for her mother. The soldier saw this and threw Kara back then nodded for her to get her little girl.

She lifted Hannah off the car. People were so panicked to get out of the car that they were pushing each other off. People fell feet to the hard ground. There were no steps or ladders to help them off. Soldiers were barking at them. Shouting obscenities. Some had rifles raised. A family in the next car stood with their hands raised, horrified at the guns being aimed at them, the father pleading with the soldiers not to hurt his family. Another mother and her two children ran in front of Kara as the guards harassed her, telling the woman and her children to make their way down the platform quickly.

She pressed Hannah up against her breast, held her close, even nervously thanked the guard for letting her take her daughter. The platform was packed. People from the train cars were being marched down toward a tall fence with a double gate. Soldiers were everywhere, rifles at the ready. Two men dressed in long gray overcoats with army hats on watched from a small dais but said nothing. As they were prodded towards the double gate Kara could see two tall towers on either side, two men up in each tower, a machine gun staring down at the long line of human beings.

"Mommy!" Hannah cried out; her arms locked tightly around Kara's neck.

The masses moved slowly. There was sobbing, confusion and cries for mercy every step of the way as they shuffled down the platform. The soldiers were indiscriminate and cruel, taunting them as they went. A man asking for help for his wife was taken out of line and Kara could see as a soldier used the butt of his rifle on the man's stomach then cracked him over the head. She shielded Hannah's eyes and whispered to her not to look.

The first gate opened, its edges rimmed with sharp razor wire, and the people were herded in. Beyond the second gate was a large brick building with an archway in its center and beyond that, who knew. The guards up in the towers looked down at the long line, laughed, spit, taunted them with insults.

She held Hannah as they walked through the first set of gates. The rusty hinges of the second gate squeaked as it opened, and the guards kept the crowd moving with threats of force. One of them looked Kara up and down as she stumbled by, licking his lips sickly. She stared down at her feet rather than look him in the eye.

"Welcome to your new home," the guard said coldly as she walked by.

Hannah buried her face in her mother's shoulder and began crying. Her little girl's tears ran down Kara's neck. She tried to console her and tell her everything was going to be alright, but the child just kept weeping. She wasn't the only one crying either. Everywhere the sound of children and old women could be heard, dozens, maybe hundreds. It was inhumane. She could feel the terror inside her like a freezing cold breeze that got worse with each step she took.

"Why are we here, Mommy?" Hannah cried to her mother. "What did we do?"

As they approached the large brick building inside the second gate Kara looked up. Just above the wide archway an eagle spreading it's wings wide was decorated into the building, a wreathed swastika clenched in its talons. The crowd filed into the long tunnel below and disappeared into shadow.

She didn't know what to say or how to answer the question. How could she? They had done nothing.

CHAPTER THIRTY-TWO

The Foreign Secretary lifted his glasses and gently massaged the lids of his eyes. The flight from London to Geneva hadn't been overly long, despite a brief stop in Orléans, France where his plane had been forced to wait while air space between there and the Swiss border had been judged safe to fly through. Not that anyone expected German planes that deep into France, but one could not be too sure. It was an unmarked flight, and the British government hadn't wish to take any chance of enemy spies, or sympathizers, getting wind of anything out of the ordinary, such as a plane being given special permission to bypass normal flight protocols.

He'd hated long flights anyway and the thought of being airborne any longer because his flight needed to be rerouted disturbed him. Arrangements of this type were difficult to make as it was. Diplomatic flight or not, in war unexpected things happened all too often. Though both the British and Italian governments had agreed on the secrecy of this little trip and the Swiss government had been nothing but helpful in arranging this first face to face meeting of the two top diplomats, it was always a major security concern when such events happened. Everything from the time and date of the affair to its location, attendance, even who was arrive first, had to be intricately worked out by the mutual staffs. In this case his and Galeazzo Ciano, Italy's Foreign Minister and subsequently, Mussolini's son-in-law.

Halifax glanced out the small window of his flight just as the plane settled into its final approach on the airport's runway. It was just after noon but under the dark, sunless sky the city had turned its streetlights on. You could see the headlights of cars driving through the city below and the airport terminal was lit up like a town unto itself. It was depressingly cloudy and cold looking outside. He hadn't caught wind of the weather report before leaving London, but he'd been to this country enough times to know just how cold Geneva this time of year could be.

He settled in his seat and took a sip of his scotch whiskey. The ice in his glass had almost completely melted and his drink was well watered down, but it helped to calm his nerves. Not from the flight, of course, but rather this meeting. There was a lot riding on this parley. The Italian Foreign Minister was second in line to the Duce, Mussolini, who had a direct line with Hitler and was eager to act as an intermediary between Berlin and the Allies. While they'd spoken many times on the telephone, this was the first face to face meeting the two ministers would have since the outbreak of war.

"Woulda' been nice if we'd chosen a warmer location for this sit-down," the man sitting across from Lord Halifax grumbled. He was Roy Keith-Falconer, Halifax's friend, bodyguard and sometimes advisor. "Greece maybe." Halifax grinned.

"No. This was appropriate," He replied. "Besides, I'd think you'd feel right at home in the cold. Just like Scotland outside." Roy chuckled. He straightened the papers he'd been pouring through and clipped them together. The flight had at least provided him with a brief interlude from his normal daily duties and given him the chance to both catch up on his reports and with his old friend who'd accompanied him. He upended the glass and swallowed the last of his scotch just as the plane's wheels touched down on the runway.

"We'll only have an hour before meeting with the Italian," Roy told him after looking at his watch. Roy was a Scottish Highlander by birth, a distant cousin to the Earl of Kintore. His thick highland accent had faded over the years by the days spent at Oxford in his teenage years and his mingling with English high society. He'd been a traveled man in his twenties and thirties and Halifax had found his advice to be quite useful over the years.

"His name is Ciano, Roy. Not the Italian." Roy laughed lightly in response. "I know that you don't like the man, but he is a fellow diplomat."

"Ach!" Roy waved his hand away. "I don't like 'im, cause I don't trust 'im. I've known too many like that. Self-important types. Nothing more than two-bit criminals. Trust me, Edward." He shook his head disparagingly. "And I don't put any faith in this man. Or 'is boss."

Halifax smiled but didn't bother to reply. He'd known Keith-Falconer long enough to know the man's mind on a variety of subjects and people. The Scotsman, for all his upper-class upbringing and education, was no fool. No black-tie diplomat, as they called them. His preferred medium for conducting business were card tables, taverns and often seedier establishments. Places where the noble lords and foreign aristocratic types would not have dared to set foot in while the sun was up, Roy had no reservations about. He'd often made more headway in a room full of low and mid-level officials who drank heavily well into the night then many a cabinet secretary could make over dinner with heads of state. His private misgivings to Halifax about this meeting reminded him of Prime Minister Churchill's feelings on the matter. Though the Prime Minister had allowed this meeting to transpire when Halifax had told him about Ciano's offer, he certainly didn't hide the fact that he didn't believe anything good would come of it.

But Halifax wasn't so sure. He firmly believed in what he was doing, and he'd stuck to his belief that a negotiated peace was better than no peace at all.

The plane slowed to a crawl and taxied up to a parking space a hundred feet from the single hangar that was reserved for British Airway flights. There were no commercial flights expected from England today and most of the airline employees had been given the day off. The only reception awaiting him were half a dozen staff from the British Embassy, five or six more diplomatic bodyguards and two uniformed police officers. Switzerland and its people were so rooted in neutrality that they gave little or no notice whatsoever to the comings and goings of foreign diplomats. The country had a centuries long tradition of hosting just such talks and foreign diplomats were as common a sight as coffee at a coffee shoppe.

Halifax unbuckled himself and grabbed his hat from the seat next to him. The plane came to a stop and its passenger door swung out to meet the short metal stair wheeled out by a pair of ground crew members. As soon as the door had opened a cold breeze of air rushed into the cabin and he shuddered slightly.

"Good thing we came prepared," Roy told him. Halifax put his arms through his thick wool trench coat and buttoned himself up. Grabbing his briefcase, he stepped out onto the metal stair first, spotted his assistant, Ivo Mallet, standing with another man halfway between the plane and the parked cars. The other man he recognized as Sir David Kelly, the British Ambassador to Switzerland. Though the man would play no part in these talks it was always customary for the residing ambassador to greet his superiors upon arrival.

Keith-Falconer followed closely behind Halifax as the two men descended the stair and Mallet and Kelly approached them as they did. Halifax felt the stinging cold breeze against his cheeks and thanked God he'd dressed appropriately. The wind out of the mountains was strong and could easily knock the warmth out of anyone not dressed for it.

'Welcome to Geneva, Mister Secretary," Sir David greeted. Halifax shook his gloved hand then Mallet's. "Glad you made it safely."

"Thank you, Sir David. Ivo. Good to see you. Sir David, I don't believe you know Roy Keith-Falconer. He's an advisor to me." Sir David extended his hand and Roy shook it.

"Yes. Your reputation does proceed you, Mister Keith-Falconer. I didn't know you were an expert on these kinds of things, though."

"I'm just tagging along today, Sir David," Roy told him and let the reference about his reputation slide. "I promise not to kick over any hornets nests."

"We have plenty of time before the meeting," Ivo said to Halifax. "The roads are mostly clear today, so we'll be at the hotel in no time. I'm sure the Italian delegation will be late, though. As they usually are."

"Well why don't we get out of this cold anyway," Halifax told them and started walking towards the Bentley parked near the hangar before the others could even offer. It was cold and he didn't want to stand out in it if there was a warm car to sit in.

The driver opened the back door and the four men filed into the extended car. It wasn't much warmer in the car than it had been outside but at least the wind wasn't blowing right into his face. Ivo Mallet sat directly across from him in the backseat and Sir David to his left. Roy sat next to Mallet, knowing that his presence here was more unofficial than anything and did not wish to interfere with the official business at hand. The three automobiles sat in a line for just over a minute then the first car honked its horn. A police car pulled out in front of the three Bentley's and escorted them from the airport and on to their destination.

"So, what do we know about his entourage?" Halifax asked aloud.

"Two of his top aides are traveling with him," Mallet replied. "Three military advisors. But we don't expect them to take part in anything."

"The Hotel Métropole has provided us with suitable accommodations," Sir David added. "It's discreet but appropriate."

"Good," Halifax replied. Mallet handed him a folder and he began to scan the pages. "The fewer people that know I'm here, the better."

Sir David and Ivo Mallet shared worried glances at each other before Ivo gave a subtle clearing of the throat cough.

"Well, sir...we may have a little problem there," Ivo Mallet informed him.

Halifax snapped a troubled look at him. The look in his eye was a mix of concern and consternation. The Lord Halifax was not a man who was given to many bursts of anger but when they did happen you could bet it was for a good reason.

"What problem?" His tone was demanding.

"Well, sir," Ivo stuttered a moment. "The French embassy got wind of this somehow. Their ambassador phoned Sir David while you were in transit. He was not pleased about their own people being left out of these talks."

Halifax grimaced, ran his fingers through his thin hair and let out a long sigh. It was too much to hope for that the French did not catch wind of any such talks taking place, but he had thought it would be after the meeting with the Italians and not before. Then he could spin it any which way he could best use it. But now...

It would be hard to explain to the French that he'd held this meeting without the consent or invite of their ally. The new French government was already walking a tight rope, and this was not going to make it any better. Daladier had been driven out of power just last week and the new Prime Minister in Paris, a man named Reynaud, had expressly told his people that France and Britain were the strongest of allies and walked together in all things.

"How?" Halifax demanded.

Sir David shrugged uselessly. "Not sure, sir. Could have been a leak from the hotel, or even someone in one of our offices not paying strict attention to protocols."

"I made very careful preparations, sir," Ivo said. "Nowhere was your name or title used in any diplomatic cable."

Halifax was completely silent for a few seconds. He looked despondently out the window at the people strolling the cold, wintry streets.

"Well, this is a damned bad start to any negotiations," he said brusquely. "By now their embassy has been in touch with Paris. By the end of the day Winston will have…" He broke off his sentence then shook his head. "I guess it doesn't matter now," his voice was low.

"These are just preliminary talks, My Lord," Ivo replied. "Any real settlement will, of course, include a French delegation. We're just…testing the water." He shrugged.

"Ha!" Halifax let out. "I doubt Reynaud will see things that way. The two top diplomats for the British and Italian Empires meet in secret in a neutral third country to discuss an end to the war?" His head shook with agitation. He couldn't believe this. "Well, we're here now and we've come too far to turn back."

The remainder of the trip was awkwardly quiet. A few points came up between the men, but Halifax's mood was already brooding. It had taken weeks just to put this thing into motion and all the care in the world had gone into its planning. While there were those back in London who would have loudly opposed this had they known about it, he was sure that it was the right thing to do. *It wasn't appeasement,* he told himself. *It was simply all part of the game.*

The Hotel Métropole was a beautiful, palatial building that sat on the southern tip of Lake Geneva. A long rectangular structure that sat between two of the busiest streets in the heart of the city. At first, he'd been apprehensive about meeting in such a visible place and in such a busy part of the city. But the Italians had systematically ruled out nearly every other reasonable location, and meeting at the private residence of a certain Portuguese businessman that they had suggested, was deemed too much of a risk by his own Foreign Office. So, it was a ritzy, glamorous hotel or nothing at all.

Halifax found himself momentarily grateful that today had been such a gloomy, dark day out when the cars pulled up to the hotel side entrance. The police escort moved on immediately and drivers jumped out of their cars to open doors for their passengers. Had it been bright and sunny out, it might have been easier for someone to see him entering the hotel. Now that it was known the French embassy knew of the meeting, there was a real possibility of someone being on the lookout. But between the dark skies and the cold weather there were few people on the streets, and nobody seemed all that interested in the three Bentley's parked on the side street.

Once the occupants were out, they hurried through a side door, opened by a single hotel bellhop, and then the cars drove out of sight. The hallways were surprisingly clear. Only here and there were there any people, hotel maids and cleaning staff mostly and a few guests who paid no attention at all to the group marching through the main floor. As far as anyone knew it was just a group of well-dressed businessmen, a common enough sight in Switzerland.

"Down this way, sir," Sir David told him, indicating to a second corridor off the main lobby. The corridor led to series of small meeting spaces, all but one of which was closed off. The last double doors at the end of the hallway were wide open, it's lights on and two hotel workers were standing outside of it. In the room was a large table next to the door with two large coffee pots, a couple dozen white coffee cups and a generous array of pastries and food.

There were six large tables pushed together to make one large one and some cloth spread out over them in the center and an array of small chairs along either wall. A large leather couch sat off to the left, between the double door and the large table setup. It was just spartan enough to meet their needs, though the generous amounts of food were a bit much and he suspected it was the Italians who had requested the pastries.

"Well, we should have some time before Ciano arrives," Ivo said to him as the staff began to setup the side of the table designated for the British.

Halifax looked at his watch. The arrangements called for the Italians to arrive after the British, but he knew already that Ciano would play the old game he who arrives later, arrives late. That was the way of diplomacy, especially when meeting with a country that was not necessarily friendly with yours. Hitler had played the same game when meeting with Chamberlain. He'd become used to such meaningless delays and paid it no heed.

The time in between was spent going over everything again and again. Sir David and his assistant and Ivo kept going over several issues that should be brought up and those that should be played down. Keith-Falconer had mostly kept quiet and to himself, speaking only when asked a question by Lord Halifax. His own contribution to this meeting would be to sit on the lone leather sofa and watch things unfold.

Half an hour later, ten minutes past the time set for the meeting, not a single member of the Italian delegation had yet arrived. Halifax resisted any urge to keep looking at his watch, he'd been doing this job for a good long time, but when two Swiss hotel workers could be heard speaking loudly in the hallway, he was half afraid it was an angry member of the French embassy barging in on the session. It was very nearly an hour after the set time before word of the Italian Foreign Minister's arrival. The entire procession had entered through the main hotel lobby as opposed to the side entrance as they'd agreed. That alone had not surprised Halifax too much, but he was perturbed when Ciano and his aides were dressed in formal military uniform.

Ciano was a sinewy man, well built, clean shaven and walked with a serious arrogance to him. His black and gray uniform was immaculate, as if he'd been dressed by a professional. He had an eerie smile on his face when he entered the large room. He reminded Halifax of some

American playboy or actor. Douglas Fairbanks perhaps. Despite being an hour late Ciano looked like a man arriving to his own surprise birthday party. Halifax had never sat, instead waiting for his counterpart on his feet. He also did not move an inch when Ciano arrived. If the Italian was so full of energy, then he could walk to where Halifax was standing.

Ciano saw him, smiled broadly and strode across the room in a few long strides.

"Lord Halifax," he greeted and the two shook hands enthusiastically. "It is a great pleasure to see you again."

"Count," Halifax replied. Aside from being the Foreign Minister he was also Italian nobility. "Thank you for coming." The man showed no sign of being even slightly conscious of the fact that he'd kept the British waiting longer than what courtesy allowed. Halifax, likewise, showed him no sign that the delay had bothered him. The dance had begun.

"Let me introduce my assistants. Signor Cappelli, who I believe you've spoken with on the telephone. And Major D'Azzo, my advisor on military affairs."

"Yes. Signor Cappelli, Major. Pleasure. Let me introduce William Mallet, my Assistant Secretary. Please call him Ivo. Sir David Kelly, our ambassador here. And this shabby looker is Mister Roy Keith-Falconer."

Ciano shook Keith-Falconer's hand and smiled in a strangely friendly manner.

"Keith-Falconer?" From his voice Roy thought he sounded slightly miffed. "Pleasure." He shook his hand and it seemed to Roy that it was a bit too tight.

"Thank you," Roy replied with a grin. "I actually had the pleasure of meeting your wife. It was years ago."

"Oh! Well...good. I'll have to ask her about this." The Count said then abruptly yanked his hand back.

"Well... shall we?" Halifax gestured to the tables. Everyone took their places, the Italians on one side and the British on the other. Roy Keith-Falconer took his leave and seated himself on the sofa away from the others. Coffee was poured and formalities exchanged. The routine diplomatic pleasantries ended at just the same time the two hotel stewards left the room and the double doors closed behind them. Ciano wasted no time taking the lead.

"I'm glad that we're here today," he opened. "It pleases us all that our British friends have chosen to reach out to us and ask for Il Duce's favor in bringing an end to a war that has already cost so much and been so bloody." He finished his short preamble then leaned in across the table from Halifax. "Lord Halifax, Prime Minister Mussolini has instructed me to convey to you his personal gratitude and is honored that you've allowed him to act as intermediary. He feels quite certain that Herr Hitler would be favorable to some sort of treaty if he found the terms to be favorable." He smiled broadly and leaned back in his chair. At first Halifax was unsure whether the other man was finished or not. Diplomatic encounters of this sort tended to be more long winded in the beginning when establishing a dialogue.

"Please pass along my thanks to your Prime Minister for his assistance," Halifax told him. "We are so fortunate to have the help of someone so close to Herr Hitler. We're prepared to lay out, what we feel are generous terms. Some of which we've already communicated to your office. However, our own foreign service has yet to receive any type of definitive reply from Rome on what guarantees Berlin is prepared to make. Obviously, the future security of Western Europe is of paramount importance to us. So, we'd like to begin there. What kind of assurances can we expect that Germany's territorial desires will extend no further?"

"Ah. Well, I've spoken personally with Minister Ribbentrop since his return from Bucharest. He made clear to me that the territorial integrity, as it currently stands, would have to be recognized by your government before Berlin gave any type of future assurances. However, he has also stated that Herr Hitler does not wish for any drawn-out conflict with the west."

Halifax recalled hearing those same words from Hitler in Munich when he had outright demanded the Sudetenland be handed over to Germany. He said then that it was necessary for securing peace and that he really had wanted no conflict with France and Britain. Hearing those words again made Halifax shift uncomfortably, but he was quick enough to make it look as if he was simply moving in his seat.

"I'm sure that given the circumstances, a de-escalation of the conflict is in everyone's best interests," Ciano continued with more than just a hint of a patronizing tone in his voice. "It would be hard for Signor Mussolini to even try and engage Berlin in talks if we cannot get at least a conditional agreement that your government would be willing to accept. Surely you can understand this?"

From where he sat, Roy Keith-Falconer sniffed the air contemptuously. For a moment he was glad to be seated so far away from the group, otherwise he might be inclined to say or do something that might have ended those negotiations.

"Minister, I must be plain with you, my government will not recognize the situation in the occupied territories," Halifax replied pointedly. He shook his head and rubbed his bottom lip. "I can tell you that the French will certainly not accept it. Any attempted peace settlement must include restoration of the pre-war borders. My own Prime Minister made that plainly clear to me before I left."

"Well..." the Italian began then petered out. "Mister Chamberlain seemed quite willing - "

"That was Chamberlain," Halifax politely intervened. "Mister Churchill is a... different sort. He isn't as amiable to such an agreement as Chamberlain might have been."

"You uh, understand don't you, that uh, we cannot go to Sir Hitler and ask him to uh, make peace without this...uh...how you say...stipulation?" Major D'Azzo asked in heavily accented, broken English, his fingers wagging around in the air as he spoke.

"As I've already said, Major D'Azzo, my Prime Minister will not accept that condition. And, if I might add, Herr Hitler made similar demands two years ago."

Count Ciano sighed and leaned back, nodding his head slowly as if agreeing with the thoughts in his head.

"Well, this certainly comes as a bit of a shock to me," he said and let out an audible breath. "Your former Prime Minister showed much more of a willingness to resolve matters. Hmm. I knew that the French would most likely decline the German position. But our conversations, Mister Secretary, have always been more direct. We see eye to eye I think, in many ways. We're both pragmatists. You do understand, don't you, that Herr Hitler's position must be recognized as part of the status quo?"

"Even if by some long chance my own government was to do just that, and that's a big if, the French would immediately reject it," Halifax told him bluntly. "Their new leader is even more of a fighter than Daladier was. Churchill obviously isn't going to distance himself from our French allies. The fact is, gentlemen, that Germany has exceeded any prior claims they might possibly have on ancestral lands when they invaded nearly every country they share a common border with. If they wish to bring the French to the negotiating table, we're ultimately going to have to put on the withdraw of their forces on it."

"I see," the Italian Count replied softly and chewed lightly on his lip. He sank back in his seat and listened as his aide, Cappelli, leaned in and whispered something into his ear, his head bobbing up and down. The two conversed in hushed voices for half a minute, occasionally Major D'Azzo would add something short into it. Ciano nodded one final time then brought his gaze back to Lord Halifax. "I believe that we may be able to find some middle ground. Prime Minister Mussolini is an incredibly talented negotiator. It might be possible for him to persuade Hitler to make a strategic withdraw. So long as such a move is reciprocated by the Allies."

Halifax's eyebrows rose slightly in surprise. He'd half expected to hear that any further attempt at diplomacy was useless. His instincts couldn't help but think that his counterpart had given in just a bit too easily. Again, all part of the dance. Diplomacy was just as often about gaining a leg up against one's opponent as it was about resolving issues between nations. But it was hard to see what kind of advantage the other man was gaining.

"Well, if Herr Hitler is open to this option, then I can inform my government and if it's made in good faith, we may be able to find some way to reciprocate," Halifax replied, an air of optimism in his tone. "Prime Minister Churchill, however, will view everything with skepticism. He'll want to see hard results before agreeing to anything longer term."

"I understand. But it will be a starting place," Ciano replied.

"It will be a starting place," Halifax agreed.

"Can you give us an idea of any kind of timeline, Minister?" Ivo Mallet inquired. Ciano shrugged and put up his hands.

"Who can say anything for certain. What is important is that we can at least broach the subject with Hitler. He is not a man who believes in giving away things before knowing what he is gaining in return."

He's not a man who gives things under any circumstance at all. Bloody bastard. The thought ran through Keith-Falconer's mind. Hitler crossed his Rubicon in Czechoslovakia as far as he was concerned, and Poland was just another nail in the coffin. He was anything but impressed by the facade taking place just feet away and he knew the Germans would not view these talks with any seriousness. Despite what the Italian had to say.

"Well," Mallet continued, "if our government agrees, at least in principle, to negotiate on those terms, then we would need to consult with Paris as well. We'd ultimately need to bring any agreement, no matter how tentative, to them. They are our allies."

"Hmm. Yes. The French." Ciano's tone was soft and contemplative. He tapped his thumbs together in rhythm with his thoughts. "The new French government seems less likely to accept a negotiated peace than the previous one. It may be best if we kept these talks alive without them for the time being. I believe that we can accomplish more without them for now."

Almost in unison all the eyebrows from the British side of the table went up in shock. Apart from Halifax each individual made a sour expression of the proposed notion. The Foreign Secretary sat expressionless for a time, studying Ciano and considering his words. He knew that Ciano understood that keeping the French out of any future talks was not just unfeasible but outright impossible. The fact that he'd even suggested it immediately made Halifax think that he'd found out the answer to whom had leaked this meeting out to the French.

Perhaps in order to gain a leg up by creating strife between the two allies?

"Well, as you said earlier, Count, this is merely a starting place," Halifax told him and gave him the most placating of grins. He had no desire to get into a fruitless back and forth with this man. "We can broach the subject of the French at a later date."

Count Ciano eyed Halifax briefly. The look on his face just barely hid a layer of concern. Finally, he smiled and graciously nodded.

"Good," he replied. "Very good." Cappelli leaned in once again and whispered into his boss's ear and the Count's head bobbed up and down as he listened.

"This would bring us to our next subject," Cappelli stated promptly. "French concessions."

That did provoke a reaction from Lord Halifax. He leaned towards the table and with all the self-control he'd learned he'd learned in thirty years of service contained a natural urge to laugh aloud.

"I beg your pardon?" He simply asked jovially.

"My Lord. Signor Mussolini is very close to Hitler," Ciano replied. "He feels very confidently that he can convince him to see the reason in your demands and bring the war to an end. However, as you know, Italy has territorial claims with France. My father-in-law is extremely adamant about this. He feels that Italy should at least be compensated for helping to bring an end to your war. I don't believe this to be unreasonable. The French would see the light much better if your government brought it to them."

By this he meant that if the British wanted peace, then they would put pressure on their ally to hand over certain territory to Italy. Italian claims in Africa and even Corsica were well known sticking points between the two nations. France had always dismissed any such claim on their territory and any concessions by them would be a boost to Italian prestige.

"Any concessions made by the French would be looked upon favorably by Hitler," Cappelli explained and produced a single envelope. "They could be the difference between having peace or not having peace." He smiled and slid the envelope across the table to Halifax.

The Foreign Secretary hesitated for the slightest of seconds then opened it up. He tried to contain his emotions as he skimmed through its contents. He couldn't believe what he was reading. It was literally nothing less than a list of demands by Italy. Land and economic concessions they were asking to be handed over to them. What they called a broker's fee he called a ransom demand. He swallowed his words down and sat with his hand over his mouth for empty long moments. He already knew what Churchill was going to say as soon as he learned of this. He didn't even wish to think about what the French reaction would be. Perhaps he had erred in his decision to leave them out of this.

He raised his eyes back at Ciano. The other man had always been the paragon of diplomacy and now his master back in Rome had sent him to the negotiating table with this? Halifax could feel the outrage swell up in him and fought to keep it contained. He folded the paper back up and breathed out silently. Either he had misread Ciano entirely or Mussolini had sent his son-in-law to this meeting against his wishes. He was content to think that it was the latter.

But either way, he'd just been boxed into a situation that he had not anticipated.

Ciano blinked and leaned forward in his seat then looked Halifax squarely in the eye and made a disingenuous smile.

"I'm sure, My Lord, that given the time to reflect upon this, you will see that the benefits far outweigh the price. Now, shall we continue?"

CHAPTER THIRTY-THREE

The sound of multiple popping gunshots rang out, both in the streets of Bucharest and from inside the royal palace complex itself. King Carol II of Romania braced himself physically but despite his resolute exterior he was terrified inside. The telephone lines to the palace had gone dead almost an hour earlier and the military men that had been dispatched to find out what was going on had neither returned nor reported in. Then had come radio reports of a division of army troops entering the city

Carol understood well how coups were carried out and didn't need the worthless advice of his military counselors about what was going on. He wasn't the fool that so many others who claimed to be loyal to him thought he was.

He sat behind his large, elaborately made desk in the over-sized palace office. His fingers tapped anxiously away on the glossy desk-top. Outside the windows he could glimpse the sight of palace guards-men coming and going, setting up roadblocks and checkpoints on the city streets. But those men would be utterly useless against the better equipped and trained regular army soldiers and would be swiftly over-run with little or no effort.

Outside the great double doors, he could hear the muffled sound of officers conversing with each other and the hurried activities of couriers leaving and arriving at the palace. The king had been awakened very early this morning with reports of troop movements and he was feeling the day's fatigue already. His primary military advisor, Colonel Hamza, had left him shortly before dawn and taken half a battalion with him to try and rally support. That was nearly three hours ago, before communications had been cut. Now, with the sounds of gunfire inside the complex itself, Carol had to believe that no help was forthcoming.

He inwardly cursed those men, those generals who were now abandoning him. He had no love for Hitler either and cursed him too, for supporting this coup. And deep down in his bowels he cursed himself for allowing control of his country to be lost as it was looking like.

His tension was evidenced when the double doors suddenly opened, and he instantly jumped up out of his chair. His back was ramrod straight and he stared, wide eyed, as a cadre of armed soldiers strolled in.

He gulped.

"Your Majesty," the first soldier called out as he strode across the large room. "Sir, for your safety we must move you."

Three more armed men were behind the man. He recognized them as palace guardsmen, but he did not know if they were loyal to him or would simply turn him over to the insurrectionists.

"Who are you?" Carol demanded, all the authority in his voice that he could muster.

Another officer pushed his way in from behind. He was a young man with a captain's rank on his uniform. The king exhaled the breath he'd been holding onto as he recognized the man as Captain Halet, one of Colonel Hamza's top aides and a man loyal to him.

"Your Majesty," Halet stammered. He was slightly out of breath. "I received word from Colonel Hamza. There is a danger to you. We need to move you to a secure site immediately."

"Colonel Hamza? The telephones are back up?" Carol asked hopefully. No one had told him. "We should call for aid."

"No, sir. A courier just arrived with a message. I can vouch for him. I'm having a car brought around for you, but we must leave now."

As he finished his words there was some activity from the courtyard outside. The sound of vehicles arriving and voices shouting. Captain Halet stepped toward the window and looked down into the open yard. He hesitated a moment then unholstered his sidearm.

Carol's heart began to beat like a drum, and he felt a great flush of excitement swell up. The other soldiers in the room moved protectively closer to him.

"We need to move. Now!" Halet said and his tone was so commanding that the king was startled.

The group of men briskly walked out of the great office and into the even greater concourse where the main hallway adjoined with others and a series of intersecting staircases that made their way down to the first floor. Offices on either level were being evacuated as quickly as possible. Scores of civilian workers made their way out side exits and down the concourse stairways.

"This way, Your Majesty," Halet said as he moved ahead of the entourage, pistol in hand.

He led them, not down the stairway, but across the upper landing toward the south side of the building. The king knew that there were any number of exits from the palace, but he'd never been through any of them except the main entrance. He was the king after all.

More palace guards were posted at the end of the hallway. A blue uniformed officer with a hilted sword stood awaiting the group. A loud pounding echoed throughout the hall as if some crowd was trying to kick in the front door.

The king's group quickened their pace. Carol felt his pulse racing and his breathing got heavier. Voices were shouting on the bottom floor and then a heavy breaking sound.

"Quickly!" Halet urged them.

On the main floor came the dull bang of a gun firing a single shot. The king glanced over the railing and saw several olive-green clad men storm into the room below and move swiftly towards the staircases. Officers among them shouted orders as they ran.

The blue royal guardsman with a sword kicked open the door he was positioned at. The king's entourage started down the concrete steps inside a squared off stairwell. The very fact that they were retreating down a dirty corner stairwell felt offensive to the king.

"There's a car waiting for us on the southern rotunda," Halet told them as they descended quickly down the steps.

The plodding sound of leather boots on concrete resounded in the empty chamber. When they reached the bottom Captain Halet motioned for the others to exit after confirming that the car in question was indeed waiting.

It was raining when King Carol II, monarch of Romania stepped outside and got into the rear of the automobile. Another army officer sat next to the driver. Captain Halet pushed the king into the car then jumped in right behind him. The driver didn't even wait for the rear door to close before peeling away. The sound of crushed gravel popping under the wheels stuck in his mind as the car shifted around. The driver steered around a large circular garden before making a sharp left towards the rear gate.

The gate was already open, and the king expected to see at least some guards around it but was concerned when he saw none. The automobile pulled out of the compound and into the empty streets beyond the tall walls of the royal palace. The car sped down the roadway and halfway between the gate and the stop sign it came to an abrupt halt. Up ahead two military trucks pulled onto the rain-washed road. In the mirror he caught the glimpse of more vehicles coming from the rear.

Through the heavy rain shapes took form. Dozens of armed soldiers came out from behind trucks and surrounded the vehicle. A single officer stepped forward alone, sidearm holstered. His insignia said that he was a colonel. His uniform was quickly becoming soaked. The bulky man bent forward and examined the car's occupants then stepped next to the king's door and knocked gently on the window.

Carol gulped visibly and hesitated at first. The colonel outside was staring through the window. The expression on his face was not one of maliciousness but was surprisingly sorrowful.

The king swallowed his pride and put his hand on the door handle. It was over and he knew it. But he was still king and if he was going, he'd damned if he was going like a coward.

CHAPTER THIRTY-FOUR

General Gerd von Rundstedt strolled through the open double doors and into the main operations room at his headquarters in Koblenz, on the eastern bank of the Rhine. He was followed in close step by his staff officers. The sound of their shoes clinking across the tiled floor as they strode across the wide-open room caused many of the men and women working in that room to stop and take notice before casually returning to work.

A group of general officers standing near a knot of small tables stiffened as Rundstedt made his way towards them. His small stature and frame were contrary to his remarkable ability as a field commander.

Beyond the group was a large wall map of their sector along the German border with France and the Low Countries. The map was strewn with markers indicating military units of all types, German and Allied alike. Men were busy handing updated information to the uniformed women standing on mobile steps, who were pushing the markers around as new information on positions changed. A large clock on the wall was silently counting backwards, the seconds hand moving counterclockwise.

General Rundstedt snapped the cap off his head and handed it to a captain who was walking behind him. The general's entourage came to a halt in front of the officers gathered. He waved away the offered formalities and took his brown leather gloves off one finger at a time. Those present reflected the bulk of Rundstedt's Army Group A. Each of them in turn brought their own staff. Together, along with several other generals not here today, these men would lead the almost six hundred-thousand-man army group into battle.

Rundstedt ran one bony hand through his wispy thin hair and cleared his throat. He glanced around the gathering, threw an examining look at the huge moving map and the downward counting clock next to it.

"I've just spoken with the Führer," he began promptly. It was never his way to preamble, preferring to get to business quickly. "He has given this operation his final blessing. I informed him that I expect this group to perform its duty and to achieve its objectives as planned. Of course, he agreed. So, let's go through this one final time." He dropped his gloves onto one of the small tables and looked into the eyes of the generals who would lead. "I want it absolutely understood just what our objectives are. From this room I will be monitoring the progress of your forces. Army Group A is the hammer. It is up to us to fell the killing blow and we will achieve this." He emphasized those last three words.

"Now, before I turn this meeting over, I want a brief update on the readiness status of your commands."

As if the routine had been rehearsed a hundred times before in their careers, each began a well-practiced report on their own respective commands.

Under Army Group A fell a multitude of other formations: armies, corps, divisions. Each with their own commanders and each with their own more limited goals and objectives, be it gaining some vital piece of ground, engaging a particular part of the enemy line or to simply act in support of another formation. High Command had designated over one hundred sixty divisions, nearly four million soldiers, to this operation with another million more involved with the Luftwaffe. With troops, trucks, armored cars, motorcycles, tanks, artillery, fighters, bombers and all else being thrown into the offensive, it was going to be the single largest military operation in history.

The original plan for the attack on the western countries of Europe had called for three large army groups to launch forward from their bases in Northwest Germany like one large wheel with a southern, center and northern group striking out in their assigned sectors with Army Group C holding down the French armies in the south, Army Group A engaging the British and Belgians in the center and the northern force of Army Group B serving as the main formation, advancing through the Netherlands and down the European coast and into France.

It was a similar strategy that had been used in the First World War.

In the months following Poland's collapse, and after much politicking with Hitler about what many in the army saw as the serious possibility of a total operational failure, the plan had been modified in favor of what had become informally known as the Manstein Plan. Under the new plan Army Group A became the dominant formation. The center of the massive German force, with the other two groups advancing on the flanks, was expected to breach the Allied lines and follow through with a breakout into Northern France.

The opportunity to command the troops that stood a very real chance of delivering a knockout blow to the French was not something that the general was going to take lightly. Rumors were swirling around in Berlin that Hitler had planned to revive the old rank of field marshal and that Rundstedt's name was on someone's short list. That, if for no other reason, assured his whole-hearted conviction to achieving success in the upcoming campaign.

The last of the general officers confirmed the readiness of the soldiers under their command. Rundstedt nodded a confirmation. In the rear of the group was General Hans Oster, the Deputy Chief of the Abwehr, German Intelligence. He stood silently observing the field commanders end their briefing. He'd come here as a representative of Berlin's main intelligence gathering apparatus.

"Very well," Rundstedt began. "Let's begin a review of operational details. Colonel Blumentritt." He motioned to the officer on his right.

Colonel Günther Blumentritt was Army Group A's chief of operations and his reputation in the German Army as an excellent military planner was well known. Despite his relatively lower rank he had, in fact, been centrally involved in the planning of both the invasion of Poland and the current operation against the west.

"Sirs," Blumentritt formally addressed the group. "I'll try and keep this as brief as possible. I wanted to take a moment and to inform you about an ongoing development. As you all know the Romanian king was just detained by Marshal Antonescu's forces. He has taken full control of the government there, with the blessing of the parliament. General Oster here," he held up his hand, "has informed me that the Führer shall announce his recognition of the new leadership there shortly. What that means for us here is a constant flow of that Romanian oil which shall keep our military moving." The news brought a generally favorable reaction. Oster nodded an affirmation to the news. Colonel Blumentritt then began the details of today's briefing. "We've all been over the plan multiple times so we should all know it by heart at this point. There have been some minor operational details that have changed but nothing that should cause us any worry. I address your attention," he pointed to the large map against the wall and continued on.

Oster grinned lightly and listened to the colonel spell out the details of the forthcoming campaign. He stood with his hands harmlessly at his sides and let his eyes drift around the room at the other officers gathered. He knew many of them. Some were his friends. Others present were of a particular mind about certain issues. People whom he shared beliefs concerning the direction that their country was currently taking.

Next to him another man, newly promoted General Henning von Tresckow, stood hands clasped behind his back. A staff officer by training, Tresckow was a man whose career was ascending quickly. There was talk of him gaining a fighting command coming out of Berlin and his personal contributions to German military planning was extremely well known. What was less known were his personal feelings on the current regime.

"The recent return of several paratrooper units from Norway has offered us an opportunity to put them to use in our area of operations," the colonel continued. "We've designed Operation Westwind, an airborne operation that shall commence in the predawn hours before our main forces kick off. Fifty-five Luftwaffe transports shall lift off from airfields near Aachen along with a dozen gliders. The transports will be carrying a regiment of elite paratroopers. Their objective will be to drop a battalion size unit near the town of Sambreville, cutting off the main road between Namur and Charleoi and another battalion at the crossroads near Philippeville. They'll be equipped with special anti-tank weapons to block any immediate advance by the Allies to reinforce Namur."

"Namur, as you all know is a vital point," Rundstedt intervened. "It'll be our crossover point. Once captured, the bulk of our forces in the northern zone shall cross the Meuse there."

"And our forces are to reach the town within thirty-six hours of the operation," Blumentritt continued. "General Hoth's panzer corps will be responsible for capturing it. Once done, and hopefully with the bridges across the Meuse intact, he'll connect with the paratroopers."

"Those paratroopers will be isolated for at least a day, perhaps more," General List, commander of the 12th Army, stated. "If the French come on in significant strength, I don't see them lasting long in a firefight."

Blumentritt nodded at the general. "Yes, sir. That is why, in addition to the para drop, the Luftwaffe will be detailing off a significant number of high-altitude bombers to stall the French advance. We don't have to stop them, merely buy a few hours for those men to dig in and prepare. Once our army crosses into Belgium the race will be on, and hours will be crucial. Each bridgehead that we capture intact will be of vital importance to us. In the case in which bridges are blown out we will have to rely upon fording where we can."

Oster listened and observed. Several of the officers present here, including Tresckow, Oster knew from some late-night meetings that covertly assembled around the outskirts of Berlin. In dimly lit rooms and basements in country homes, civilians and officers alike were gathering in secret. The topic was, of course, Hitler and the Nazi party. Many of these people were registered party members but had come to believe that the regime they supported was corrupt and dishonorable. Most greatly disfavored the idea of war and conquest and had argued with Hitler and the top leadership for years against such an action.

Now, in a time when any dissent whatsoever was reason enough for the Gestapo to whisk people away in the night, these people still found the courage to discuss a need for change.

General Kluge, commander of the 4th Army grumbled. "What of all that engineering we were promised? We had plenty going into Poland."

Colonel Blumentritt nodded in slight concession. "Yes, sir. We did. Most of that has been assigned to Army Group B for use in the Netherlands. A sizable amount of bridging materiel has also been assigned to

General Kleist's panzer divisions in the south. We've allotted the remainder as best as we possibly can, with the intent of keeping our infantry moving as fast as possible behind the armor. As more bridgeheads are established, we will obviously shift resources where they are needed the most."

Oster and Tresckow exchanged eye glances for the briefest of moments. Tresckow was a high-ranking member of General Manstein's staff and had carefully placed himself in a position where he could observe or influence others to take action against what he believed was a highly dangerous autocrat who had taken control of the country. Though it was never lost upon anyone that the Nazis had come to power by being voted in.

General Rundstedt held up a single finger. "Speed! Speed is the key. We MUST move fast and seize vital river crossings and choke points as fast as possible. The Belgians are not the problem. The French and British armies are the problem. And when they take up positions in Belgium it will be even more difficult to force them back. Our objective is to engage them at every turn. To keep them off balance and, more than everything else, to keep the Allies from linking up with the Dutch and Belgian forces. Remember, both of those countries are neutral, for now. But very shortly, we will be at war with them."

The other generals and their staff officers nodded silently in understanding. The German Army had perfected the art of the fast-moving blitzkrieg in the past couple of years. First in field exercises in bases and training grounds all over Germany and then on the battlefields of Poland, Denmark and Norway. The lessons learned had been so drilled and instilled into the German military that it had become second nature to them now. The upcoming campaign was seen by many officers as the ultimate test of this new form of warfare. If Germany could crush the Allied armies here and now, then there would be no enemy that they could not overcome.

"The old man's got his blood up now," Tresckow whispered to him, referring to Rundstedt's animated body movements. Oster listened but didn't reply.

While Rundstedt had no real love for the Nazi Party, he had certainly hitched himself to them since they came into power. Only to his most intimate comrades he confessed utter contempt for what the Germany Army had become. But beyond that the man's loyalties to the Führer seemed ironclad. At least for now. Oster considered him to be out of reach as far as approaching him about certain ideas. But he also knew that Rundstedt was aware of some activities that state security would love to know about and was staying quiet.

Rundstedt turned and pointed his stick at the map of planned German advances into the Low Countries and continued his oration. Though for right now at least both the Netherlands and Belgium were still technically neutral in the conflict, both nations had gone to extra lengths in order to secure their sovereignty to the point of vocally warning the Allies not to cross their borders or risk a diplomatic incident. At first such warnings seemed to suffice as the British and French leaders did not risk isolating the Low Countries, despite having drawn up plans to confront any German attack through those nations by occupying them preemptively.

Even Churchill had been grudgingly forced to concede the fact that they could not just stroll into those neighboring countries and risk moving them into a Pro-German stance, or worse yet, outright alliance with Germany. But now, with four million German troops amassed and ready to invade come the spring, the political situation was changing. Should the British and French decide to move into Belgium, it could very well slow down any German attack. Though so far, the Allies showed no signs of doing that, and the Abwehr was not aware of any plans to do so either. And though the German government was repeatedly denying claims that it too was poised to invade those neutral nations, in a matter of weeks the gig would be up and the Nazi penchant for lies, and deceitfulness will have been cemented in the eyes of the world.

But who was the German Army to speak out against such things? Such dishonorable behavior, or against the men in power, like the Führer? They were soldiers after all, and a soldier did what he was ordered to do without question. Whatever those orders entailed.

"Another change in our operation will be here," Blumentritt continued, crossing around the group, picked up a short pointing stick and indicated an area on the map. "Dinant. Once we move on Namur it'll become a vital focal point for an enemy counterattack. Even if we can cross there it will become necessary to secure Dinant, which is already fortified. We cannot risk an Allied attack on Fourth Army's flank coming at us from there. Therefore, General Hoth shall detach a single division, Fifth Panzer. It is to sweep southwest, assault the fortifications and with luck seize yet another bridge there. Intelligence believes the number of defenders to be minimal."

"What kind of support will he have?" asked General List. "In case intelligence is incorrect in their estimate."

"We feel very confident about the information, General List," the colonel replied. "However, artillery from several batteries here, here and here should be sufficient to reduce the defender's resistance. If further support is needed, then we can always shift Rommel's Thirteenth Panzer north from its position."

"But preferably we don't want to involve Rommel's division if we don't have to," General Rundstedt added. "His unit is a strategic reserve and I want it to be available should we have the opportunity to exploit any opening we have further south towards Sedan." He said the words and he meant most of them. Though he liked Rommel personally, the man was brand new to panzer command and was thus far untested. He'd seen no combat in Poland and he'd spent too many years on staff to be effective in the upcoming campaign.

"Still, it wouldn't be a terrible idea to have the Thirteenth engage from the south," General Kleist offered. Kleist commanded many of all panzer units going into Belgium. "Attack from both directions simultaneously."

General Rundstedt waved his hands in front of him. "We're getting ahead of ourselves. We won't know what kind of resistance will be encountered until we're fully engaged. Intelligence believes there are minimal defenders and until proven wrong we will assume this to be the case. I expect to engage with the French Army within two days, three at the most. When we do it's important that we adhere to the strategy as we've planned it out. The changes made today are but minor ones, forced on us only by the recent reports of enemy movements. Everything else stays just as we've played it out for weeks now. Did you have anything else, Colonel?"

"Only one last small detail. We've recently unearthed a stockpile of rubberized rafts sitting in warehouses around our rear. We've gone ahead and issued many of them to our vanguard units." He shrugged innocently. "Perhaps some of the first wave units can find some use for them."

Rundstedt threw his hands up jokingly. "There you go. Maybe Rommel can float his tanks across the river on them." The gathered officers laughed aloud at the joke.

As General Rundstedt began to wrap up his briefing others began to murmur to themselves about their thoughts on the upcoming campaign.

"When were you planning to return to Berlin?" Tresckow asked.

"Day after tomorrow," Oster answered him. "I told my wife that I'd visit in on her cousin." He stared back into the other man's eyes and Tresckow nodded approvingly.

"Well, I hope your wife's cousin is in good health and that you enjoy the visit." He smiled just as the group began to break up and walked away. Oster looked innocently around the room. Men were busy congratulating each other on the mother of all battle plans that they had conceived. Most of them were arrogantly unaware of the death that would follow in the next few weeks. It made him uneasy to think that hundreds of thousands more people might have to die before those gathered here might see the light. He put on the outward appearance of a man happily serving the Reich as he grinned and approached Rundstedt, congratulating the older man on the brilliance of the operation.

CHAPTER THIRTY-FIVE

Prime Minister Churchill let out a belly shaking laugh then took a puff from his cigar. In one hand he had one of his famed stogies burning and in the other he held the telephone to his head. He was in a particularly happy mood this morning and it showed to the men assembled in his private office. News from the war front was less than good. The constant stalemate on the continent was overshadowed by the spike in losses at sea. U-boats were sinking Allied transports at an unsustainable rate and reports were that even more of those deadly subs were preparing to stream out into the Atlantic. On top of that the Romanian coup of the previous month had put that country firmly in the German camp. Its king had been detained in some mountainous castle and was now nothing more than a puppet for the new government there. An army general named Antonescu was now in control and had wasted little time in throwing his country's support behind Hitler, bucking twenty years of Anglo-French alignment. And there was damn little that either Paris or London could do about it right now. The new government seemed eager to solidify its relationship with Berlin and its inclusion to the Axis Powers now seemed imminent.

But it was despite these setbacks that Churchill was in a good mood. On the other end of the phone was Franklin Delano Roosevelt. The American President was preparing for his third inauguration after he and his party won sweeping elections across that country. Despite American isolationism, the voters had re-elected the man and the party most likely to support Great Britain in this desperate hour. President Roosevelt's re-election could not have come sooner and his commitment to Churchill to continue supporting the country was welcome news indeed. As was the sizable loan that the administration had promised was coming.

"Well, that is wonderful news to us over here, Mister President," Winston said into the phone. Around the office heads were nodding indeed. Half a dozen staff and military leaders present silently agreed to that statement. Secretary Halifax sat across the room, observing and remaining silent. The naval leadership would have the most reason to be happy. A new loan from the American government almost assuredly meant that much of that money would be spent purchasing new ships and equipment to update older ones.

"I certainly am anxious to have a face-to-face meeting of our own," Winston continued. "As soon as the situation here is a bit more manageable, we'll have to arrange something. In Canada perhaps?"

Since the very beginning of the conflict the Americans had walked a very tight rope between elements of its population who wanted nothing to do with the wars in Asia and Europe and those who thought it was their obligation to stand with their old allies. It certainly wasn't a shoo-in but ultimately they had decided to stick with the Democratic President, to the great delight of the man occupying this office. Though no one knew for sure just how much aid the US was prepared to give and in what form, anything was welcome.

"I like that idea very much, Mister President," Winston said and chuckled his unique laugh. "I shall, I shall. Please pass along my warmest regards to the First Lady. Yes. Thank you. Goodbye." He burned more of his cigar and hung up the phone. An almost boy like grin graced his features. "Well, that was certainly welcome news!"

"Have you any idea about the type of support we can expect, sir?" Anthony Eden inquired.

"The details will be worked out, but Mister Roosevelt is adamant that he'll be pushing for increased aid. His support in Congress is stronger now than ever before."

"Well, with his party in control of three-fifths of their Congress, hopefully it'll come sooner rather than later," Eden added. "We certainly could use it. What about the French?"

"That's between Paris and Washington," Winston replied, the cigar in his mouth wobbled as he spoke. "There's some talk of supplying aircraft. Right now, I'm more interested in securing our own supply lines. Any loans need to be directed towards our own shipbuilding efforts." An aide sitting next to him nodded and wrote that down. "The President also feels confident about getting through a more direct aid bill. I offered to allow the American Navy basing rights in the South Pacific in exchange for some of their obsolete destroyers. We'll just have to wait to see how that goes."

"I for one would like nothing more than that," Admiral Cunningham commented. "God knows we're in desperate need of escort vessels. Getting our shipyards to full capacity is one thing, but it'll take us some time for those yards to produce any results. We're already two months into nineteen forty-one. It'll be Christmas before any substantial number of ships start rolling out."

"And if our intelligence reports are even half accurate about German U-boat construction, we're going to be even more desperate in the coming weeks and months," Eden added in getting affirming nods from others present.

Naval Intelligence had estimated the number of German subs operating at sea was just about one hundred thirty. Reports out of Germany itself believed that their own submarine pens were pushing out an additional half dozen every two weeks. The Admiralty had a very real fear that in the next few weeks alone a new U-boat offensive might well come close to strangling off the overseas supply routes that the nation depended upon. Word from German sources was that the man who had succeeded Todt as Armaments Minister, a man named Speer, was working economic miracles in that country. German economic output since late '39 had skyrocketed under the man who had instituted immediate changes while Hitler lie in a coma. Should the Kriegsmarine reach parity with the Royal Navy...

"The President understands all that," Winston told him. "We'll be broaching that subject again soon. For now, we'll take whatever other aid the Americans can give us. Arms, ammunition, radar. Anything. I want you to work up a list of priorities, Anthony. Things that we need most. Give it to Tommy as soon as you can. We'll coordinate with the Americans." More smoke swirled around his head. "Well, I think this was as productive a morning as we could have asked for. I'll brief the king on the good news this afternoon. Were there any other matters?"

"Reynaud?" Eden asked thoughtfully. Churchill shook his head.

"We'll discuss that later on," he replied. His scheduled meet with the French leader was upcoming. Another grand strategy session before the spring thaw. Halifax was due to accompany him to the meeting in Normandy next week. All the top military leadership of both countries was scheduled to be there as well to plan out the spring offensive.

"If that's all then?" Churchill scanned the room then nodded. "Good day."

The meeting had convened, and everyone began to file out the office door. Everyone, that is, except Halifax. The Foreign Minister stood up from his chair and lingered behind the group. Eden looked at him curiously then gave him a half friendly nod before leaving the room.

"May I have a moment of your time, Prime Minister?" He asked and silently closed the door when Winston nodded.

"Something was on your mind during the phone call," Churchill surmised.

Halifax pouted slightly.

"I said nothing during the meeting, Prime Minister," he replied innocently.

"Precisely. Your silence was deafening." Halifax scowled slightly. "What exactly is on your mind, My Lord?" Churchill sank into his chair and crossed his legs.

"Thought I was just being respectfully quiet," Halifax replied. "Prime Minister, I've been giving a lot of thought recently to the diplomatic situation. When it comes to Germany, I mean. Your relations with the Americans are most commendable. But I'm at a loss when it comes to negotiating an end of the war with Germany. There's no need to rehash our differences there." He paused momentarily, rubbed his nose. "It's my feeling that I've failed to persuade you on this course of action. That these negotiations we've been conducting have had...well, lackluster support from you. Am I wrong?"

Churchill puffed on his stogie for a moment then stood up from his chair, a single hand rested on his hip. The two men stood across the small space from each other.

"My Lord Halifax, as you say there is no need for us to rehash our differences. I would answer your question this way. Was it not your Italian friends who sabotaged your attempted meeting? And what has happened with that? Demands for lands, for economic concessions. A broker fee paid to that man in Rome in return for securing a peace agreement?"

"Count Ciano was acting as an intermediary," Halifax retorted. "His position has always been negotiation-"

"Yes, yes! Negotiate, negotiate," Churchill cut him off harshly. "I'm sick to death with settlements and negotiations. Hitler's never been interested in settling anything, except his own ego! What are we to negotiate, My Lord?"

"An end to the conflict. A reasonable exchange-"

"Reasonable?!" Winston coughed the word. "Bugger that. Hitler is not a reasonable man. Those Nazis are not reasonable people. Their kind of negotiation comes in the form of oppression. Have you forgotten about what they've done to their own people? Or the Jewish population? Now we're hearing news of detention camps being built all over Germany. Have you forgotten about the people in the occupied territories?"

Halifax's eyes widened and he met Winston's glare head on. He'd felt trepidation about approaching this with him before, but not now. Edward Wood, Lord Halifax, could be just as formidable as anyone.

"I have NOT forgotten about anyone, sir! I'm as disgusted by it all as anyone. But what is the answer? Hmm? War? Back and forth conflict that goes on for generations? Half of Europe torn apart? No, sir. There must be a final solution to it all."

Winston nodded.

"Well, you're right about one thing. There does have to be a solution to it all. But it's not the way you think, Edward. You've always gone about this dance as if can just write off someone else's bit of land or country, give it to that bastard, and leave it at that. Negotiate! Ha." He spat the last words out. "Munich was a negotiation. You may even call it a success at that. You and Chamberlain did manage to give Czechoslovakia away with the flick of a pen."

"Then why give me leave to try? Why let me go to Geneva to meet Ciano? You've never once told me to cease the diplomatic option. If you're that convinced it can't work, why let me continue to try and keep dialogue going? Why?"

Churchill bit down on the stub and grunted. His temper was notorious. But he let out a deep breath and let it fade away like the smoke from his cigar.

"Because, My Lord. There are those who believed, and still do, that your policy was the correct one." His voice was calm and sturdy, without a hint of anger. "Time after time we've exchanged words with those people. Tried to find peace with those people. And time after time they've violated the peace. Subjugated their own opposition, invaded foreign countries, snubbed populations out of existence. But where once most of the people of this island felt as you do, now they see the truth. They understand, as I do, that there can be no peace without victory. That peace will either be reached when the German Army is standing in London, or the British Army is in Berlin. There are some fights that we simply cannot negotiate. Some people that we cannot negotiate with."

His gaze was stern and in his eyes, Halifax could see nothing but steely resolve. Halifax stood motionless. He couldn't feel his extremities after that. He was numb. He batted his eyelids, feebly tried to find his words. But he couldn't.

"We've reached the eleventh hour, Prime Minister," Halifax said, his voice weak and shaky. "The time to decide which road we go down."

Churchill blew out noisily and snatched the cigar from his mouth.

"And that is what you've never understood, My Lord. The eleventh hour has come and gone. The road that we're on now is the only road."

CHAPTER THIRTY-SIX

General Maxime Weygand tossed in his bed. In his dream's lights were flashing and there was a ceaseless pounding sound. He flipped to one side, then the other and let out an uncomfortable sigh in his sleep. There was another booming, then another. Finally, a high pitch whining. He could feel himself shake in the dream and then his eyes popped open suddenly and his head jerked upward.

The pounding had been real. The door to his small upstairs apartment, just above his field headquarters, was made with a heavy, thick wood and the banging was muffled but still loud enough to rouse him from his sleep. Outside the building was the sound of a winding siren. He tossed the blanket off him just as the door swung open and three aides entered the small room. One man hit the light switch and nearly blinded him.

"What-?!" He shouted out, startled by the sudden intrusion.

"General, you must get up, sir," his chief of staff, Brigadier Goulet told him. There was a strain of urgency in his voice. Another aide opened the closet and reached inside for a fresh tunic.

"What's going on?" General Weygand demanded. He swung his legs out of bed and put his bare feet on the floor. "What the hell is that noise?" He asked, referring to the siren going off outdoors. Through the closed window he could hear raised voices and inside the lights of vehicles passed across his bedroom wall.

"We need you to get up, General Weygand," Goulet said insistently. "We have a situation brewing. Reports of a German attack."

"What?" Weygand replied almost dismissively. He calmly grabbed his shoes and socks and began to get himself up from his bed.

It was absolutely inconceivable to him that the German Army was making any attack so serious it called for him to be awake at. . . he wasn't even sure what time it was, but he knew that he hadn't gotten more than a couple of hours sleep. It was the middle of March, and it was well known that the Germans were giving the front line a wide berth. Intelligence had not only dismissed the possibility that the Wehrmacht was in position for an attack but had outright claimed that the bulk of their forces were sitting in defensive fortifications of their own.

"Sir," the aide holding his tunic said as Weygand stood up and put his arms through the jacket.

"What's going on?" He asked. He put his kepi hat on and buttoned up his jacket.

"Reports from the front of heavy artillery fire," Goulet replied. "General Besson reports massive barrages in his sector that began half an hour ago."

"Pssh." Weygand shook his head dismissively. It didn't sound like anything to get out of bed over. Besson was an excellent officer, but his defensive lines were more than adequate against anything the Germans might throw at him. The Maginot Line was the single most impressive defensive structure in the entire world. It was impregnable.

He put straightened his uniform out just before stepping out in the dimly lit hallway and down a flight of creaking wooden stairs. The lower floors of his HQ in the city of Metz were bustling with activity. Couriers and aides were entering and leaving, motorcycles pulled up to the front of the building only to leave moments later after dropping off dispatches. The telephones rung off the hook. It was no wonder he could hear it in his dreams.

Men barely glanced at the general as he strode down the stairs, Brigadier Goulet right behind. A laminated map was clipped to a wheel mounted chalkboard. On it were drawn several red circles that had not been there the night before, marking the defensive forts along the

Franco-German line. The 3rd and 4th Armies were getting the brunt of it. Red circles pocked the line from Luxembourg all the way east to Strasbourg and down the dividing Rhine River.

"Shut that damn thing off!" Weygand hollered, referring to the siren blaring outdoors. He looked at the clock on the table. It was just now three in the morning. One hell of a time to begin an artillery offensive. He rubbed the tiredness from his eyes. "Somebody get me General Conde on the line." He scanned the busy room and turned back to Goulet. "What do we know?"

Goulet stepped forward and nodded toward the map.

"Reports of heavy shelling. Possibly railroad guns among them." He motioned his hand towards a lieutenant and took a note from the young officer's hand. "Aerial lookouts from the Luxembourg sector report bombers in the sky. Some reports of bombings in rear areas. Confirmed sightings of massive Luftwaffe air fleets flying into our territory."

Weygand took the note and glanced at it skeptically. Enemy bombers striking behind their lines at this hour? He took in the information, breathed heavily through his nose.

Could this be the beginning of an offensive against our lines? he asked himself.

Outside the winding siren ceased its wail. Weygand was grateful for the silence. 3rd Army was holding the vital stretch between Sedan and the Rhine River. A line almost two hundred kilometers long. Any bombardment might just be a prelude to a major attack. A breach by the Germans would be disastrous. If intelligence was incorrect about the German Army location, this could be only the beginning. The winter snows had only just melted. Common military sense said it was unwise to launch an offensive this early in Spring. But the German Army was anything but common.

"Can someone get me General Conde on the phone!" he repeated. A staff sergeant nodded, picked up the telephone and double tapped for an open line.

Another staff officer, headset pinned to his ear by shoulder, quickly wrote out a short note and held out his hand. "General," he whispered to Goulet.

"General," Goulet began, reading the new information coming in. "We have confirmation of German infantry crossing the Rhine in masse." He looked up from the paper. "Colmar and Belfort are being bombed."

Weygand shot him a shocked look and snatched it from his hand. Across the room, more red circles were drawn on the map. Weygand looked at Brigadier Goulet and blinked absently.

"What the hell is happening?" He said to him quietly.

Goulet didn't utter a single word. Weygand let his hand with the note fall to his side and tried to clear his mind of the flurry of disorganized thoughts. Infantry crossing the river in large numbers would only be the beginning of any potential attack. They'd have to be supported by massive amounts of artillery and air support just to make a dent against those defenses. All bridges across that river were well defended and the French had placed enough of their own artillery on their side to inflict serious casualties on any Germans crossing.

General Weygand stepped in closer to the board just as another red circle was marked. It wasn't the infantry that concerned him. What worried him most were the dozen or so German panzer divisions that were somewhere on that map, that no one could account for.

"Should we alert our other commands, sir?" Goulet inquired. The natural reaction to this type of situation would be to put the entire army on high alert and ready the reserves.

Weygand didn't answer right away. His predecessor would have no doubt rushed right in to try and meet any attack head on. But that was him. However, if this were some kind of feint, it could be used to lure his reserves into range of a bombing attack. He gave thought to the situation then slowly shook his head at the question.

"I want to speak to General Conde first," he replied softly. Conde commanded 3rd Army, one of the formations holding that line. If anybody had reliable information about what was happening, it was him.

The brigadier was stunned. His eyes widened and his jaw dropped open. Had he heard correctly?

"Sir?"

General Weygand shot Goulet a look and waved a finger at him.

"I want a full report from Conde before I order anything. I want to know exactly what's going on. After that I'll call Paris."

"I would highly recommend we at least mobilize our reserves, sir. At the very least coordinate-"

"When I know exactly what we're dealing with," Weygand snapped. "Will someone get General Conde on the line. Now!"

It was just after sunrise when General Pownall entered the private mess at Lord Gort's headquarters. The commander of the British Expeditionary Force was sitting with several of his senior officers at the breakfast table, along with General Georges of the French High Command, eating when Pownall strode across the room. Gort saw his facial expression and knew immediately that something was not right.

"Sir." Pownall came to a halt at the end of the table.

"Henry," Gort replied. He was disturbed by the look on his chief of staff's face. "What's the matter?"

"I've got with me some very urgent reports, sir," Pownall told him and held up a collection of typed papers. "Reports of German infantry divisions crossing the Rhine early this morning. Massive bombing raids behind the Maginot Line."

Pownall handed him the first few pages to sift through. Gort perused through the information contained in the pages. Massive artillery barrages in the pre-dawn morning, infantry in small boats observed, dive bombers hitting French fortifications with pinpoint accuracy. The list went on. More than a dozen independent reports from front line commanders detailing skirmishes all along the line.

"Why are we just now getting this?" He asked Pownall after noting the first reports went to Weygand's HQ almost four hours earlier.

"Unsure, sir. General Weygand called Paris before sending out a general alert." Gort sighed heavily. "There's more," Pownall continued. "The Luftwaffe's struck at several of our forward airfields on the front. Hundreds of our planes have been hit on the ground. Metz, Strasbourg, Colmar have all been hit by bombing raids."

Lord Gort stood up at the news, his silver fork falling to the floor, his face turning flush.

"My God!" Another general listening in on the conversation gasped. Everyone had stopped their meals. Even General Georges had given up trying to finish his breakfast to listen in.

Gort continued to excitedly read through the shuffle of papers. He simply couldn't believe what he was seeing. It didn't seem possible to him that the Germans could pull off an attack like that with such overwhelming strength. Hundreds of enemy bombers were reported in a score of attacks across eastern France. Barely a fifth of the RAF and French Air Force units assigned to that region had gotten airborne to meet any attack. Those that did had been decimated by German fighter squadrons.

To make matters worse General Weygand, commander-in-chief of the entire French Army, had not put his reserve divisions on stand-by yet. Fifteen divisions were sitting idly by in quarters while the front was being shelled into dust.

"Damn that man," Gort cursed, not caring if Georges overhead him. There was no love lost between Georges and Weygand anyhow.

Pownall frowned and held up one last paper.

"More bad news?" Gort asked pessimistically.

"Afraid so. Last to come in. Not from Paris either, sir. Intercepted transmissions from Holland. Civilian broadcasts. Reports of paratroopers dropping into that country as well."

The room became eerily silent. General Gort felt his heart sink and the ground shift beneath his feet at the news.

"Why would they be doing that?" General Georges asked as he picked a sliver of meat from between his teeth.

"Because they're going after the bridges, general," Pownall replied to him coolly.

The bridges over the north Rhine crossed through the Netherlands. If the Germans were to seize even a handful of them, they could storm through Belgium and straight into Northern France. The Allies had anticipated a possible German thrust into Belgium, but the Netherlands were vehemently neutral. It's occupation by the Nazis would be disastrous.

"Send out orders immediately, general," Gort ordered. "All units are to prepare to move out immediately. Execute Plan D, Henry." Pownall nodded at the order. "I want Prime Minister Churchill on the line as soon as possible. Call Air Marshall Barratt's headquarters. Ask him to get us some air cover." He handed the shuffle of reports back to Pownall. "As soon as possible the entire expedition will be heading out."

He swung back to the men still sitting at the breakfast table.

"Gentlemen, I want you all at your posts!" The group didn't waste a moment and began vacating the table in haste. "I want this entire army on the move by this time tomorrow. Unless God or the king intervene, we'll be moving into Belgium."

Like a giant chess board, the briefing room at the Führer's bunker in Berlin was adorned with ever moving pieces that shuffled around the map in a constant move, countermove. Only in this case his pieces held the advantage. It had been two days since the campaign had kicked off. He'd given his field commanders his blessing and personally sent a message to his armies, encouraging them on to triumphant victory.

The millions of soldiers now swarming into the Low Countries had the initiative from the very beginning. His troops quickly seized the vital bridgeheads in Holland and even now the northern arm of his invasion force was pushing into the last pockets of resistance in that country. On the southern front, the foolish French had fallen for the faint his military planners had devised and been lulled into thinking that was the main attack. A million French soldiers along their pathetic Maginot Line were now pinned down by relentless attacks from the air. But Belgium was proving to be a tougher nut to crack then they had planned for.

Even taken by surprise that country's army had managed to deflect some of the deadliest attacks by the Wehrmacht. But despite their tenacious defense soon they would simply be overwhelmed by the sheer number of attackers. Even now General Rundstedt's armored forces were sweeping across that country, crossing river after river in their path. The Belgian defenders would be useless in a fight against the German Army once their greatest disadvantage, the rivers that they were forced to cross, was no more.

Hitler laughed at the arrogance of it all.

Around the room his generals were gathered. His top military leaders and inner circle members were together once more to update him on the progress of the giant operation. Halder, Jodl and Göring were all present. Jeschonnek, the Luftwaffe's number two man was also there, as was General Manstein, the man who had ultimately devised the operation they had gathered to discuss. Manstein's calm, emotionless demeanor was legendary and even Hitler scoffed at him.

"Tremendous," Hitler mumbled. "Absolutely tremendous." He marveled at the progress of the operation.

"It has been quite the successful campaign thus far," Halder, head of the German Army, commented. Hitler nodded and chuckled like a boy. "The success of Army Group B has exceeded our initial estimates. Organized resistance in Holland and northern Belgium has crumbled. I expect that the Dutch will last no more than a day or two at most. Already their army is fleeing and it's simply a matter of mopping up isolated pockets."

"The Luftwaffe has cleared the airspace all the way to Amsterdam," Jeschonnek reported, causing Göring to grin enthusiastically. The head of the German Air Force liked nothing more than to bask in victory. "The Allies are still contesting the air in western Belgium, but I believe that we'll have supremacy there within a couple of days. Our bombers have pounded their supply lines endlessly. Sooner or later, they'll be forced to cede. Once they do, we can refocus our bombers further south. They can reduce whatever fortifications are ahead of the army. If we achieve a breakthrough-"

"When we achieve a breakthrough," Halder instantly interjected.

"Once we achieve a breakthrough," Jeschonnek corrected, "the Allied airfields in the south will simply fall right into our hands."

"Then we can use their own fields against them," Göring added. "The Luftwaffe will have uncontested control of the skies from Alsace in the east all the way to the French coast."

Hitler nodded approvingly. It was all happening so fast. By the day after tomorrow his armies would have occupied Holland and driven almost as deep into Belgium as the Kaiser's armies had gotten in four years of war. Even reports that the Dutch queen had been whisked away on a plane to London could not sour his mood. Some meager Dutch monarch in exile could not possibly pose a threat to him once his men were in control of that country. And all this was taking place on the heels of the news of the Soviet defeat in Finland. Reports of an entire Red Army corps being forced into surrender had come just days earlier and given him reason to be hopeful. After all, he'd secretly supplied the Finns with much of the weaponry used to fight off the Russians.

Of all present today only Manstein seemed apathetic to the success of the past two days. The brilliant strategic planner was as cold as one of his mathematical equations. But Hitler suspected that even he would be equally enthusiastic when the campaign ended with success.

"What of the British?" Hitler asked. He leaned down on the table, studying the pieces on the board.

"Our latest reports have the British force right about here, pushing towards Belgium," General Jodl reported. "Their lead elements will probably cross the border tonight. Though we don't have an exact makeup of their army on the continent, we can expect that between them and the French First Army, they will have substantial armor forces. If we do not cross the Meuse River before they arrive, it could cause a problem."

Hitler sneered and shook his head, ran his fingers through his oily hair. He studied the map as if his thoughts could dictate reality. As if he could simply will the Allied forces from reaching that river before his own forces did. Though he'd been reminded time and again of the superiority of German tanks he could remember well the British tanks rolling through the fields of Flanders in 1916. Those slow-moving tanks did plenty of damage and he cringed at the memory.

"I would not be so confident in the enemy. My planes can pound them from the air long before they reach the Meuse," Göring boasted. Hitler eyeballed him but said nothing.

"What do you think, Manstein?" Hitler asked.

"I believe," Manstein hesitated, he hated making predictions without reliable information, "that our lead units should be able to make a reasonable attempt to gain a foothold on the western bank. We only need a couple of intact bridgeheads. Remember that we had additional engineering available to us that we didn't have a year ago." He chewed his lip, ran through the numbers in his head, calculating the speed of the advancing panzer units, number of enemy defenders, cross points, logistical support and any factor he could conceive, then nodded his head smartly. "I believe we stand a better than even chance of crossing at various points before the Allies can be in position to launch any counter-attack."

"Good!" Hitler said and pounded the table with a closed fist. "Haha! Very good indeed. So, it's just a matter of time now." He straightened back up. His own enthusiasm aside, the uniformed men around him would always harbor doubts. Hitler rocked up and down on his heels. "When we meet the enemy on the battlefield, we will be victorious." He pumped his arms up and down in the awkward way he seemed to do from time to time. "I wonder how that fat man in London is taking the news."

CHAPTER THIRTY-SEVEN

The city of Liege, Belgium had been laid to ruins. The city's age-old buildings, many of which had existed since the Roman Empire and had withstood war, plague and nature's wrath, had now crumbled into bits and pieces of rubble. It had been one of the first to fall to the Nazis just days earlier. Half of its former inhabitants had fled and were even now streaming west, clogging the roads from here all the way back to the French border.

Joseph Portier was a twenty-nine-year-old policeman on the day the Germans invaded, only one short week ago. Most of his daily routines included directing traffic in the streets of Liege. The worst thing he'd ever seen on the job had been a horrific tour bus accident that had claimed the lives of several school children. He thought that experience was bad enough when he'd first witnessed the bodies of little boys and girls being carted away with white sheets draped over their little bodies.

But the world had turned upside down a week ago. The gray uniforms of the German war machine had brought death and destruction on a scale that Joseph had only read about in the Old Testament.

German bombers had leveled much of Liege on that first day. Buildings, schools, churches and homes were reduced to heaping piles of rubble. Though there had been little actual fighting around the city, fortifications nearby had fallen to the invaders quickly and the defenders all killed or captured. The German Army panzer division that had passed through with lightning speed and pressed on toward Brussels and Namur to the west, left only a token force to garrison the town. With no Belgian military presence to oppose them, the civilian population had been left to fend for itself.

But already there were those among them that could not sit still and do nothing. Those who had to act no matter what happened.

Through the muddy reeds Joseph hauled the body of a single German soldier. The dead man's boots dragged its heels into the thick mud, leaving behind a trail that stretched back to the main road a hundred meters away. And this man had been a heavy one. The first had been much lighter.

Behind him he heard the gentle splashing of his companion exiting the stream and coming to lend a hand. The other man, Jules, was a little younger than Joseph and stockier. He wore waders that came up passed his waistline and his rubber boots were covered in mud and river weeds. Jules, having sunk the first body, took the dead German by the legs and they both waded into the cold river.

No word was uttered between the two men. It was clear enough between them what had to be done. Joseph had done the hard part and the most difficult thing that he'd ever had to do. Killing those two soldiers had been the hardest thing he'd ever done. He'd used a knife and caught either man from behind. Even held them down and watched as the life went out of their eyes while he muffled their cries. That alone had been difficult enough but what had been even truly more shocking was the fact that he felt absolutely no remorse for doing it. Now they simply had to dispose of the evidence.

Joseph stepped into the frigid water first then Jules swung his end out. When the body became light enough in the river Joseph let go and Jules pushed the corpse under water for several seconds before letting go and allowing the current to sweep it away.

It was nearly dawn. The two walked back through the reeds and parted ways after disposing of the rubber boots they wore. The only noise that morning near the river was that of crickets chirping.

The roar of the engine from the German Army vehicles was loud and ferocity of the soldiers exiting from the convoy of trucks and cars fright ened the villages in the early morning hours. Outside, two dozen troop- ers, armed with machine guns, fanned out into the streets. Villagers in the open were corralled together. Rifle butts beat against wooden doors as troopers went from house to house, violently ushering their occupants out into the open street. In less than half an hour there must have been nearly fifty armed soldiers who'd arrived and almost two hundred vil- lage residents standing out in the chilly village square. Many still wore their bed clothes. The tiny hamlet in west Wallonia, just kilometers from Liege, was nowhere. Literally. Its small population subsisted of farmers and those employed at a local wool mill nearby. Nobody went there and its location didn't even sit near any of the major roadways. So, when a company of heavily armed Nazis showed up unexpectedly no one could quite understand why.

It was over an hour after the first of them had arrived, after the sun began to warm up the early morning that additional cars rolled into the center of town and more men turned up. Most wore the gray uniforms of the German Army, others were dressed in jet black. Two wore the red and white armband with swastika that had become so notorious. On the front of one of the cars was the death's head emblem.

An officer opened the rear door of the middle car and a medium built man wearing charcoal gray stepped out. He was immaculately groomed. His mustache was so narrow and trim that many villagers thought that Hitler himself had arrived. The man looked around before putting a gray cap on his head. A skull and crossbones patch was affixed to his collar and on his hat was not the roundel of the Germany Army but the silver eagle with swastika of the Nazi Party.

Orders began to be barked out and the soldiers aligned the civilians along two sides of the street. The man in charge stood there and watched, his hands in his trench coat pockets, seemingly callous to the terror his troops were causing. Men, women, children, young and old were sepa- rated into two groups with armed troops between them. A cold spring wind picked up and blew down the length of the road. The civilians hud- dled together to keep warm.

Finally, after long minutes in silence the man in charge walked into the middle of the road. His dark eyes seemed to scan the people with a chill that only made the cold morning air worse.

"My name," he began slowly, turning his head to the people on either side of the street, "is Major Meyer. This village and all others in this area are now under my charge." His words were slow and monotonous. "My authority here is final." He shifted his head from right to left, making sure his words were heard by everyone present.

"Yesterday, people from this village aided enemies of the Third Reich. Dutch and Belgian soldiers were given aid and comfort by some of you. We have reports of locals helping enemy soldiers escape from the fighting. Even passing along information of German positions in Liege. We cannot tolerate such behavior. As subjects of the Third Reich, it is your responsibility to provide any SS or army unit with information on such activities." He paused for a dramatic effect and investigated the faces of the gathered. "I wish to know whom among you is responsible for this. Who here is responsible for this treason?"

His words were sharp, and his demeanor was like some inquisitor getting ready to inflict some religious punishment. Villagers looked at one another and began murmuring lowly to themselves. Some shrugged away the major's suggestion, others shook their heads in confusion or ignorance.

"Nobody here lent aid to anyone," a single voice spoke up.

Major Meyer snapped his head around towards the voice. He was a diminutive man. Middle aged with thinning blonde hair and a pointy nose. The man adjusted his round spectacles as the major gazed at him appraisingly.

"Who are you?" Meyer asked.

"Me? I am Claude de Trooz," he answered nervously. "I... I am the mayor here." He gulped visibly.

Meyer eyed him for a moment then put a smile, of all things, on his face. He walked steadily towards de Trooz, and the mayor's features turned pale as the blood rushed out of his face.

The Nazi major stopped and placed a gloved hand on the mayor's shoulder. The look on his face was friendly but the hand on his shoulder felt anything but that. There was a coldness that surrounded the Nazi that terrified the smaller man. Despite the friendly grin, there was an illegitimacy to it.

"Mayor? I see." Meyer nodded approvingly. "So as mayor here would you have firsthand knowledge of everything that goes on? Who comes and who goes?"

de Trooz blinked and shook his head slowly.

"Everything? No. But...," he faltered, tried to exhale his nervousness away. "I can assure you, major, that no enemies of your Reich came through here. No soldiers of any kind. All of the fighting has been far away from here."

The two men locked eyes. The major's stare was unnerving. His brown eyes were piercing.

Finally, the major patted the shorter man lightly on the shoulder and let out a relieving sigh. He stepped back and nodded his head at the group assembled on the left side of the road.

"Well," he began to say, "that is very good to hear." He sounded almost relieved and de Trooz tried to overcome his fear and return the other man's smile. "That is very good to hear indeed. So, am I to take your word that no one from this village has ever or would ever lend comfort to our enemies?"

"Of...of course," the mayor replied nervously. "We would never do that. We are peaceful people."

Major Meyer nodded and began to take off his left glove one finger at a time.

"Excellent. Peaceful neighbors are what Germany wants. Then my job here is finished. I can report to my superiors that this town and its people are loyal, and they do not present any threat to our brave soldiers in the region. Thank you very much for your assurances, mayor." He turned and walked back towards his vehicle. The tension in the air seemed to evaporate with each step and the townspeople began to relax visibly. The major had gotten perhaps half a dozen paces and came to a stop. He looked another officer in the eye, nodded his head slightly and with a flick of his thumb across his throat the troops raised their machine guns at the hundred people on the side of the road opposite the mayor, and opened fire.

It was violent and terrifyingly loud. Hundreds of rounds swept across the line of civilians and the people began to fall as bullets riddled each one of their bodies. Men of all ages, mothers with babes in their arms, elderly, all fell to the Nazi bullets. On the opposite side of the road others cried out at the butchery. Some men stepped into the road as if to run across only to be clubbed by a soldier with a rifle. The firing only lasted seconds but felt like forever to those who were there that day. It was beyond horrific, and it was the first of a long line of SS atrocities and that of a man named Kurt Meyer, avid Nazi and devoted son of the Fatherland.

In the thick bush just a couple hundred meters away, Joseph Portier was hiding. He had observed the line of cars approaching the village and hidden in a ditch before they could spot him then snuck through the countryside to observe what was going on. Though he wasn't related to any of these people and as far as he knew, he wasn't familiar with any of them either. But when he saw what he saw today he told himself that he would never stop until every one of those Nazis were dead or out of his country.

CHAPTER THIRTY-EIGHT

General!" The voice called from fifty paces behind him, but Rommel ignored it. "Sir! We're dangerously close to the enemy lines!"

General Erwin Rommel studied the map he was holding then compared it with the landscape before him. He mumbled to himself and ran half a hundred thoughts through his mind as he did. He understood the terrain, he knew the points that would be heavily fortified and which ones wouldn't be. As large as the Allied armies might have been they couldn't defend every piece of land. Rommel traced his finger along the Meuse River on the map. He could almost feel where the enemy were.

"Sir!" The voice called again, closer this time. He could hear the huffing and puffing of the man running up from behind him. "We're very close to the enemy positions, general. Please, let me drive you back. Just a bit. Please."

At first Rommel didn't answer, he finished running the thoughts he was having through his mind. He needed to see the terrain firsthand, needed to know what exactly was ahead of him. Things that no map could tell him. Besides, any general that sought safety in battle was no true general at all.

"Sir?"

"Hush," Rommel replied quietly. "I need to see for my own eyes, major. Besides," he scanned the plain in all directions, "I don't see any enemy troops."

Major Otter looked around the horizon. "Well, artillery perhaps. Sir, I...."

Rommel held up his hand and Major Otter fell silent. The general was known to be a bit eccentric when it came to leading his men. His inclination was to stay mobile and as far ahead of the main columns as was possible. He didn't sit in a chair or even follow along from the back of his division in a cushy car somewhere. He had to be up front. If his division was in the lead, then he had to be out front leading it. For Rommel there was no other way. He received reports of course but preferred to see things for himself.

The town of Givet was only five kilometers south of his present location. It was a small town that sat on the Meuse River. The French had units there occupying the fortifications on that side of the river. To his rear was the thick Ardennes Forest and further south the Meuse bent and twisted around the town of Sedan. He knew Guderian's corps was down there and would no doubt try and cross there. Rommel had studied the French defenses and knew from reconnaissance reports that the area around Sedan was weakly defended. Guderian would only have to push through with some tanks and be across and once across he could flank the entire French First Army.

Rommel's single division was miles ahead of the rest of the army. Never one to slow down or dig in, he'd kept the men moving for five days straight now with little rest but plenty of enemy prisoners to show for the progress they'd made.

Just two hundred meters behind him the first of the lead tanks were making their way down the dirt roads hugging the rolling hills of the Franco-Belgian countryside. The column stretched back for miles.

"Come," Rommel told him and stomped back towards the staff waiting near the command car, all the time he continued studying the map in his hands. "Guderian should be down here, around Sedan," he told the group as he put the map on top of hood of his car. "If he hasn't already done so, he'll attack southwards to try and force his way across the river. We're going to cross right here, at Givet. Cross here, hold the town and once the whole division is over the river, we'll press on into France."

"The French armor divisions are over there somewhere, general," a junior aide pointed out. "Shouldn't we wait for support?"

Rommel folded up the map and stuffed it back into his tunic. "There is no support." He hoisted himself up into the armored car he'd been riding in and pointed back at the upcoming tanks. "Get those tanks into line. Have them form a battery on our side of the Meuse. Bring up our infantry. It'll be dark in a few hours, and I want some of those rubber rafts up here. Tonight, under darkness, we're sending some men across. There are some villages both north and south of here on our side. I'm going to scout upriver right now. When I get back, I expect you to have captured them. Flush out the inhabitants and send them on their way. Be prepared to burn the buildings down."

"Sir?" A junior aide asked confusingly.

Rommel shot a look at the man. "The wind is blowing west, Lieutenant. We're going to need cover for crossing that damn river. Smoke screen, Lieutenant, smoke screen. Major Otter, you're in command until I get back." He thumped the driver's shoulder. "North."

With him in one car and his escort in a second, for the better part of the afternoon the general drove northwards, along the eastern bank of the river, stopping here and there to scan the landscape. On the opposite side of the Meuse, he could make out enemy fortifications, enemy troops moving up and down along their side of the river and even an enemy patrol who were observing him from their side. He gave them a friendly wave, which was of course not returned.

By three o'clock he'd gotten as far as ten miles away from his division and he knew that both his escort and the staff he'd left behind were not happy by his absence, but he didn't care. He'd deliberately moved his division so fast that he'd gotten out of support range by the main body of the army in order to get the element of surprise on the enemy. A single division, even a panzer division, posed little risk to the French defensive lines. He had hoped against hope that with the major fighting taking place far to the north and south of him, the French would leave this area lightly defended and he could make his crossing here.

By mid-afternoon they'd gotten as far north as the village of Houyet. Rommel found the main bridges here also blown as the French had retreated out of Belgium. Across the river the landscape was made up of heavily wooded hills and beyond that a low flatland that went all the way into France. Rommel had studied his maps again and again and felt he knew what the terrain was like for miles but there really was no substitute for viewing it himself. He'd been here once before as a young officer in the Kaiser's armies, remembered vaguely the fighting that took place in this area back then. The long plodding armies fighting in those forests in 1914 and '15 had been bloody, and he had no wish to see that happen again.

At just before four he'd stopped his car once again at the top of a steep hill overlooking a bend in the Meuse River just southwest of the town of Dinant. At the bottom of the escarpment, just north of the bend was a narrow metal bridge. Rommel scanned through his binoculars. The bridge was made of grated metal and linked the east bank to what looked like some sort of water pumping station on the opposite bank, surrounded by miles of forest. There were some bodies moving here and there on side of the river, but he couldn't make out whether they were soldier or civilian.

Far behind the trees on the west side there were several roads running north and south, but he saw no sign of any heavy use. What he wouldn't give for a couple of reconnaissance planes right now to know just what awaited him over there.

"Sir," his escort said to him. The young lieutenant by his side was holding up his own field glasses and pointing down at the metal bridge below.

"What is it?" Rommel asked him.

"Below that bridging, sir. Do you see it?"

Rommel squinted and refocused his lens. He wasn't sure what he was seeing at first but then it occurred to him. The metal walkway was barely obscuring a concrete wall underneath it, where the water was flowing downriver. It was a levee. He grinned as he realized that the pump station was part of a dam. He felt a sudden swell of excitement.

"Lieutenant, I want a rifle battalion up here. Immediately!"

Prince Charles, Count of Flanders and younger brother to King Leopold III of Belgium, paced back and forth along a wooden walkway a hundred feet from an elevated train platform. He was anxious. His inners felt like jelly and though it had been almost two full days since he'd last had a decent meal, he felt absolutely no hunger whatsoever. He was far too depressed to eat anything. Outwardly too he was sure that his emotions were on display. He was nervous, angry and melancholic all at the same time. Despite his royal upbringing and the leadership skills that he'd been taught his entire life, he was allowing his emotional state to get the better of him and he knew it and disliked it. He was a Prince of Belgium, younger brother to the king. He had an obligation to his family and to his country to be strong. He could almost hear the voice of his deceased father schooling him on the responsibilities of being a royal.

But the past several days had simply been overwhelming. Pacing around a nearly abandoned train depot in the backwater of his own country didn't help his disposition either. Though not a smoker right now he wished desperately that he had a cigarette on him. He could ask for one, of course, and any number of two dozen aides would kindly oblige him, but he swallowed the urge down. Everyone around him knew he didn't smoke and starting now would only send the message that was already painfully obvious to so many.

He and his entourage were at one of the last few train stations left in free Belgium. That is, the small, westernmost part of his country that was not yet occupied by the Germans. Just fifty kilometers north was the city of Ypres, which had been the scene of brutal fighting during the First World War. He'd only been a small child then, but he could remember the horrors that war had brought with it. The countryside had been torn apart, the people killed or scattered, the land scorched. It had taken a generation for the land and the people to recover from that war and now another conflict reared its head and threatened to do the same.

Near him was his principal aide, Albert De Grun, half a dozen minor functionaries, several government officials and nearly twenty armed guards. The village nearby had been all but abandoned and very few of the townsfolk remained and even fewer bothered at all to pay heed to the prince. He didn't blame them. Who was he anyway? Fourth in line to the throne, for all the good that would do. A nobody prince against the German Army which was right now only miles away and rolling west.

De Grun, a hefty man in his middle forties and dressed in a thick wool suit, sat in a tiny chair just under the train depot's tin roof canopy, fanning himself with his brimmed hat. He was a good man but not in the shape that he'd been in his youth. The last few days had taken a toll on him as well and though the prince was sure the man had come down with pneumonia, De Grun had waved away attempts by doctors to get him to the hospital.

High above them, in the thick clouds, one could hear planes flying high. He couldn't tell which way they were going but he was quite sure they were not bombers; they were flying too slow. Reconnaissance planes most likely. He'd come to learn quickly the different sounds of war. The education that he'd received since being forced to flee Brussels had been nothing that he'd prepared for when at any number of private schools in Britain as a youth.

From out of the main depot office a man stepped out onto the platform and walked down the rampway toward him. De Grun turned his head at the man as he walked past.

"My Prince," the man began. Karl Francois had been a recent addition to his staff. A former Brussels city police detective turned royal attendant and bodyguard. Charles found the man's directness to be a refreshing change from his normal company. Like most royals, people around them seemed to walk on eggshell. But not Francois.

"Yes?" Charles asked, a hint of nervousness in his voice. He stunned himself with how much of a frightened child he was acting like.

"I'm sorry, My Prince," he paused, and his face turned dour, "but I have some terrible news. Telegraph lines to Ypres are still up and running and I thought I'd get whatever updates that I could before the Germans took the city. I must be the one to inform you. . ." He stopped, hesitated.

Charles looked at him. His stomach turned to cold stone. He could sense the distress that the other man was in.

My God, what's happened?

"The king is dead. He and his family were on their way here when his automobile was strafed by German planes. I'm very sorry."

Charles went into total shock. He felt as if he'd been hit with a hammer. His breath left him, and it felt as if his heart had stopped beating. He brought his hand up to his face and tried to cover his eyes as tears instantly welled up in them. He held down a sudden urge to openly sob.

"What about," he tried to begin. His words were broken, and he found he had no voice. It took several moments for him to compose himself. He turned his head towards the line of trees on the opposite side of the train tracks, where nobody could see his face, and wiped the tear away with a finger. "What about his children? What about the queen?"

Francois gave a single, silent shake of his head and shrugged.

"I'm sorry. We believe that they too were all killed but no one really knows for sure. The king and queen were traveling together. But for the royal princes and princesses, we just don't know."

My God, he thought. *The children as well?*

The two men stood there for a minute, quietly and undisturbed. He was so overcome with emotion right now that he barely even heard the crunching footsteps over the gravel. Albert De Grun had watched from under the canopy at the scene and walked over the join his prince. His own face was even more gaunt than Prince Charles right now, beads of sweat ran down his plump cheeks.

"Highness?" De Grun asked gently. His eyes shifted between Karl Francois and Prince Charles.

"It was the king," Francois told him softly and De Grun blinked away his shock.

"And the children?"

"Nobody knows for sure," the prince replied. He rubbed away the tear at the end of his nose and turned back to face the two men, then straightened his shoulders and peered at his longtime aide. "They just don't know."

De Grun was silent for several seconds then said, "If it's true, then we need to move you now, Highness. Quickly. For your own safety." He looked at Francois who seemed to agree. He patted his face with his handkerchief again.

"Did you not hear what I just said?" Charles asked him curtly. "My nieces, my nephews may also be dead. Do you understand me?"

"Yes, I do understand," De Grun replied to him gently. "That is exactly why we must go. Prime Minister Pierlot has escaped the country. Even now he's in Paris meeting with Reynaud with most of the cabinet. Parliament has also fled. The king," he crossed himself, "was a brave man but rumors were he was preparing to surrender the nation and the army."

Next to him Francois nodded in understanding.

"He's correct. Right now, as far as anyone knows, you are the heir to the throne. That makes you the de facto head of state. My Prince, we must get away from here now. We can be in France in an hour. We can take refuge in Paris."

"Better yet, London," De Brun added quickly. His face was turning red, and his breath was intermittent. He coughed into a handkerchief.

Prince Charles looked at them both with astonishment. His eyes floated between the two men and in the skies above he heard yet another plane pass overhead.

"Flee? This is my country. We don't know if any of my brother's children are still alive. If even one is then they will be heir, not me. My father didn't flee in the face of the old Kaiser."

"Highness, the Kaiser didn't have tanks and planes like Herr Hitler does," Francois rebutted him. The old police detective in him was beginning to show and his voice had an air of authority in it. "The government can be reformed far away from here. Please listen to me. It is far better to have a government in exile than some puppet regime run by Berlin."

"What about my brother's children? What if they turn out to be alive?"

Francois hesitated a moment. He was no fool. He understood just what would happen to them should they still be alive. If they were captured then the Nazis would simply use them as tools, install one on the Belgian throne and call him or her the legitimate ruler. On the other hand, most of the parliament had left the country and Belgian law called for a new monarch to be sworn in by them and to rule by their authority. The voice of the deceased king's brother would lend much weight to that legitimacy even if he had to rule from another country.

In the distance, as if by providence, a train whistle blew faintly. Prince Charles, heard it sound, heard Francois's words of advice. His love for his brother and his loyalty to his people told him to stay and not to leave while a single part of Belgium remained free. But his instincts and conscience said something else. His moral dilemma lasted right up until the train whistle signaled its turn into the depot. Then, slowly and with much reluctance, he nodded his head. They were right and he knew that. Should any of his brother's children have survived then they could always have hope for them. If not, then it didn't matter.

The train let out a last steam whistle then came to a stop. The escort began to huddle around the platform of the wooden depot station. A small stop on the rail line between Ypres and Paris.

"You're right," Prince Charles replied to them in a soft tone. He inhaled sharply and found his voice again. "You're right. We have a duty. It's to Belgium."

"Highness we must move you immediately," De Grun said insistently. He broke protocol by touching the prince on the shoulder, urging him towards the platform. "Please."

They wasted no time. The three men were followed closely by two dozen others up the ramp. The train sat at the station for no more than a few minutes. Just enough time to get everyone aboard before it started forward again. With one last blow of its whistle, it moved on, leaving behind the final sliver of free Belgian soil.

The train ride all the way to Paris went unimpeded, to the surprise and relief of those aboard. The prince, and possible new King of the Belgians, sat mostly in silence in that time. The French countryside looked much like Belgium had, with plumes of smoke in the distance and long lines of refugees traversing the roadways. Even large cities and towns were mostly empty these days. Soldiers and armies moved east as the train sped west.

It took four hours for them to reach the outskirts of Paris. The city was as open and vibrant as any of them had ever seen it. Cafes and restaurants were still teeming with people. Civilians lined the streets as the train came into the enormous central station. It was almost relieving in a way to see the marvelous city, still teeming with life. It's people oblivious to the fighting. Whether that was a blessing or a curse, he didn't know. Parisians were strange that way.

A drive from there to the Belgian Embassy was a mere twenty minutes. Charles was surprised to see just how incredibly packed the city streets were. How alive with energy. How ignorant the populace was. He'd been in Paris before, knew its occupants to be blissfully arrogant. Did they know that the German Army was literally only hours from here? That their tanks and planes had crushed Holland and Belgium in mere days?

The Belgian Embassy was on the north side of the River Seine. Five cars pulled up in front of the four storied building. A bevy of embassy workers, uniformed guards and press correspondents were already assembled as the cars pulled up. Bodyguards leapt out of cars before they even came to a stop, pushed away the photographers as they snapped pictures and opened car doors for their occupants.

Outside, a balding man with a cleft chin stood with hat in hand as the prince arrived. The man offered his hand and Prince Charles took it warmly. The hours traveling between Ypres and Paris had given him the time to find his strength again. He put aside the mourning his brother's loss for the present and put on the face of a man who'd been born to the royal household.

"Highness." The man said. "I'm Ambassador Jaspar. Welcome to Paris." The embassy guards outside snapped to attention at the prince's approach.

"I'm sorry to greet you under these circumstances," the ambassador continued. "We had very little warning of your arrival."

"I'm pleased to be here. I am the bearer of grave news unfortunately." He gulped his grief away. "The king, my brother, is dead. We got word of it right before coming here."

"Yes. I heard," Jaspar told him. "We are all very sorry for your loss. We will do all in our power to offer you whatever comfort we can. Again, I am very sorry."

"You must not be sorry for me," the prince said. His voice was much more confident than it had been this morning upon hearing the news. "It's the people we must take care of. Please tell me where is Prime Minister Pierlot? He and I have much to discuss."

The group stopped in the main foyer of the embassy. Ambassador Jaspar parted his coat as he put his hands on his hips. The group filed into the building behind the prince.

"Prime Minister Pierlot is not here, My Prince. He's meeting with Reynaud as we speak. After that we'll be leaving for London."

"London?" Charles asked confused by this. "Was the Prime Minister not informed of my arrival?"

"Yes, sir. He was indeed. Unfortunately, the situation has changed since you left Belgium this morning. He's been with Prime Minister Reynaud since noon discussing the situation."

"What situation?" Charles asked him.

"My Prince, I'm afraid the news today is not good. The Germans have broken through the lines. Some general named Rommel even now is driving towards Arras."

"Arras?" The prince replied. They had passed by Arras on their way to Paris. It seemed this day had no end to bad news.

"The British and French are falling back. The situation is not good." Jaspar shrugged uselessly. "If the French cannot hold the line, then Paris itself will be threatened. It might be less than a week that German tanks roll into the city."

Prince Charles was visibly shocked by this. The people in the streets had looked painfully oblivious to the threat of occupation. As it was bits and pieces of the northern part of their country was already living in occupied territory. How could the Allies, with nearly three million troops in the field have suffered such a defeat so soon? He inwardly cursed his country's decision to remain neutral early on. Could today become any worse?

"I understand," he told Jaspar. "I'm going to need to speak with Mister Pierlot as soon as humanly possible. In the meantime," he gestured back to the company of escorts squeezing through the doorway behind him and those still outside, "we're going to need accommodations. And I think that you and I should go somewhere and speak in private. We have a lot to discuss, and it seems that time is running out."

CHAPTER THIRTY-NINE

It was hot. Damn hot. The heat made Ernst think briefly of the battle-fields in Poland from last summer. A lot of the heat was coming from the huge engines of the tanks that were riding forth to war, constantly running, constantly heating up. It made the times when the panzer divisions crawled slowly across the French countryside grueling. Krauss took the final bite of his apple then tossed the core to the ground.

The whole XIX Corps was pressing forward like some massive human wave washing over the grassy landscape of Northeastern France. 2nd Panzer was smack in the center of the formation and the 3rd Regiment was on point for the division. They'd crossed into France two days earlier and despite making a halfway decent 40 kilometer advance they encountered a resistance that they'd barely experienced in Poland the year before. The enthusiasm and excitement that so many of the boys had first set out with a mere week earlier was now gone. This wasn't going to be the simple operation that many of them had thought it would be and the French Army wasn't going to be the pushovers the Polish Army had been. Indeed, it was even said some of those Polish units that had escaped from the fall of their own country were now fighting in the ranks of the French and British forces.

The treads of his Panzer IV squeaked as it rolled through the muddy ground, a result of the hit it had taken in Belgium, the large ding still on the side of the tank a badge of honor of their first time in combat. They'd been a tough opponent those Belgians. The 2nd had hit them head on like a sledgehammer but somehow, they'd managed to stop the roll of those panzers and get in some damn fine hits. It didn't hurt either that the British were fighting alongside them and were outfitted with some halfway decent anti-armor guns. Something else the Poles hadn't had last summer.

"Corporal, do you know where we are?" newly promoted Senior Private Albrecht asked from below.

Krauss couldn't help but smile at the question. "Yes," he called back down. He could hear the others in the tank laugh a few moments later when no further answer came. Truth be told he had no idea exactly where they were. France was all he knew. The forests off to their right might have been the famed Ardennes but he wasn't sure. He didn't care either. He was in charge of a single tank crew, not the entire army.

Five hundred meters off the ground a flight of Messerschmitt's flew overhead heading west. The army had had plenty of air cover since the offensive began, that was for sure. More than they'd even had in Poland it seemed. Every day for the past eight days fleets of high-flying bombers were seen heading deeper and deeper into France. It was said that the bombers had totaled most of Belgium. Some of the men in the regimental radio unit had been overhead saying that the entire city of Rotterdam in Holland had been completely destroyed by the bombing.

Krauss couldn't imagine it. *An entire city destroyed? Allied propaganda.*

He held up his binoculars and viewed the countryside. It was green and lush and quite beautiful. One would hardly know that they weren't in Germany anymore. The landscape all looked the same. The few towns and villages they'd passed through also looked much like those on the east side of the Moselle River. Some of the civilians they'd encountered even spoke decent German.

Smoke rose in steady streams in the far distance ahead. Not the little plumes of smoke like they'd seen in Poland either, this was thick black smoke that could be seen miles and miles away. They were towns burning. The Luftwaffe had spared nothing. Hundreds of their aircraft were flying twice a day every day into the west, leveling everything in the path of the advancing ground forces.

From across the entire countryside, he could hear the far-off sound of artillery fire. Both the German and Allied armies had been exchanging fire like this since the start of the campaign. The artillery had been bad in Belgium, but it had gotten much, much worse since crossing into France. Now it never ceased, not even at night when the sound of thunder was coupled with fire lights set against the night sky.

The entire division was spread out over several kilometers and rolled steadily forward. Ernst had trained with the panzers his entire time in the army but even he had never seen so many tanks before. The 2nd alone had five hundred and the 3rd Panzer Division was just south of them with another five hundred. There were fifteen other panzer divisions in this operation as well that was spread out from here all the way to the North Sea through Belgium and the Netherlands.

The German offensive was massive and had taken the Low Countries completely by surprise. There was no force on earth that was going to stop the German Army today. But the Allies certainly weren't going to just sit back and do nothing either. Everyone knew that the British, French and Belgian forces were in retreat and falling back towards the French coast, but they were putting up one hell of a rearguard. In the past two days alone they'd passed dozens of their own vehicles, destroyed wrecks that now littered the countryside. But there had been hundreds more Allied wrecks, burnt out shells of trucks, cars, tanks of all sorts, even planes shot down by the Luftwaffe still smoldering in empty fields all over.

Along the way he and his men watched as whole companies of surrendered Dutch and Belgian soldiers sat in large clumps of grassy areas off the muddy roads. Their uniforms were torn and bloody, many of them were themselves wounded with bloodied bandages splattered with mud. Some were smoking on cigarettes, others sitting quietly as the Germans marched past. They all looked exhausted.

Ernst looked down at a wooden sign that had broken and fallen to the ground. Nearly covered with mud as men marched over it, he could still make out what it said as his tank rolled by: **Amiens – 122 km**

So they were heading for Amiens. Ernst pulled out the map that was stuffed into his tunic breast pocket and unfolded it as his tank continued to roll along at a slow pace. Amiens was a city on the Somme River. In the First World War it had seen some of the very worst fighting and its location was strategic, even he could see that. He ran his fingers over the map straight south from Amiens to Paris. Less than two hundred kilometers away.

That had to be it, he told himself. *They must be planning for us to take Paris.*

He found that he actually got excited thinking about the prospect of riding into that city atop his Panzer IV. The Frenchies wouldn't like it, but he could already see himself telling Papa about it when he got back to Germany after they had beaten France and the war was won.

In the next tank ahead of them Sergeant Wagner sat atop the turret and pointed this way and that way. The stout sergeant was always moving his arms about. He turned his head back, saw Krauss looking back at him and the round-faced sergeant smiled broadly back.

"Just like in Poland!" He bellowed back. His arms stretched outwards to indicate the prisoners lining the roadside and laughed heartily.

Ernst had thought about Poland and what he'd seen there. He was still disturbed by the things that happened there. He'd told Papa about it when he was home in Dresden, but he didn't understand. How could he? *They're not like us,* Papa had said speaking about the Polish. When he'd tried to talk to him about what he'd seen happen to those Jewish people, Papa had only shrugged. He'd never admit it, but he'd had more than one nightmare about that day, those people and that little boy.

He shook the thoughts away.

"Corporal," Private Nicholas shouted up. "Do you think we'll be stopping for the night soon? I'd like to help myself to some of that nice French wine."

"I don't think you need any more of that French wine," Schmidt countered him.

Krauss barely listened. There was a flurry of activity coming up from the rear of the column. Even over the noise of the engine and the squeaking treads he could catch little sounds of commotion on the breeze, sounds that were not typical of what he'd experienced in combat zones. It almost sounded like...cheering. He turned his head around to try and see what the commotion was but all he could make out was the occasional sight of someone waving their hand high or some far off soldiers taking his helmet off and holding it above their heads.

Then came the muffled blare of a horn blowing. Ernst looked and listened, initially dismissing it as perhaps a fight that had broken out between some men, or perhaps some bit of good news making its way up the ranks from the rear. A loud honking sound was coming up from behind. The shrilling of the horn repeated every few seconds and Krauss had become accustomed to it's annoying sound. It meant that some general officer was making his way through and that everyone else had to clear out of his way. He'd heard the sound so many times over that he barely paid it any attention these days. Just another dog wagging his tail.

But as the honking drew closer there also came the sound of men cheering. He turned his head and watched the vehicle hugging the road, infantry and vehicles alike moving aside as it weaved its way through. Had it been General Veiel in the car he'd never have been cheered on that way. He was too strict and disapproved of such things.

Another cheer went up and another. A hand rose in a clenched fist from the back seat of the car and another cheer from the men. Ernst frowned at first and watched the car bop behind the following tank then rode around its right side.

"It's Guderian!" A voice called out from somewhere and men waved their hands at the passing car.

It was true too. The car passed by the following tank, its commander waving down at the general. Guderian, smiling, waved back and threw out encouraging words to the men on foot, telling them to keep up with him or miss the party, which led to laughter. His car pulled up almost besides Ernst's Panzer IV, the blonde haired general in the backseat laughed and held up his fist again.

Ernst couldn't help but stare. He'd been with Guderian since the beginning, since before the war had even begun and had never once glimpsed the famed general. Now he was literally just feet away and it was sublime. He couldn't help but feel a bit overwhelmed at the sight of the great man going by. Guderian tipped his hat to the men walking along on his right then turned left and looked up. Ernst wasn't sure but he thought that the general had grinned at him. He froze, didn't know what to do. Then instinctively he straightened up and snapped off a crisp salute. Guderian saw this and brought his own hand up to the brim of his hat and returned it evenly.

Ernst stood there with his hand up to his eyebrow even after the General's car passed by and he watched it go, the long line of soldiers cheering him on as he rode on towards the front of the column.

"No! No!" Brigadier General Charles de Gaulle shouted into the telephone and waved his finger up in the air. He stomped his feet around on the dusty ground and occasionally slapped his thighs as he argued with the person on the other end of the telephone. At times the discussion had become an all-out shouting match and his staff quietly went about their duties, trying not to gawk at their commander as he unashamedly launched into a full-fledged, foul mouth tirade.

The division's command post consisted of an old run-down post office and a few abandoned garages on the road to Roye. Most of the country people had abandoned the area days earlier at the first sight of German bombers flying overhead and were even now clogging the main road arteries on the way to Paris. Millions of French citizens had now become displaced refugees and the sight of the tired and ragged looking souls they had passed on the way to the front lay heavily on the hearts of the soldiers.

Brigadier de Gaulle had earned a reputation for himself as one of the premier armored commanders in the French Army. But his reputation had frequently come into conflict with the more traditional old guards of the establishment. His notorious temper had gotten him in more trouble more than a handful of times and he knew that his only recent promotion from colonel had been held up on strictly political grounds. But when it came to fighting the enemy, he put aside any grudges that he held. But now, in the face of an overwhelming German advance, he felt once again like a man apart.

All morning long he'd had a non-stop confab with command, urging, in fact begging, for those lazy generals sitting around Paris and Amiens to take to the offensive rather than fall back to the defensive positions that he considered to be inadequate. He knew this part of the country, it had been his home in fact, he didn't need any map to tell him what the terrain was. If the damned German army crossed the Somme with resistance and gained a foothold on the south bank....

"Bring up some god damn heavy guns! Artillery support. We've got to have Artillery support!" General de Gaulle shouted into his phone.

On the other end of the telephone line an exasperated General Weygand let out an aggravated sigh. De Gaulle thought he could hear a muffled swear under the other man's breath.

"What was that?" He asked his tone edging on the verge of insubordination.

"De Gaulle, you fool! I have no artillery to send to you," Weygand told him sternly. "Everything I have left is going Reims. Corap is preparing--"

"Reims?" He interrupted General Weygand, his voice incredulous. "Reims? There's no one to fight at Reims. The enemy is here. In hours they are going to cross the river. After that nobody is going to be able to stop them. There will be an open road all the way to Paris."

"Listen to me!" General Weygand shouted back. De Gaulle could hear the man's panting breath over the line. "Corap is regrouping to the south of you. Once he's reinforced, we'll launch an attack northward and regain the ground we've lost. We need time, De Gaulle. We go charging head long into the German lines and we'll lose. Not just one battle but the whole thing." The other man grumbled on the line, and he fell silent for a moment. For one good moment he thought very hard about hanging up on his superior, the man who was, in theory, directing the defense of the entire country. "Hold your position. I'll get you reinforcements just as soon as we can organize it. Do not attack under any circumstances!"

General de Gaulle, looked around him, but remained silent for the moment. His officers were within earshot, and he knew they could hear every word that he said. He couldn't believe what he was hearing. He'd warned them, warned them all against these static defense strategies and he understood better than any of them the kind of tactics the Nazis were going to employ, hell they'd used it to great effect against the Polish. He licked his dry lips and his eyes drifted around.

"When?" He asked calmly and with as much respect as he could bring himself to muster. "Sir." He added.

"I don't know," General Weygand replied. "Two, maybe three days."

De Gaulle groaned and nodded his head, giving the impression as though the general was giving him good news, putting on the appearance for his men of a general who was getting exactly what he wanted. Inside, however, was a completely different story. He was fuming over. He held up his other hand and motioned for an aide to come over.

"I see," he said back to the general then placed his hand over the phone as a first lieutenant reported to him. "Get General Dupré on the line," he whispered to him then went back to Weygand. "I see, general. And air support?"

"What?" Weygand replied confused. "I don't know what you're talking about! De Gaulle just do as I've ordered. Hold your position. Wait for the reinforcements. I repeat you are NOT to attack."

"I understand, sir," he replied then hung up the line before Weygand had time to say anything further. He unsnapped the top pocket of his khaki field uniform and produced a long cigarette from his silver case. With a metallic flick of his zippo he lit it to life and let out a long stream of smoke. Around him were parked the tanks and vehicles of the 3rd Cuirassiers battalion. It's soldiers and vehicles were filthy, muddy and looked like hell but despite their outward appearances he knew that every man was ready to fight, and every vehicle was serviced and ready to go.

5th Armored Division had been assembled only weeks earlier, just prior to the German offensive, after much imploring by men like De Gaulle, commanders who understood the future ways of warfare. It hadn't been easy to get the command either. The traditionalists who ran the French army were so stuck in the past that just getting them military and political leadership to put together the new tank corps had been just as taxing a fight as he was now facing against the Nazis. And now that there was a full-scale war going on, the likes of which France had not seen since the days of Bonaparte, that same leadership was timid and showing signs of weakness in the face of the invasion. But Charles de Gaulle was determined to lead his troops into the fight, alone if necessary.

From out of the abandoned post office his aide-de-camp, Major Henri Toussaint, strode, a bundle of papers tucked under his arm as he strode towards the general. De Gaulle blew out a stream of cigarette smoke with one hand and put his other hand behind his back. Toussaint was a steady hand and a good officer who, though new to the armored corps, showed a quick grasp of the advantages tanks and armored warfare offered over the traditional infantry. He was almost as eager as the general was to get into the fight. It didn't hurt that his whole family had resided in Lille, which was now behind enemy lines.

"Telegraph lines have been busy today," he told De Gaulle. "The situation is bad, sir."

"I know, major," he replied icily.

"We're hanging onto our link with the British by a thread. Half of First Army has either been destroyed or surrendered. I've got the casualty lists and the update intelligence reports here if you wish." He indicated to the papers under his arm and De Gaulle merely shook his head. "May I ask, sir, what General Weygand had to say."

"He's ordered us to immediately attack," De Gaulle said back without thinking about it. Though he regretted having to lie to his subordinate he did not regret the decision he'd made to take to the offensive. If he could persuade his old friend General Dupré who commanded the 17th Infantry Division to follow him into battle, then there was a halfway good chance of heading off disaster.

"Really?" Toussaint's face looked shocked by the general's response.

"Oui. That's what he told me to do," De Gaulle said with a straight face. "I want the whole division ready to move out in one hour. Phone Colonel Sarrut. Order his Tenth Cuirassiers to take the point. We'll move straight to the crossroads at Ablaincourt." He exhaled again and put his free hand on Toussaint's shoulder. "Any word from your family."

The major's face looked immediately distressed at the mere mention of his family and he simply shook his head. De Gaulle patted his shoulder lightly.

"Sir," Lieutenant Tautou said respectfully and quietly. He was standing under a camouflaged net strewn across a pair of trees. "We have General Dupré on the line."

The general took another draw and walked across the crushed gravel. "Merci," he said and took the phone. He looked at the lieutenant and said, "See if you can get my wife on the line." Then put the phone against his ear. "Andre? It's Charles."

"Yes, Charles."

"Andre, I'm getting ready to move north toward Péronne. I could use your infantry to back me up. What can you get here and how fast?"

"Move to Péronne?" Dupré gasped. "Charles, I have no orders to advance, and I don't have the supplies I'd need. My division is in shambles right now."

"Andre, listen to me. Those fools at headquarters are leading us to disaster." He kept his voice down but knew that the others could hear what he was saying but didn't care. "If we don't take action now, we'll never get the chance again. The idiots in charge have chosen cowardice. There's no line that we can dig ourselves into this time, Andre. We need to act now or France is done."

Over the telephone line General Dupré could be heard sighing. De Gaulle could almost picture his old friend shaking his head furiously. Andre was a good man and a good fighter, but he'd always been a little more conservative than he would have liked.

"Charles, I don't have the fighting power and I cannot disobey my orders. If I move an inch General Corap will relieve me in a minute."

De Gaulle rolled his eyes. "Look, we must move now. The enemy crosses the Somme and everything is done. Give me support. Once we're in position along the south bank headquarters will have to back us up. They'll have to send the rest of the army northward. Dammit! The enemy is on their way, we can't delay!"

"De Gaulle," General Dupré began then faltered. "General Weygand called me less than half an hour ago." De Gaulle instantly knew what was coming next. "He gave me direct instructions not to move my command. I'm sorry. I can't help you, Charles."

"Weygand is a fool!" He snapped back, his voice carried, and heads turned towards him at the words. "Andre, for the love of France. Once they're on our side of the river we've already lost."

"I'm sorry, Charles," Andre told him, softly but sternly. "I can't help you."

A rush of frustration swelled up inside of him and he flung his half-finished cigarette to the ground in disgust then rubbed the tops of his brow as if doing so would massage away the stress that he was feeling. General Dupré was no fool, he knew how to read a map, had to know what would happen if those German tanks weren't stopped. Charles couldn't wait any longer it was already the middle of the day and every minute now counted.

"You can tell that to the millions of women and children you meet on the road fleeing their homes!" He hung up the phone angrily and shook his head in loathing. Men were gazing at him sporadically then averted their eyes as he looked around. He could feel their looks but didn't care. Weygand and those old fools at headquarters were obviously too stupid to see the strategic situation.

"Have you gotten through to my wife?" He asked the Lieutenant.

"No, sir," Tautou replied, holding the receiver to his ear and shaking his head. "There's a lot of lines down."

"You're to remain here," he ordered then took a moment to compose himself. "Keep trying, Lieutenant. Tell me wife..." He hesitated. "tell my wife to get to Brittany or Bordeaux if she can. She'll know what to do after that."

"Yes, sir."

De Gaulle stomped off towards the long line of armored vehicles and tanks that straddled the roadside. He tapped Major Toussaint on the back as he walked past, grabbed his helmet off the top of a car hood and hoisted himself up onto the side of an S35 tank in one easy movement.

"I'm going up forward," he told Toussaint before strapping his helmet on. "As soon as we've finished fueling up, get this column moving. NO STRAGGLERS!" He snapped a quick finger at the tank driver who started up the engine. "I want the whole division on the road and moving north by the time I reach Colonel Sarrut." He tapped a knuckled against the hull and returned a quick salute just as the driver applied the gas and drove off.

CHAPTER FORTY

General Rommel grinned wolfishly and let out a short, rapacious sigh. To the west of his position he could see the first of two French armored columns making its way over a shallow ridge. The two roads that led from here all the way back to Philippeville were the only causeways that French armor could have possibly used to make the counterattack that he had suspected would come. It was the only real option open to the French commander that made any sense.

Just hours earlier he'd sent in three machine gun companies to push forward and function as a recon force. Its goal was two-fold. The first to function as a forward picket and to warn him when the attack he suspected was coming materialized. The second, was to be a decoy, luring the French forward. Three companies were just enough to be a picket for a division sized unit but was also enough of a tempting target for an armored unit to want to cut to pieces given the chance.

Overhead he'd observed Allied reconnaissance planes making their way east just an hour earlier and he had purposely kept his panzers back just far enough to convince the Allies that his own armor units were far enough away that they posed no immediate threat. But the threat had not been the panzers that he was holding back, they could be brought up into attack position in less than an hour. Rommel wasn't interested in getting into a tank for tank battle with the French, no matter how much better his own tanks were. He knew that some of those French tanks could give almost as good as they got.

The general crouched down behind a wide, tall oak tree and kept those advance units in his sights. The dual causeways ran straight through small wooded patches of land and continued all the way back to the Meuse, kilometers away. After forcing his way across the river two days earlier, he'd expected to encounter heavier opposition. His own scouts and forward units had brushed aside a single Dutch battalion but had encountered no other resistance of any kind. But Rommel was not one to take chances and had prioritized getting the single battery of anti-tank guns to the front of his division as rapidly as possible. It had not been easy either. Moving those eighty-eights through uphill, wooded terrain had taken a lot of time and effort but they'd finally gotten them to his current position just before sunrise this morning, kilometers ahead of the tanks waiting in reserve for his order.

There was a staccato of heavy machine gun fire from the road ahead. Here and there he could make out distant images of men moving about. His forward troops were falling back as he had instructed them to. Slow and in good order. Each company covering the other as they tried to keep those French vehicles at bay. It was useless, he knew, but he had to keep enemy tanks from coming unopposed. A cautious enemy might have time to observe the geography ahead and even a few shells fired on his position could have disastrous consequences for his own men concealed in the thickets of trees. Even now twenty guns were positioned and ready to open up on the enemy as soon as they put their head into the noose.

He had handpicked those infantry commanders ahead because of their reputations for ferociousness. They were going to be chopped to pieces and he regretted the loss of those men, but the rewards were going to be far greater than the price paid. All he needed was a little more time.

A German mortar shell dropped down just ahead of the lead tank and exploded, sending out chunks of earth and asphalt. The column didn't even slow a bit. The two lead Renault's just rolled right through the smoke and kept firing on the retreating enemy troops. On the northern road the situation was much the same. De Gaulle's vehicle was right in the middle of his column so that he could observe both forces going forward. The German infantry on the ridge were putting up a good fight, but they were simply no match for his armored vehicles. His own infantry, supported by the two tank columns kicked them right off and it had now degenerated into a full-fledged retreat for the Germans.

A few mortars rounds came winding down here and there but he'd only lost a handful of men so far. He observed his forward tanks breaking into line formation, peeling off the roads on either side of the roads and making their way down the depressed hillside. His blood was up, and his adrenaline was flowing. The high ground was now his and any enemy tanks that might show up would be fighting uphill. Though the reports that came in said the German panzers were still miles east of here and no threat to him. Though he didn't wish to waste a moment. Now that the momentum was with him maybe his actions and those of his division might inspire those fools in leadership to follow his example and get back into the fight.

If Corap moved his corps forward now he might arrive in time to cut off the German advance toward Paris. De Gaulle had every intention of driving his division straight into the enemy line no matter what backup he might or might not have coming to aid him. Aerial scouts believed that the panzer division ahead of him was not yet consolidated on this side of the Meuse River and was spread out too much to adequately defend their foothold.

And he planned to drive straight into them and defeat them piece-meal.

He laughed at the sight of the enemy infantry fleeing before his tanks and the useless pinging of bullets against their armor. The division was quite spread out now, the infantry hugging close to their tank support. Up ahead, the roadways twisted and bent around a number of wooded areas. Beyond that was a wide open plain for miles. They were either going to kill or capture those fleeing Germans long before they reached the wooded cover.

His own vehicle reached the edge of the ridge and came revving down the slope. Another couple of mortar shells exploded to no effect. The forward most tanks advanced, machine guns blaring.

What was left of those rifle companies were out in the open and running for their lives. The first tanks were infantry support vehicles, armed with heavy machine guns only. But they were pressing into his retreating soldiers ferociously. All the while they were getting closer and closer to where Rommel wanted them to be.

His gunners had orders not to fire on the first line and to wait until the French had committed themselves to finishing off the retreating Germans. And he had just given the order for his radio operator to signal his own tanks to move forward. His whole division was not yet consolidated but he knew it didn't matter. A third of his armored force, over a hundred and fifty tanks were in position and were now racing ahead. The French still had the advantage and controlled the high ground, but this was about to change.

"Hold," he whispered to no one. He didn't even need his binoculars anymore; the French were so close. There must have been over a hundred enemy tanks now racing his way in a line of battle a kilometer and a half wide. He would have given his rank for another dozen eighty-eights or a battery of artillery backing him up. But it was too late for that, and he knew his gunners were the best. They must have been, he had trained them for the better part of a year now and molded them to perfection.

The German troops were finished. Some were already standing still on the field, their arms held up above them and their rifles flung to the ground. A few were still racing away but they were exhausted, and his lead vehicles were closing in on them quickly. The column's pace had slowed slightly as the foot infantry made their way to the ridge behind him and tried to catch up to the mechanized forces. The infantry was spread back three miles at least and he was a little worried they would not be in position in time to stop a German attack or were exhausted when they did get into place.

De Gaulle tapped his driver on the shoulder.

"Stop here," he ordered. The helmet on him was making him sweat and he was thirsty. De Gaulle reached down and grabbed his canteen. The water was cool, and his mouth was dry. He unbuckled his helmet strap and was about to wipe the sweat from his forehead when the unexpected happened.

Fifty paces ahead one of his advancing tanks split in two, its turret upended, and the tank exploded. What came next happened so suddenly that it startled him, and he ended up dropping his canteen on the ground. A moment later, to the left of the line a second tank exploded then a third in the center. Off to his left and right the unmistakable sound of heavy artillery reverberated across the landscape. Anti-tank guns ripped into his lines, turning his tanks up into fiery wrecks.

Almost in unison half a dozen vehicles blew apart. The attack had come so fast and unexpectedly that it took everyone unprepared. Hot shrapnel cut down infantry and the entire force came to an abrupt halt.

De Gaulle quickly put aside his own shock and let his instincts take over.

"Go! Go!" He ordered his driver who floored the gas. The general waved to his other units, pointing them forward, ordering them to advance. The trees in the woods nearly shook apart by the recoiling of the cannons hiding beneath them. Birds flocked away as the concealed guns unleashed hell.

The line that had paused now jolted forward again. One tank fired off a salvo into the line of trees only to be picked off by an enemy shell instead. A round tore straight through its hull like a train through aluminum. Methodically, the enemy guns picked off the moving targets. French tanks fired back, and one must have hit because a line of smoke erupted behind a tree. But the Germans were reloading rapidly and aiming their guns with deadly accuracy. Nearly every time one of them fired another vehicle was lost.

"Fire!" He shouted. The turret shifted and the main gun recoiled as a single shell fired at the closest woods. Another tank fired, then another.

And the exchange was on. The thinning line of tanks closed in on their targets, each side firing away at each other like an old-fashioned cannon duel. Two shells collided on a tank to his immediate right and the vehicle exploded into a fireball.

His own tank fired again, a shudder running through it. If they could close the distance, then he could open up with his own machine guns. Maybe even capture that battery. But the closer his division got the easier a target they became for those German gunners. Out of the almost two hundred and twenty tanks that had charged forward with him no less than forty of them were now burnt-out wrecks and there was still a kilometer between him and them.

"Keep moving!" The general shouted to the infantry units running alongside of the tanks. Infantry and armor alike charged in together. For a moment he thought the scene looked like something out of the Napoleonic Wars, with cavalry charging forward to break an enemy formation. But this was far deadlier than Napoleon could have imagined.

A single shell brought one of the heavier Char B1's to a sudden halt. Then small arms fire opened up. The closest pair of tanks and the German positions got to within meters of one another and machine guns tore into each other. For a moment it looked as if his tankers were about to push into a German position when guns from the north took them both out.

"Faster!" He screamed down to his driver as his tank passed the burning wreck to the right. "Faster! Get us in close."

The driver put the pedal to the floor and the tank bore straight in, its treads tearing up the damp ground beneath it. The main gun recoiled again. Ahead a single tree nearly shook apart as the round passed through it.

Almost there.

Just as dared to think victory was within reach his body was thrown against the side of the cupola. Their forward momentum came to a dead stop and the hulk upended. The driver was killed instantly. The bulk of the tank rose up off the ground then its giant metal frame slammed back down, killing the gunner and General de Gaulle. Neither of them felt a thing.

The earth seemed to explode all at one time. Everywhere around Private Thomas Bagshaw the ground erupted as artillery shelled their positions. He ran, rifle in his hand, into a deep crater that had been hollowed out by an exploded shell, then hit the dirt. Everywhere around him there was confusion and madness. Soldiers were running for their very lives in the opposite direction as they'd been going just two days earlier.

Tommy covered his helmet as he poked his head up slightly from his position. The Germans had systematically taken out nearly all of the armored vehicles. Everywhere there was the sight of smoking devastation, hulks of twisted metal and bodies of the dead. The Queen's Own Royal West Kent Regiment had only today been ordered into the fray, having remained behind in France when the rest of the army advanced into Belgium. But now the only thing advancing were the German panzer divisions, chasing after the BEF that was falling back to the coast toward Boulogne.

Dirt fell down like rain, there were thick clouds of smoke off in the distance, but he could still make out shadowy movements of enemy tanks coming out of a covered bridge. Behind them, God only knew. He jumped and lifted his rifle up as another person dove into the pit with him, then visibly relaxed when he recognized him as Sam Giles, his platoon mate and one his best friends since childhood.

"Bloody crazy!" Sam said and crawled next to him. His face was covered with dirt and blood. "Damn Huns. Thought we had 'em all bottled up in Belgium."

Tommy scanned the field. Everywhere there were men in the brown uniforms of the British and Commonwealth armies or the dark blue uniforms of the French making their way to the rear, many wounded, mostly on foot. Only here and there were there any vehicles or horses with officers. A wagon went by, pulled by a single mule, with half a dozen wounded in its rear and a French officer riding close behind on horseback. Tommy couldn't believe what he was seeing. It was impossible.

The rumors had been true after all, and the army had been defeated. All he could feel was terror.

"Please, God," he prayed silently.

The shelling increased and the retreating men picked up their pace. Then came short-range machine-gun fire. Bright tracer rounds skipped across the field like fireflies. The scene was like something out of some old book. The battlefield littered with dead, cries of the dying, smoking craters, and dark skies. All of a sudden Tennyson's poem about some heroic charge into battle seemed less romantic.

"Here they come!" A voice shouted through the smoke.

Tommy gripped his rifle and swallowed his nervousness down. He was only eighteen. For the past several months he'd spent his days unrolling barbed wire and building fortifications. He'd never even heard the sound of artillery fire or seen a single German soldier before today. When he and his mates had arrived in France last year he'd been told over and over that there would be no war, at least not like the old war that his father had fought in. That there would only be some light fighting at best and the Germans wouldn't attack because they knew France was too well defended. But now, as he lay down in the dirt, he could see the dead and the dying, could hear the sound of thunder just beyond that layer of smoke, all his thoughts turned to home.

The first German tank rolled into sight, and he could hear the squeaking of its treads. It was followed closely behind by what looked like a rifle platoon. Those friendly soldiers that couldn't make it out of the way of the advancing tank were mowed down by its machine gun. His own mates, men of 1st Battalion were beginning to trade shots with the Germans as they covered the retreat.

He was scared stiff and could barely move. Sam was next to him but wasn't moving either, just watching. The first of the enemy soldiers were moving forward in a line, crouching down, firing then advancing a few steps before firing again. Mortar and artillery shells exploded just feet away. Poking his head up from the crater he saw more Germans emerging through the smoke, an armored car behind them.

Sam propped his rifle up against his shoulder, took aim and fired. When he had emptied his cartridge, he popped in another and kept firing.

Tommy watched him, was afraid to move, tried to fight down the fear. Dozens of enemy infantry were moving in his general direction and more tanks rolled into sight, firing into the British defenders. A single tank shell tore straight through a small house that had been occupied, ripping a man in half and sending his entrails splattering out into the street.

Along the line more of his mates, his friends, got hit and Tommy had had enough. He was frightened out of his mind but what else was there to do but fight or run? He unslung his rifle, brought it up to his shoulder and began searching for a target to shoot at. It was difficult to see with all the confusion going on, but he settled his sights on one perhaps fifty yards out. The broad-shouldered German was crouched down in the open, his fast-moving hands firing and reloading his own rifle in quick succession.

Tommy zeroed in on him, inhaled through his nose just as he'd been taught, brought his finger up to the trigger and just as he squeezed it his hand jerked away. The shock was only momentary. The German bullet had passed straight through his right eye and with his last breath he slumped face forward into the dirt and was gone.

CHAPTER FORTY-ONE

There was a profound sense of urgency in the underground this morning, and an atmosphere of alarm as well. There were always rumors swirling about, most of them were untrue, of course. But not today. Churchill was used to people giving him looks as he made his way through the maze of tunnels that connected the vast complex, but today was different. Today their eyes were glued on him as if they each knew that whatever was waiting for him behind those closed doors, he wasn't going to like it. Not at all.

The thick metal door to the war room was pulled open by the guard standing outside. Inside the room the smell was musky. As often as the room had been used in recent weeks it still felt damp and wet. Eden was already present as were Generals Dill and Ismay, Air Marshal Newall and Admiral Cunningham, gathered in front of the pieced together maps that adorned the tack boards on the wall across from the door. The uniformed men came to attention as the Prime Minister entered the room, a swirl of cigar smoke in his wake.

There was an odd look on their faces this morning and he knew Anthony Eden well enough to know that something was not right with him.

"So gentlemen, I'm very distressed by what I'm hearing." He crossed the small, cramped space, puffing away. Behind him Halifax walked briskly into the room, half out of breath.

"Is it true?" Halifax asked hurriedly.

"General Dill?" Churchill asked.

Dill cleared his throat. "I'm afraid it's not good, sir. The Germans panzers hit our forces at Arras just after dawn. That was the focal point of our own counterattack. We've taken heavy casualties, sir."

"How heavy?" He demanded to know, and Dill sighed.

"Most of our armored forces," he answered. "Reports from the battle say that the German eighty-eights cut them and elements of the French First Army right into pieces. Enemy tanks are now reportedly driving hard for the French coast."

"Good lord," Winston said bleakly. He pinched the bridge of his nose. "What about the rest of our expeditionary force? What's Gort's next step?"

Dill shook his head. "He hasn't one, sir. He's ordered a general withdrawal back to Fruges. He's going to re-establish the line there."

Churchill was rattled at the report. On the map red markers had replaced black ones as enemy units pushed through defensive lines. Panzer divisions were in the lead. No doubt by now they would be moving fast towards the beaches in the north, squeezing the almost four hundred thousand Allied soldiers until General Gort was forced to call a surrender. This was a nightmare scenario.

"What happened?" Halifax asked. "I thought we outnumbered the enemy."

"We did, sir," General Ismay replied. "But it was an uncoordinated attack. The French tanks went in in waves rather than a single assault. As for ourselves, our tanks are simply no real match for those heavy panzers. Too slow and too lightly armed."

"So what's the state of our position on the continent?" Winston asked.

"Precarious, sir," Dill replied then immediately shook his head. "Actually...more like doubtful. We'll be forced to retreat almost fifty kilometers. Between our expeditionary force and the French Army our pocket will now go from Abbeville in the south to Dunkirk in the north. I expect that within a day, two at most, it will be completely cut off from the main French Armies in the south. When that happens, the Nazis will simply squeeze our troops from all sides. They'll be forced to surrender or be annihilated."

There, it was said and nobody in the room dare say another word more. Halifax stood, mouth gaping and rubbing his jaw. A sharp chill ran up Churchill's spine. He couldn't allow such a complete disaster to take place. Defeat was not in his nature nor, was it in the cards.

"What are our options?"

"Very limited, Prime Minister," Ismay answered. "We could try to punch our way out. If Gort can regroup in time then push his forces south, then he might be able to escape the pocket. Link up south of the Seine River. But the chances of that are slim to none. His forces are scattered across too wide an area. He'd face a German advance force long before he could even begin to coordinate such a thing."

"Any other options?" Halifax asked.

Dill grumbled. "Yes, sir. Evacuation. Mister Prime Minister, if we begin evacuating our boys now, we could get a decent portion of our army out before that pocket collapses on them."

"How long would we need?" Churchill asked.

Dill shrugged. "Five, perhaps six days. More if we're to save our heavy equipment."

"But we wouldn't have six days," Ismay added. "Once the Germans regroup, they could punch right through whatever defenses we put up and force a capitulation. Two, perhaps three days at most. Rundstedt isn't going to pull his punches now. Not after pinning us against the coast."

"To hell with the equipment. Just get those boys out of there," Eden retorted. Winston nodded emphatically.

"The problem, sirs," Ismay continued, "Is that there are only a couple of ports large enough for our troop ships to dock at. It would take hours for us to load up just one transport ship. It's a tedious business."

"Three days," Winston quietly muttered. His eyes drifted absently around the room.

"You said we could get a decent number of our army out," Halifax said. "What does that mean?"

Dill thought about it for a moment then shrugged slightly. "Twenty, perhaps thirty percent of our force."

There was a sudden feeling of consternation and even Winston, ever the optimist, became distressed at what he was being told. The thought of leaving behind nearly three quarters of the British Army in France made him physically sick. He could feel himself breathing heavy as the anxiety built up in him. For once he was at a loss for words.

"If I may, Mister Prime Minister," a voice spoke up and Winston looked over at Admiral Cunningham. "We may be able to speed that process up. A few months back the Navy informed the Chamberlain government of the need to develop flat bottomed boats. At the time they were to be used in Norway. It took some arm-twisting to get the former First Lord to agree to it and we only ever developed a handful, but we can certainly employ those. They can land in shallow water and pull men right off the beaches. Ferry them right out to destroyers and cruisers off the coast. It wouldn't take long for them to load and unload. They're sitting around in Margate right now. They could be in Dover in only a couple of hours and from there straight across the Channel in no time."

Winston warmed at the idea and a grin touched his features. "Yes. Well there you go. We can haul them from the beaches to the transports off the coast. How many men can we get aboard each one?"

"Perhaps thirty," the admiral answered. "I can have them transferred to Admiral Ramsay's command immediately."

"Do it!" Churchill snapped and pointed at the phone on the nearest desk. "I want as many of those boys off those beaches as we can!" Cunningham didn't waste another moment and went about making phone calls. Winston turned back to the map, and it seemed to him that the red arrows and markers resembled dripping blood. He hated it. Hated looking at it, hated what was on it and hated what it meant. And for a string of moments he found that he didn't know what to do about it. If the army, or a substantial portion of it, was left behind and forced to surrender it would leave Britain defenseless in the case of a German invasion. As it was, it was obvious what the next step for Hitler would be: swing south and capture Paris, thereby causing a French capitulation and leaving Great Britain to stand alone. It was an unacceptable situation, and he did not intend to be the Prime Minister who allowed the great British Empire to collapse into ruin. The end of his cigar burnt out and he shook himself out of his mental reverie. "We cannot allow this to happen," he muttered under his breath then turned to the other officers in the room and repeated himself. "We cannot allow this to happen. Surely, we must be able to do something that can buy us another day. Perhaps two."

Generals Dill and Ismay stared back at him, their faces expressionless. Even Eden looked at him and frowned. Eden, as much as he himself understood military operations. He could see the looks on their faces and any lack of a response was telling of their minds. Winston was just about to speak up again when he was preempted.

"There may be something we can do," Air Marshal Newall said in a soft voice. All eyes turned to him. "There is one tool in our box that we haven't employed yet." He started to lay out his plan and as unpleasant an idea as it seemed to him, Churchill reluctantly found he had no choice but to agree.

General Henry Pownall reached into his pouch, produced a small whiskey flask and uncorked it, then took a generous swig before stuffing it away again. He let the liquor settle down his throat and felt a profound sense of relief as he did. He was quite exhausted, as was everyone. The British army in France was now forced to withdraw back to the coast and was wasting no time taking any road that it could to get there. According to his watch it was now an hour past midnight. In the darkness behind him were the shadowy silhouettes of soldiers marching past.

General Gort and his detachment had gone missing and any attempt at locating him had come up short. Until he could be found, or a replacement appointed, then that meant that Pownall was senior officer. Though he disliked the thought of it, he certainly wasn't going to shirk his duties either. As senior officer it was his responsibility now to get whatever was left of his command out of its current predicament and, if possible, link back up with the French. Though based upon all the reports that had come through during the course of the day the odds were getting slimmer as time went on.

Any German divisions not in hot pursuit of the BEF were right now pushing south towards the Seine River. And when they got there he knew any chance of connecting back up would be impossible. The pocket was collapsing quickly.

He stood in the dark, under the limbs of a large oak tree and pondered the situation as the troops marched or drove by in the moonlit night. Morale had collapsed, organization had broken down and the supplies were quickly running out. Another day or two and they'd be forced to reassess their situation and that meant surrender or die.

"Sir," a familiar voice called out from the shadows. Lieutenant Colonel Duncan Callum walked up next to him, his face barely visible in the moonlight. "Sir. A message just came in on the wireless. I think you're going to want to read this." He held out a paper.

Pownall took it then opened it up. Callum offered him a zippo lighter, which he took, flicked it to life and viewed the message. His eyes narrowed as he digested the information. He read it twice just to make sure that he'd understood what it said then thumbed the lighter closed and stood in the dark for a moment before replying to the colonel.

"Colonel, gather together whatever general officers you can. And find me a map. We're going to have a terribly busy night I'm afraid."

CHAPTER FORTY-TWO

The evacuation was being called Operation Cartwheel. At least that's what they had told Captain William Tennant of the Royal Navy. The ships of the fleet were holding position just off the coast of Boulogne. Forty-five destroyers and a half dozen light cruisers were providing evacuation cover for the men crammed into the town and on the beaches. Three light transports and a single steamship docked in the harbor rocked steadily as hundreds of exhausted men silently made their way aboard. Their running lights were off in the overnight darkness and long lines of soldiers packed the pier from end to end. Just beyond the seawall another transport was limping past the outer mole. The night was pitch black, the moon was covered by thick clouds. Every man of the expeditionary force had been given strict orders not to use a flashlight or even light up a cigarette. There was no point in giving any German off the coast or in the skies any opportunities. They'd get plenty of chances when daylight came back around.

Captain Tennant looked down at his watch. 0331. He put his hands back into the pockets of his pea coat and tapped his foot softly against the wood of the pier beneath him. He felt desperate right now. Watching the slow, agonizing pace of the evacuation was taking its toll on him. He kept running the numbers in his head. Each transport carried an average of eight hundred-fifteen men, including the crew. It took just about an hour to load each one and then it took nearly that long for it to make its way back out into open sea. They couldn't bring another transport into harbor until one had cleared out, like playing a game of musical chairs.

Thankfully, however, the Port of Boulogne had survived mostly intact and was a perfect disembarkation point. It was certainly much better than, say, Dunkirk to the east, which had suffered terrible bombing damage. Where, even now, a much smaller force of forty-thousand Allied soldiers was waiting desperately to escape from that pocket as well.

Two small freighters swung at anchor just off the coast and the Royal Navy had managed to produce three dozen of their flat bottom boats to take men straight off the beaches and out to the waiting vessels. All the while an enemy U-boat could be lurking just beneath the waves. It was tedious work and there were nearly three-hundred and fifty-thousand more men squeezed into a pocket that was daily becoming smaller and smaller, waiting to be rescued. If half the soldiers waiting on the beach here were saved, it would be a miracle.

Upon his arrival he'd given charge of the evacuation situation, thrown together a makeshift staff and gone right to work. Luckily, transports ranging from Dutch passenger liners to small freighters were already waiting in the harbor and a screen of Royal Navy warships were keeping German subs and aircraft at bay. But every hour the German panzers were inching closer and closer. It had taken him the first half of the day just to get the operation organized into something that resembled orderly. Troops had been packed so close to the loading docks that they literally swamped the boats trying to get aboard. He'd had to slow the process down just to untangle the situation, then assembled the men into four long lines stretching from the town to the ships in port.

Only a dozen miles from here the remnants of the French were still holding the rear. Keeping the German Army at bay and the RAF was spending bombers like crazy to try and cease the incoming assault. Friendly aircraft losses were tremendous. So much so that the RAF had been forced to cut back on sending more fighters across the Channel due to the losses they'd taken.

The soldiers continued to file up the gangplank. He stood and watched from the top of the overlook he was standing on. The night breeze was frigid, and he was cold and felt slightly guilty for at least having a wool coat on while most of the lads were garbed in the same uniforms most had been wearing for days now, muddy and wet.

He'd been up all day long and he was terribly exhausted. He'd been overseeing this dull process for so long that he barely registered the soft footsteps of heeled shoes approach him from behind.

"Sir," a voice whispered. Tennant, startled, swung around to the navy lieutenant standing before him, paper held up in his hand. "Message came in, sir."

Tennant grimaced faintly at the younger officer.

"Lieutenant, how am I supposed to read that in pitch black?" He asked him and gave the young man a look an inquisitive look.

"Uh, yes, sir," the lieutenant feebly replied and lowered his hand. "It's from Dover Command. The Admiralty's dispatched an armada of civilian ships. They're coming to help with the evacuation, sir."

"What?" Captain Tennant asked suspiciously.

"Yes, sir. Fishing boats, trawlers, private yachts. Anything and everything sitting between Dover and Ramsgate. They're on the way now. Should be here by dawn, sir."

"Jesus Christ," Tennant whispered into the night. "How many?"

"Doesn't say exactly, sir," the lieutenant answered. "Every seaworthy vessel they can get their hands on."

Boats? Civilian boats were on their way?

If there was even five hundred of them he get another twenty-four thousand men out each day. Between those boats and the ones already loading up the boys, they might stand a real chance of getting very nearly all of them away. He ran some numbers in his head. If he could get even a dozen men on each of those civvies, each with a four-hour turnaround time they could get over twenty thousand off this damn beach by this time tomorrow. All he needed was four or five days. That's all. Only four or five days.

The flight was level and steady. The mix of light and medium bombers turned in on their final attack approach and wave after wave of RAF bomber settled into formation. Bomb doors opened and bombardiers rechecked their sights. They were in highly contested airspace now and the target zone up ahead was considered a vital choke point. Bomber Command had designated the German units holding the vital crossroads as priority targets. Though only the higher-ups themselves knew how critical the area about to be bombed was, the crews of those bombers understood how to read a map. And the map said that this was an important crossroad for the advancing tanks, and the slower the Germans were advancing down it, the longer it would take them to get to the coast. To the west the remnants of the British Expeditionary Force and its allies were desperately waiting to be rescued by the Royal Navy. To the east the German war machine was rolling ahead relentlessly.

There were eighty bombers in this flight and there were five more just like it on similar runs. In order to buy time to evacuate those waiting in Boulogne and on Dunkirk beach, the generals in charge had chosen to abandon their normal standing policy of not launching large scale daylight bombing attacks. But this was no ordinary attack, and every flier knew it. Instead of dropping bombs on strategic or industrial targets from thirty thousand feet, as they'd done for months now, they were coming in much lower and hitting tactical targets on the ground. The targets being those roads and those panzer divisions advancing along them.

The captain of the lead plane looked at his gauges then his watch. The wing was holding at six thousand feet and their speed would put them above the target zone in minutes. Only a mile below them was the pock-marked French countryside. Burnt homes and farms dotted the squared off landscape. Fire had burned hundreds of acres of woodlands and wide stretches of land had been left blackened and charred.

"One minute to target," the co-pilot said into his mic.

The pilot's hands shook slightly. Not much but enough that the co-pilot took notice of it. This was not anyone's first mission, but they also weren't sneaking hundreds of miles around the front line to bomb targets along the German coast either. No. This time they were flying straight into the jaws of the Luftwaffe. A number of their fighter airfields were only miles away.

Up ahead the six-way crossroad came into sight. The lead bomber was going to cut straight across it, then make a mad dash back to the coast. Each crew knew the plan. Drop the bombs then run like hell. Hopefully, before the fighters had time to react.

Far, below them the long lines of gray-clad vehicles could be seen scattering as the bomber flight approached. A few bursts of anti-aircraft fire erupted in the skies, but it wasn't much. Obviously, the Germans had been caught off guard.

The bombardier began the ten second countdown. His finger was steady on the switch, the bombs were armed and ready to go. It was only seconds now.

"...four...three...two...one... Bombs away!"

One by one the flight began dumping their bombs over the target below and one by one they began their evasive pullout just as soon as they'd dropped their loads. The noise a bomb makes when dropping is a very unique one. They streamed down from the underbelly of each plane as they reached the target zone.

The plane almost felt lighter as soon as the last bomb released, and the pilot began to bank his craft away and head back north. He wasn't sure if it was truly the weight or his anxiety, but he wasn't going to wait around and figure it out now. The flight began to break up now and head both north and northwest. If they were lucky, they could make it the hundred miles before the Luftwaffe reacted to them. If not...

"Bandits!" A voice called over the headset. "Bandits! Three o'clock high." Heads turned and searched the air frantically.

And then there they were. Eight of them were coming down on them. The flight was already at max speed and no bomber was going to outrun any fighter. The group of bombers maneuvered as fast as they could, but they were sitting ducks, at the mercy of those eight fighters now coming in.

They swooped down from twelve-thousand feet, flying in a single line formation. They must have been on patrol, spotted the bombers and figured they'd gotten lucky. The noses of the German planes were painted a bright yellow that made them look like a swarm of hornets. As soon as they reached optimum firing range the tracer rounds tore into the slow flying British bombers and began cutting the formation into pieces.

CHAPTER FORTY-THREE

Prime Minister Churchill puffed away vigorously on his cigar and stared intently at the map on the bunker wall. It was absolutely impossible to believe just what he was looking at, impossible. France had fallen. Belgium and the Netherlands were occupied, and the German army now controlled everything from Denmark all the way down to the western coasts of France. The French capitulation had given Germany every single French port along the English Channel and the Atlantic. With Italy's declaration of war and invasion of Southern France Mussolini's forces were now in control of the Savoy and Provence regions of France, including the seaside city of Toulon. Along with that had come the capture of several French navy ships by them which would no doubt be incorporated into the Italian fleet.

The news of France's terms of surrender had come in yesterday via the embassy in Switzerland and they had been harsh, but surprisingly lighter than they could have been. The French would keep control of almost half their country which would govern from the town of Vichy. Their precious naval fleet would be all but disarmed and their once mighty army would be reduced to nothing more than a mere token force. The Germans and Italians would also be allowed basing rights in their North African territories.

He scanned the faces of the uniformed men standing around the war room and exhaled noisily as he shook his head.

"What's the meat of it, general?" He asked General Dill.

Dill cleared his throat. "The French Army is completely annihilated." Churchill bristled at the word. "Paris is occupied and all organized resistance in France, Belgium and the Netherlands has ceased. The Germans now control all the coastline from Denmark down to the French Atlantic coast. Our own military position on the continent is now untenable, sir."

Winston grunted his reply and puffed away again. The lightning speed of it all had been truly overwhelming and nobody had really been prepared for it. The British and French on the continent had been planning for a defensive war while Berlin was playing a completely different game.

"What about our final evacuation numbers?" Churchill asked.

Admiral Cunningham flipped through a small notebook. "My most recent update came in just after midnight. Operation Cartwheel is still underway so this number will go up, but so far two hundred and twenty thousand of our boys have been evacuated back to England so far. We're also hosting a hundred thousand Frenchmen, fifteen thousand Belgians. Twenty-two thousand Dutch troops were rescued along with nine patrol boats, three corvettes and three frigates with some two thousand sailors in all. By tomorrow afternoon, barring German intervention, we should have the bulk of the rest of our expeditionary force evacuated from Normandy, Brittany and Bordeaux. Along with the Czechs and the Poles and whatever other forces would choose to evacuate, we could be looking at an additional one hundred and fifty thousand."

Winston nodded. "Leaving all their heavy equipment on the beaches around Boulogne," he countered, and Admiral Cunningham nodded.

"As well as our bomber crews, we've suffered considerable losses," General Dill stated. "But things could have been far, far worse, Prime Minister. Considering that on April Fifteenth the thought that we may lose our entire expeditionary force seemed like a reality. I've spoken with General Giraud, he expects a sizable number of those French troops to repatriate back to France once the armistice goes into effect. He's of course outraged with the French government. Called their capitulation treason. He's vowing to continue the fight."

"Well, that may be useful when the time comes," Churchill replied. He grimaced at the sight of the map on the wall.

Hitler had done in months what the Roman Empire had failed to do in five hundred years. The entire western half of the continent had been brought to heel and everything from the French coast in the west to the border with Russia in the east would be controlled by that madman in Berlin. Now the most modernized military force in the world held hostage nearly three hundred million people and just like that the global political situation had been turned on its head to the horror of the free world.

Churchill had conferred briefly with President Roosevelt just prior to the evacuations and both men had agreed that if France were to fall to the Germans then the safety and security of the entire hemisphere, United States included, was indeed at risk. While Roosevelt had pledged to do all that he could to offer assistance to London, both men knew his hands were largely tied by law. Their so-called neutrality act had been amended but not repealed and American involvement in this conflict was anything but assured.

I wonder how many Americans will still remain neutral when Axis bombs drop on Boston or New York, he wondered to himself. In the end, if Britain fell, that's exactly what would happen, be it in a year or ten or twenty. If Europe fell into darkness Nazism would find new targets in North America.

"What of our own defenses?" Winston asked. "Hitler won't stop at the beaches of France."

"The Channel Squadron has put to sea," Cunningham answered. "We're still involved in retrieving the last of our troops from France. Once that operation is complete I'll re-task those ships for patrol duty. However, our recent losses of light cruisers and destroyers have been quite high. The Luftwaffe inflicted a heavy toll on us at Boulogne and Dunkirk. It's going to take us a while to recover from that. The Home Fleet I'm holding back and keeping them in northern waters. We can't risk bringing our big ships within striking range of the Luftwaffe and I've ordered that nothing larger than a light cruiser enters the Channel at this point."

"The army is not in good shape, that's no secret, sir," General Dill said and indicated to points on the map in Southern England. "Like you said we left most of our heavy equipment in France when we retreated.

Right now we have one of our own combat divisions fully equipped and ready for action plus the First Canadian Division. Four hundred tanks in all. Nearly two hundred thousand troops have returned home from France but are in a rather sorry state of affairs. We're going to need time to reorganize them into something that resembles a fighting force." The general gave the Prime Minister a hard gaze. "Sir, if the Germans were to land a force on our coasts right now, corps sized, there'd be damn little we could realistically do about it. Our Home Guard is made up of older men and invalids and our regular units are simply exhausted."

Churchill blew another stream of smoke from his cigar and nodded his head in grave agreement. "Not a very rosy picture at all," he said to which Dill and Cunningham both nodded in agreement. Churchill finally looked at Marshal Cyril Newall, the head of the RAF. "I'm depending upon you for some good news, Marshal."

Newall quickly obliged. "Well Prime Minister, we do have some good news. Because of our decision to cease sending our fighters over to France in the final days of the fighting there we have over two hundred more than what we would otherwise have. We have eight hundred fighters currently on our airfields in country that are combat ready. So there is that. However, right now my chief concern is qualified pilots. We have enough to man them for a sortie or two but if the Luftwaffe begins a full-scale offensive on us, we'll need to cycle through pilots or risk losing fighting strength."

"How many pilots do we need?" Churchill asked.

"I'd like to see another four hundred. We're putting trainees through the flight programs as quick as we can, cutting the training time down to bare minimum but I believe we're going to come up short. Even with our Commonwealth and foreign volunteers we'll be hard pressed for the near future."

"Hmmm. And they'll be green," Churchill added. "With no combat experience. Whereas those Luftwaffe pilots they'll be flying against have had years to perfect their craft."

Air Marshal Newall agreed. "And they'll have numbers that surpass our own. We estimate a three to one advantage in fighter strength. As for bombers," he shook his head gravely, "we may be looking at as many as twenty-five hundred."

"My God," Admiral Cunningham said, and Churchill rubbed the bridge of his nose in dismay at the information.

"There's more," Newall continued. "Production estimates for our Hurricanes and Spitfires in the next month are only two hundred sixty-seven. Beyond that the numbers aren't much better. We simply cannot afford too many fighter losses in the near future. I know that may sound redundant but we're scratching the bottom of the barrel for manpower as it is. That situation will not change for the better anytime soon. We do have some advantages, however, the first being that we'll be fighting in our own skies above our own country. Meaning any of our pilots that manage to bailout would land safely in friendly territory. Any German shot down would go straight into captivity. It also means we won't have to stretch our supply lines. Fuel and ammunition are in high supply right now. The second advantage we have is our Chain Home radar system. It beats the devil out of anything Jerry has, and we'll be able to see them coming all the way from the French coast."

"That's something," Churchill replied. "But in the numbers they have they can simply swamp us completely. Isn't that right, Cyril? Hit us everywhere at once?"

"At least at the beginning that would certainly be true," Newall answered. "As battle commences and their aircrews tire and supplies are used up they'll have to slow down their attacks. But knowing which direction they're coming from would provide us with a tactical advantage. Provided our radar stations stay operational. We can expect them to be targeted by the Luftwaffe as well. Our airfields too would be priority targets for enemy bombers. If they can hit our fields in the south, force us to move further north, they'd control the airspace in Southern England."

"And that's when any invasion would come," Cunningham added. "Once they have control of our skies."

"Which is why we cannot allow that under any circumstance," Churchill told them all. "Control of our skies is going to be paramount."

Churchill walked away from the table he'd been leaning against and studied the map for several seconds, tapping his finger along the French coast. Known Luftwaffe airfields were marked with red X's and German army staging areas in black ones. The Normandy coasts directly south and the Pas-de-Calais to the southeast, opposite Dover, were where most of the Germans were located and both offered the greatest opportunity for a cross channel invasion of the United Kingdom.

"The navy is our shield and the air force our sword," he said to no one in particular. "Our chief concern right now will be to prevent a full-scale invasion of this country. Hitler's taken everywhere else in Europe but he's not coming here. Not this far. The Channel is our moat and by God I'll turn the whole of this island into a fortress."

"Well, neither time nor resources are on our side," Admiral Cunningham said. "Momentum is with the Jerries right now. The smart money says that once they solidify their grasp in France they'll come at us. It's the best chance they're going to get. We're at our weakest right now. Every day they delay the likelihood of a successful invasion will decrease."

"It's not going to be easy on our end, Prime Minister," General Dill added in. "The army needs time. Time to reorganize and rearm. Right now we couldn't stop a Hitler Youth parade marching through Trafalgar Square."

"How much time?"

Dill gave it some thought then shook his head. "Best estimate for a full reorganization, three perhaps four months. That's just to get the army we've got back into fighting condition. Calling up even more men for service is barely an option right now. As soon as Cartwheel is over with we'll have upwards of four hundred thousand of our own soldiers back and possibly as many as two hundred thousand foreign. But they'll be exhausted. They'll have the uniforms on their backs and the rifles they held in France but that's about all."

Churchill finished off his cigar. "Hmmm. Then we'd better get some damn more troops here as quick as possible. Australian, New Zealander, South African. Whoever and wherever we can bring them in from. India if needs be!" He tapped his finger against the map of England and General Dill nodded in acknowledgment. "We've been kicked from the continent, gentlemen, and there are those in Britain who would still have us negotiate a truce with Berlin. There are dark days ahead, but I'm determined that we shall fight on. There can be no retreat. In a couple of hours it shall be dawn and I will meet with the king to brief him and this afternoon I will address Parliament and the nation. My advice is to get some rest, gentlemen. We're going to need all of our strength in the coming weeks."

The gathering of officers was silent as Hitler walked across the crushed gravel surface that made up the road overlooking the beaches around Calais. Hitler was in a good mood this morning as he'd arrived to inspect his troops and meet with the generals. He'd been overjoyed after touring Paris for the last few days and rubbing the French noses in their own shit. Now it was back to business, and he'd ordered this final stop in Northern France before leaving back to Berlin.

Field Marshall Rundstedt happily greeted the Führer with a handshake and a few words of congratulations were exchanged between them. Hitler was seldom in such a happy mood and the men who spent the most time around him became used to his mood swings. But not today. Today was a joyful day.

In the port around Calais hundreds of small boats swung at anchor. Behind the town new anti-aircraft guns had been placed and everywhere along the beach, east and west, the construction of defensive forts were already being erected. Overhead flew a squadron of fighters and fluttering in the breeze above the town center was the swastika flag, a reminder to all of whom was in charge now. Hitler could see the enlisted men working on the fortifications stop to glare at him and he gave them a wave. It was always good to be seen by his soldiers.

"Mein Führer," Rundstedt indicated to a set of large binoculars that had been set up atop a tripod overlooking the beach below. "The view from here is the best."

Hitler smiled and patted Field Marshall von Rundstedt on the shoulder. He peered through the huge binoculars across the English Channel. It was hazy with a cloud of mist at first but after a few moments the mist lifted and then he could see it clearly, as though God himself blew the mist out of the way so that he might see.

The White Cliffs of Dover rose straight up from the seas like a great wall built by some ancient giant. They were quite beautiful actually. He knew that Napoleon himself had gazed at them through his own eyeglass in his own time, possibly from the very spot Hitler was now standing on. But this was as close to England as Napoleon had ever gotten.

"How far away?" Hitler asked in a muffled voice.

"Thirty-four kilometers," Rundstedt answered.

Thirty-four kilometers. An hour is all that separates us!

The English Channel. He'd only barely glimpsed it during his own time in the trenches as a young soldier himself and now he was here. It was calm today and there was hardly any wind but the Channel, he knew, had a way of turning quickly against those seeking to cross it. One reason why Napoleon had never crossed it. Hitler was not so timid. His armies had conquered the land of Napoleon and now the land of Henry the Fifth lay a mere one hour away.

"Spectacular," he said then turned back to the group of men standing behind him. "Absolutely spectacular." He smiled warmly. "If those people over there do not come to their senses then we will have to bring them to it. Come. Let us speak awhile. We have many plans to make."

Mister Edward Bagshaw adjusted his eyeglasses as he looked at the picture of Thomas on the fireplace mantle. His boy, smiling wide, his father's arm over his shoulder. It was taken on Thomas's graduation from school. Edward wiped the tears from his left eye as he looked at the photograph. Next to it was the single photo of Thomas in uniform, taken that day at the train depot. The day Tommy had left for the war. The last day they'd seen him. He still couldn't believe he was gone. His boy.

In the next room there came the sound of talking and greeting. He could hear Mary's voice and Simon's too. Their neighbors the Pipers had arrived. Sharing meals together with the neighbors was becoming tradition in this house now with the rationing and all.

He wiped the layer of dust off the picture frame then turned and walked into the next room where his family and the neighbors were waiting.

"Oh, hello George," he greeted Mister Piper. "Cordelia."

"Hello, Edward," they greeted him back. Mrs. Piper smiled and put a dish on the large table, children of both families were roaming around the table. The two fathers shook hands.

"Thank you for coming. It's nice to have everyone together," Edward told him. "Please won't you sit."

"Mary, let me help you in the kitchen," Cordelia Piper said, and the two mothers left.

George and Edward spoke for several minutes, though it had only been two days since the families last met. But small talk was the only way to avoid the unavoidable subject of the war and of Thomas. The children played on the floor, toy soldiers fought small battles, until Misses Bagshaw and Piper re-emerged from the kitchen, carrying a basket of bread and small dishes of food and put them on the table.

"Children, dinner," Mrs. Bagshaw called out. She sat down and smiled at the gathering. "Simon."

Edward poured George a cup of tea then Mary and Cordelia. The children sat themselves up at the table, except for Simon who was still in the living room. Edward rubbed the Piper boys head as he took a toy soldier out of the kid's mouth and laughed lightly when he did.

"Simon," Mary called again. "Dinner!"

Simon, the Bagshaw's now oldest son, stuck his head into the dining room. "Mum, Dad. On the radio. Come quickly. He's on the BBC."

"Hmmm? Who's on?" Edward asked.

"Mister Churchill. He's on the BBC!" Simon said anxiously.

The adults in the room looked at each other in surprise then ordered the children to not touch any of the food until they'd returned. Edward, Mary, George, and Cordelia moved into the living room where Simon turned the radio volume up. There was a crackling over the speaker and the voice was at first broken and distant but cleared up after a moment.

"...have sustained a terrible loss in France...not lost the will to fight on..."

"I didn't know Parliament was meeting today," Mary said. Edward shrugged and shook his head.

Another crackling on the radio, then, "...*Poles, Norwegians, Dutch....* *joined their causes to our own...*"

Simon thumped the side of the radio with the palm of his hand. There was a moment of silence then the broadcast came through loudly and clearly.

"*We shall not stop, and we shall not fail. Though at times the days ahead may seem dark, we shall persevere. Our allies have not abandoned us, and we shall not abandon them. While the Battle of France may be over, I believe that the Battle of Britain is about to begin...*"

EPILOGUE

Tokyo Bay
June 1941

The skies above Tokyo were overcast this morning, but the rain coming down had been gentle, a welcome relief to the sailors aboard the mighty Japanese aircraft carriers that were anchored in the harbor. The enormous carriers and their escort vessels rose and fell on the ocean tide and a fleet of small fishing boats were off in the distance coming and going from the harbor in the early morning hours just after the first rays of sunshine rose over the eastern horizon. The Japanese had been a seafaring people for their entire history and those who ventured out to sea were as revered now as their ancestors had been for generations. The pride of the Japanese Empire now rode on those ships in the harbor. The huge flattop carriers, the heavily armed and armored battleships, cruisers, destroyers and all other classes of warship built for the glory of Japan were all manned by the absolute best and brightest in the land and all hope for a glorious future rode with them.

Small droplets of rain softly beat against the starboard porthole of the battleship *Yamato's* main briefing room. The small, enclosed room was as silent as the grave, and one could clearly hear every raindrop that pelted against the double thick window. Not so much as a whisper was made from the group of naval officers standing in a horseshoe around the large table in the center of the room. The man hovering over that table had his eyes glued intently on the map of the Pacific Ocean, islands and land masses dotted across it, studying every detail no matter how minute and reflected on it in utter silence.

Admiral Isoroku Yamamoto, with his white gloved hands gripping the edge of the table, studied the map before him for what seemed like forever. Models of Japanese and American warships played out an elaborate wargame on the table where movements and counter-movements were made, pieces withdrawn, and battles won or lost entirely in the mind of the observer. Mathematics calculated losses just as arbitrarily as a child might roll a pair of dice to any set of numbers. Blind chance was all that stood between victory or defeat when playing these games.

Many plans and preparations were made in war, particularly when fought at sea. Weather, wind direction, lines of supply, communications with other ships, avoiding detection by the enemy, the skill of the pilots, the fighting spirit of the sailors, the cautiousness or boldness of the commander, the list went on and on and on. It was all but impossible for anyone to calculate all the factors involved and to produce any kind of conclusion that even resembled reality.

But if forty years of service in the Imperial Navy had taught Admiral Yamamoto one thing it was that none of those things counted nearly as much as one thing: Surprise. If surprise was on one's side, then that was as good as having the blessing of the God of War. Because surprise meant one thing, that your enemy was unprepared for battle. If your enemy was unprepared for battle, then victory was most assuredly yours.

Finally, after long minutes in silence, Yamamoto stirred. He stood up straight, nodded lightly and gave up a small grunt.

"Impressive. Most impressive, gentlemen."

The officers gathered, all utter professionals, gave only the most modest of nods in return to the admiral's compliment. It was neither customary nor acceptable for a proper son of Japan to be thankful for doing one's duty. It was enough just to be acknowledged by their superiors.

"Commander Genda," Yamamoto looked at the young naval aviator standing to his immediate right. Genda was an excellent aviator and one of the best tactical planners in the Imperial Navy. "Your additions to my plan are exemplary. You are to be commended."

Genda bowed his head in thanks. "It was your plan, Admiral. All I did was add on to what you had already done."

"You are humble," Yamamoto replied. "A trait to be commended for sure, but you deserve the credit for this. My original plan was not this intricate. I planned for a massive aerial attack on the Americans. One that would hurt them yes. But this. . ." he stretched his arms out over the table, "this would devastate them."

Genda nodded in agreement. "I believe so, yes. A three-wave attack launched from our carriers here, north of Oahu, should be sufficient to destroy the American fleet." He picked up a model of an American aircraft carrier off the battle map and held it in his hand. "Once our first and second air strikes eliminate the American ships in the harbor our third wave will concentrate on destroying the facilities themselves. Drydocks, fuel storage tanks, repair shops, airfields etc."

"And once their Pacific Fleet is annihilated, they will be in no position to intervene in our other operations," Admiral Kusaka added, hovering his hand over the Philippines and East Indies.

Admiral Yamamoto looked at the officers grouped around the table. To his left were Vice Admiral Chichi Nagumo, Rear Admirals Tamon Yamaguchi and Chichi Hara, the men who led Japan's aircraft carrier groups, members of their staffs standing silently behind them. To his right was Rear Admiral Kusaka, Nagumo's Chief of Staff and an excellent military planner in his own right and Commander Minoru Genda. Genda was a professional naval aviator and had been specifically requested by Admiral Yamamoto to help develop what was known as Operation AI, the attack on the American fleet.

Commander Genda continued. "Once we sink the American battleships at Pearl Harbor, their offensive capability in the Pacific will be crippled." He took the American battleships from the map as he said this. "Leaving no threat to come at us from the east."

"As I said, most impressive," the admiral complimented. "After the attack has been resolved we will make back for Japan and be ready to support the Philippines Campaign."

Admiral Kusaka and Commander Genda nodded in agreement along with some of the junior staff. The plan was brilliant and if it were successful, it would all but assure Japanese supremacy in the western Pacific, at least for the time being. Nobody in the room was more aware of the formidable industrial might that the United States could weld than Yamamoto. Industrial power that dwarfed Japan.

If there was going to be a war with the Americans it would have to be a short and decisive one.

Yamamoto scanned the room; his eyes fell inevitably on the admirals who would be responsible for leading any attack.

"Admiral Nagumo, what are your thoughts?" The admiral inquired. Nagumo, hesitant to answer held his hand up to his jaw as if studying the plan again. "Speak freely. I must hear all viewpoints."

Nagumo shrugged. "Admiral, this plan that you and Admiral Kusaka and Commander Genda have come up with is audacious. It is bold. However," he hesitated sightly but knew he must say what he felt, "I do not believe that this course of action would be best. I agree with you and with all the other officers who think that a war with America is inevitable, and I am quite certain that it will come in time. But I must speak truthfully now that I do not put the faith in this plan that others do."

Yamamoto gave him a confused look. "What exactly is it that you put no faith in, Nagumo?"

"First, sir, the strike itself I believe is flawed. I commend Commander Genda for his brilliance in working out the details for an aerial attack, but I strongly believe that its chances to successfully achieve the objectives are slim. An attack from the air will not have the strength that we need to deliver such a knockout blow. That can only come from the guns of our battleships. Furthermore, even if we manage to hit the naval base and inflict considerable damage there is still the matter of their island airfields. American bombers would be poised to strike back at us immediately."

"Excuse me, Admiral Nagumo," Genda began, "But that would be most difficult to accomplish. If I may, sir. As I explained during our demonstration our pilots would be making a series of course changes while in route to the American naval base. Our carriers will launch north of the Hawaiian Islands, however, our aircraft will be coming in from the west in the first and third attack and from the east in the second.

The American forces in Hawaii will not even know which direction the attack is being launched from. Furthermore, we will sortie with enough fighters to cover the American airfields on Oahu. If they do manage to get their bombers airborne, our fighters can pick them apart in the skies. Commander Fuchida is an excellent flight leader. He knows how to train his pilots."

"I understand these things, Genda and I know Commander Fuchida to be an excellent pilot and leader. But such an attack has never been attempted in naval warfare. We are betting the future of the empire on an untested battle plan." Nagumo shook his head. "Of course, Admiral Yamamoto, I will lead wherever you wish me to go. But I have stated my concerns."

Yamamoto nodded then looked at Yamaguchi. Surely Yamaguchi would give his endorsement. "What do you think, admiral?"

The other man was silent for a few moments in considerate thought then nodded.

"I agree with you, Admiral Yamamoto," he replied. "Admiral Nagumo is correct when he says that such an attack has never taken place in naval history. But we have bombed targets routinely on land and our torpedo bombers are better than anything that the Americans have. I feel certain that properly trained pilots can launch such a strike as this. We will have the element of surprise on our side. There are some minor details that I would like more time to study, however. But overall, I believe in the plan and in the courage of our pilots."

"Admiral Hana?"

Hana shrugged. "I have mixed feelings about this operation, sir. Respectfully, I do agree with Admiral Nagumo's point that an aerial attack might not have the strength we need to completely destroy the American fleet. We must inflict overwhelming damage on the enemy in those first two strikes and a third strike would be crucial. My concern, however, is what happens after the first wave. The Americans will be woken to our attack and will get everything they can off the ground in order to retaliate. The second and third waves could suffer considerable losses."

Yamamoto looked again at Commander Genda to address Hana's concerns. Again, Genda failed to disappoint.

"Admiral Hana, you are quite correct that after the first wave the Americans will undoubtedly be alert and eager to retaliate," Genda told him. "We can expect their army airfields to get every available pilot in the air. However, consider that the American aircraft are vastly inferior to our own, especially in fighters. Our new Zeros can outperform the Americans in every aspect. Also, recall that I said our own fighters will be flying circles above the island once the attack commences. They can blow apart anything that tries to lift off from one of their airfields. Also, any attack we commence must fall on a Sunday. This day has a special importance for the Americans. That may also play a part in the battle readiness of the enemy forces."

"I remind you as well that the Americans have only recently deployed the bulk of their Pacific forces to Hawaii," Admiral Yamamoto added. "They may not be fully established as of yet." Though he said the words he knew that to almost not be the case. The Americans had been in possession of the Hawaiian Islands for decades now and they'd had plenty of time to establish defenses there. The moving of their main fleet from the west coast to Honolulu last year was made partly due of the ring of defenses around the island harbor.

"Then my next concern would be anti-aircraft fire," Admiral Hana continued. "Surely the island batteries and those from shipboard anti-aircraft will present us with a problem."

Commander Genda sighed before answering. "You are quite correct, sir. That is also my concern. Anti-aircraft guns from their warships can be quite formidable. Commander Fuchida and I are still working this detail out. What I can say is this, that one of the reasons for alternating the direction from where our attacks are coming from is to keep the Americans confused and to keep their anti-aircraft fire from being too concentrated against us. The first wave will come in from the west and hopefully it will draw some of the American destroyers and cruisers away from the east where the second wave will approach from. All our pilots have trained repeatedly for low altitude flying to avoid radar detection. Unfortunately, Admiral Hana, we will not know the extent of enemy fire until the operation commences."

"Which always happens in battle," Admiral Kusaka added. "Nobody can ever foresee all contingencies all we can do is plan and prepare as best we can. Commander Fuchida will command the strike force and we all know his reputation. If anyone can deal with a changing situation, Fuchida can."

"Then, under those circumstance, Admiral Yamamoto, I can endorse this plan," Hana said. "If this operation goes as Commander Genda and Admiral Kusaka have said, then yes I can see it doing irreparable damage to the enemy. Two strikes to cripple their fleet and a third to destroy the support facilities." He nodded once.

Yamamoto turned his gaze back to the battle played out across the map. Six Japanese aircraft carriers would sortie for this mission. That would be over four hundred attack aircraft and over twenty submarines positioned near the entrance to the harbor ready to torpedo any American warship that was lucky enough to escape the aerial attack. More than sufficient strength to cripple them in the Pacific. Once their mighty battleships and carriers were nothing more than burning wrecks, Japan would be free to conduct whatever expansion into the south that they deemed necessary in order to secure the resources they would need, including the precious oil in the Dutch East Indies.

"Good," Yamamoto said. "Then we are agreed to how to proceed. There are a few details to work out, but I am most confidant in you Kusaka and you Genda to work them out." He nodded to the admirals at his left. "Gentlemen." He turned and removed a linen off a tray filled with cups of sake. Each of the senior officers present took a cup. "To the Emperor and to victory."

"To the Emperor," the others echoed then swallowed their sake.

The officers mingled around the table. Admirals Nagumo and Yamaguchi debated between them the details of the operation. Admiral Nagumo, ever doubtful, expressed his deep concerns to the younger man. Admiral Hara conferred with Kusaka and Genda and the junior staffers began making talk amongst themselves. Admiral Yamamoto put his empty cup down and lost himself in thought. War with the United States was not anything that he actually wished for of course. Japan was still bogged down in China and the thought of more war was not something that sat easy with him. He knew the United States would crush Japan in a long-drawn-out conflict and that it would be bloody and brutal.

From behind him and to his left the doorway hatch opened and a young officer entered the room practically unnoticed.

"Admiral," he whispered and bowed his head respectfully.

Yamamoto, turned to him, the ensign was holding out a small note. He took it and the other man disappeared through the hatch as quietly as he'd come through it. The admiral unfolded the note and read its message. It was from the palace directly. He gave no outward indication of emotion whatsoever, he was far too practiced for that, but for a handful of moments he could swear that his heart had stopped beating. His eyes read, reread and reread the message again. He stood there like a frozen statue, his white gloved hands holding the note he'd been slipped, and he'd had to fight to contain the emotion swelling up in him.

"Sir?" It was Genda's voice, he knew it as well as he knew his own. Yamamoto, the old sailor and poker player mustered up his best face and turned towards him. The admiral licked his lips and looked at the young officer who had joined him at his side, a hint of a grin on his face. Genda looked at his superior and intuitively knew something was not right by the look in the other man's eyes.

"It would seem, gentlemen," Admiral Yamamoto began in a low tone, "that the Gods of War have seen fit to make us wait a little longer for our victory." The officers gathered stopped their chatting and all eyes in the room turned to him. "The emperor has spoken. It would appear that our new war will be to the north. In Siberia."